Tales of the Barf Table

Book Three: Diamonds and Stone

Tales of the Barf Table

Book Three:

Diamonds and Stone

RAHN & TIMBERLEY ADAMS

Written by Rahn and Timberley Adams

Illustrations by Timberley Adams

Manga illustration by Amelia Dowdle

Published by Gaillardia Press

Copyright © 2025 Rahn and Timberley Adams

ISBN: 979-8-9869431-4-5

First Edition, November 2025

All that's important is that the individual does the best he can. . . . The only victory for me is in the quality of the competition, not in the final score.

—Mike Marshall, pitcher

CHAPTER 1

THE WIND ROARED LIKE A LOCOMOTIVE as the two teenagers scrambled toward the back of the small, steel structure. Built like a Quonset hut, the round roof of the batting cage could withstand the tornado, but big Artie Bauer knew from having grown up in farm country that a twister could lift the building off the ground and toss it like a Tinkertoy across the red-clay diamond and into the green outfield grass.

Pitcher Ty Green—tall like Artie, his best friend and catcher, but much slimmer—dove behind the big wooden desk that the baseball and softball coaches shared, and tried to fit into the empty space underneath. On the dirt floor, a broken-down chair lay on its side, its tiny wheels spinning.

"It *does* sound like a train!" shouted Ty, reaching back to pull Artie toward him in the darkness. The power had gone out less than a minute before the terrible storm reached the school campus on the outskirts of Monk's Landing. Their first clue had been the rattle of hail on the steel roof.

Artie yelled back, "Move over!" The desk was oak and heavier than a wooden coffin, and Artie figured there was enough space for at least their upper bodies. "Make some room!"

"Oh, come on," said Ty. "You have catcher's gear on. I'm not wearing anything like that." But he moved his legs and twisted his torso to let Artie crawl in beside him.

The sheets of corrugated metal above and around them groaned under pressure as the howling wind intensified. The earth shook for a moment at the crash of something against the back wall of the steel building, only feet from where the two boys lay.

"A tree?!" Artie shouted.

Ty waited an instant to answer. "Or a set of lights," he said. "The main pole's right outside. I bet it broke in two."

They could still hear the roar, but it was moving away from them. The wind continued to whip debris against the sloping sides of the metal structure.

Artie Bauer and Ty Green waited for the lights to come back on, but they never did that April night, not even after the tornado had moved away from the Arbor High baseball stadium and into the swamps of Oleander County.

With more effort than usual, Artie pulled inward the front door to the batting cage. "My gosh," he said, shaking his head. "The wind warped the door." Brushing sand and cobwebs from his short, light-brown hair, Artie stepped outside to survey the damage around the stadium complex. He waited for his buddy to join him before moving away from the small building that separated the school's baseball and softball fields. Ty patted his own coarse, dark curls to even them out as he caught up with Artie.

Gray bleachers along the two adjoining outfields lay in mangled piles of aluminum. What had been arrow-straight lines of chain-link fencing lay crushed and broken wherever the twister had fired a heavy-enough projectile. A giant hemlock that had stood between the green center-field fence and the highway now rested on what was left of the baseball team's crumpled scoreboard.

Ty whistled at the devastation around the stadium, most of it on the baseball side. "Dang," he said. "That scoreboard wasn't even a year old. It was just a baby." The three flagpoles in center field, however, remained standing.

Hearing the relief in his friend's voice, Artie smiled and nodded, then turned and looked across the parking lot at the school building. "Ty?" he said, with a note of concern. "Is there any chance Nicie's dad still likes you—I mean, even though you guys aren't dating now?"

"Why's that?" Ty asked, following Artie's gaze toward the parking lot where they had left their vehicles. He stepped forward to peer around his pal. "Can you see *The Whale*? Is it okay?"

"Well," said Artie, "let's put it this way. You're gonna be riding home with me tonight—and *every* night until you talk Nicie's dad into doing body work on your car. Some *major* body work. *The White Whale* has been, well, *harpooned*. Sorry, buddy."

The night sky had cleared enough that the two boys could make out a long section of a stadium light pole resting lengthwise on Ty's white Ford LTD. The old car wasn't going anywhere that night after having been crushed and skewered by the post of creosote-stained pine, as if Captain Ahab himself had called down this retribution upon Ty Green's pride and joy.

"Well, at least we aren't hurt—just our feelings," said Ty, pausing as the wailing of sirens grew in the distance. "You know, we'd better get home. Mom and Dad are probably worried sick."

Artie nodded again, this time in all seriousness. "Yeah, Grandpa, too. Gee, I hope *he's* all right, but the Durans will check on him—or Minnie, if she's still out there." Artie thought for a moment. "We'll come back and take care of *The Whale* tomorrow, buddy, no kidding around. I do know what that old car means to you. We've had some good times in it."

"From your lips to God's ears," said Ty, again with a smile. "I'm just glad we didn't have a game or team practice tonight—it being Good Friday and all." He chuckled. "Can you imagine us trying to pry Jug Johnson out from under that oak desk?"

Artie laughed. "Well, it is his desk—and Coach Carson's. But, yeah, let's get on home. There's nothing else we can do here."

"Yeah, we were lucky tonight," said Ty. "It's just a car." He nodded toward *The Whale* and then shook his head sadly.

On the highway, three emergency vehicles heading out of town flew past the high school, their red lights whirling and sirens blaring. They were going the same direction that Artie and Ty would be traveling together within minutes. The Bauer and Green farms were located beyond the big swamp but not too far from Ebenezerville, the next town over.

After retrieving some papers and other items from the crushed car, the two friends climbed into Artie's old red pickup truck and started toward their homes in the farm country off Ebenezerville Road. Both of them were worried that someone else's luck that night hadn't been as good as their own.

* * *

When the boys reached the Bauer farm road, they had to wait for the Durans' white van to pull over and make room for them on the narrow, dirt lane. Little Ricky Duran—not his father, Ricardo—was driving the battered work vehicle with ladders on top. In the passenger seat next to Ricky was 68-year-old Harry Bauer, Artie's grandfather. He appeared fine, nodding and lifting one calloused hand to acknowledge his grandson. With the other hand, the old farmer scratched the graying bristles of his crew-cut head. Both drivers stopped their vehicles and rolled down their windows to talk.

"Everything is okay, but the power is out," said Ricky. "The phones still work. Mother called Mr. Bauer to come stay with us. Father is hooking up the generator for us now."

Artie was relieved. "How close did it come?" he asked. "The tornado."

"Close enough," said Ricky. "We heard there was more than one. There is a lot of damage in E-ville. The church called Father. He's going there to help as soon as we get to the house. I may go with him."

Grandpa leaned forward and, with a frown, squinted past Ricky and Artie. "Ty Green," shouted Harry Bauer, "your mama called and asked if Artie had got home yet. She's worried to death."

"I figured she would be," said Ty. "Artie has to take me home. A light pole at the school fell on my car. Can you guys call and tell her we're on our way?"

Ricky nodded. "Yes, we will," he said, then waved, put the van in gear and started to pull away.

"Hold on!" Artie called. "Was Minnie out here in the storm? And Wilma? Has anybody checked on them—and the animals?"

"Yes," said Ricky, "Father checked on them, and they are okay, too. Dr. Marecek and Wilma are putting the horses and cows back in the barn now. They had turned them out into the pasture when the tornado warning sounded on the radio. It was really scary."

Grandpa broke the tension with a laugh. "Yeah," he said, "but Frick and Frack enjoyed it. They rolled around in the mud and had 'em a good ol' time in the thunderstorm—once the hail stopped."

Ricky smiled at Grandpa's mention of the hogs, rolled up his window and threw up his hand again before driving on.

Artie backed up enough to turn his truck around to get back on the main highway toward Ebenezerville. The Greens lived only two farms over; however, to get there, Artie and Ty had to continue on for a mile, turn left off E-ville Road and travel another mile to the Greens' split-level rancher sitting just off winding Little Swamp Road. When they pulled in, Ty's mother, a nurse, stood on the front porch waiting for them. A pretty lady but a tired one, Rachel Green still wore her nursing outfit, as if she hadn't had time to change from her day shift at the hospital in Ebenezerville.

"I'm so glad to see you two," Rachel called, heading toward the truck. "Don't get out. I need a ride to the hospital." She crossed in front of the pickup, its headlights shining off her white slacks as she passed. Ty jumped out and helped his mother into the cab. She slid over next to Artie and said, "You're fine. Plenty of room on this bench seat."

She reached out and punched a button on the radio, and twisted a knob to find Ebenezerville's AM station on the dial. "They've been giving reports about the damage," she said. "It's pretty bad."

Ty scooted in next to her and slammed the door twice to get it shut. "Where's Dad?" he asked, as Artie backed down the driveway to the road.

"One of the steers ran off when he let them out of the barn," she said. "He's looking for it now. It couldn't have wandered too far away."

Artie touched the brake to slow the truck. "Do we need to hold up and go help Mr. Green?" he asked. "With the steer, I mean."

"No," said Rachel, "I talked to him a minute ago on the walkie-talkie after Ricky called. He said I should go on to work. I'll call home later when things settle down. The ER is packed right now. And my boss said to be careful driving in. There's a lot of damage all over town."

Artie nodded and stepped on the gas, but had to watch his speed on the curvy road. Once they reached the stop sign and took a left back onto Ebenezerville Road, the pavement straightened out and let Artie drive faster. They were about two miles outside the town limits when he was forced to slow the pickup to a crawl behind a line of traffic that had formed.

"Can you see what's going on up there?" Artie asked his passengers.

Ty sat up straight and tried to see past the glowing taillights of cars and trucks in front of them. "I think it's a wreck," Ty said. "I see somebody standing on the shoulder with a flashlight—on your side. Must be a deputy or first responder."

"Yeah, I see him," said Artie. "Looks like some cars are trying to turn around. The highway must be blocked up there."

Both lanes of Ebenezerville Road were, in fact, completely blocked, but there was no wreck, as such. The barrier was a huge oak tree that the storm had uprooted on the left side of the roadway and laid across the pavement, with the upper limbs and their smaller branches covering a dark sedan sitting to the right at the end of a paved drive leading into a gated subdivision. The three emergency vehicles—two rescue trucks from the town's volunteer fire department and a sheriff's department cruiser—were also unable to get past the fallen oak; however, the firemen were already busy with chainsaws, cutting through the limbs that had trapped the driver and passengers inside the sedan. Portable lights had been set up so that the firemen could see to work at freeing the motorists.

"Some of our doctors live in Oakhurst Manor," said Rachel Green, "and that sure does look like a nice car under all those branches."

Artie nodded. "Yeah, they could've been called in to the hospital, just like you," Artie said. "The deputy is headed this way. I'll ask him if those folks are okay and if we can help."

"Is your chainsaw in back—in the toolbox?" asked Ty. "I can grab it and help with the tree."

"No," Artie said, "but there are some work gloves. We can carry limbs away as the guys cut them. That'll make things go faster."

Artie rolled down his window and leaned his head out when the deputy got close enough to hear him above the chainsaws. "Are the people in the car okay?" Artie shouted. "We have a nurse here."

The deputy stepped closer and shined his light into the pickup's cab. Seeing that Rachel was wearing a nurse's smock with a hospital ID attached, he volunteered, "Two injuries, but they aren't life-threatening. We called it in, and the ER said it'll be a few minutes before an ambulance is free and can head this way. Come with me, ma'am."

Ty and Rachel exited the cab and stepped away so that Artie could move the pickup onto the shoulder. Rachel followed the deputy toward the firemen working on the tree. The boys retrieved thick gloves from the toolbox in the bed of the truck and helped the tree crew. Thirty minutes later, enough branches had been cleared that the car's doors could be pried open for access to all four occupants. They included a father and mother, and their two teenage children—a boy and a girl. The father, in the driver's seat, and the son, seated behind him, were the two injured ones. They stayed in their seats and awaited help. The mother and daughter appeared fine, just shaken, once they could get out of the car.

Using a first-aid kit from one of the rescue trucks, Rachel tended to the father first, cleaning his bloody head and face before lightly pressing on his shoulders, arms, torso and legs to check for injuries. Whenever Artie glanced over at them, he noticed that the man seemed to be giving Rachel instructions and that she appeared to be following them. Then she moved back to the injured boy, whose wound wasn't bloody like his father's but was causing him more pain. Again, Artie saw that Rachel seemed to be consulting with the man as she worked on the boy, whose left shoulder was what the nurse became focused on. She used an elastic bandage to secure the teen's left arm against his torso to keep the arm from moving. By then, the father had gotten out of the car to help Rachel with his son, and they moved the boy's legs first and set them on the ground so that he could stand. It was then that Artie noticed just how tall the boy was—several inches taller than his good-sized father.

Artie also recognized the boy from school—not from Arbor High, but from Solid Rock Christian Academy, where the tall, lean teenager was a Harvesters baseball player that spring. It was his first semester at Solid Rock and his first season on the baseball squad, and he had quickly become the team's star as its best pitcher and one of its best hitters. The Harvesters had already played Artie and Ty's Bruins twice that season, home and away, the latter meeting just over two weeks earlier. Thanks to Ty Green's superb pitching, Arbor had won both games but only by a total of three runs—2-1 at Solid Rock and 4-2 at Arbor. This boy, Michi "Mike" Inouye, an 11th grader, had started both contests on the mound for the Harvesters and, as a hitter, had driven in all their runs.

The wail of a siren signaled the approach of an ambulance from Ebenezerville; however, the emergency vehicle was on the opposite side of the fallen oak's huge trunk that had not yet been cleared from the roadway. Having freed the trapped motorists, the firemen had turned their attention to the tree trunk but still had much work to do before the road would be open. Rachel Green and the father helped the injured boy climb over the downed tree, and they met the ambulance there when it came to a stop, its red lights still flashing even after the driver had silenced the vehicle's siren. Rachel waved Ty over to her and pulled him close so he could hear her. They hugged, and she got into the back of the ambulance with the father and the boy, who used his free arm to wave to his mother and sister, and to give them a thumbs-up that he would be okay.

Ty Green scrambled back over the tree trunk and returned to where Artie was standing with the woman and girl. "Mrs. Inouye?" Ty said. "Rachel Green is my mom. She's riding to the hospital with Dr. Inouye and Mike—I mean, Michi. Your husband asked if we'd give you and your daughter a ride back to your house. He said to tell you they'll be okay."

Ty looked over at Artie, since they hadn't talked yet. "Well, sure," said Artie, to the woman, as much as to his friend. "You guys go climb into my pickup. It's the old red one over there." The woman smiled weakly and thanked both boys. The girl, standing close to her mother, remained silent.

Artie pointed at his truck and watched as the mother and daughter started in that direction. Turning to his friend, Artie said, "I'll drive them home as quick as I can and be right back. Maybe the road will be clear by then, and we can head on into E-ville."

"Yeah," Ty said, "there's probably a lot we can do to help out. Maybe we'll run into Ricky and his dad. From what I've been hearing on the firemen's radios, E-ville looks like a war zone—like somebody dropped a bomb on it."

"Somebody *did*," said Artie, reaching into his pocket for his truck keys. "And that somebody was Mother Nature."

CHAPTER 2

'THE GOOD FRIDAY STORM,' as it would be called for years to come, had turned lives upside down in the minutes that the line of tornadoes spun across coastal Oleander County. The recovery began that night, as emergency workers and volunteers reopened roads to traffic, cleared debris off residences and other structures to rescue people and animals that had been trapped, and searched for those individuals who had gone missing in the twisters. No part of the county was spared, but much of the destruction in and around Ebenezerville was so bad that it could not be fully assessed until the sun rose on Saturday.

Most Saturday morning activities that had been scheduled in advance—Easter weekend check-ins at beach rentals, golf outings, Easter egg hunts, Little League games, shopping trips and sightseeing excursions—were either postponed or canceled altogether in the cities and towns of Iron Harbor, Port Oleander, Monk's Landing and Mimosa Beach, depending upon the activity's importance. But in storm-ravaged Ebenezerville, no everyday activities were possible that day and for days to come, except for rescue and recovery efforts, especially in the downtown business district. Due to the extent of tornado damage, not even rebuilding could start right away. Emergency officials met at sunrise on that grim Saturday morning to survey the damage and assign search-and-rescue teams with dogs to the worst-hit blocks downtown.

Around eight o'clock that Saturday morning, Artie and Harry Bauer, Minnie and Wilma Marecek, and Ty Green toyed with their coffee cups around the long kitchen table in the Bauer farmhouse. Artie and Ty had already been back to the school campus and had waited for a wrecker to come and haul off Ty's totaled car, *The White Whale*. His ex-girlfriend's father, Donnell Evans, had been happy to pick up the white LTD, though he warned Ty that body work might cost more than the old Ford was worth. He also encouraged him not to give up on Nicie, Donnell's daughter—that she was anxious about her own future and was "going through a phase," he said.

Looking across the kitchen table at Artie, his best friend, Ty said, "Thanks for the lift, buddy. I need to run to your bathroom before Dad gets here in a few minutes." He also nodded to Minnie Marecek and her niece, Wilma, also a senior at Arbor High. "Oh, and thanks for the coffee, ladies," Ty said, tipping his lidded cup at them. "I hope the power comes back on around here soon. Hauling water from the creek gets old quick." He stood to leave.

"Yeah," said Artie, "not to mention, Grandpa gets grumpy when he can't make himself a good cup of coffee."

Harry Bauer snorted. "I like a strong cup of Joe, young man," he said, holding up the coffee that Dr. Marecek had brought him from town. "This here is pretty good for store-bought brew."

As Ty Green stepped into Grandpa's bedroom off the kitchen to use its half-bath, the telephone rang. Artie jumped up and grabbed the handset from the phone mounted on the wall behind him. The caller was Bennie Pressler, another friend from school. For some privacy, Artie pulled the handset's coiled cord taut and stepped just around the corner into the hallway that led to the farmhouse's front door. The conversation took only a couple of minutes, after which the big farm boy reset the receiver on its hook and sat back down at the kitchen table. Ty opened the bedroom door and rejoined them.

Artie looked at Ty, then at Wilma. "Bennie needs our help," said Artie. "The tornado destroyed his family's store in E-ville—you know, the old store downtown. Bennie wants *us*—the Barf Table gang, as many of us as can—to help his father look for some important stuff where his office used to be. He said they'll pay us. I mean, they have a crew on the way to gather up clothes and other merchandise that hasn't been damaged, to give to storm victims. But Mr. Pressler wants us to work with him in the office area. I guess he trusts us not to blab about what we find."

Artie added, "Oh, and Minnie . . . Bennie said he needs to take a rain check—well, a *tornado* check, he should've said—on his horse-therapy session this morning."

The other two teens—and the two adults—agreed that they should help the Presslers however they could, because Abe Pressler had done so much over the past year to help them. Sure, he was the richest person in Oleander County and one of the wealthiest individuals in the region. In addition to the original store in downtown Ebenezerville, the Pressler's Department Store chain maintained locations in Iron Harbor and Mimosa Beach, as well as in almost every good-sized city or town with a shopping mall, including Capital City. But Abe and Deborah Pressler also donated more time and money to local causes than any other business in Oleander County. In fact, Deborah Pressler's main job was to coordinate the company's community outreach. Now the community needed to reach out to them.

"What can we do to help?" asked Minnie Marecek. "I wouldn't have such a successful practice out here on the farm if not for Abe. He helped me move my horses here from Stark Stables."

In her early fifties, rawboned Minnie had worked in other towns and counseling practices during her long career, even in Capital City. She was one of the most positive people that Artie had ever known, always looking at the bright side of things. Equine therapy also suited her, with her love of horses and the outdoors. Eighteen-year-old Wilma had told Artie that she might follow in her Aunt Minnie's footsteps as a horse therapist. A certified assistant, she was now half a head taller and twenty pounds heavier than her aunt, definite attributes in the stables, paddock and corral.

"And the Barf Table wouldn't have a real clubhouse," said Wilma, "just that little round table in the lunchroom at school."

Artie nodded. "I know," he said. "We owe Mr. and Mrs. Pressler—and Bennie—a lot. I'll try to get hold of Ricky, if he and Ricardo haven't left yet."

"I'll run out to the office trailer and call Leah," said Wilma. "We can't have her therapy session this morning, either, not with everything else going on. Right, Aunt Minnie?"

Dr. Marecek nodded. "Right," she said. "Tell you what. I'll stay here to exercise and groom our horses—yours, too, Mr. Bauer—and you kids can take the Suburban to E-ville. It'll hold the whole gang, or whoever can come."

Harry Bauer didn't want to be outdone. "I'll exercise and groom my *own* horses, thank you very much," he said to Minnie, a grin on his weathered face. "I ain't a cripple no more. And my workhorses only stand still for me or Artie or Ricardo to use a currycomb on them. Tom and Dick are particular like that. They don't let nice-smelling women handle them—not for long, anyways."

Minnie laughed. "Okay, Harry," she said. "We'll *both* work with the horses." She turned to Ty Green and asked, "Is all your livestock accounted for now— over on your farm?"

"Yeah," Ty said, "it took him a while, but Dad finally found a steer that ran off last night. It was down by the creek. We were gonna walk the fence line today, but I'm sure Dad will let me go help Mr. Pressler. He knows how important that family is to me—to *all* of us. I wouldn't have my weight room out there in the trailer, if it wasn't for Mr. Pressler. He's the man."

Minutes later, Ty Green jogged outside to meet his father, who had just pulled into the parking area at the farmhouse. While they talked, Artie Bauer made his calls—to little Ricky Duran, whose family lived in the old Bauer homeplace across the highway, and to Brett Woods, whose father, Woody Woods, ran Woody's Surf Shop & Grill at Sandpiper Beach. Artie caught little Ricky at home and got his father Ricardo's permission to join them. No one answered the phone at Brett's house on the beach, and the line to the surf shop was busy. But when Wilma Marecek returned to the farmhouse, she informed the boys that Leah Russo, Nicie Evans and Brett Woods would meet them at the Pressler's site downtown after they finished passing out food and water to emergency workers. Brett had worked for his father for a couple of years; Leah and Nicie had just gone to work for Woody. He had closed the surf shop and grill at least for that day.

Like the Pressler's chain, Woody Woods's three surf shops—on the strand at Sandpiper Beach and in Iron Harbor and Mimosa Beach—didn't hesitate to do community service, whether it was keeping the beaches clean or making sure that local teenagers had wholesome fun in the sand and surf. Woody sponsored events at the county's beaches in the summer. He also fed Arbor High's sports teams during seasons when his only grill—the one at Sandpiper Beach—was open. It was only coincidental that his son, Brett Woods, a 10th grader, had become a star on the Arbor Bruins football team the previous fall. The shaggy-headed teen was a surfer at heart, but he could carry and catch a football like few other boys in Oleander County. How he ended up sitting at the school cafeteria's Barf Table—where the student body's so-called losers and misfits sat—was hardly coincidental. It had to do with the most definite of intentions—those involving a teenage boy's heart.

* * *

A mile before Ebenezerville Road's two lanes became Commerce Avenue's four lanes, the wide swath of tornado damage that cut across the small town was breathtaking to the four friends in Wilma Marecek's white Suburban. Outside town, trees large and small lay on the ground everywhere, twisted and broken, or uprooted, leaving deep holes at what had once been their bases. Anything that had been mobile—manufactured homes, campers, cars, trucks, boats and trailers—looked like playthings that a petulant child had tossed aside. A number of houses along E-ville Road—frame and brick structures alike—sat in ruins, their roofs ripped off and one or more of their walls collapsed. The twister also had crushed metal storage sheds like soda cans and had flattened farm buildings as if they were made of matchsticks. Along Commerce Avenue, fast-food joints, convenience stores, strip malls, shopping centers and motels were all heavily damaged, if not destroyed. None of those businesses were open that morning. Overturned vehicles, including two eighteen-wheelers—a tractor-trailer rig and a tanker truck—made driving into the business district something like navigating a video game maze without a joystick or reset button.

Turning onto Main Street into the heart of Ebenezerville's downtown, Wilma

Marecek looked up into her rear-view mirror at Ty Green sitting behind her. "Ty, when does your mother's next shift start?" Wilma asked. "She's off duty right now, isn't she?"

"Yeah, Dad told me she's off until noon," said Ty, seeing the red brick of the three-story hospital building up ahead on the left. "Holy cow, it didn't have much damage at all, but look at the church—and the high school. Oh, my gosh."

Ebenezerville General Hospital and Solid Rock Christian Church faced each other on opposite sides of the once tree-lined Main Street. The church's high school—Solid Rock Christian Academy—sat behind the church building. On a side street, the sprawling school campus consisted of a sixty-year-old, two-story brick building that had been the old Ebenezerville High School; a modern, prefabricated steel gymnasium with metal siding; and a stadium with a central press box and tall sets of metal bleachers that could be moved to accommodate football or baseball, in season. Solid Rock's softball team played across town on one of the fields at E-ville Community Park.

No trees were left standing on that section of Main Street. The church's white, wooden steeple lay on the green front lawn, its point and the golden cross at the tip extending well into the roadway, an obstacle to be avoided. Two men in work clothes and hard hats stood beside the steeple and shouted at the driver of a yellow backhoe, waving for him to turn around and use the front-loader instead. Behind the church with its damaged roof and crumbling walls, the entire school campus had been razed. There was nothing left except the sections of brick and pieces of metal on the ground that the tornado hadn't carried away in its maw-like vortex.

Across the street from the church, the hospital had stood sentinel over nature's destruction but had been inexplicably spared no more than cosmetic damage to covered walkways out front and to the entrance's plate-glass windows facing the devastated church and obliterated school campus.

"Do we need to stop, Ty?" asked Wilma. "Do you want to see your mom?"

Ty looked away from the storm damage outside and caught Wilma's eye in the rear-view mirror. "Not right now," he said. "I'm sure she needs to rest. I'll try to call her later."

Now it was little Ricky Duran's turn to talk, having been quiet since leaving the Bauer farm. Artie Bauer twisted in his front seat to face the diminutive 9th grader and asked, "Where did you and Ricardo work last night? He came through the barn this morning when I was doing the milking, but we didn't get a chance to talk."

Ricky's eyes showed his weariness, and he sadly shook his head. "We started at the church," he said, "but then we heard that there were people trapped in cars and in stores up ahead on Main Street." He paused for a second as he appeared to recall horrible scenes from the night before. Until right then, he hadn't described the worst of what he'd encountered. "Father and I found an old man in a car," Ricky continued. "He was alive when Father ran to get help for him because he was bleeding." Ricky was silent again for a moment. "The man died before the EMTs came. I was holding his hand."

Wilma looked up into the mirror again. "Oh, Ricky," she said. "I'm so sorry."

Ty reached over and squeezed Ricky's shoulder. "You did what you could, buddy," Ty said. "That kind of thing really bothers Mom, too, and it happens pretty often to a nurse. She says that's all you can do sometimes—just hold their hand and be there with them."

Artie regretted making the boy relive that painful experience. "Yeah, Ricky, I'm sorry, too," said Artie. "I shouldn't have pushed you to talk."

"That is okay, my friend," Ricky said, turning away to look out his window. "I needed to share it with someone, and I trust you—all three of you."

Before the previous night's storm, Ebenezerville was known as having one of the most charming downtown business districts in the state, with two rows of historic, turn-of-the-century storefronts and office buildings that supported the community's two main industries, a commercial bakery and a textile mill, both located on the other side of town. The first Pressler's Department Store—originally known as Pressler & Company—started in the 1930s and was located in the heart of downtown, at 100 West Main Street. Bennie Pressler had once told his friends that this first "general" store carried everything—food, sundries, hardware, clothing, jewelry, musical instruments, fine furniture and even coffins—and that the original proprietor was his great-grandfather, Noah Pressler, an immigrant from Bavaria. As the business was passed down from father to son, then again from father to son, the store expanded its physical size on Main Street and modernized the facility, but narrowed its inventory in keeping with that of a modern department store. Bennie's father Abe, the second son to inherit the business, was proud that Pressler's served everyone in the community, whether they were doctors at the hospital, lawyers with Main Street offices, or hourly workers at the bakery and mill.

Wilma parked the white Suburban next to the old fountain, now dry, in the middle of town, part of a downtown plaza or bench-lined park across the street from what was left of Pressler's Department Store. The damage was on par with what the teenagers had seen minutes earlier at Solid Rock Christian Church, except that there was much more roof damage to the business. All the display windows along Main Street had been blown out, with headless and limbless mannequins lying here and there. It was as if the funnel cloud had skipped over one of the newer sections of the store, but then had dropped like a drill press through the original storefront's roof, square in the middle of the historic building. The suite of rooms upstairs where through the decades all three Pressler men, including Abe, had kept their main office appeared intact but heavily damaged.

Ty whistled softly at the sight. "Dang," he muttered. "No wonder Bennie called us to come help. That's almost as bad as the school."

"At least part of it is still standing," said Artie. "I mean, part of the old store. Mr. Pressler was so proud of it—that he was still using the same space where his grandfather and father had done business. That's how I feel about our farm."

With that, Ricky perked up. "It *is* the same thing, isn't it?" the small boy said. "It is *tradition*—what my parents are trying to build for me here in this country. I would be very sad if what I had built for my children was destroyed all at once like this. Bennie must feel very bad, too."

Wilma, who had noted the damage across the street and then looked away, spoke up. "Well, we could ask him," she said. "He's sitting on that bench right over there—with his dad." She paused. "But I think that sad picture says it all."

Side by side on the bench, Bennie leaned into his father, with one hand touching Abe's shoulder and the other holding the man's hand. Abe Pressler, a friend of all his neighbors across Oleander County, sat on the square of his family's American hometown and wept openly, in broad daylight.

After his blunder with Ricky minutes earlier, Artie knew exactly what to say and do. "They'll see us when they're ready," he said. "We're here, and that's what's important."

* * *

That evening, as Wilma Marecek wheeled the white Suburban down Bauer farm lane and drove around the barn to park, she and her passengers saw that lights were on in the doublewide trailer whose back half served as their clubhouse. The front half housed the office and waiting room for Minnie Marecek's horse-therapy practice. Dr. Marecek herself stood outside her door on the front deck and leaned on its flat, top rail, as if she were worn out and in need of both rest and a breath of fresh night air. She looked up and waved the teenagers onto the deck, where they all took seats on two long benches that farm handyman Ricardo Duran had made and given them. The indigo sky was clear and growing darker by the minute, so that more and more points of starlight were visible.

"This has been some kind of day, hasn't it?" Dr. Marecek said. "I'd be happy to just sit out here in the dark and look up at the stars." She waited. When no one spoke, she added, "We should turn off the porch light, I guess."

Just then, the door to Minnie's waiting room opened, and Bennie Pressler walked outside to join his friends. He was followed by a tall, husky youth with tousled blond hair. It was Tommy White, a 9th grader, who lived with the Presslers as their foster son and had been an indispensible help the previous semester while Bennie was confined to a wheelchair after an accident. Like Minnie, both boys appeared to be bushed. Bennie had assisted his father Abe at the downtown store all day; Tommy had helped his foster mother Deborah set up and man a relief tent at a fire station on the outskirts of town.

"Hi, guys," said Bennie, taking a seat next to Wilma. "Where have you been? You left before we did. And where is everybody? I thought Brett and the girls would be with you."

Ty spoke up. "You must have passed us when we stopped for sodas," he said. "And Nicie nixed riding with us. Artie said there was more than enough room for her and Leah in Wilma's Suburban—in *Moby*—but they wanted to ride back to the beach with Brett and Woody. And Nicie had left her car at the surf shop. Who knows? They may show up here yet."

"Well," said Bennie, "that makes sense, then. And Leah wants to spend as much time with Brett as she can. That's why she's working at Woody's, isn't it—to hang out with him?"

Wilma nudged the dark-haired boy sitting beside her. "Don't be jealous, Bennie," she said. "Leah wants a weekend job so she doesn't have to ask her dad for money all the time. Besides, Leah says Brett doesn't spend all that much time in the store *or* the grill on Saturdays and Sundays. He's always out on the beach surfing or delivering pizzas in *The Woody Wagon*."

At her mention of the grill's legendary delivery vehicle—an old, wood-paneled station wagon that Woody had owned since his own youth—Wilma turned to Ty and said, "I'm still not sure *Moby* is the best name for my Suburban. You're the one into whales. Minnie and I are into horses. What famous horse could we name the truck after?"

"*Mister Ed*?" said Bennie and then whinnied, "Wi-i-i-i-ilma," like the famous talking horse.

The big girl tried not to laugh. "No," Wilma said, "but that's what it sounds like sometimes when I can't get it started. Gimme some other ideas, guys."

Artie scratched his head. "*Silver*?" he said. "*Trigger*? How about *Tornado*? But then you'd have to paint the truck black."

"No, no," said Ricky Duran. "It would look like a hearse, and we have had enough death." The boy's reminder about the storm's fatalities that weekend—five deaths in Oleander County alone—hushed the group momentarily.

Seated on the other bench, Tommy leaned forward and waved at Wilma.

"*Goblin*," he said, "you know, like in *Thunderhead*. That was my favorite book when I was a kid."

Tuning in again from stargazing, Minnie Marecek exclaimed, "Oh, Tommy, that was my favorite book, too, when I was a girl—so much better than *My Friend, Flicka*. But, no, if the Suburban must have a name, let's just stick with *Moby*. That's short and sweet."

Minnie seemed anxious to talk again about that day's activities, as difficult as they had been. "Artie, your grandfather and I worked really hard today," she said. "After we exercised the horses and got them all groomed, we hopped into your pickup truck and drove over to that quaint little country church of yours. Harry was worried about your grandmother's grave—well, about *all* the graves in that old cemetery. You do have a lot of family buried there."

"Shin's Grove isn't our church, not anymore," said Artie, his face suddenly warm, though no one else could see in the darkness that it was flushed. "We stopped going there when I was a baby," he said. "Those people gave my mother a hard time because she wasn't married."

Raising her hand, Minnie nodded. "I know, Artie," she said, "and I'm sorry. I misspoke to say it was *your* church." When Artie nodded, she continued, "There *were* some trees down, and I was able to call Ricardo to bring his chainsaw and cut the ones that had fallen in the cemetery. We also had to set some headstones back up that had been pushed over."

"Was Grandma's stone knocked down?" asked Artie. "I didn't even think about that."

"No, it was fine," Minnie said. "There were other family graves that needed fixing, but Pearl's grave and headstone weren't damaged. I think just seeing her stone and reading his own name there—you know, without that last big date on it—well, that bothered him. So, remember that when you go back to the house later. He's still mourning her, as I'm sure you are, too."

The therapist rose from the bench and prepared to go back into her office. "I hope you all can come back here tomorrow, even though it's Easter," she said. "I have an activity in mind that I think will help us out." Artie wondered what all

Minnie knew about the teenagers' experiences helping others that day in E-ville, but he figured that Bennie and Tommy must have filled her in before *Moby* got to the farm with the others.

Minnie finished her thought: "I'll go ahead and call the ones that aren't here—Leah and Nicie, Jamie and Brett—and ask them to be here around, oh, let's say, around six. That'll give us a couple of hours before dark. As far as the rest of the group goes, that just leaves Julia, and she probably won't be home until late tomorrow night, if she makes the finals again. She told me today on the phone that her draw looks really good and that she's playing well."

Hearing about tennis phenom Julia Safin made Artie Bauer blush once again. Not only was this girl good at tennis, she was beautiful, not to mention more mature than any other 18-year-old girl that Artie had ever known. A Russian exchange student at Arbor High, she lived with the Mareceks and was chaperoned at junior tennis tournaments in and out of state by Wilma's mother, Lena. The reference to Julia embarrassed Artie because the next day, Easter Sunday, would be their three-week anniversary—of their breakup, that is.

"I don't want to sound vindictive or anything," said Artie, "but is Julia still a member of the Barf Table?" He looked at the other teens for some support. "I mean, she's hardly ever at school, and when she is there, she doesn't eat lunch with us. She's always in the guidance office or with a teacher, and when she does come to the cafeteria, she sits with other friends."

"Come on, Artie," said Wilma, growing irritated at her friend. "She *thinks* she's still a member of the group." Wilma glanced over at Ty Green. "I mean, *Nicie* doesn't even sit with us all the time now—right, Ty?—not since you guys broke up. But Nicie is still a part of the group, so why not Julia?" The big girl looked to her aunt for input.

Minnie Marecek raised both palms to the night sky. "That's not for me to decide," Minnie said. "Who is or isn't a part of your group is something that you all have to answer for yourselves. Maybe you should wait and talk to Julia. At the start of the year, none of you—well, nobody except Artie—wanted to sit at the Barf Table. You wanted to sit somewhere else so you could show the other kids that you really did fit in with them. But you showed them anyway and built something special for yourselves individually and as a group of friends. Trust me, you don't want to throw that away."

Artie reached over and patted Wilma on the knee. "I'm sorry, friend," he said. "I'm new at this break-up stuff. I'm still Julia's friend, and she can still be mine if she wants to be." He looked over at his best buddy, Ty Green. "Right, Ty? Is that how you feel about Nicie?"

"Sure," Ty said, "as long as her dad still fixes *The Whale*. I mean, a good mechanic is worth his weight in girlfriends—or gold, or diamonds." He laughed. "Nah, just kidding. But I do miss the peanut butter and jelly sandwiches she used to bring for our lunch."

Dr. Marecek smiled. "You're hopeless, Ty Green," she said. "No, I'll give the others a call, and hopefully everybody can be here tomorrow night." As she stepped back into the trailer, the light from inside showed a mischievous gleam in her eyes. She added, "Now we have *two* agenda items—what I had originally planned and showing Ty here how to make the perfect PB&J sandwich. We don't want our star pitcher to go hungry, do we?"

"Or his catcher," said Artie Bauer. "I'm still a growing boy."

Bennie Pressler laughed and pointed at Ricky and Tommy, and then touched his own chest. "Or his new second baseman. Or his new first baseman. Or his public address announcer. And, don't forget, Brett's playing third." Then to Wilma, Bennie said, "You and Nicie and Leah and Jamie—all you softball girls—you can get Julia to show you how to make some kind of weird Russian sandwich, since Nicie is already an expert at PB&J. Maybe Julia will get home early."

"She won't be here," said Artie. "She'll be in the championship match, and if she doesn't win it, she'll give it her best." He nodded to Minnie as she started to turn away, and he added, "That's what it means to be a member of the Barf Table—always has, always will. We're Barf Table strong."

CHAPTER 3

BUT ARTIE WAS WRONG about his former girlfriend Julia Safin—in more ways than one. After seeing Saturday's news reports on the Oleander County storms, Julia had gone into both of her matches that day more than a bit distracted. She won both matches, but not in her usual impressive fashion.

On Easter Sunday morning, she had risen early to watch the news updates from Ebenezerville. The TV reporter had interviewed Deborah Pressler with Tommy White and other volunteers in the relief tent. The news story also showed scenes of the devastation downtown, including the damage done to the Solid Rock church and school, and to the old Pressler's store. In those shots, Julia had spotted Artie Bauer and other Barf Table friends working with Abe Pressler in the rubble.

That was when Julia decided to withdraw from the tournament, though she had been favored to win her semi-final match that morning and also the championship match that afternoon. She didn't care. Without calling home, she and Lena Marecek were on the highway back to Monk's Landing before most of the churches along the way had finished their Easter sunrise services and fellowship breakfasts.

Some of those churches had erected flower-covered crosses on their front lawns to symbolize the Resurrection, as well as nature's rebirth. In the passenger seat of Lena's car, Julia stared out at the colorful spring blossoms—on the crosses and in yards, gardens and fields—and she hoped against hope that her new home of Oleander County could experience that same resurrection and rebirth from the deadly Good Friday Storm.

* * *

Even seated in the bathroom upstairs, Artie heard the knock on the back door to the farmhouse. Being indisposed at the moment, he hoped Grandpa was awake and could answer the door before the visitor left. Artie sat up straight to peer out the bathroom window toward the back yard, but he could see neither the back walkway nor the parking area.

The knock sounded again. This time, Harry Bauer's gruff voice greeted the visitor. "Hold your horses!" Grandpa shouted from his bedroom downstairs. "Gimme a minute to get my pants on!" That was followed by bumping and banging as the old farmer moved from his bedroom, through the kitchen and onto the enclosed back porch, to the back door. Artie could hear muffled voices, but he couldn't tell who had come to visit.

"Artie!" called Grandpa, back in the kitchen. "Get down here! You've got company!"

When Artie emerged from the bathroom and started down the stairs, he saw Julia Safin waiting for him in the hallway below. Grandpa was nowhere in sight, either having stayed in the kitchen or gone back to his bedroom. The tall, dark-haired Russian girl's natural beauty—as she wore neither makeup nor flattering clothes, just a white warm-up suit and tennis shoes—made Artie's heart skip a beat and his breathing quicken.

"What are you doing here?" said Artie. When he realized how the question sounded, he added, "I mean, I'm happy to see you, but . . . aren't you supposed to be playing tennis?"

There were tears in her eyes, and she dropped her head to dab them with her sleeve. "I saw pictures of what happened in Ebenezerville," Julia said, looking up again. "I saw you all working together to help Bennie and his parents. I, too, should have been there."

"Why?" asked Artie. He stopped at the bottom of the stairs and rested one hand on the post cap of the dark wooden banister. When he saw that she was struggling to answer, he said, "We knew if you hadn't been away at a tournament, you would've been right there with us. You're still part of our group, right? That hasn't changed, has it?" She began to cry again.

As he waited for her answers, Artie took his eyes off Julia for an instant and saw his grandfather step out onto the back porch and close the door behind himself. Artie took Julia's arm and led her into the simple living room, with its old, overstuffed sofa, fake-leather recliner and console television. They sat together on the sofa, their knees pointing toward one another but not touching. He pulled a tissue from the box on the end table near him and gave it to her.

"Don't cry," Artie said. "Just because you broke up with me, doesn't mean you broke up with the whole gang. And it doesn't mean we can't still be friends— you and me—if that's what you want."

"Yes, Arthur," said Julia, "that *is* what I want. I *do* want to be your friend." She took a breath. "But I want you to understand *why* I cannot keep dating you while I am playing tennis."

"*While you're playing tennis?*" Artie repeated. "Isn't that what you want to do for the rest of your life—play tennis?"

"Yes," she said again, "just as you want to stay here and run your family's farm, and to make it a successful business. You are doing this as much for your grandfather as for yourself. You want to honor him and make him proud." She paused and checked to see where Harry Bauer had gone. "I want to do the same for *my* father—to honor his memory. He was a great athlete."

Artie nodded and smiled sadly. "Yeah, we *are* alike," he said. "By the way, Grandpa hasn't said so, but he misses you a bunch. He asked what I did to *run you off.*"

"Did you tell him you did not *run me off?*" said Julia. She glanced toward the back porch again.

"Don't worry," Artie said. "He's out there in his old chair reading a farmer magazine so we have some privacy." He winked. "When we started going out, he said he'd do that so I wouldn't have to *run out of gas*, just to be alone with you."

They both smiled, knowing that "running out of gas" on a date was an inside joke within their circle of friends—something Ty Green had been accused of doing with different girls he had dated. Even Grandpa had admitted using the ruse with Grandma before they were married.

"I love Meester Bauer, your grandfather," said Julia. "I truly do. But you understand why I cannot date you now. You talked much about wanting to study agriculture at Iron Harbor A&M, and about your hopes for this farm. I do not want to come between you and your dreams—to make you feel as if you must attend all my matches now and, next year, follow me to State College. Your future is right here, close to your grandfather, for as long as that is possible. Is that not true?"

Artie recalled Minnie Marecek's advice the night before about making important decisions that affected others, but without their input. "Shouldn't that be *my* choice—I mean, about *my* future?" he asked. "That is, if we want to be more than just friends, and if we . . . *love* each other?" It was the first time he had used that word in that way with her, and he feared he had just asked a question whose answer he did not want to hear.

But, again, Julia surprised him. "That is the problem, Arthur," she said. "I *do* love you. But you and I have *separate* dreams, and they will keep us apart if we pursue them as we should. Just as I do not want to hurt you, I do not wish to be hurt *by* you—by being away from you when I am lonely and when I need to feel loved. I am afraid we will resent each other, and then not even friendship will be possible."

"What if I want to play ball or wrestle for State College?" he asked. "What if I get a scholarship offer from there—maybe in baseball—and then we're both in Capital City next year?"

She shook her head. "I may not be there more than a year," she said, "or maybe two. My dream is to play on the women's tour—to be a professional—and then I would have to travel all around the world, all year round." No longer crying, she appeared stronger. "But it is just a dream right now, and I must do all I can to achieve it—despite what I did today. I cannot quit, Arthur, every time I want to be somewhere else."

"No, you can't do that," said Artie, agreeing with her. "But today was a different situation, and everyone will be happy you decided to come back early. You know, we're meeting tonight at six—in the clubhouse. Now the whole gang can be there." He touched her smooth, tanned hand resting on the sofa cushion. "Are you sure? About us?"

"Trust me, Arthur," she said. "This will be what is best—for both of us. We must both be patient about what the future holds."

Julia rose from the sofa and started to leave, but stopped short. "Arthur?" she asked, turning to face him again. "Wilma and I are accompanying Dr. Marecek to Ebenezerville this afternoon. Would you like to go with us? Dr. Marecek will meet with others about the school there, and Wilma and I will assist Bennie and Tommy in the relief tent while Mrs. Pressler attends the same meeting."

Artie wasn't certain how well their new friendship arrangement would work, but he was willing to give it a try. "Sure," he said. "Just give me a buzz from Minnie's office when you're ready to leave. I'll let Grandpa know I'm going with you—with Minnie, I mean."

Julia smiled and nodded, and Artie followed her into the kitchen to see her onto the back porch, where Grandpa was, in fact, sitting and reading a farm journal. The old man dropped the magazine and stood at his chair as the pretty girl approached him on her way toward the back door. Artie remained in the kitchen and listened as the two people he cared for the most—his grandfather and his former girlfriend—exchanged pleasantries about the beautiful spring weather that Easter morning.

Then Artie watched out the kitchen window as Julia walked through the yard and up the farm lane toward the barn and the doublewide trailer behind it. All he could think about right then was what might have been—for better or for worse. She would always be his first true love, and now they could at least be friends.

* * *

The group activities that Dr. Minnie Marecek had planned for the Barf Table gang changed as a result of the meeting she had attended that afternoon in Ebenezerville. Everyone was present, even Jamie Foxx, who had been helping her mother, a real estate agent, inspect Sandpiper Realty's rental houses on the beach all weekend before spring vacationers checked in. The rental company had also been having trouble with septic problems at their houses.

Delayed by the storm, tourists streamed into Oleander County late Saturday and all day Sunday, jamming local roadways and also the local businesses that had managed to reopen. However, even on Sunday, Woody's Surf Shop & Grill remained closed so that Woody Woods, Brett Woods, Leah Russo and Nicie Evans could keep fixing food for storm victims and emergency crews. They delivered boxes of food and drinks late Sunday morning and again that afternoon.

Both Ty Green and Little Ricky Duran attended church services separately with their families in the morning, and then spent the early afternoon helping their fathers. Though Ty hadn't hiked from his family's farm to Artie's since their middle school years, he did so that Sunday afternoon, stopping to rest at the old homeplace where Little Ricky and his family lived out by the highway. With *The White Whale* out of commission, Ty would have to either walk, get out his old ten-speed bike, or catch a ride with someone, just as Artie had done until Harry Bauer's accident the previous fall freed up the farm's pickup for Artie's own use.

Ricky walked down the farm lane with Ty, and the pair arrived at the clubhouse just as *Moby* and *The Woody Wagon* pulled in from E-ville. Minutes later, Jamie Foxx was dropped off after her long day at Sandpiper Beach with her mother.

Jamie was thrilled to see her former exchange sister Julia Safin, who had lived with the Foxxes in the fall and winter. "Julia, you're here!" said Jamie, taking a seat on the doublewide's deck. "I thought you'd still be on the road— even though I figured you'd win your match this afternoon in straight sets."

"I did not win," Julia said matter-of-factly. "I forfeited this morning's match so that I could come home and be with my friends. The storm damage looked so horrible on television that I could not have played my best. I needed to come home." She glanced at Artie sitting on the other bench.

Bennie Pressler, usually the group's comedian, was dead serious when he offered, "Dad told me to thank all of you. What that tornado did to our store downtown was almost more than he could bear." He paused to catch his breath. "It meant the world to him—and to me—that you guys would help us like you did. I mean, that hundred-year-old safe was a bear to move. But thanks. You, too, Julia. Thank you." His voice cracked on those last words. Foster brother Tommy White patted Bennie on the shoulder.

Still mourning the death a year earlier of her older brother, Leah Russo also tried to comfort Bennie. "That's how my dad and I felt before Christmas when everyone helped us pack up Reuben's things," said Leah. "It hurt Mom and Dad so much—well, it hurt me, too—just to walk into his room. I think I sent you and Brett an email about that when you two were in Hawaii last winter, Bennie."

"You did," Bennie said. "I'm glad we were able to stay in such good touch, even though we were so far apart. Isn't email wonderful? And the internet?"

Dr. Minnie Marecek had been standing at her office door, listening to the teens' conversation. When Bennie mentioned the advances in computer technology and communications, she opened the screen door and stuck her head outside. "Come on in, everyone," Minnie said. "Let's get started. I set up another table, so I think everyone can find a place to sit."

As the eleven teens took their places at the two round tables in their clubhouse—one, an old, round, dining-room table; the other, a portable table, also round—Minnie handed out sheets of lined notebook paper and pencils.

"Since we don't have eleven computers for you to use," began Minnie, "we're going to do this 'old-school'—on paper. And, yes, these are No. 2 pencils, Bennie." She looked at the now serious, dark-haired boy and winked, as if she were priming his comedic pump.

He managed a grin. "Are we gonna be tested?" asked Bennie. "Should we take good notes?"

"This is the test," Minnie replied. "Well, it's a test, but you can't fail it—if you do your best." When everyone was ready, she continued, "I want you all to answer three questions for me. Your answers don't have to be long—just a sentence or two—but I want you to think a minute before you write each answer down. Use complete sentences so that if someone else reads it, they'll understand it. I'll read all three questions at once—write them down on your paper—and then I'll give you fifteen minutes to think and write your answers before we share them."

She paused for a few seconds and looked around the room, making eye contact with as many of the teens as she could. "Here's the first question," she said. "Other than the tornadoes themselves or, maybe, that the storm was really scary or that people got hurt, even killed … what was one thing that happened this weekend that had the biggest *negative* impact on you personally? For example, Bennie just told you how personally devastating the storm was for his father—through the destruction of his family's first department store. That might be how Abe Pressler would answer this question. Seeing the store that had meant so much to him and to generations of his family—seeing that building destroyed—had the most negative impact on Abe, we'll say. Now, Bennie's answer to that question might be a little different. How do *you* answer it? That's question number one."

She waited until they all finished writing. "Okay, here's number two," said Minnie. "What was the one thing that happened this weekend that brought you the most joy or hope or inspiration—the most *positive* thing from this weekend? And, again, be specific. Don't just say, for instance, that nobody close to you got hurt, or that *you* didn't get hurt in the storm, or that people came together and helped each other. What, specifically, gave you a *good* feeling this weekend? That's number two."

Again, she waited. Finally, she told them the last question. "Here's number three," she said. "Students from Solid Rock Christian Academy have been reassigned to finish the year at the county's other four high schools. That means that on Tuesday—there's no school tomorrow—you will receive about a hundred new students at Arbor High. Many of them are just like you, as far as damage to their homes and farms and places of employment go. But many others are like Bennie and his father, with much more storm damage around Ebenezerville than in other parts of the county. Many of them lost homes and vehicles and farm buildings and animals and the list could go on and on. There were many injuries and—what was the latest number . . . *eleven*? Eleven deaths. And *all* of the Solid Rock students have one other loss in common—the loss of their school and, for many, their church as well. Those young people are *grieving* those losses, and we must do our part to help them. Right?"

She looked around the room again and seemed gratified to see most of the teens nodding in agreement. "Okay," she continued, "here's the actual question: What can *you* do to help even one of those grieving students? For example, Wilma and I use our horses to help people overcome various challenges. I know from personal experience that caring for a horse and riding it helps me deal with my problems. But there's also art therapy and music therapy and dance therapy."

When Minnie said the word *dance*, everyone turned and looked at Little Ricky, and he raised his arms in celebration at having found his talent to share with others. "Yes!" he said, a big grin on this face. Everyone there knew that Ricky Duran was no slouch on the dance floor. He was the best male dancer at Arbor High. And Julia Safin was the best female dancer, as she had inherited her Russian mother's gift as a ballerina and modern dancer.

Minnie went on. "What we're doing right now—journaling—can also help us face our problems. How? By putting our problems into words and becoming mindful of ways to approach them. You know, when you share how you feel with someone who cares, you can feel that tightness in your chest—that weight on your *heart*—begin to ease. It's true."

She continued, "Reading can help, too. Maybe you can head up a book club. And if you aren't the studious type, some sort of physical activity also helps to relieve stress—like weight-lifting or yoga or *tai chi*." This time it was Ty Green's turn to let out a restrained *whoop*, as he'd already outfitted one side of the clubhouse with weight equipment.

"So, again," Minnie concluded, "what can *you* do to help these students you'll meet on Tuesday to deal with their grief and to help them feel as if they're a part of Arbor High? Maybe you can do more than one thing. That would be great. But give us one thing this evening, so that we have a place to start. Then we can move on from there. Someone has to lead."

Minnie gave the friends time to write—more than fifteen minutes, it turned out—and she didn't stand over them to see what they were writing or how much they wrote. In fact, she left the clubhouse trailer entirely and walked to the farmhouse to talk with Harry Bauer about a discussion she'd had that afternoon with another school committee member. That's what she told the teenagers as she went out the door at the start of their writing session.

When the therapist hadn't returned after twenty minutes, Wilma Marecek stood at her table, took up the paper she'd written on, and walked to the front. The big girl with dark, shoulder-length hair looked around the room, much as her aunt had done earlier in reading the questions. "Aunt Minnie asked me to get us started," she said. "I'll read my answers first, and then you take turns reading yours. If you want, I'll read your papers out loud for you—or not, if you'd rather keep them private. Okay?"

It was natural that Wilma would lead. In addition to being Dr. Marecek's niece, Wilma was the best female student grade-wise in the senior class at Arbor. Artie Bauer was best in academics for the boys. In fact, the two of them were competing for the school's top academic honor, valedictorian, the graduating senior with the best grades. As student-athletes, they also vied for the prestigious Ebenezer Endowment scholarship for a full, four-year ride to Iron Harbor A&M. Each school in the county awarded one such scholarship each year. The Ebenezer Endowment program had been funded for years mainly by local corporations and businesses like Pressler's Department Stores, Inc.

"What had the biggest negative impact on me?" Wilma read aloud. *"I will never forget the fear that I felt when Aunt Minnie and I heard the weather radio alarm go off Friday evening. We were doing paperwork in her office, and we heard the tornado warning on the radio. We knew we had to get out of this trailer right away, and that we had to let the horses and cows out of the barn so that they wouldn't be trapped if a tornado hit here. And we ran to the house to get Mr. Bauer and bring him back here. We hunkered down in the little block building next to the barn until the storm passed."*

As she hadn't followed Minnie's instructions to keep her answer short, Wilma looked around the room again, shrugged and finished. *"The worst thing was the fear of what might happen,"* she said, *"and not knowing what was happening, being completely in the dark in that building."*

Reading her answers to the second and third questions, Wilma explained that her greatest relief was emerging with Minnie and Mr. Bauer from the small, cinderblock-built creamery and seeing that the trailer, barn, farmhouse and other structures nearby had not been damaged much—that they were still standing. For question number three, she said she would continue working as an assistant in Minnie's horse-therapy practice, but she added that she would gladly tutor any students—not just the new ones from Solid Rock—who might need academic help.

When Wilma finished reading her answers, she looked up and waited for one of the other teens to share what they had written. As everyone might have expected, Artie Bauer stood and joined Wilma up front. "I'll go next," the big farm boy said. "I know it's not cool for guys to show their emotions, but I was so scared when me and Ty were hiding under the desk in the batting cage that I felt like crying. I—"

"Read what you wrote, Artie," interrupted Wilma. "That'll be enough."

He nodded and cleared his throat. "Okay," he said, looking down at his paper. *"When the storm hit Monk's Landing, I was afraid that Ty and I were about to die. Then we saw three emergency vehicles fly past the school on the highway headed this way, and I was afraid that my grandfather had been hurt, like last fall, and that he might die this time."* He looked up, his eyes moist.

"Number two," he continued, *"the best thing was seeing Grandpa sitting in the van with Ricky, and seeing that he was okay."* He smiled and added, despite Wilma's admonition not to ad-lib, "Simple as that. And I made sure to tell Grandpa later how much I love him and how much I appreciate what he's done for me my whole life." Several of the girls—Julia Safin among them—sobbed aloud at the big guy's confession.

"Number three," Artie read, *"I will do anything my friends and fellow*

students need me to do, but my grandfather and this farm have to come first." Feeling the need to explain, he added, "Ricky, we love you and Gabby and Ricardo like family, but my grandpa and I are the only *real* family we have left." Little Ricky Duran smiled and nodded that he understood.

"Thanks, Artie," said Wilma, as he went back to his seat. "Who's next? You don't have to come up here. You don't even have to stand up. Anybody?"

Ty Green raised his hand. He began by saying, "Well, I was afraid, too, Artie, and maybe this is being really selfish, but here's what I wrote: *The biggest negative for me personally was seeing what happened to my car."*

No one had made a sound, but he looked up from his paper and said, "Don't laugh. I need that car to play sports and help my folks. I don't know what I'm gonna do now. They can't buy me another car with all the bills Dad has to pay, and I can't get a job until this summer, not until baseball is over." He glanced over at Nicie, whose father was rebuilding *The Whale*, as Ty took up his paper to keep reading.

"The positive thing was seeing Mom help the family trapped in their car. I was so proud of her," Ty read, adding, "It makes me want to go into some kind of healthcare career, maybe physical therapy, maybe something else—after I'm done with baseball, I mean. What I wrote was: *I want to be like my mom. I want to help people."*

"Me, too," volunteered Nicie Evans, sitting at the other table away from Ty. When their eyes met for an instant, she looked away.

One by one, the others shared their answers. As Dr. Marecek had suggested, Bennie Pressler's responses dealt with the loss of his family's store, though his "worst thing" was seeing his father cry for the first time. Ricky Duran was next. Again, he mentioned being with the old man who died on Main Street, but he added that he and his father had helped to rescue five other people in a wrecked van, including three children, before they encountered the old man's demolished car. Brett Woods, Leah Russo and Nicie Evans all wrote about some aspect of their efforts helping Woody Woods make and distribute food in Ebenezerville. Julia Safin again described her horror at first seeing on television the destruction in Oleander County and her guilt at not having been with her friends in their time of need.

In turn, those group members' statements of what they might do to continue helping the Solid Rock transfers at Arbor High were predictable, based on each teen's interests and abilities. For instance, Bennie wanted to set up a computer bulletin board to help connect animal owners with their lost pets or livestock. Both Ricky and Julia were enthusiastic about Minnie's dance therapy suggestion. Brett admitted that he had started playing ukulele in Hawaii that winter, drawing some jibes from the others until he said music therapy sounded like fun. Being an introvert and an avid reader, Leah said she would head up a book club and practice journal writing with other students, too. As Nicie had indicated, she was interested in nursing, maybe starting out by learning first aid and CPR, and then by helping with classes for other students.

The only surprising responses came from Tommy White and Jamie Foxx. Always the quiet one, Tommy asked Bennie to read his answers aloud for him. Bennie agreed and took the single sheet from Tommy and looked over the three responses for a minute, glancing up at his foster brother a couple of times as if he didn't want to believe the words that Tommy had written.

"Really?" Bennie asked Tommy. When the straw-haired boy nodded, Bennie pursed his lips for a second before starting to read: "*I feel like a jerk 'cause I didn't even think about my real parents up in prison, like if they were okay or not. But I felt even worse when we were moving stuff out of my foster father's office, like that big old safe and all those pictures and paintings of the other Presslers, and I realized that I don't belong anywhere. The Presslers have been good to me, a lot better than my own family ever was, but I'm just in the way now.*" The room was silent.

Bennie continued reading, "*My good thing was helping my foster mother set up the big tent so she could help other people. That made me feel good to be needed like that. That was how I always felt when Bennie needed me to help him get around. I don't know what I can do for those kids from Solid Rock unless they need me to push a wheelchair or carry something or build something for them like that tent or my old beehives. I'm strong and good with my hands, and that's about it."*

Shaking his head, Bennie handed back the paper and said, "No, Tommy. You're wrong. You *do* belong, and you *do* have a lot to offer other people—not just kids in wheelchairs, like I was. I'm so sorry you feel that way." Tommy looked even sadder than before and dropped his eyes, as if he wished he hadn't been so honest about his feelings. Sitting beside him, Nicie leaned over and gave him a hug.

The biggest shocks were Jamie Foxx's three answers. It was almost as if she and Tommy had talked before they put down their thoughts, but they hadn't. Unlike Tommy, Jamie wasn't afraid to read out loud, even though she didn't waste any words making her points. Waiting until last to read her paper, the tomboyish athlete refused to make eye contact with any of her friends, not even with Julia, her former exchange sister. With short, brown hair curling over her softball visor, she pulled the brim down low to hide her eyes, and she didn't bother to sit up straight in her chair off to one side. She wore a dirty white T-shirt and torn jeans, both soiled from checking and cleaning rental properties all weekend with her mother at Sandpiper Beach. They had worked hard.

"The worst thing wasn't NOT hearing from my father," Jamie read in a tired voice. *"We couldn't reach him at the halfway house in Mimosa Beach, and he didn't call Mom's cell phone all weekend. The WORST thing was realizing that I just don't care about him anymore. He was probably dead drunk at a tornado party or something. I hate him. Maybe my good thing is, now I can admit to myself that I hate him and that I've hated him for years. I'm not in a position to help anybody. I'm the one who needs help."*

CHAPTER 4

AS MINNIE MARECEK HAD SAID, schools in Oleander County were closed on Easter Monday, not due to the holiday, but because of the Good Friday Storm. At the very least, most school buildings had cosmetic damage; a number of them, like Arbor High, needed to fix athletic facilities and other auxiliary structures before they could be used again. Also, the ad-hoc storm recovery committee's recommendation to send Solid Rock students to other high schools had to be approved by the board of education that morning in emergency session and then publicized on local news media. School administrators might have been too optimistic about reopening their doors so soon, but they wanted students and teachers alike to get back into familiar routines in safe environments as soon as possible. The longer they stayed out of school, the harder it would be to return.

Artie Bauer honked the horn of his red pickup as he pulled into the Greens' driveway. Although it was still early, Ty Green came out of his house carrying a plastic grocery bag that contained a baseball glove and shoes. He would need them for team practice late that afternoon. Except for his shoes, Artie kept most of his catcher's gear in his open locker in the team clubhouse. On this brisk spring morning, both boys wore their green-and-gold Arbor Bruins caps, as well as their gray practice pants and white baseball tees with three-quarter-length green sleeves, but no jackets.

"I like your Arbor High duffel bag, buddy," teased Artie, as Ty dropped the bulging grocery bag on the floorboard as he started to get into the truck. "Hold on a second," said Artie. "Look over there in that stand of redbud trees. What is that?" He pointed back in the direction he had just traveled on Little Swamp

Road, at some spindly trees with tiny, red flowers. Near the end of one limb not too high off the ground, a dark, amorphous shape hung down.

"Whoa," said Ty. "I'll go see." Leaving the truck door standing open, Ty jogged toward the trees which stood near the shoulder of the road. He stopped abruptly and studied the limb's odd appendage for a moment. Then he backed away without taking his eyes off the dark clump. When he got back to the truck, he leaned into the cab and said, "I think we just found Tommy's bees that he lost in the storm. Give me a minute to go call him. Maybe he can get out here quick and catch them before they fly away."

Artie nodded. "Yeah," he said, "*I'm* not gonna mess with them. Tell him we can come get him if he needs a ride. Coach will understand."

Ty disappeared into the house and was gone for a couple of minutes. When he reappeared, he was smiling. "I made that boy's day," said Ty. "He asked if we'd stay put and watch the bees until he gets here, just in case they *do* fly off. Then he'll know which direction to look for them."

"We can do that," Artie said. "He was really proud of those bees and the hives that Mr. Pressler bought him. I'm glad Grandpa agreed to let Tommy keep them on our farm, but I'm still kinda scared of them. How's he gonna get here?"

"The Presslers," said Ty. "They were getting ready to leave for E-ville, anyway, and were gonna drop Tommy off at school. He said they can just bring him over here instead, and then he can ride back to Arbor with us. I asked Mom to call the school and send word to Coach about what's going on."

When Tommy White arrived, he held a grocery bag similar to one Ty had stowed in Artie's truck. The tall, blond-haired boy dropped his shoes and first-baseman's mitt into the truck bed. He also carried a five-gallon bucket from which he took a curved pruning saw, a folded white sheet, leather gloves and a simple beekeeping veil.

"Hey, Ty," said Tommy, with a grin, "how 'bout we go over there, and you give me a boost? The limb they're on isn't all that high."

Shaking his head, Ty replied, "How 'bout I go get you a stepladder? Dad has one in the carport." He added, "I'm having a hard enough time with girls. I don't need a face full of welts." Ty turned toward the house.

"These girls aren't gonna sting you, Ty," said Tommy, as Ty walked away, "not right now. They're full of honey, and they're too fat and happy to sting anybody." He pulled on the long gloves and donned the veil over his ball cap.

"Well, why'd they swarm, then," asked Artie, "if they're so content?"

Tommy shrugged. "It's usually when something's going on in the hive," he said. "If the bees get too crowded or if something disturbs them, they'll leave. But they take as much of their honey as they can. That's why they're fat and happy."

"That makes sense," said Artie. "That storm sure did disturb me."

When Ty returned with the short stepladder, Tommy carried it and the bucket toward the swarm of honey bees.

Artie and Ty watched from inside the truck—with their windows rolled up—as their friend and teammate unfolded and spread the sheet beneath the overhanging limb. He set up the ladder, climbed it, and cut off the limb that held the swarm, holding the branch with his other hand so that it didn't fall. Descending the ladder with the limb in hand, he tipped it toward the ground and then shook the ball of bees onto the white sheet.

"I hope he knows what he's doing," said Ty. "He isn't wearing one of those big white moon suits like you see on TV. He has one, doesn't he?"

"Yeah," Artie said, "and he usually wears it—or a jacket, at least. What's he doing now?" Tommy had bent over, as if he'd dropped something into the dark mass of bees on the white sheet.

"What's he looking for?" asked Ty.

Artie chuckled. "I don't know," he said, "but I wouldn't be picking it up until all those bees are gone. Look, he's taking off one of his gloves!"

Crouching over the sheet, Tommy reached down and took something between his bare thumb and forefinger—one of the bees, it appeared—and gently placed it inside the bucket. He had already laid the bucket on its side and had tucked one corner of the sheet into it. The tall teenager then sat back on his heels, as if he were waiting for something to happen—and it did.

"Look at that!" Ty said. "They're going into the bucket all by themselves! He doesn't even have to do anything! It's like a parade!"

Within minutes, the swarm was inside the five-gallon container. Tommy tilted it upright and put on the bucket's lid containing holes that were just large enough to give the bees air without letting them escape. He folded the ladder, picked up his sheet, glove and saw, and carried everything to the truck. He secured the bucket of bees in a corner of the pickup bed.

"I'm glad I straightened up the bee yard yesterday," Tommy said to Artie, as they waited for Ty to return from the carport. "And these bees do look like mine—they're Russians. It won't take me long to shake them back into the hive box. Then we can head into town. You think Coach Johnson will make us run for being late?"

Artie shook his head. "Nah, he won't," Artie said. "Ty's mom called the school. Besides, this isn't a regular practice. It's more like work—picking up wood and metal and stuff that blew onto the field, so we *can* practice this afternoon without somebody getting hurt. The softball girls are gonna be doing the same thing, I heard."

"Weren't we supposed to play at Solid Rock tomorrow?" asked Tommy, moving over to make room for Ty in the cab.

Slamming the truck door shut, Ty gave Tommy the once-over before getting too close. "You don't have any stowaway bees in your clothes, do you?" Ty said, relaxing when the boy laughed. "I'm supposed to pitch tomorrow, but it won't be at Solid Rock—that's for sure. Coach hasn't said who we're gonna play yet, or where. I don't think we *can* play any home games, not until we get that light pole and the fence fixed, and bring in some new bleachers."

Artie nodded as he cranked the truck and started backing down the driveway. "I talked to Coach last night after our meeting," said Artie. "He told me he was still making calls about tomorrow's game. I don't know anything except we *won't* be playing Solid Rock. I mean, they don't even have a team now."

"What about their players?" Tommy said. "They're good—especially that Japanese kid you guys helped rescue the other night from the smashed-up car."

"Yeah, Inouye," said Ty. "I forgot to ask Mom how bad his shoulder is hurt. He's a good pitcher, and he's an even better batter—almost as good at the plate as Jimmy Gore used to be."

By then, the red pickup truck was back on the highway headed toward the Bauer farm. Tommy squinted at Ty and asked, "What d'ya mean *used to be*? Jimmy Gore's probably the best athlete at Solid Rock—in football and baseball, anyway. He looked okay in the two games against us this spring. He got a couple hits and made some good plays at third. He's got an arm."

"Oh, he's still good," said Ty, "but after he signed this winter to play football at State College, he started acting like baseball wasn't as important—like he didn't want to get hurt and blow his scholarship or something. Other years, he could always get a hit or two off *me*, but he's oh-for-six against yours truly this season. That was Smitty he got those hits off of, after I sat down. I figure Jimmy Gore would be oh-for-nine or ten if we played that third game tomorrow, but we'll never know now, will we?"

* * *

Both Arbor teams—the Bruins baseballers and Bruinettes softballers—worked hard on their separate ball fields through the morning. They labored under the supervision of baseball coach Jug Johnson and softball coach Joe Carson. The two coaches, however, didn't actively direct the work, as they spent most of the morning jogging back and forth from their shared desk in the metal, batting-cage building to the school office to use the telephone. They were still trying to schedule makeup games for the next day.

Describing the two men's gaits as "jogging" would be generous. At 350 pounds, Coach Johnson had trouble even walking fast, supporting his jug-shaped frame on stout legs with knees and ankles weakened from carrying such a large load. It didn't take much for sweat beads to pop out on Jug's balding head, seen outdoors only on the rare occasions when he doffed his ever-present Arbor ball cap, whether on the baseball diamond in the spring or the football gridiron in the fall. In the winter when he coached wrestling, he observed Arbor High's "hat rule" and didn't wear a cap in the gymnasium. In fact, his attire in the gym on match days proved that he could dress up when he wanted to.

Coach Carson's nickname at Arbor was "Bozo Joe," which students in years past had picked for him, not because he liked to clown around, but because of his receding hairline and red face from the least exertion, and because the nickname rhymed. He and Jug were best friends, and whether in school or on the athletic field, they regularly hung out together and pursued a common interest: tobacco use. While Jug dipped snuff—with often more than a pinch between his cheek and gums—Joe smoked cigarettes as if they were going out of style, which, of course, they were. Even if the smoking did elevate Joe's blood pressure and cause shortness of breath, it kept him trim—at least compared to his best friend, Jug. Side by side, the two looked like Laurel and Hardy, but wearing ball caps and coaching togs.

With the school campus basically closed on this Easter Monday, the baseball and softball teams had the cafeteria to themselves at lunch. As a result, the friends who usually sat together at the round Barf Table up front near the trash cans and tray-return window took seats at the long, rectangular tables where the rest of the student body sat on school days. Cafeteria worker Frankie Hughes was on duty this day, though he didn't have to do his usual job of running the cash register. This day's meal was donated by Woody Woods—the barbecue sandwiches, fries and drinks dropped off on his way to Ebenezerville with another load of food for needy families. One familiar thing that day in the lunchroom was what Frankie Hughes wore—a black, death-metal music T-shirt and black jeans to go with his long, dark hair and black mustache and beard. Everyone knew, though, that scary-looking Frankie was a sweet guy and their best friend on the cafeteria staff.

On her way to sit with the softball girls, Nicie Evans stopped next to Ty Green as she passed the baseball team's table. The tall, well-built girl looked down on her ex-boyfriend with a bemused smile. "I have good news," Nicie told Ty. "Daddy said he found you something to drive while he's working on *The Whale*—a pickup truck. He's gonna bring it here after practice. If you like it, he can ride home with me."

Artie Bauer, sitting next to Ty, spoke up before his best friend did. "Hey, that's great," Artie said. "What kind of truck?" While he didn't mind giving Ty rides, Artie usually had little Ricky Duran as a daily passenger, since the 9th grader lived in the old homeplace on the Bauer farm. That day Ricky had ridden into town with his father, who had needed to pick up some building supplies.

"I don't know," said Nicie, shrugging. "A blue one? Does it matter?" She started to move on to join her softball teammates.

"Blue?" Ty said. "You don't see many blue pickups. But, no, I don't care about the color. How new is it? How many miles? Where'd Donnell find it?"

"Again, Ty, I don't know," Nicie said pointedly, as she drifted away. "You're just gonna have to wait until Daddy gets here with it."

Artie tried to defuse whatever tension was building. "I'm sure he'll love it, Nicie," he said, "just as long as it has four wheels and gets him where he's going."

Her dark eyes softened. "Oh, he'll *love* it all right," she said, grinning again. "That's for sure." She carried her tray to the softball table and sat with Leah Russo, Jamie Foxx and Wilma Marecek. Artie saw her whisper something to her friends that made them laugh.

When they weren't standing in the breezeway outside, the two old coaches sat together at the faculty table near the front of the cafeteria—a round table near the cashier's stand outside the door to the serving area. It matched the Barf Table, except for fewer scratches and stains on its laminated top. Jug Johnson grunted as he pushed himself away from the table and stood to address both teams.

"Let me have your attention, guys and gals," said Jug Johnson. "First of all, me and Coach Carson want to say a big thank-you to Woody's Grill for this fine spread today." Jug nodded at 10th grader Brett Woods, seated at one end of the baseball table. "Tell your daddy it was good, as usual—best barbecue and fries in Oleander County, hands down."

Jug studied his athletic shoes for a moment—that is, if he could see them— then looked up and continued, "We also appreciate all the hard work you young people did this morning, getting our fields picked up and in shape for practice this afternoon. We'll get started in about thirty minutes. You can rest a little and change or do whatever you need to do." He blushed as he glanced over at the girls' table.

"Coach Carson and I got some good news this morning," Jug went on. "As you know, we were all set to play at Solid Rock tomorrow—our third games with them—but that won't happen now, obviously. So, we did some switching around with the other schools, and tomorrow we're heading up the road to, well, to Capital City High to play them non-conference. We weren't scheduled to play them this year—Solid Rock was—but it'll be a good test for us, for *both* teams."

At that point in the season, the Arbor High Bruins baseball team was 10-1, while the Capital City Red Caps were undefeated at 13-0. Arbor's only loss had been on the road at Iron Harbor High, an extra-inning affair that came down to a questionable call at home plate. Artie was positive that he hadn't been blocking the plate on the throw home. He had clearly tagged the runner out, but the home-plate umpire ruled against him and awarded the walk-off win to the Gray Dukes.

The Bruinettes, with a 5-6 record so far, weren't nearly as excited as the boys about playing the Red Caps, but they were thrilled to be visiting the capital, with its historic buildings, its state university, and Capital City's larger stores and nicer restaurants frequented by the college crowd.

Jug Johnson promptly doused those thoughts in the softball girls' heads. "Now, we aren't going up there to shop or socialize," he said, looking down at Joe Carson for support in the murky waters he had just jumped into. "We're going up there to play two good teams. It'll make us both better—baseball and softball—as we finish up this season. It'll be like the state playoffs."

Coach Carson was okay with everything Jug said until he mentioned the state playoffs. Then Joe winced. Several of the girls looked at each other and frowned, as most of them had played basketball for Carson the previous winter. For all intents and purposes, their team had won the conference basketball championship, but had been forced to forfeit their games and were barred from post-season play due to having an ineligible player on the roster all season. That player was Russian exchange student Julia Safin, who had transferred to Arbor from Mimosa Beach High, along with her exchange sister Jamie Foxx. Julia had been ineligible through no fault of her own—a paperwork snafu that had also ruined the Mimosa Beach girls' hoops season. The blame lay on Jamie's estranged father, MBHS coach Jimmy Foxx. He had been the Lady Waverunners girls' basketball coach. This spring, he was Mimosa Beach's baseball coach.

"One last thing before we give you that thirty-minute break," Jug Johnson said. "Coach Carson and I learned this morning that three Solid Rock ballplayers—one young lady and two young men—are interested in joining us for the remainder of the season. We weren't told their names, just that they might come and watch us practice this afternoon so they can make a decision. These kids and their parents could show up at any time, so be on your best behavior." He looked around the room. "Any questions before we turn you loose?"

As a team captain, Artie Bauer raised his hand to ask the two questions on every starting player's mind. "Any idea what position the two guys play, Coach?" asked Artie. "And will they be eligible to play tomorrow in our game at Capital City?"

Jug Johnson shrugged. "Your guess is as good as mine, Yogi—about the positions," the coach said. "Now, if they tell me they want to play, I can put them on the eligibility list and get it filed before the bus leaves tomorrow. It kinda depends on who they are, Yogi. You know?"

Johnson was the only person who insisted on calling his star catcher *Yogi*, after his Major League Baseball hero, the legendary New York Yankees catcher, Yogi Berra. In fact, all of Jug's favorite players in MLB history had great nicknames—like Shoeless Joe Jackson, Moonlight Graham, Slats Ledbetter and, of course, the one and only Babe Ruth. Other people who weren't baseball fans might hear Jug's nickname for Artie and assume that the reference was to the famous cartoon bear because of the similarity to the big farm boy's surname, Bauer. And Artie *did* look kind of like a bear. But Artie just wanted to be plain *Artie*—or *Arthur*, as his ex-girlfriend, Julia Safin, called him.

"Yeah, Coach, I understand," said Artie, "but do you even know what grade they're in—the two guys? We've got some young players this season, but they're doing a great job for us."

Jug nodded and held up his hand to quiet Artie. "I know what you're saying, bud," said Johnson, "and I'm right there with you on that, but all we can do is wait and see." He turned to look at Joe Carson. "Anything you want to add, Coach?" When Joe shook his head, Jug reminded the players to be dressed and ready to practice thirty minutes later.

As the baseball boys were headed outside to lounge in the shaded breezeway, Ty Green, the other co-captain, sidled over to Artie and said, "*Wait and see. Wait and see.* I'm tired of hearing that."

Artie smiled. "Don't worry, Ty," he said. "You're the best pitcher in the whole county, and the second-best pitcher—that Inouye kid from Solid Rock—well, he's hurt. You don't have to worry about your starting spot."

"Worry?" said Ty Green. "I'm not worried about *that*." He shot a look across the breezeway at Nicie and a gaggle of softball girls tying each other's hair up in ribbons and adjusting their green-and-gold visors. "I'm worried about Nicie's dad bringing me an old hoopdie to drive and not being able to turn it down. I've got a reputation with the ladies, you know."

"Oh, come on, Ty," said Artie. "Most girls don't care about that. Nicie didn't care, and neither did Julia—well, unless you want to date Vicki Duke over there." Nodding toward another cluster of giggling softball players, he continued, "And even then you and I aren't what *she's* looking for. She's looking for somebody with money—like Brett or Bennie, even though they're both younger than her. I mean, hey, I heard she's been seeing Josh Stark again, on weekends when he comes home from military school. Julia and I saw them at the movies in Mimosa Beach one Saturday night."

Vicki Duke was a senior and had been head cheerleader and homecoming queen at Arbor High that year. Josh Stark, a 10th grader, was the spoiled only child of the man who now owned Sandpiper Realty. His father, developer Joel Stark, liked to throw his weight around in Oleander County. So when young Josh got into big legal trouble the previous fall—trouble that involved the Barf

Table gang—the family's high-priced lawyers made a deal to ship the boy off to Hawthorn Military Academy two counties over. Otherwise, he would have been sentenced to finish the year and maybe spend the next one at the School for Troubled Youth up the highway in Capital City.

As fate would have it, Josh Stark was a starting pitcher that season on the Hawthorn baseball team, and he would get a homecoming of sorts in the final game of the regular season at Arbor High, assuming the baseball stadium—the scoreboard, fences and stands—could be repaired by then. It would be the Bruins' only home game before the state playoffs, if they did, in fact, qualify for post-season play. Right then, making the playoffs appeared inevitable, but the young athletes at Arbor High had learned that year not to take anything for granted, not after what had happened to the girls' basketball team.

"I'm not worried about that jerk Josh Stark, either," said Ty Green. "Tell you what, Artie. Since my back is to the highway when I'm on the mound, call timeout and come talk to me if you see Nicie's pop pull up in a blue pickup while I'm pitching. If it's a piece of junk, I might need some help coming up with an excuse not to take it."

Artie laughed. "You got it, buddy," he said. "But just remember, Ty, if you don't have your own wheels, Grandpa's pickup can get awfully crowded. It doesn't have a back seat, so a double date means one couple would have to sit in back *if we run out of gas*—and that's where we haul chickens and bags of fertilizer and all sorts of smelly stuff."

"Well," said Ty, with a sigh, "maybe I *will* love this truck Donnell is bringing me. I'll just have to wait and see."

CHAPTER 5

JIMMY GORE SHOWED UP ready to practice that afternoon. A senior, the former Solid Rock Harvesters third baseman didn't need his parents to speak for him, nor did Jimmy's little sister, Jenny, an outfielder who came along to join the Bruinettes softball team. Over the four years of Jimmy's sterling high school career, his parents had observed Jug Johnson every time their teams met on the football gridiron or the baseball diamond, and they knew Jug was a fine coach in both sports. They also knew Joe Carson from having watched Jenny, a natural athlete like her brother, play for the Lady Harvesters basketball team over the past two winters. Despite their nicotine addictions, both Jug and Joe were two of the best coaches in Oleander County's five-team, now four-team, Suncoast Conference.

It was a different story, however, for Michi "Mike" Inouye, the injured Harvesters pitcher and slugger who Artie Bauer and Ty Green had helped rescue after the Good Friday Storm. The boy's whole family came to Arbor High that Easter Monday afternoon, though not just to watch baseball practice. Dr. Kato Inouye, still looking banged up from the car accident, stood with his son behind the backstop and watched the Bruins take infield practice. The 11th grader's left arm—not his pitching arm—was in a sling to give his hurt shoulder relief, but the injury didn't appear to be too serious. Mrs. Inouye took Mike's twin sister, Kimi, into the school building to meet with Principal Jerry Church and guidance counselor Thelma Hopper. Just as Solid Rock's student body was being dispersed to the county's other four high schools, so were the Christian academy's faculty and staff. Mrs. Hiroko Inouye would teach math at Arbor

High for the rest of that year. She might even choose to stay on permanently if juniors Mike and Kimi grew to like Arbor High. Kimi was no athlete, but she did enjoy supporting her talented brother.

Swinging his fungo bat with minimum effort, Jug Johnson slapped grounders and pop flies at the infielders. At third base, sophomore Brett Woods and senior Jimmy Gore took turns in the "hot corner," even though Jug's fungoes during infield practice were lukewarm at best.

During the short break before batting practice, Artie and Ty approached Jimmy Gore in the home dugout. "Hey, man," said Artie. "How does it feel?"

"How does *what* feel?" asked Jimmy, drawing a cup of water from the big orange cooler.

"Being in *this* dugout instead of the one over there on the visitor side," Artie said. "We've played some good games against each other on this field—and over at your place."

Jimmy nodded and sipped his water. "Well, considering the way things are," he began, "I feel pretty darn good. I tried to get some of the other boys to come with me, but they couldn't get past all the bad blood between you guys and Stark last fall. He did a real number on you, running his mouth—even on ol' Jug. Said he was senile. The boys were afraid you'd hold it against them—all of them but Mike."

Ty Green got a cup for himself. "Josh Stark never learns," Ty said. "So, how'd things go when you played Hawthorn last week? We saw you won, but we wondered if Josh behaved himself."

"Yeah," said Artie, "how many of your guys did he hit? The paper didn't have a box score."

The former Harvester laughed. "He threw at *me* in the first inning," said Jimmy, "but that didn't keep me from crowding the plate. I took him yard second time up and watched it all the way—even did a bat flip. And then he *did* hit me the next time I batted. I got even with him, though."

"What?" asked Artie. "Did you rip some foul balls at his father in the stands?" All three boys chuckled at that, and Artie added, "That's like our football game last fall. I can still see you tackling Mr. Stark when he ran onto the field to scream at Josh."

"No," said Jimmy, "I got Josh when he had to cover home plate with me on third. He threw a wild pitch, and I blasted him at the plate, like I was Pete Rose or somebody. Knocked Josh out of the game, but he was done, anyway."

Artie looked across the field at the visiting on-deck circle, where Jug Johnson was talking to Dr. Inouye and his son. "So, what's *his* story," Artie asked Jimmy, nodding toward Mike Inouye. "Will he help us? Or is he just out for himself—like Josh Stark?"

Jimmy shook his head. "Nope, not one bit," he said. "He's all about team and working together, giving it all we got—even calls it some Japanese word. It's *wa*, I think. He's a good kid. His *father*, on the other hand, is kinda pushy, but he's a doctor, and he's just looking out for Mike."

"What do you mean?" asked Ty Green. "You talking about starts? Is he gonna push for Mike to be the top starter—to take *my* place?"

"Nah, it's not like that," said Jimmy. "It's more about his arm—not letting him pitch too much, not even when we needed him to go a little longer. The doc would get all over Coach Knight's case until he pulled Mike."

With this insight, Artie tried to make out what the doctor was saying to Coach Johnson, but they were too far away. "How does Mike feel about that?" Artie said. "From what I've read about Japanese baseball, those guys give it all they've got. They even play hurt."

"He doesn't like it—you can tell," said Jimmy, "but there's not a lot he can do. Besides, his dad is probably right. He comes to every game and uses one of those little golf clickers to count Mike's pitches. When he gets close to fifty, the doc starts sending notes to the coach, no matter what the score is."

"Notes?" asked Ty. "What do they say? And who delivers them?"

Jimmy laughed again. "Mike's twin sister, Kimi," he said. "She's a real trip. She's quiet—well, if she doesn't know you—and she's always reading those weird Japanese comic books. She draws, too—really good, but it's that same kind of stuff, you know, kids with big eyes and all."

"Anime?" asked Artie. "Or is it, what, manga? They do baseball stories that way, too."

"Who knows," Jimmy replied, dumping out his water. "Not my cup of tea. But I like Kimi. I took her to the homecoming concert last fall—that's a big thing at Solid Rock—and I was gonna ask her to the junior-senior banquet this spring, but, well, you know."

Ty shook his head. "I forgot about that," he said, "that you guys don't have proms or sock hops or any kind of dance over there. No wonder Josh Stark went off the deep end and decided to come ruin our homecoming dance. You know about that, right?"

"*Everybody* does," said Jimmy, looking through the bats in the bin near the dugout entrance. "I heard he swung like King Kong from one end of the gym to the other. And you should have heard all the stories about him and his girlfriend, what they used to do."

"Vicki?" asked Artie. "Vicki Duke? You know she plays on our softball team, right?" He pointed through the mangled fence toward the softball field. "That's her pitching right now. She's not bad."

"Yeah, that's what Josh said," Jimmy quipped, pulling an aluminum bat from the bin and hefting it. "She *is* good-looking. I'd go out with her in a heartbeat."

"That's not what I meant," said Artie, "but aren't you dating Mike's sister? What's her name?"

Jimmy shook his head. "Kimi," he replied. "I wish. But her folks won't let her go out with me on a real date, not unless it's an official school thing—you know, with all the teachers standing around acting like prison guards. And Mrs. Inouye kept an eye on Kimi at school, to make sure she didn't sneak around between classes or at lunch. I'm sure it'll be that way here, too."

Just then, Artie saw Coach Johnson shake Dr. Inouye's hand and pat Mike on his good shoulder, the boy's head down as if he were sad. The two visitors left the field and strode toward the parking lot, where Mrs. Inouye and Kimi waited at a shiny sedan with rental tags. As Jug headed toward the dugout, Artie said, "Well, I wonder what *that* means—them leaving now. And Mike didn't look happy."

Jimmy Gore walked over to the nearby on-deck circle and took a few tentative swings with the bat he had selected. "Don't worry about Mike," said Jimmy. "He'll play as soon as he can. It's that *wa-a-a-a* thing. He'll do what's best for the team. It's his over-protective dad we have to worry about—no *wa* in that man."

Checking his watch, Coach Johnson hollered, "Okay, all you rookies lazying around! Let's get to it! Duran, get the ball cart out to the mound and make sure there aren't any balls laying around. I don't want to fall and bust my butt today."

The old coach pointed at Tommy White and Brett Woods seated at the far end of the dugout. "Hey, White! Woods!" Jug shouted. "How 'bout you two set up the pitching screen, and then get your rusty dusties to your spots? We're running behind here."

The instructions continued. "Let's have Jimmy boy leading off, Yogi on deck, and Ty Green in the hole," said Jug. "Three bunts, three hit-and-run, six balls swinging away—running on number six, three strikes and you're out. Jimmy, take over at third when Brett comes to bat. Everything else, the same."

As usual, Ty alternated with fellow hurler Johnny Smith in right field, the position both usually played when the other boy was on the mound. Both Ty and Smitty were right-handers. The Bruins' third regular pitcher, lefty Phil Waters, "closed" most games, coming in fresh for the 7th inning to get the last three outs of the contest. Phil, almost as wide as he was tall, preferred not to play a regular defensive position but had been pressed into service in left field. Like Artie Bauer and Johnny Smith, Phil Waters had earned all-conference football honors on the Arbor offensive line, but he was known more for his strength than his speed. If the Bruins outfield had a weak spot, it was Phil in left.

Other starters included 11th grader Manny Freeman in center field. Manny, the fastest boy on the team, was a true utility man who could play any position well enough, even pitcher or catcher, if necessary. In addition to Brett Woods at third base, Ozzie Maye, another 11th grader and the lineup's weakest hitter, played shortstop; little Ricky Duran, almost as fast on the base paths as Manny, handled second base; and Tommy White manned first base.

First up, Jimmy Gore dutifully laid down his bunts and smacked three balls on the ground to the right side of the infield. Then he proceeded to tag each of Jug's next six pitches to him over the damaged fence in center, the deepest part of the outfield. The last one rolled all the way to the highway.

"Nice ones, Jay," shouted Jug, as Jimmy jogged down to first base to practice his base-running and work his way over to third, where he would take Brett's defensive post. "Keep that up, Jimmy, and we'll have to stop traffic when you come to bat. But they didn't call me Rag-Arm Johnson for nothin'. Ty will give you some *good* pitches to look at later, okay?"

Taking a lead at first base, Jimmy smiled and nodded. The rest of batting practice wasn't nearly as encouraging, partly because the other players were paying so much attention to their new teammate whenever he took over for Brett Woods at third. In his own first at-bat, Brett couldn't get solid wood on Jug's short-armed, batting-practice pitches, and he struck out after four attempts to swing for the fence. Shaking his head in embarrassment, Brett flung his bat toward the dugout, almost hitting Tommy White in the on-deck circle. Brett muttered to himself all the way down the line to first.

"Enough of that," said Jug, without looking directly at Brett. "We don't throw our bats, in BP or any other time. Why not? 'Cause bats are expensive— just like visits to the emergency room. And you can get tossed out of the game for doing it." Jug was taking a chance, fussing at Brett Woods, whose father fed the team before home games, but the old coach knew it would be too late to say anything *after* someone got hurt. Besides, even though he was a 10th grader, this was Brett's first year of high school baseball. He had decided to play due to his friendship with Artie, Ty and the other Barf Tablers.

Eventually, Coach Johnson put Ty Green on the mound without the screen and cart. He put Artie Bauer behind the plate in full gear and Jimmy Gore in the batter's box. The other starters took their positions in the field and watched to see how Jimmy handled Ty's pitching now that they were teammates. Ty couldn't resist muttering "oh-for-seven" to himself, like a mantra, as he looked in for

Artie's pitch sign. Even though he had warmed up on only eight pitches—the number he'd be allowed coming into a game as a reliever—Ty nodded when he saw his big catcher put down just his index finger to call for a fastball down the middle. Batting right-handed, Jimmy Gore dug into the red clay of the batter's box, tapped his bat on the outside edges of the plate before taking three easy practice swings. With the barrel of the bat on his right shoulder, he waited for Ty's first pitch.

Ty Green's pitching motion was unusual in that he didn't go into a full windup, nor did he pitch from what was called "the stretch," an abbreviated delivery that pitchers used with runners on base. His odd motion had him stepping toward home plate and bringing his pitching arm forward like an inverted pendulum, then finishing with his elbow popping out and up, instead of twisting his arm and snapping it across his body. Artie knew that his friend had learned the motion after reading an old magazine article about his hero, Cy Young Award winner "Iron Mike" Marshall of the Los Angeles Dodgers. That was what got Ty interested in weight training and kinesiology—how to pitch without hurting his arm.

Jimmy Gore made contact with Ty's first pitch, but his timing was off after having seen so many batting-practice pitches from the coach. He swung early and pulled the ball foul down the left-field line. Strike one. Jug tossed Artie another ball, and he snapped it to Ty on the mound. Artie called for another fastball but put down his pinky instead of his index finger to direct the next pitch to the outer half of the plate. This time Jimmy's bat was a bit slow, and he fouled the ball off to the right. No balls, two strikes.

"Okay," called Jug Johnson from the dugout, clapping his hands, "it's oh-and-two, oh-and-two. Let's be smart with this pitch, boys. We got a good batter at the plate, and he's getting wood on the ball. What kinda pitch you gonna call on oh-and-two, Yogi boy? Make it a good'un."

In this situation with most pitchers, Artie would call for either a curveball or a changeup—a pitch that looks like a fastball but is thrown with less velocity. While Ty did have a good changeup, Artie didn't call for one because that speed of pitch was basically all Jug had thrown in batting practice. Also, Ty did not throw a regular curveball. He had learned to throw a *screwball*—a breaking pitch that spun in the opposite direction and moved toward a right-handed batter instead of away from him, as regular curves did. That had been his hero Mike Marshall's pet pitch. Ty knew about Mike Marshall not from watching him play, but from reading about him in old *Sports Illustrated* magazines and in the book *Ball Four*.

Artie decided to call for the screwball, but before he put down the sign for Ty to see, a flash of light off a windshield and a dash of color against the green trees across the highway caught Artie's attention. Remembering the instructions that Ty had given him before practice, Artie called timeout, rose from his crouch and lifted his mask. After jogging to the mound, he pretended to confer with Ty about the next pitch they would offer Jimmy Gore in this practice at-bat.

"What are you doing?" Ty said, still focused on the batter. "I'm about to strike him out. He'll be oh-and-seven on the season, buddy. Oh-and-seven."

Artie smiled and shook his head. "Nah," he said, "you told me to call time if a blue pickup turned off the highway." He nodded toward the parking lot. "Well, there it is—the truck you're *gonna love*."

Holding his fielder's glove up to block his face from Coach Johnson's view, Ty cut his eyes toward the parking lot and saw Nicie Evans's father getting out of the smallest pickup truck he had ever seen—a light blue, older-model Chevrolet L.U.V. truck. Artie chuckled and said, "Nicie did say that you'd *love* the pickup Donnell found for you. We just didn't know she was spelling it *L.U.V.*"

Frowning, Ty said, "*L.U.V.*? Why's it spelled that way?"

"I don't know," Artie replied. "Maybe to be cute—just like that tiny little truck over there. But I betcha girls will like it—well, a lot better than they do my big old dirty pickup."

Ty's frown faded. "You think?" he said, showing the beginnings of a smile. "Hey, and it doesn't even need a new name. It's got one. It's *The Luuuvvv Truck*." Ty laughed. "I would call it *The Luuuvvv Machine*, but that's what Nicie called *me* whenever I'd say we ran out of gas. Don't you dare tell her I told you that."

He grinned from ear to ear as Artie turned and trotted back to home plate.

"Awright, ladies," shouted Jug Johnson from the dugout. "Now that you had your tea party, let's get back to work. Count is no balls and two strikes. Play ball!"

Artie went back into his crouch and put down two fingers—the usual sign for a curve—and then he waggled them for a screwball. But Ty wasn't looking. He had turned his head to take another peek at his new pickup—*The Luuuvvv Truck*—that would get him back on the road to romance. Smiling, Ty faced Artie again and nodded as the catcher repeated the screwball sign. He went into his motion and flung the ball toward Artie's glove. Perhaps Ty Green was just being too careful to aim at the outer half of the plate so that he couldn't be accused of throwing at his new teammate. Or maybe he was too distracted by thoughts of how his cute new pickup truck would get his love life back on track.

Whatever the reason, Jimmy Gore's eyes lit up when he saw the pitch and could even make out how the ball's red laces were rotating as the white horsehide sphere spun toward him. He hesitated just a beat before stepping into the pitch, and crushed it over the left-field fence. Since this was practice, he didn't run the bases as a home run hitter would in a game, but Jimmy did watch the ball sail all the way out of the stadium and bounce once, twice, three times on the parking lot pavement. Leaning against a fender of the blue pickup parked close to the ball field, Donnell Evans raised his hands high and clapped at the batter's feat, and then jogged away to retrieve the home run ball.

As the next batter moved toward the plate from the on-deck circle, Artie trotted out to Ty to take him another ball and to talk about the dinger that Jimmy had just launched. "One-for-seven isn't bad," the catcher assured his friend. "That's .143—better than his average against Smitty this season. You still got it." He dropped the ball into Ty's glove and turned away.

"Still got what, Artie?" said Ty. "A knack for throwing gopher balls?"

Artie knew that Ty was still sensitive about the only other long home run he had given up that season. In the Bruins' lone loss, Ty had entered the Iron Harbor game in relief of starter Johnny Smith, who had gotten into trouble early. With a one-run lead, Ty performed well until his pitch count reached seventy—at which point Coach Johnson had called time to hold a quick conference on the mound. Jug's main concern was whether or not Ty felt strong enough to face one more batter to finish the sixth inning before letting Phil Waters close out the win in the seventh. Ty had assured Jug—along with Artie and all the infielders joining them on the mound—that he would sit down the Gray Dukes' cleanup hitter, Louis Hines, once again, having already struck him out twice that day. As it happened, the veteran slugger's solo blast on the very first pitch of his at-bat tied the score and set up the controversial game-ending play at home plate an inning later.

"Two," said Artie. "You've thrown *two* gopher balls all season, and this one didn't even count. Besides, you probably would've been okay in both cases if we'd just left you alone—no conferences on the mound, no distractions, period. Like I said, you still got it. You've *always* had it, buddy."

* * *

Donnell Evans had to wait thirty minutes for the two teams' practices to end, so that he could talk to Ty Green about *The White Whale*'s repairs and catch a ride home with his daughter. Nicie was driving a small green SUV that Donnell had found for her a couple of weeks earlier. The vehicle had already come in handy with giving younger teammates rides and with hauling boxes of food and emergency supplies in her job at Woody's Surf Shop & Grill. Donnell also needed to inform Ty about *The Luuuvvv Truck*'s quirks, since the teen would be driving the tiny pickup for an extended period, it turned out.

"Your car needs more than just body work," Donnell told his daughter's ex-boyfriend. "I finally got under the hood this morning, and there's a lot of damage there, maybe more than you want to fix. You'll probably need a new engine, especially if the block's cracked. Now, I can get you a rebuilt motor, but they're expensive."

Ty looked over at Artie and raised his eyebrows, as if his friend might help him decide whether to repair *The Whale* or declare it dead. "Don't ask me," said Artie, holding up his hands. "I'm as broke as you are. You need to talk to your folks."

"That's why I brought you *this* truck," Donnell said. "It's seen better days as far as its looks go—heck, it's twenty years old—but it runs good. I did an oil change and a tune-up for you. We can settle up later on. The tires have some good tread left on them, and I changed out the spare for you. It was shot. But I got a good deal on this little old L.U.V. truck—that stands for Light Utility Vehicle, by the way—and it won't break the bank if you do decide to buy it."

He held out two keys on the same ring. "Now, there's one other thing," he continued. "I noticed that the control panel lights come on real slow when the engine's cold, and you have a hard time seeing the gauges—like the gas gauge." There was a sparkle in his eye. "So I went ahead and filled 'er up before I left the house, and I even filled a gallon can and put it in the bed—just in case you're out on a date, say, and run out of gas." He winked.

Seeing a group of softball girls headed their way, Artie slapped Ty on the back. "Well, buddy, it looks like you're all set," said Artie. "I need to go find Ricky and head on home. I'll try to give you a call after I finish milking the cows. I just hope Bessie and Bossie are in a good *moo-o-o-d* tonight." With a laugh, Artie nudged his friend and threw up his hand to Donnell Evans.

Looking around the ballpark grounds, Artie saw that Ricky Duran was already waiting for him in the parking lot at the red pickup. With him stood Tommy White, a forlorn expression on the tall boy's soft face. Artie wondered what was up, but he took his time walking over to the truck.

"Hey, guys," said Artie. "What's going on?"

Tommy got right to the point. "I need to stay at the farm tonight, Artie," he said. "The Presslers are stuck in E-ville until really late—don't know why. But Deborah called the school this afternoon, and Miss Hopper sent me a note saying I should see if you guys can put me up tonight."

"You know we can," Artie said. "Do we need to run over to the Presslers' house—I mean, to *your* house—and grab some clothes and your toothbrush?"

Tommy nodded. "Yeah," he said, "I'll need some clothes for school tomorrow, and I'll need my backpack. I'm in enough trouble for forgetting my books and homework."

Ricky Duran had another idea. "Maybe you should get enough clothes for *two* days, Tommy," he said. "Remember, we have a game in Capital City tomorrow, and then *we* will be the ones who are late getting home. You can stay with Artie tonight and with me tomorrow night. We'll have fun."

The tall boy nodded again. He looked relieved but still somewhat dejected. "Yeah," Artie said, "we'll have fun *both* nights. So, cheer up, Tommy. That gloomy look might rub off on the girls."

"Girls?" said Tommy, his eyes widening a bit. "Are you and Ty throwing a party tonight at the clubhouse? Are you and Julia back together? And him and Nicie?" He seemed hopeful.

"No," Artie said, "not *those* girls. But you and I *do* have dates tonight—with a milk bucket and two of the sweetest ladies standing on four legs—well, make that *eight* legs."

Tommy shook his head and said, "Bessie and Bossie? Now I *am* sad. When I stayed with you and Grandpa before, I never could get any milk out, like they were holding back. I don't think they like me."

Artie held up both hands and showed the two younger boys his sturdy palms and strong fingers. "It's all in the touch, boys," he said. "All in the touch."

CHAPTER 6

THE NEXT DAY AT LUNCH, freshman Leah Russo beat senior Artie Bauer to the Barf Table, as usual. At Arbor High, students were released to the cafeteria by grade level—12th graders first, on down to 9th graders—but Leah always got to the table right away because she never went through the lunch line. Actually, until Valentine's Day when she and Brett Woods became an item, Leah didn't eat much at all, anytime. She preferred to read paperbacks at lunch. This day's title was *Jaws*. Her eating disorder was why she was in therapy with Dr. Minnie Marecek, and why she still needed help dealing with the death of her older brother the previous school year. Now, too, she had to make sense of her parents splitting up and talking about divorce. For Leah Russo, the Barf Table had become family.

"Are you looking forward to the road trip this afternoon?" Artie asked, as he set his tray down at his regular spot. "We don't usually go to Capital City during the week—in any sport. It's a long bus ride."

As Artie pulled out his chair and sat down, he noticed Nicie Evans making her way across the lunchroom, a brown paper bag in one hand. She headed toward a chair next to Leah and greeted both friends. "Hi, guys," she said, then addressed Artie. "Don't look so surprised, big guy. Ty is so happy with that little truck Daddy loaned him that he gave me permission to sit here again."

Artie laughed. "Yeah," he said, "the poor guy didn't know what to think at first until I told him girls would like riding in it. I made him think it's a chick magnet."

"Well, it *is* cute," said Leah Russo, "but, Nicie, since when do you need Ty

Green's permission—or anyone's—to sit here? I mean, this is the Barf Table."

Nicie shrugged. "Since when?" she began. "Since he started getting attention from colleges and pro scouts. He was so mad when we first broke up that I knew to stay away from him. It just kept him stirred up, and he couldn't focus on playing ball. But he's getting used to us being apart, and we're even friends again."

As if on cue, Ty Green himself emerged from the serving area and paid cashier Frankie Hughes for his heaping tray of food. Right behind Ty was Jimmy Gore, also with food piled high on his tray. Like old friends, they walked side by side to the round table down front and then separated. Ty sat beside Artie; Jimmy, across the table beside Nicie.

"Did you guys leave any food for anybody else?" said Artie. "You know, this *is* Krakatoa Tuesday, and those mounds of mashed potatoes *do* look like volcanoes. Good thing they aren't serving them with gravy today, just butter."

"Krakatoa Tuesday?" Jimmy Gore said, confused. "What's that?"

Nicie shook her head. "Oh," she said, "the kids at this school are goofy— and mean. They made us sit here at the loser table, and then they started picking on us. Every day it was something different, like Krakatoa Tuesday and Waisin Wednesday—silly stuff like that. But we put a stop to it. Right, Artie?"

"Yeah, I guess so," Artie said. "Now it's almost like *everybody* wants to sit here."

"Well, why not?" said Jimmy. "You guys aren't losers. Two state wrestling champions? Yeah, the Iron Harbor paper gets delivered to E-ville, too." He turned his head and smiled at Nicie and Leah. "And such fine-looking ladies." He winked at Ty Green to let him know he was just teasing.

Nicie snorted. "I thought you had the hots for Kimi Inouye," she said, grinning. "Yes, ol' buddy. Your sister done told on you. I like Jenny. She's gonna help us keep you in line, pal."

"*Sisters*," said Jimmy, shaking his head but still smiling. "Speaking of Kimi, I guess her mom is still making her eat lunch in her classroom, even here at Arbor. The Inouyes are just too protective of Kimi—*and* of Mike. I wonder where Mike is right now."

Wilma Marecek, Julia Safin and Jamie Foxx arrived then, taking the last three seats at the round table. Having overheard Jimmy's remark about Mike Inouye, Wilma volunteered, "I saw him on my way over here in the office with his father. I guess he was checking out. They were talking to Mr. Church."

"Ol' Lurch Church," said Ty Green, for Jimmy's benefit. "He's kinda wishy-washy, but he usually figures out the right thing to do—well, except where Josh Stark was concerned last fall. Lurch just made that situation worse for everybody."

Jamie Foxx spoke up. "That's because Jerry—Mr. Church—is working for Josh's dad part-time," she said, "you know, at Sandpiper Realty, well, like my mom, even though she's *full*-time now. But Jerry Church is okay. Mom likes him. She says he's good at handling complaints, especially all the ones they're getting now—about backed-up toilets and stuff like that. And he's nice to me whenever I'm over there."

The teenagers had just gotten started on their lunches when the rest of the gang—Brett Woods, Bennie Pressler, Ricky Duran and Tommy White—showed up with their trays. With all eight seats already taken, newcomer Jimmy Gore jumped up to make room for at least one old Barf Tabler. "Nah, stay where you are," said Brett. "We're used to this happening." He and the other three boys laid down their trays and retrieved chairs from the empty faculty table near the cashier's stand. That table also was round with eight actual chairs, not attached stools like the long, student tables in the lunchroom.

Ordinarily, Jug Johnson and Joe Carson would be the only teachers eating lunch in the cafeteria, mainly because they had gotten into trouble with Principal Church the previous fall and had been put on permanent lunch duty. But this day was different due to the upcoming road trip to Capital City for the baseball and softball teams. Neither Jug nor Joe was anywhere close to the cafeteria, not even outside in the breezeway dipping snuff and smoking cigarettes. The coaches were packing the school's activity bus so that their teams could leave as soon as lunch period ended.

There already wasn't much elbow room around the Barf Table, but the teens who had sat down first didn't mind squeezing together to let the four latecomers join them. Still, after getting jostled a few times while trying to read, Leah Russo looked up from her paperback and said dryly, "We're gonna need a bigger table." The ones who had seen *Jaws* laughed. The others readily agreed.

* * *

The bus ride from Monk's Landing to Capital City started out with energy and excited chatter from the young athletes. They sat in pairs behind their two coaches who sat in separate seats up front. The driver was Frankie Hughes, still wearing his usual black attire despite Jug Johnson's admonition to cover his death-metal T-shirt with a green-and-gold Arbor Bruins warm-up jacket once they got to the ballpark. After the first hour on the road, most of the students had settled down and were either napping or quietly talking to their seatmates. After two hours, everyone—including Frankie, now also the death-metal bus driver—was tired of seeing cars, pickups and tractor-trailer rigs blow past them. But that was travel in the slow lane to the state capital, and there was little they could do.

Nicie Evans and Leah Russo turned in their seat to ask Artie Bauer a question that was bothering them—not about the tiresome ride, not about the big games they were about to play, but about what a member of the Barf Table had written and shared in their meeting Sunday night on the farm. Nicie made sure that Tommy White was sitting out of earshot. "Have you talked to Tommy?" Nicie asked, whispering to keep from waking Ty Green, who was curled up against the bus window.

From the girls' concerned expressions, Artie didn't need Nicie to explain herself. He nodded and said softly, "Yeah, Tommy was with me and Grandpa last night. We talked about him thinking he doesn't belong and thinking he's in the way at the Presslers."

"Did it help?" asked Leah. "We're worried about him."

"I think so," said Artie. "Part of what went on was that he'd overheard Deborah Pressler talking to Minnie Marecek about how hard it was gonna be to pick him up at school after our road games—like tonight. The home games aren't a problem, because we don't have any until the last game of the season against Hawthorn. The storm took care of that."

"I don't understand why's it so hard for them to pick Tommy up?" asked Nicie, trying not to let her voice rise. "Besides, all they have to do is ask one of us to help out."

"That's right," said Leah. "We could give him a ride home—me and Brett—as long as he doesn't mind riding in the back of *The Woody Wagon* and smelling like pizza for a day or two."

Artie smiled. "Tommy didn't understand either," he said, "but he didn't know that Mrs. Pressler had asked Minnie to ask Grandpa if he'd mind having Tommy stay with us on game nights. The Presslers are even having a hard time figuring out how Bennie's gonna keep coming to therapy on the farm. With everything they're up against right now, it's a real mess. Mr. Pressler is tied up with cleanup crews and contractors and permitting issues, and Mrs. Pressler is trying to get her emergency relief center running. She wants to do more than just hand out water and food."

"So what's the solution?" asked Leah.

Artie replied, "Starting today—about right now, as a matter of fact—Bennie's riding one of the school buses from Arbor to E-ville with the Solid Rock kids. Then he can help out his folks and ride back home with them at whatever time. And tonight Tommy's staying with Ricky." He turned to glance back at Tommy before continuing. "He doesn't know it yet," Artie said, "but tomorrow we're gonna go to the Presslers and pick up enough stuff for him to stay with us until this string of road games ends. After two weeks on the farm with me and Grandpa, Tommy will be *glad* to not be needed for anything."

Then he got serious again. "So, what about Jamie?" he asked. "She seemed okay today at lunch. Did you guys talk to her about what *she* wrote the other night? That was disturbing, too."

Leah nodded. "Yeah, we talked," said Leah. "I know how she feels, even though my *mom* is the one being the big jerk. Jamie wrote that she couldn't help anybody else—that *she* needed therapy. Well, that's me, too. That's why

I've been going to sessions twice a week since last summer. And that's what I told Jamie—to take Minnie's advice and look for a way to help other people, just like me learning how to take care of my horse. If you're focused on helping somebody else solve their problems, you don't have as much time feel sorry for yourself."

"Then how's Jamie gonna help out with the Solid Rock kids?" asked Artie. "She didn't seem to have any idea the other night."

Nicie's eyebrows rose. "Believe it or not," she began, "me and Jamie are gonna work together. Never thought you'd hear that, did you, big guy?"

Before Artie could respond, Ty Green's eyes popped open. "I've got to hear this," Ty said, sitting up straight next to Artie. "Not even a year ago, you and Jamie were sworn enemies."

"Well, we're friends now," said Nicie, "and we're even gonna do something together—start a beach volleyball league on the strand at Woody's. He said he likes that idea, and it's right down my alley. We can practice with the Solid Rock transfers during the extracurricular period at the end of school, and the best teams can play at Woody's on the weekend. Woody said he'll put up the prizes."

"That *is* a good idea," said Ty. "Maybe me and Artie will enter as a team."

Artie was already shaking his head *no*, but Nicie headed off Ty's wisecrack. "Sorry, pal," she said. "All the teams will be co-ed—one guy and one girl. So, do you know any girls who are champion beach volleyball players, other than me?" That was a fact, as Nicie Evans—Arbor's most athletic girl—had won tournaments the past two summers in a women's league at Mimosa Beach.

Ty scratched his head and yawned wide. "Gee, aren't we there yet?" he said, looking out the bus window at the outskirts of Capital City. "It'll be good to finally get off this bus. I'm ready to pitch."

CHAPTER 7

IT LOOKED LIKE A RECIPE FOR DISASTER that the Barf Table teens—the baseball players, anyway—had to sit with Jug Johnson the following day at lunch. Joe Carson was there, too, but his girls had played better than anyone would have expected the previous afternoon in Capital City. The Lady Red Caps had underestimated the Bruinettes, and the Arbor girls had taken an early lead. The more powerful home team finally found its footing and ground out a narrow win. Still, Coach Carson was pleased with his players' performances as they had given their best efforts. The baseball game that followed had been another story entirely, as Arbor High—even with the Bruins' star hurler on the mound—never had a chance against the undefeated Capital City nine after a disastrous first inning. Ty's poor performance in that first inning had been the result of misguided decisions by several people. Jimmy Gore's efforts on the diamond—or lack thereof—were also partly to blame. Why Jug and Joe had to sit at the Barf Table that Wednesday was, like so many other things, out of their control, but it turned out for the best.

The two coaches had been called to the principal's office at the start of Wednesday's lunch period, so they weren't in the cafeteria when the Barf Table gang gathered to eat together. Principal Church had summoned Jug Johnson and Joe Carson to reprimand them for having used tobacco the previous day while loading the activity bus. Guidance office assistant and general busybody Vicki Duke had seen the two coaches taking a break to dip and smoke, and had tattled to perky guidance counselor Thelma Hopper, who, in turn, had informed the principal of Jug and Joe's indiscretion. In their meeting, the principal fussed at the coaches for their tobacco use and reiterated their supervisory responsibilities as cafeteria monitors. Also, he dared them *not* to be seated at the faculty table whenever he happened to check on them.

Before the chastened coaches reported to the cafeteria, the newest member of the Barf Table troupe, Jimmy Gore, told the others that he had invited the Inouye twins—Mike and Kimi—to join the group for lunch. He said they had accepted his invitation but needed to get Mrs. Inouye's permission first. "They're in her room right now," Jimmy said. "Let's drag that other round table and some chairs over here so we'll have room for them."

"That's the faculty table," said Artie. "Besides, how do you know Mrs. Inouye will say *yes*?"

Jimmy shrugged. "Because all of Kimi's crowd went to Mimosa Beach," he said, "and her mom wants her to have friends—just not a *boyfriend* right now. I told them to tell her that I promise not to sit with Kimi—that I'm interested in another girl at this table." Like the day before, he winked at Ty Green.

"Why are you winking at *him*?" asked Nicie Evans, pointedly. "Shouldn't you ask *me* if I mind being your fake girlfriend?" Jimmy was quickly getting on Nicie's bad side, especially after his lackluster first-inning effort the previous day against Capital City High.

Artie still wasn't sure they should push the two round tables together without permission, even if teachers rarely dined in the cafeteria. "Let me go ask Frankie about this," said Artie, rising to walk over to the cashier's stand. "Maybe he has a card table stored in the back that teachers can use."

When Artie returned to the Barf Table, he was smiling and nodding. "Frankie said to go for it," Artie announced, "and we can move all eight chairs. Frankie's gonna bring something in tomorrow for the coaches. They're the only ones who ever sit at the faculty table, anyway."

With the two round tables pushed up against one another near the tray-return window and trash bins, the six Barf Table seniors—Artie, Ty, Jimmy, Nicie, Julia and Wilma—sat at one table, leaving two chairs vacant for when the coaches showed up. The other six members of the gang stayed at the old Barf

Table, leaving empty seats for the Inouye twins in case they got permission to join them.

Sure enough, within minutes Mike and Kimi appeared at the cafeteria door. They carried their lunches in brown paper bags. Mike's left arm was still in a sling. Behind them stood Jug Johnson and Joe Carson, bearing nothing but frowns at seeing that the faculty table had been commandeered. Muttering, they headed toward the serving area to get their lunches.

Being 11th graders, the twins appeared confused about which pair of vacant chairs to take. But then they recognized fellow junior Jamie Foxx from their classes that morning, and they headed for her table. Mike sat between Jamie and Brett; Kimi, between Leah and Bennie. There at the old Barf Table, the younger teens greeted the twins warmly and didn't hesitate to include them in their conversations.

Having jumped what was left of the lunch line, Jug Johnson and Joe Carson took the two seats between Artie on one side and Wilma on the other. The six seniors were silent, waiting for the coaches either to begin working on their food or to pick a topic of discussion. None of the teenagers wanted to broach the subject of the baseball team's mercy-rule defeat—a ten-run loss that was stopped after four-and-a-half innings. But that was what Jug Johnson wanted to talk about.

"Yogi, my boy," said Jug, "I admired your spirit yesterday—to just put your head down and do your job behind the plate. That's what a leader does." The old coach glanced first at Ty Green and then at Jimmy Gore around the table. "I'm sorry if I let all you boys down," Jug added. "That was a mighty big opportunity for us, and I blew it."

Artie shook his head. "No, Coach," he said, "*we* blew it. I should've called time a lot sooner and got everybody on the mound to talk things over and settle down. That first inning got out of hand faster than in any game I've ever played, even going back to Little League."

"*Heh*," said Jug, begging to disagree with his catcher. "It happens more often than you think, if you stick around this game as long as I have." He loaded his plastic spork with green peas and shoveled them into his mouth. When he was ready to continue, he pointed the utensil at Ty Green. "That was the most discombobulated start I've ever seen you make," the coach said. "I hope you don't mind me saying so in front of everybody sitting here, but I've been warned not to leave the cafeteria until the bell rings. And, shoot, we were all there last night, so what happened isn't any big secret."

"I know," said Ty Green. "I'm sorry, Coach. I just couldn't get the ball across the plate on those first two batters, and then we got what looked like a double-play or even a triple-play ball, but . . ."

Jimmy Gore spoke up. " . . . but then *I* let the ball get past me down the line," he said, "and both runners scored. That was *my* fault, not yours, Ty. I should've dove for it."

Ty shook his head. "No, what I was *gonna* say was, the game got away from me, like Artie said, and I started thinking about all those college coaches—like Coach Landis—and that scout in the stands, and I just couldn't reel it all back in. I've never let a team bat around on me before. That was embarrassing."

"Ty Green, I've told you before to quit thinking so much," said Jug. "Don't think. Just throw the pitches that Yogi here calls for."

Across the table, Nicie Evans couldn't help but laugh. "That's what I always told him, Coach," she said. "He wouldn't listen to me, either."

"From your lips to God's ears, young lady," Jug said, turning now to Jimmy Gore. "Young man, did I not give you enough time to recover from that horrible storm? Did I make a mistake by pushing you to play third base last night?"

To Artie's surprise, Jimmy answered in the affirmative. "Yes, sir," he said, "I think you *did* make a mistake playing me there—last night, anyway. My head wasn't in the game after talking to Coach Landis before batting practice. My brain was out in left field somewhere."

"Why's that, you think?" asked Jug. "He's a good coach—the best football coach State College has ever had. You'd think he'd know better than to mess with a high school player right before a game. You mind telling me what he said that got you so mixed up?"

"He told me to be careful," said Jimmy, "and not to take any chances that might get me hurt. He said football's gonna pay my way, not baseball, so I should keep that in mind. Actually, he said that same thing back on Signing Day after he found out I played baseball, too, at Solid Rock."

"*Huh,*" Jug grunted. "Now, you see? That's where I messed up. I should've trusted my gut and run Landis off when I saw him hanging around the batting cage, but I didn't because he's a big college coach and I'm not. I knew better than to let him talk to you boys right then. I saw him talk to Yogi here and Ty Green, too."

"Sorry, Coach," said Jimmy. "It won't happen again. I'll apologize to the whole team—and to Brett, for taking his spot and then not doing my best. I'll talk to him before lunch is over."

Studying the young man's face, Jug nodded slowly. "I appreciate that," said the coach, "and I can respect the courage it takes for you to admit you didn't give us a hundred percent yesterday." He looked down at his tray for a moment. "Jimmy, I want you to do one other thing for me," said Jug. "I want you to take some time over the next couple days and decide if being an Arbor Bruin truly is the right thing for you. We only got four regular season games left, and whether we make the state playoffs or not, I don't want you to do anything that doesn't feel right. Coach Landis was dead-on correct yesterday—football is your bread and butter. Matter of fact, there isn't a better linebacker in this whole state, if you ask me. But on a baseball field, you're a fine, pure hitter, too—you showed that yesterday. We sure can use your bat, especially going up against teams like Capital City High. You decide what's right for you this spring, young man, and I'll back you up one hundred and ten percent, whatever your decision is. Just let me know before Friday's game."

Jug Johnson ate another sporkful of peas and turned to his best buddy and coaching colleague, Joe Carson. "Did I cover everything, Joe?" he asked. "This is a good group of guys, and if we can get this ship back on course, it should be smooth sailing the next two weeks." He didn't mind that the boys and softball girls heard him say that. They knew it was true.

Joe looked up from his tray and nodded thoughtfully. "From your lips to God's ears, old buddy," he said, turning his head at the sound of the cafeteria doors opening and closing. "Don't look now, but God just walked into the room, and I think he's checking to see if we're still here. Let's wave at him."

* * *

The sun was setting on Oleander County as the old red pickup carrying Artie Bauer, Ricky Duran and Tommy White turned off Ebenezerville Road onto the farm lane. There, they stopped for a moment to let Ricky out. The boys were running late because after practice they had driven to the Presslers' house at Sandpiper Beach to pick up more clothes for Tommy. The Presslers hadn't been home—all of them, including Bennie, were in E-ville—but Tommy used his own key to get into the house. While they were gathering up Tommy's things, he had commented that his having a key to the large oceanfront home had never been an issue, because Abe and Deborah Pressler had always treated him like family. And Bennie was like a brother. They had even let him participate in their recent Passover Seder. But Tommy had said again that he didn't feel as if he belonged—that a poor boy like him with both parents in prison didn't deserve any part of the Presslers' hard-earned wealth or good name. "I know why the Presslers weren't there yesterday," he had said, "but my real mom didn't even try to come see me play. She's on work release *in* Capital City. She could've asked them to bring her by." Neither Artie nor Ricky had been able to say anything helpful.

Harry Bauer wasn't alone in the farmhouse kitchen when the boys arrived. Grandpa and Minnie Marecek sat facing each other at one end of the long table with a stack of papers between them on the red-and-white checkered tablecloth, as if they were negotiating a contract or sale of property. "Howdy, boys," said Grandpa. "Give me and Miss Minnie a few more minutes, and then we need to have a word with you—with *both* of you."

The boys moved Tommy's things from the pickup truck to a spare bedroom upstairs, using the front door to the farmhouse so that the two adults could finish whatever they were doing without being disturbed. Artie and Tommy were still upstairs when they heard Grandpa's gruff voice. "Come on down, boys," Harry called. "Me and Minnie have some big news."

At that announcement, Artie and Tommy exchanged a quizzical look. "You don't think . . . ?" Artie said. "I mean, I know Grandpa's lonely, but he wouldn't . . . . Would he?"

"I don't know," said Tommy. "He said they need to talk to *both* of us. Why would your grandpa dating Dr. Marecek involve me?"

Artie laughed and said, "Well, there's only one way to find out. Let's go." The pair hurried down the stairs to the kitchen as if a pizza had just come out of the oven. They *were* hungry, having not eaten supper yet, but they were more interested in hearing Grandpa and Minnie's "big news."

Once the boys were seated, Grandpa motioned for Minnie to begin. "I'm glad that the three of you were able to talk about Tommy's concerns—what he wrote Sunday night," she said. "I have been very concerned, too, so when Harry asked me yesterday to look into something for him, I was glad to help out." She pointed to the papers on the table. "I drove up to Iron Harbor today, to the Oleander County Courthouse, and I found several important documents."

Minnie took the paper on top of the stack and handed it to Artie. It was a photocopy of his birth certificate. "I know you have your original birth certificate," said Minnie. "Harry got it out and showed it to me yesterday morning." She paused to point at the copy in Artie's hands. "But this birth certificate is different. This one *does* list your biological father, and his identity does go along with what you and your grandfather found in your mother's old diary—where Ingrid wrote 'I love P.J.,' remember?"

Artie nodded as he read the name "Peter Jacob White" in the space identifying his father. It also showed that this man—the older brother of Tommy's father, Bob White—was 24 years old at the time of Artie's birth, and that Ingrid, his mother, was 16. Both listed Ebenezerville as their place of birth.

Handing him the next sheet of paper, Minnie said, "This is a copy of what's called an affidavit of parentage. It's how your biological father's name was added to your birth certificate. You'll notice that it's dated about six months after you were born, and that it was signed by both parents—by *Ingrid Ann Bauer* and *Peter Jacob White*—and also, there above Ingrid's signature, is your grandmother's signature, *Mrs. Pearl Stone Bauer*. Harry tells me that he knew absolutely nothing about this—that Pearl did it all on her own. That makes perfect sense, especially in this case."

"That's right, Artie," said Grandpa. "I would never keep something like that from you, son. A man has a right to know where he comes from. And if Pearl *had* told me how old P.J. was, I would've had me a word of prayer with him—at the very least." He shook his head in dismay. "But I *do* remember this next paper that Miss Minnie's gonna show you. We got a lawyer to help us with it before you went off to kindygarden. I didn't read it, but I signed it where Pearl told me to."

"It's an official custody agreement," Minnie said, handing Artie the document. "It says that your grandparents take full legal and financial responsibility for you. As your grandfather said, this was done long after your mother disappeared—and your biological father, too. You may even remember this. It was handled at the county courthouse."

Artie shook his head. "Not really," he said. "Well, I *do* remember having to dress up and go with Grandma and Grandpa to Iron Harbor, but I didn't understand why. I was more excited about seeing the naval base and all the ships. Back then, I wanted to be a sailor. I always figured that's what happened to my father—that he was in the navy and that he had sailed off to sea. Now that I know his name, maybe I can find out what happened to him."

That was when Tommy spoke up. "No, you don't want to do that," he said. "Remember? I asked my dad about P.J., and he said to shut up about him—that it could get me killed. I don't know what kind of drug deals P.J. was involved in, but they must have been bad. Or maybe P.J. doesn't want anybody to find *him*, for whatever reason." He looked away from Artie, and back to Minnie and Harry. "So," Tommy said, "is that the *big news*—that me and Artie are real cousins?"

Minnie Marecek nodded. "Yes, Tommy," she said, "and, however alone you were feeling the other night when you wrote your paper, this proves that you do have *real* family here that cares about you, not just a foster family that also loves and cares so much about your well-being. And, yes, I did talk to Deborah Pressler about you on Sunday, and she did express some concern about scheduling conflicts. She didn't want you to feel as if your baseball was a problem. She didn't want you to feel guilty and quit baseball because the Presslers have so much to do now in Ebenezerville."

Tommy dropped his head, but nodded that he understood. Minnie continued, "And that leads me to the last thing I found today at the courthouse. Tommy, this is something else that Deborah told me the other day." Minnie pushed the last few papers across the table toward the straw-haired boy. "I found this at the register of deeds office," she said. "It's a copy of the deed to your family farm. You already knew that the farm had been seized by the government and auctioned off after your parents were arrested. Didn't Abe Pressler tell you that?"

The big boy nodded again, this time lifting his eyes from the photocopy to look at Minnie. "*Uh-huh,*" Tommy replied, "and Mr. Pressler told me he'll help me find out who bought our farm, and then he'll help me buy it back someday— you know, when I'm older and have a good job."

Minnie smiled. "Well, he's done just that," she said. "Abe Pressler bought your family's farm at auction, and then he set up a trust fund for you and you alone—not for your parents or for any of your relatives, just for you. When you turn 21, that entire farm—or the land, at least—will be yours. In the meantime, Abe will manage the property for you. It's just that right now, Deborah said, Abe is awfully preoccupied with rebuilding their department store and downtown E-ville itself."

"That's great!" Artie Bauer said. "Tommy, we're cousins! And we'll both have a farm to run someday!" Then he looked at Harry Bauer and added, "I mean, whenever Grandpa's ready to retire. Right, Grandpa?"

Harry laughed. "Darn tootin'," he said. "Well, all of this *is* big news, now isn't it? Artie, you have a new cousin; and, Tommy, turns out you *are* one of the family—official." He thought for a second. "I tell you what, though. Those honey bees of yours, Tommy, will be good for the crops, but you need some experience with bigger livestock. So, Artie, maybe you two better grab you a sandwich and go on out to the barn so you can show him how to milk a cow again. You two know how fussy Bessie and Bossie can be. And on your way back to the house, how about sloppin' Frick and Frack for me? I've already fed the chickens, so you don't have to worry about that. But right now, if you boys don't mind, I'd like to sit here and talk to Miss Minnie for just a while longer. Sometimes just talking to her does me a world of good. I might even take up riding horses again and get her to give me some of that fancy *ee-quine* therapy—if she don't charge too much."

Minnie smiled. "Don't you worry about that, Harry," she said. "What you've given me by letting me work out here at your farm is worth a lot more than what I pay in rent."

CHAPTER 8

FRANKIE THE DEATH-METAL CASHIER had the new "faculty table" all set for Jug Johnson and Joe Carson when the first lunch bell rang on Thursday. It wasn't a table, as such—instead, two old recliners that Frankie said he and his wife had replaced in their living room with a sectional sofa. The faux-leather chairs were in good shape but had few features other than being able to recline—no built-in heating pads, no lower-back vibrators, not even cup holders. The recliners did, however, have swiveling tray-tables that swung up from the sides like the little writing desks in auditorium seats. Frankie said those trays had gotten more use at his house than their mahogany dining table.

The recliners caused a stir among the student body as they filed into the cafeteria, whether they headed for the serving line or straight for their seats in the two sections—the raised level for seniors and juniors, and floor level for the lower grades. Frankie had positioned the recliners in the exact spot where the old faculty table had stood before it was merged with the Barf Table the previous day. The two large chairs were turned so that Jug and Joe could watch the serving line as students passed by. The two men could also survey the whole cafeteria, including the double door to the hallway and the school clock on the wall above the entrance.

Jug and Joe were thrilled at Frankie's initiative, as they had always joked about needing a nap after a good meal in the cafeteria. "Now you can take naps *during* lunch," said the cashier, with a laugh as he sat the coaches down and demonstrated the tray tables.

When Artie Bauer got to the enlarged, double Barf Table—now shaped like an *8* instead of a big *0*—he greeted Leah Russo and Kimi Inouye, who were already seated. "Hi, ladies," Artie said. "What do you think of the new faculty table? It suits those guys perfectly, doesn't it?"

The girls barely looked up from a sketchbook on the table between them to answer. "Not for long," said Leah. "Lurch hasn't seen it yet." She pointed to a figure that Kimi had drawn on the page they were studying, and added, "I love your artwork, Kimi. You're really good."

Artie laid his tray down at his new spot on the "senior" side of the figure eight and walked to the other table where the girls sat. "That *is* good, Kimi," he said. "Is that Mike?"

The manga-style drawing showed her brother—taller and more muscular with dark, spiky hair—throwing a flaming ball from a mountaintop. "No," said Kimi, "this is Zircon. See his blue eyes? They are gemstones—like diamonds. My brother's eyes are brown."

"And he only throws fastballs," added Leah Russo. "Well, before he hurt his arm. Where is he? I didn't see him around school this morning."

Kimi closed her sketchbook and opened her lunch bag. "Father took Michi to the hospital to get his shoulder checked," she said. "He should be here soon." She took a sandwich from her paper bag and offered half to Leah.

"No, thanks," said Leah. "I brought my lunch today." She went into her book bag and took out a small slice of cheese pizza wrapped in wax paper. Artie recognized Woody Woods's distinctive crust.

"Are you working more hours at the grill?" Artie asked, heading back to his seat. "I thought you only worked there on weekends."

Leah shrugged. "Brett brought us a pizza when he came over last night," she said, not seeming to mind Artie's curiosity. "It was so late that he and Dad couldn't eat it all."

Taking his seat, Artie looked down at his tray—whose entrée was mystery meat—and just shook his head for a second. "Man," he muttered. "I need to find a girl who works at a steakhouse."

With the exception of Mike Inouye, all the Barf Table teens were seated at their new spots when Principal Church entered the cafeteria, accompanied by school tattletale Vicki Duke. As they stood inside the doorway, Vicki pointed at the two old coaches in their recliners and put one fist on her hip in a show of defiance. She hadn't liked Jug Johnson ever since she accidentally drank from a spit cup he had left on a table at the homecoming dance. Vicki got along well enough with Joe Carson on the softball team, but she couldn't burn Jug without scorching Joe a bit, too.

"What's this, gentlemen?" asked Mr. Church sternly, as he neared the coaches' chairs. Vicki Duke had peeled off to avoid a direct confrontation with Coach Carson, because she wanted to pitch in Friday's game at Port Oleander. She slid into an open Barf Table seat next to Brett Woods. It was where Mike Inouye had sat the previous day.

Both coaches had finished their lunches, returned their empty trays, and tucked their swiveling tables back out of sight. "Hi, Jerry," said Jug, with a grin. "Good of you to come join us. How do you like the new faculty table?"

"That doesn't look like a table to me," the principal said. "Those are pretty nice recliners—nicer than you two old rascals deserve. I thought I made myself clear yesterday."

"You did," said Jug. "You told us that our butts had better be sitting at the faculty table. Well, this is the new faculty table. The old one is sitting over there now." When he pointed at the expanded Barf Table, his eyes shifted to a tall, lean boy making his way across the cafeteria. It was Mike Inouye. Jug lifted his hand to acknowledge his new player.

Church also noticed Mike, but the principal wasn't finished reprimanding Jug and Joe. "I said faculty *table*," snapped Church. "Those are chairs."

That was the cue for the coaches to return their tray tables back into place on their laps. "See," said Joe Carson, patting the small laminated surface, "this isn't just a recliner, Jerry. It's a table, too—and a mighty comfortable one at that." Joe then flipped his table straight up to show its bottom side. It had that very word—*TABLE*—printed there in black marker.

Jerry Church's face began to flush, as he hated being outsmarted. "I said *faculty* table, Joe," insisted Church. "No one in their right mind would call this the *faculty* table."

"Well, *somebody* did," said Jug Johnson, flipping up his tray to reveal the word *FACULTY* in the same block letters as Joe's *TABLE*. "You can read, can't you, Jerry? This is the faculty table now." Jug laughed nervously, because he had to know that the argument wasn't over.

That is, until Jamie Foxx rose from the Barf Table. The softball player gave Mike Inouye her seat and moved to where Principal Church stood. She took advantage of his exasperated silence, as he tried to come up with an appropriate response to Jug Johnson's pronouncement. She tugged at his coat sleeve and said something in his ear. As she spoke, the redness in his face deepened. When she finished, he simply nodded that he understood her. She returned to her table and stood between Mike and Vicki, and waited for the principal to settle his dispute with the coaches.

"Well," began Mr. Church, studying the recliners and the men occupying them, "I'd better not catch you two sleeping during lunch—or you'll be retiring sooner than you planned. You're supposed to be our lunchroom monitors." He turned on his heel and left the cafeteria as quickly as he could, without stopping to correct any students for anything.

Still standing behind Vicki's and Mike's seats, Jamie Foxx kicked the leg of the chair occupied by her softball teammate. "That was a crummy thing to do, Vicki," said Jamie. "Now that you got Lurch to fuss at Jug and Joe, you can go back to your seat up in the senior section."

Without even looking back at the girl, Vicki Duke flashed a big smile at Brett Woods. "I'm not going anywhere," she said, batting her long lashes. "I like sitting here. I may sit here every day."

Brett shook his head. "Oh, no, you won't," he said. "You're in Mike's seat. Jamie gave Mike her spot after you came in from tattling to Lurch. The coaches weren't hurting anyone. The recliners are a great idea." He looked over at the cashier's stand and gave Frankie Hughes a big thumbs-up.

Rising, Vicki harrumphed and stomped off to her regular table on the upper level. Mike got up to give Jamie her chair. When Mike stood, the others noticed that he no longer wore his left arm in a sling.

"Hey, Coach!" said Artie. "Take a look at Mike. Notice anything different?"

Jug Johnson nodded. "No sling," he said. "Yeah, I saw that when he walked in. A good baseball coach notices that kind of thing—even when we're in the middle of a good *brouhaha*."

"We aren't out on the diamond, Jug," said Joe Carson, "and Jerry Church isn't an ump. He's our boss. But that's an awful good baseball word—*brouhaha*. Haven't heard that one in a long time."

Jug waved Joe off and called Artie over for a conference with the two men. "Tell me something, Yogi," said Jug. "Did you happen to hear what Jamie said to the principal?"

"No, sir," said Artie, kneeling between the two recliners.

Jug looked over at Joe and asked, "Do you have any idea?" When Joe shook his head, Jug said, "I'd like to know what in the Sam Hill that girl told Jerry Church to make him back down. I've only seen him do that in two other situations, and they were both when he was neck-deep in some real hot water. I wonder what kind of mess he's in now."

* * *

Mike Inouye had good news Thursday afternoon for Coach Johnson and the Bruins baseball team. His doctor—a colleague of his father at Ebenezerville Hospital—had given Mike the okay to play baseball again on a limited basis. He could bat but was still not allowed to pitch just yet. Even though he threw right-handed, the injury to his left shoulder affected his pitching windup and risked keeping the muscle from fully healing. So, Jug Johnson's plan was to use Mike as the team's designated hitter—a definite plus because the Bruins needed another left-handed batter, which Mike was. Also, his injured shoulder would face away from the pitcher when Mike batted, making it less likely to be hit by a wild pitch.

The team's other transfer from Solid Rock—third baseman Jimmy Gore— had been as good as his word and had apologized at practice on Wednesday for his lack of effort on defense against Capital City High. At Thursday's practice, after two days of reflection, Jimmy told Coach Johnson privately that, yes, he did want to stay on the team, but he asked Jug if he could either DH or play somewhere other than at third base. With the coach having decided to give Mike Inouye the designated hitter spot to get him in the lineup, Jimmy Gore's other suggestion—that Brett Woods start at third base, as he had done before the storm—needed more thought.

As it turned out, Brett Woods and left fielder Phil Waters came up with the best solution to the problem of where Jimmy Gore should play. During batting practice, with Brett playing third and Phil in left, Jimmy smacked one ball after another into the hot corner. Brett handled the first two balls, both grounders right to him. With the third pitch, he dove and knocked down a hot line drive but didn't field it cleanly. On the very next ball, he muffed a hard grounder that was hit closer to him than to shortstop Ozzie Maye. Brett had leaned the wrong way, in case Jimmy sent another laser shot down the line. The fifth pitch saw Jimmy bloop the ball over Brett's head into shallow left field for what would have been a "Texas League single." After chugging forward at full speed and watching the ball drop yards in front of him, Phil Waters looked up at Brett Woods and just shook his head. Jimmy's last ball in that round of BP sailed down the left-field line toward the tall, yellow foul pole, but stayed in the park. The ball bounced off the warning track into the outfield fence and then skittered away. Phil, who had played shallow to give himself a better chance of catching another bloop single, had trouble chasing the ball down. Jimmy stopped at third base, even though he could have made it all the way home.

At catcher, Artie Bauer repositioned himself in foul territory to back up Phil Waters's throw to Brett Woods on the bag at third. "Good hitting, Jimmy!" said Artie. "Hang in there, Brett! You, too, Phil!" Both fielders hung their heads, as if they'd bungled more than just one player's at-bat in BP.

Jimmy nudged Brett with his elbow and said, "You're doing fine, bud. You're still learning this position. I'll help you out any way I can."

Brett snorted. "You could hit a few balls the other way," he said, but added,

"Nah, I need the practice. So does Big Phil—along with a breather." The rotund left fielder was bent over, hands on his knees and breathing hard from all the running that Jimmy Gore had made him do.

"Hey, Phil!" called Artie Bauer, noticing that his tired teammate needed a break before the next batter, Mike Inouye. "Phil! Come over here a minute! "

There was no rush. At home plate, Coach Johnson talked to new DH Mike Inouye as the former Solid Rock star took some easy practice swings to test his shoulder. Phil Waters lumbered over to third base, where Artie Bauer, Jimmy Gore and Brett Woods were gathered. Middle infielders Ozzie Maye and Ricky Duran took the opportunity to chat with Tommy White at first base. The other two outfielders—Ty Green in right and Manny Freeman in center—played catch while everyone else talked.

"I have a question, Artie," said Big Phil, still trying to catch his breath, "but I'm afraid to ask the Jugster. Don't want him mad at me." Artie told him to go ahead, and Phil continued, "Why am I standing out there in left field when we got two guys—these two guys here—playing third?" Turning to Brett and Jimmy, Phil added, "Wouldn't one of you boys like to play a little bit deeper and let me just pitch? Am I a good pitcher or not, Artie? I know I'm not a particularly good outfielder."

Artie nodded. "You're a *great* pitcher," he said, "for one or two innings. But that's all a closer is supposed to do." Raising his eyebrows as he considered Phil's suggestion, Artie looked over at Jimmy, who nodded in agreement. "Well, I'll talk to Coach then," said Artie. "It'll also give Phil more of a chance to warm up before coming in as closer."

"And I don't mind left field," said Jimmy Gore. "Matter of fact, I can holler at Brett better from left field than from the dugout." He nudged Brett again. "You won't mind, will you?"

Adjusting his ball cap on his shaggy head, Brett asked, "Hey, man, why would I mind? It's like surfing. If you want to get better, you surf with somebody who's better than you are. You can give me some pointers at the plate, too—so I can return the favor in BP and hit some line drives at you on third." Brett smiled.

Before batting practice ended, Artie Bauer talked to Coach Johnson about the boys' discussion at third base. Jug liked the idea of having Jimmy Gore in left, Brett Woods at third, and Phil Waters as the team's dedicated closer. But what Jug Johnson liked most from that afternoon's practice was seeing Mike Inouye, their designated hitter, launch one baseball after another over the outfield fence—in left, center and right.

* * *

Later, behind the wheel of the red pickup truck, Artie smiled as he drove Ricky and Tommy home. "Boy, oh, boy," Artie said. "Port Oleander doesn't know what's gonna hit them tomorrow. We've got an awful good team now, don't you think?"

"Yeah, buddy," said Tommy White. "Jimmy and Mike were Solid Rock's best players. We were already good, but we've got that team's strength now."

Ricky Duran nodded. "Yes," he said. "Now, we are Solid Rock strong."

Hearing it put that way gave Artie another idea that he was sure Coach Johnson and the rest of the team would like. It turned out that all of Oleander County liked what Little Ricky Duran had just said.

CHAPTER 9

THE SIMPLE SQUARE OF BLACK TAPE that appeared on the left sleeve of each Arbor High baseball and softball uniform at Friday's game was nothing compared to the stitched, full-color *We Are Solid Rock Strong* patch that would adorn every Oleander County player's shoulder at their games the next week. On Friday morning, Artie Bauer talked to both Coach Johnson and Coach Carson. They went to Principal Church, who phoned the school system office in Iron Harbor. Artie also got word to Bennie Pressler, who called his mother at her storm recovery office in Ebenezerville. Everyone loved Ricky Duran's motto that summed up how all Oleander County residents felt in the week after the deadly tornadoes.

The black tape was the best the Bruins and Bruinettes could do Friday on short notice. But in the cafeteria on Friday, the Barf Table gang—the artistic ones, especially newcomer Kimi Inouye—sketched out the perfect patch design for Bennie to take to his mother. Deborah Pressler had said that if she got their design by the end of the workday, she could order the patches and have them on hand by Tuesday. The round patch would have a black background with *We Are Solid Rock Strong* sewn in white in the outer ring. Inside that would be an infield-colored heart with a grass-green diamond, three white bases and home plate at the points. Each of the four points would bear the initials of the four high schools that had absorbed the Solid Rock students. In the center of the green diamond would be an intertwined *S* and *R*, the logo that had appeared on Solid Rock baseball and softball caps since the school's start. Mrs. Pressler had said she would also order T-shirts to be sold at each school and in the various communities to raise funds for storm relief.

Artie Bauer was right about Friday's road game with the Port Oleander Pilots. He and his Arbor Bruins were unstoppable, with Ty Green starting on the mound. Ty hurled four innings of shutout ball, giving up only one hit and no walks this time out. He was relieved by Johnny Smith, who pitched two innings and gave up a single run on two hits and two walks. Rested for a change, Big Phil Waters shut down Port Oleander in the seventh inning by striking out the side. On offense, each of the Bruins' big bats had at least one home run. Inspired by the symbolic gesture to recognize the Solid Rock players—with the black tape that night and the new patch coming—former Harvesters Mike Inouye and Jimmy Gore hit two dingers apiece, with Jimmy's home run being a grand slam in the top of the seventh inning. The final score was Arbor 13, Port Oleander 1.

"I heard Coach Johnson say that was a *lucky* thirteen runs," said Artie Bauer, as he drove Ricky Duran and Tommy White from Arbor High to Sandpiper Beach late Friday night.

Woody Woods was keeping the grill open late so that both Arbor teams could celebrate. The Bruinettes had also won in softball, topping the Lady Pilots 15-13. Their winning pitcher was junior Jamie Foxx, who had started the game and was pitching when the Bruinettes took the lead for good. After five hard-fought innings, senior Vicki Duke relieved Jamie—that is, if Vicki's disastrous one-third of an inning could be called relief. Getting only one batter out, Vicki gave up five runs and all but relinquished their lead. At that point, freshman Leah Russo came in and managed to close out that inning and the next one to preserve the win. Seniors Nicie Evans, Wilma Marecek and Mel Grayson homered for the Bruinettes. Jamie Foxx and sophomore Jenny Gore—Jimmy's sister and a former Lady Harvester—tallied three hits, three stolen bases and three runs apiece. Coach Carson was thrilled about everything except Vicki's brief appearance in the pitching circle.

"And that was a very *unlucky* thirteen runs—for Icky Vicki," said Tommy White, as the red pickup crossed the tall bridge onto the barrier island. "That's what she gets for being a tattletale."

Sitting between his two friends, Ricky Duran looked out the windshield at the lights of Sandpiper Beach. "Look at all those houses," said Little Ricky. "That is beautiful. But I like where we live—out in the country—much better." He was quiet for a moment. "Tommy, you should not call Vicki mean names like that. She helped bring many students to see us wrestle in the state championships last winter. She was trying to become a good person."

"Yeah," said Artie Bauer, "that's all any of us can do—try our best—whether it's playing ball or being a good person. But I hope she doesn't feel too bad about the way she played. That was how *we* looked Tuesday in Capital City—or some of us did, anyway."

Tommy nodded. "You're right," he said, as the truck tires thumped onto the island causeway at the bottom of the bridge. "She's good-looking, but her family doesn't have much money—just like ours. Well, like either of *yours*. Bennie told me that her dad works for the county."

"Remember, Tommy," scolded Artie. "It's *our* family now." Tommy nodded.

Ricky broke the silence. "I wonder if Vicki will be at Woody's tonight," he said, still looking with wonder at the beautiful homes on Sandpiper Beach.

"Why?" teased Artie. "Are you gonna ask her out?"

"I may do that," said Ricky, as they turned into the parking area at Woody's on the oceanfront. "The prom is coming up. I may be a freshman, but I am a good dancer. And she may *need* a date."

That was when Artie's headlights shone on a red convertible, its top down. "Or she may *not*," Artie said soberly. "That's Josh Stark's car, and I'll bet he isn't here alone."

* * *

Vicki Duke and Josh Stark sat in a dark, corner booth away from the counter, with its cash register at one end and pickup window at the other. In between, all six stools at the counter were taken by Arbor Bruins baseball players. The dining area's four square tables had been pushed together so that the softball girls could sit as a group. Along the wall were three booths in addition to the one holding Vicki and Josh. Only one booth—the one next to the couple—was empty.

Nicie Evans, Wilma Marecek, Jamie Foxx and Leah Russo sat with the girls at the tables, though Nicie and Leah soon jumped up to help Woody and Brett Woods handle the big crowd. Ty Green hadn't arrived yet. He was supposed to give Mike Inouye a ride since the two lived not that far apart off E-ville Road. The Gore siblings also weren't there yet, as they were following Ty in his new vehicle—*The Luuuvvv Truck*. Artie Bauer, Ricky Duran and Tommy White headed toward the empty booth. Artie took care not to make eye contact with Josh Stark, who sat on the side facing the Arbor boys' seats.

"Did you see his hair?" whispered Tommy across the table. "Buzz cut, like in the army."

Artie raised his head to peak over the back of Tommy's seat. "Yeah," Artie said, "or in prison." When he realized what he'd just said—that he might have embarrassed Tommy—Artie blushed. "Sorry, I wasn't thinking."

"No problem, cousin Artie," said Tommy, with a crooked grin. "I mean, he's *your* family, too. Remember?"

Ricky was confused. "Josh?" he mouthed at Artie across the table, then asked, "You three are related?"

"No," Artie said, cringing, "not *him*. Tommy's *dad* is my *uncle*. We just found that out the other day. So, yeah, Tommy and I are cousins. Isn't that neat?"

"This is good news," Ricky said in a normal tone, then got louder. "This has been a *great* day!"

Right then, it wasn't Josh Stark that Ricky had to worry about upsetting with his exclamation. It was Vicki Duke. She heard his remark and blew up. "What was so great about it, shrimp?" she snapped, twisting to look back around her seat into their booth.

"You are right," said Ricky, smiling. "I am small, but I am strong. You know that, Vicki, because you cheered for me." He was referring to his state title that year in wrestling—won in a finals match that Vicki Duke had attended in Capital City, along with two busloads of Arbor High students that she had put together as head cheerleader. Likewise, Artie Bauer had won his weight class's championship. Tommy White had finished sixth in his own division.

Those facts apparently kept Josh Stark from getting involved in Vicki Duke's little spat with Ricky Duran. However, when the glass door into the grill from the outside deck opened, Josh's eyes cut in that direction and caught fire. Into the building stepped Ty Green, Mike Inouye, Jimmy Gore and Jenny Gore.

During football season, Jimmy had kept Josh, his teammate, from being assaulted on the gridiron by his father, Joel Stark, who had burst onto the field late in the game at Arbor High. Jimmy had blindsided the crazed elder Stark before he reached his son. That led to Mr. Stark's ejection from the stadium and near arrest and, indirectly, to Josh's later transfer to Hawthorn Military Academy. More recently, baserunner Jimmy Gore had blasted pitcher Josh Stark in a play at the plate in Solid Rock's last home game before the previous week's storm.

Artie remembered chuckling about the collision at home plate when Jimmy had told him and Ty about the incident, but no one was laughing now, not with Josh sitting in the next booth.

"Whoever owns the red convertible outside . . . ," said Jimmy Gore loudly, pausing to brush drops of water off his jacket, " . . . needs to put the top up. It's starting to rain." Like every other teenager in the room, he had to know that the shiny sports car belonged to Josh Stark, but the older boy didn't want everyone—including Josh—to know that he was doing his former teammate any kind of favor.

It would be a tight squeeze, but Jimmy, Mike and Ty headed for the booth where Artie and the younger boys sat. Artie got up to let Ty slide next to the wall in the booth. Jenny took one of the chairs that Nicie and Leah had vacated at the softball table. As Josh Stark hurried past them to his car outside, Jenny Gore called to her brother, "Hey, Jimmy. There's an extra chair here for you to use over there. It isn't a contest to see how many baseball players can sit in a booth."

Josh Stark stopped at the door and looked back at Jenny Gore. "Don't you mean *clowns*?" he said, with a sneer. "Like at the circus?" He was out the door before Jenny or the boys could respond.

Jimmy Gore took his sister's advice and pulled the extra chair over to the booth, and then sat in it himself at the end of the table. Wet from his trip outside,

Josh Stark returned to his seat in the corner, bumping Jimmy's chair as he passed. Jimmy had seen him coming and had scooted forward, but Josh hit up against him anyway.

"You're in the way, man," said Josh Stark, taking off his own jacket before sitting back down. He shook the jacket to shed water from it. "Where's Woody? The clientele here is really falling off. You can see it in the parking lot—nothing but hoopties and crappy old pickup trucks. One isn't even big enough to be *called* a truck. Next thing you know, it'll be rice-burners and low-riders out there. Jeez." He eyed Artie, Ty, Mike and Ricky to see if they took his bait. Then he snapped his jacket twice to get the last of the water out.

Jimmy rose and moved back a step. "Hey, watch it," he said. "Look, you got water all over the floor. Somebody's gonna slip and get hurt."

Still seated, Artie Bauer could tell from the gleam in Josh Stark's eyes that he was spoiling for a fight—just *not* with Jimmy Gore. Artie wondered if Josh was drunk as Josh always caused trouble when he had been drinking. So Artie tried to defuse the situation. "Don't worry about it, Jimmy," Artie said. "I'll go back to the kitchen and get a mop."

That was when Josh Stark crossed the line. "Keep your seat, fatso," said Josh. "Why don't you let one of your *boys* there go after the mop bucket? Their kind is good at doing scut work." Then he looked at Tommy. "Or send the big, dumb, blond kid. He needs to learn how to mop the floor—before he gets sent to prison like the rest of his stupid family."

Artie stood up and placed one hand on Jimmy Gore's chest to keep him from stepping forward. "I'll take care of this, bud," Artie said evenly. "This kid's had it coming for a long time."

"If you touch me," Josh Stark said, "you'll regret it." But when he made the threat, he was already leaning backwards, whether from intoxication or fear.

Artie laughed. "I don't have to hit you—not first, anyway," said the big farm boy. "All I have to do is wait for you to screw up, like you did at homecoming and at Halloween. Third strike and you'll be out, just like in baseball."

"Third strike?" said Josh. "What are you talking about? Dad made sure I don't have *any* strikes on my record. I'm clean. I can do whatever I want, and nobody can touch me."

"Well," said Artie, "then take your best shot—in front of everybody here—and we'll see what happens." The room was silent. Behind the counter, Nicie Evans took off her apron and laid it next to the cash register. Leah Russo slipped back into the kitchen.

Artie Bauer knew that Josh Stark was no fool. Josh was arrogant, reckless and hotheaded, but he was smart enough, even when drunk, to know when he was outgunned and outnumbered. Josh always tried to have backup. That night, with only Vicki Duke on his side, he couldn't have liked the odds of him getting out of Woody's Grill in one piece.

"Come on, Vicki," said Josh, putting his jacket back on. "Let's go. The food here sucks, anyway."

Again, all heads turned as another door—the one to the kitchen—flew open and then slammed shut behind Woody Woods himself, armed with a baseball bat. By the time Woody reached the corner booth, Brett Woods had also emerged from the kitchen and was moving to block the door outside. Leah rejoined Nicie at the cash register.

Woody pointed the bat at Josh Stark. "Well, then you don't have to come back here—ever," he said. "As a matter of fact, you're banned from the surf shop *and* the grill. I don't care if your father's real estate office *is* next door. You're not welcome here."

Pulling Vicki to her feet, Josh shouted, "My dad is gonna sue you for everything you have." He pointed at the baseball bat. "And that's assault."

"You should know," said Woody. "You were charged with enough counts of it at Halloween. Now get out of here."

Josh jerked Vicki away from the booth. Her shoes hit the water that he had shed on the floor minutes earlier, and the girl skidded awkwardly, losing her balance and falling backwards toward the booth. As she went down, the back of her head struck the table. Josh bent down and yelled at her. "Get up, Vicki," he snarled. "You're okay. If you don't get up, I'm leaving."

But she wasn't okay. The blow had knocked her out cold. Nicie Evans grabbed the first-aid kit from under the counter and ran toward her teammate. "Get out of the way, creep," shouted Nicie at Josh. "If you aren't gonna help, just go ahead and leave." She yelled for Leah to call 9-1-1. Having tossed the bat aside, Woody knelt down to help Nicie with the unconscious girl. The boys kept Vicki warm with their jackets and rolled one up under her head.

At the door to the deck outside, Brett grabbed Josh by the arm. "I hope you heard what Dad said loud and clear," Brett warned. "Step one foot on our property again, and I'll take care of you."

Josh jerked his arm away. "Oh, yeah?" he said. "Well, old buddy, you just went from assault to assault-and-*battery* by laying your hands on me. We'll see who takes care of who. What goes around, comes around. You can tell Jimmy Gore that, too."

Before Brett could respond, Josh was out the door and running through the rain to his car. Brett just shook his head and watched his former friend leave. The squeal of tires peeling out of the marl lot onto the wet pavement and the fading whine of the sports car's engine in the night told everyone inside the grill that they were rid of Josh Stark, at least for the time being.

A few minutes before the ambulance from Mimosa Beach pulled up outside, Vicki Duke regained consciousness, sat up shakily, and, ditzier than usual, asked Nicie Evans where "the boy I came with" had gone off to. When Nicie said Josh had left without her, it was clear that Vicki's erstwhile boyfriend would have more to worry about than a baseball bat if he returned to Woody's that night.

Brett Woods did, in fact, pass along Josh Stark's parting words to Jimmy Gore, but the Solid Rock standout just laughed. "What goes around, comes around?" said Jimmy. "The boy's full of crap. He's the one who has payback coming."

CHAPTER 10

CALL IT PAYBACK OR FATE, but the Barf Table gang learned Saturday that Josh Stark's karma broke down the night before on his way home from Woody's Grill. For the first time since the storm, Leah Russo and Bennie Pressler came to the Bauer farm for their therapy sessions with Dr. Minnie Marecek. As usual, Wilma Marecek assisted her aunt with Leah and Bennie. Tommy White, who had moved to the farm earlier in the week, was on hand but wasn't needed to help as much as he had when Bennie was disabled. Artie Bauer and Ricky Duran did regular farm chores, along with Ricky's father, Ricardo. Still using a cane outside, Grandpa Bauer sat on the deck of the clubhouse trailer near the corral and prepared to watch the Saturday morning activity on his farm. Minnie and Tommy joined him as they waited for the sessions to begin. The news about Josh Stark came from the group member who hadn't been at Woody's on Friday night.

Bennie Pressler and Leah Russo talked as they brushed their horses in the stable. "I'd like to have seen that," said Bennie, of the gang's run-in with Josh Stark. "Artie should have cleaned his clock. Then Josh might not have caused the wreck later."

"Wreck?" said Leah. "Josh was in a wreck?"

Bennie nodded. "He sure was," he said, "and you'll never guess who was in the other car—well, in the minivan, actually." He waited a second. "Miss Hopper from school. She was on a date with Deputy Ross. He got hurt pretty bad."

"Who?" Leah asked. "Josh?"

"No," said Bennie, "Deputy Ross. You remember Skip Ross. He was the cop at the homecoming dance, and he also handled Josh's mess here at our Halloween festival. The radio news this morning said he's in the hospital—in serious but stable condition. Miss Hopper and Josh were treated and released. Charges are pending, the news guy said."

As she entered the stable to summon the riders, Wilma Marecek heard the last part of Bennie's report. "Thelma Hopper and Josh Stark were taken to the ER?" she asked. "I *thought* I heard a siren last night when we were leaving Woody's. Where was the wreck?"

"According to the radio, it was at that big intersection near the Starks' golf course development on the river," said Bennie. "What's it called? Sandpiper Shores? Anyway, Josh ran a stop sign and got T-boned by the minivan. The news guy said there was extensive damage to the passenger side of Josh's car, also to the minivan's front end. Good thing it had airbags—but Miss Hopper's boyfriend got hurt, anyway."

"Well, I'm glad the man's stable, at least," said Wilma. "So, what does 'charges are pending' mean? Have any idea?"

Bennie shook his head. "Nope," he said, "but when Josh is involved, it probably means *nothing* will happen. Joel Stark will get the cops to drop the worst charges—even for driving while impaired. Josh probably won't even be charged with running the stop sign."

"Yeah," said Leah Russo, "before it's over, the deputy will get blamed for messing up Josh's car. Besides, Mr. Stark has it out for Skip Ross. He stood up to Mr. Stark at the Halloween festival *and* at our last football game—you know, the big game with Solid Rock."

"*Deputy* Skip Ross?" said Wilma. "Didn't he arrest Josh and his father at that football game? And didn't Jimmy Gore body-slam *both* of them out on the field before the deputy hauled them off?"

Bennie laughed and said, "Yeah, there must be a mysterious force that pulls poor Skip Ross into whatever mess Josh Stark gets himself into." He made a face at Leah. "How did I ever forget about that football game?" he said. "You and I both were up in the press box."

Just then, a familiar voice called down to the trio from the hayloft. "Hey, Bennie!" yelled Artie Bauer, peering through an open trapdoor above them. "You'd better not forget that game! It was the best ever! And Little Ricky here was the hero."

Ricky Duran's smiling face popped into the opening on the side opposite Artie. "And Jimmy Gore body-slammed me, too," said Ricky, still smiling. "But I like Jimmy Gore. He plays hard, and he does not cheat like Josh Stark does. Jimmy is a good person. I am glad he is on our team now."

* * *

The horse-therapy sessions ended around noon, and everyone went their separate ways. Headed back to River Bend outside Monk's Landing, Minnie and Wilma Marecek gave neighbor Leah Russo a ride home—in *Moby* the Suburban, not on horseback—so she could leave for work at Woody's. That spring Leah had enjoyed more freedom than she'd ever had, not only dating Brett Woods but also borrowing her father's new johnboat to cruise from their house on the river to the marina on the inland side of Sandpiper Beach. In a pinch, she could also take the small, flat-bottomed boat up the Oleander River to the riverfront park in Monk's Landing, not far from Arbor High. Fellow horseman Bennie Pressler needed a new kind of ride in the opposite direction that day—to Ebenezerville to rejoin his hardworking parents. Artie Bauer volunteered to take Bennie to E-ville after they all had lunch on the farm. Little Ricky Duran had plans for that afternoon with his parents. Ricardo and Gabrielle Duran planned to host three storm-impacted families from Solid Rock Christian Church at their house for a meal and bible study. The church building had been destroyed, but the actual church—the people—remained strong.

Grandpa Bauer had four bowls of vegetable soup and a platter of pimento-cheese sandwiches ready in the farmhouse kitchen when the boys got there for lunch. Tommy White had returned to the farmhouse early with Grandpa to help fix the food. When they arrived, Artie and Bennie washed up at the sink just inside the back door from the porch and were ready to eat.

"I'm glad you could stay for lunch, Bennie," said Grandpa. "I hope all this good food meets your approval. It's not fancy, but it's filling."

Bennie nodded. "Thank you for having me, Mr. Bauer," he said. "It looks good—just like Mom makes for us. Isn't that right, Tommy?"

The big, blond-haired boy's face reddened. "Well," Tommy began, "the pimento spread I used isn't exactly, uh, *kosher*, but I'm sure it's good."

"No, no," said Bennie, shaking his head, "I wasn't referring to *that*. You know we don't worry about that kind of thing all the time. If we did, I'd never be able to eat at school." He laughed. "No, this looks like a feast, Mr. Bauer."

"Well, good," said Grandpa, taking a sandwich off the top of the stack and placing it on his plate. "Artie," he continued, turning to his grandson, "what's on the agenda for this afternoon? Where are you and Tommy going after you drop Bennie off in town? I know you won't come straight back home."

"We will if you need us to," Artie said. "No, Grandpa, we thought we'd run over to Shin's Grove and put some fresh flowers on Grandma's grave. Her two-tone irises are blooming now. They'll look nice tomorrow when people are there for church. Maybe you, me and Tommy could go for a drive tomorrow and see how it looks. What do you say?"

Grandpa took a bite of sandwich and chewed deliberately. After swallowing, he looked at Artie and smiled sadly. "I really miss her," said Harry Bauer. "I miss talking to her in the mornings before I go out, and in the evenings when I come in. Since my accident, she really was everything to me—my nurse, my cook, my friend, my sweetheart." He laid his sandwich down and fell silent.

"Sorry, Grandpa," said Artie, glancing at Tommy and Bennie to see how they were absorbing this sad moment. "We don't have to go over to the church—not tomorrow, anyway. Or today, if you'd rather drive over there by yourself. We can come right back from E-ville."

The old man shook his head. "No," Harry said, "those were Pearl's favorite irises, and she'd want to show them off on our headstone over there. Now, isn't that something—such soft, pretty blossoms in that cold, hard, stone vase? I want you to go ahead and do that for us today, whether I see how it looks or not. I'll be sure and run over there one day while you're at school."

Artie laughed. "Well, you'll *have* to run," Artie said, breaking the tension, "because I'll have the truck at school. How will you get over there without our pickup? The tractor?"

Not hesitating, Grandpa replied, "Me and Miss Minnie go for rides sometimes. That's when we do some of our best talking—when we don't have to sit and stare at each other. Besides, her pickup is newer and nicer than that old red heap of ours." He paused for a spoonful of soup, blowing on it first. "So, are you gonna cut some flowers here before you leave?" he asked. "Be sure to leave me a few."

"No, actually," Artie began, "Tommy and I are gonna go over to his family's farm—or what's left of it—and see if the irises his mother planted there are blooming like the ones here. Didn't you tell us that Grandma gave Connie White some iris bulbs from the flowerbed right outside the kitchen window here, and that Connie transplanted them over there on the White farm?"

Grandpa nodded. "That's what Connie said when she called me, back in February," he replied. Then he looked at Tommy. "That's right, son. She got permission to call me after she saw that picture we found in the attic—you know, of her and Ingrid going to the prom. We had a good talk." He took another bite of sandwich. "I remember Pearl giving lots of folks bulbs and cuttings and seeds. That's how my wife was. Pearl believed in sharing the beauty of God's green earth instead of keeping it to herself. She was just like one of your little worker bees, Tom, my boy."

Tommy smiled. "I wish I could take some of those irises to my mom," he said, "but since I can't, we can cut every last one that's blooming now and take them over to Miss Pearl. Mom would like that. Mom's why I started gardening and keeping bees a couple years before Mom and Dad got arrested. My old flower garden and beeyard were toward the back of the farm where no one could see it but me and my bees. So, in a way, Miss Pearl was responsible for me liking flowers, too."

Bennie had finished his soup and was working on the last of his sandwich.

"How about if we go over there *before* you take me to E-ville?" he asked. "I can call Mom and let her know we'll be a little bit later than I thought. Dad's still tied up with insurance adjusters and the FEMA people. There's so much paperwork, it isn't funny. So, he won't miss me, as long as we aren't too late—even though he did ask me to bring my camera this afternoon."

Artie asked, "Did he find everything he needed in that old safe we helped you guys move?"

"Yes and no," said Bennie, in an uncertain tone. "Dad found all the important documents—the deeds and blueprints and stuff, even an old scrapbook with pictures and clippings from the Old Country. So, the papers he needed were in the safe. All the money drawers and bank bags from each department's cash register were there. But Dad acted like something was wrong—like he *hadn't* found something that was supposed to be in the safe."

"Have any idea what it was?" Artie said. "Maybe it's still in the office or somewhere in the building. That tornado made an awful mess of things."

"Maybe," said Bennie, "but Dad wouldn't talk about it, not even with Mom. He told us to stop asking him so many questions about it. We're kinda worried. He isn't usually that way."

Grandpa slid his soup bowl aside. "Well, boys," he said, "loss hits people in different ways, and this was a *huge* loss. Right, Bennie? It wasn't just *a* store; it was your family's *first* store. And it's a big loss for the whole community. Me and Pearl shopped there all our lives. In fact, Pearl bought her wedding gown there, and Old Man Pressler himself sold us our rings. I would've bought a diamond ring from him, too, if I could've afforded it. He was a fine gentleman. So, under the circumstances, Bennie, I'd say your daddy is handling things pretty good. It just takes time. At least, that's what everybody tells *me*."

"You're right," said Bennie. "I'm just curious, Mr. Bauer. Which one of my grandfathers was *Old Man Pressler* to you—grandfather Elisha or great-grandfather Noah? I kinda see them *both* that way—you know, from those bald heads and white beards in their portraits."

Harry Bauer smiled at the memory. "It was Noah, son," Grandpa said.

"Until the day he died, we couldn't go to town without stopping at Pressler's Department Store and seeing old Noah Pressler. He'd hold court with whoever was there and start handing out combs and pens to the little boys and pink hair ribbons and such to the little girls. Everybody loved him. He even gave me a pocketknife one time when we were there—a nice little peanut knife. That's what he'd give grown men."

"*Peanut* knife?" asked Bennie. "Like for eating peanuts?"

Grandpa chuckled and replied, "No, it's shaped kind of like a peanut. For some reason, that was your great-granddaddy's favorite little knife. He must have give out hundreds of them, even though they sure didn't *cost* peanuts. Funny, you don't see them much now."

"Okay then," said Artie Bauer. "We'll all go flower-hunting on Tommy's farm, and then we'll take the flowers we find to Shin's Grove Church. Grandpa, are you sure you don't want to go with us?"

"Yeah, come with us," Tommy said. "I'll ride in the back."

"No," said Grandpa, "I'll stay right here, if you don't mind. I have to make a call. I need to see a man about a dog."

All three boys laughed. "Oh, okay, Grandpa," said Artie. "We'll give you some privacy. I'll call you from E-ville before we start back home." He thought to add, "And if you don't answer right away—if you're still talking to that same man—I'll give you a few minutes and then call again."

Shaking his head, Harry Bauer gave his grandson a confused look, and got up to take his soup bowl and plate to the sink. "Well, whatever," he said. "You boys have a safe trip. Behave yourselves."

* * *

Ty Green's light-blue *Luuuvvv Truck* was parked on the shoulder of Little Swamp Road just beyond the Cairn Creek bridge. Before leaving the farm, Artie Bauer had called Ty and asked him to meet them at Tommy White's old home farther down the winding road into the swamp. From its intersection with busy Ebenezerville Road, two-lane Little Swamp Road was paved and easy to travel until it reached Cairn Creek. Then the roadway turned to gravel and was maintained as a service road by the timber and paper companies that owned much of the swampland. The old White farm sat on high ground that was called an "island," as it was bounded on three sides by Little Swamp and the creek, a tributary of the Oleander River. The blackened foundations and forlorn stone chimney of the White farmhouse and barn could be seen from the road, but the remote place where the boys were headed—to Tommy's old flower garden and beeyard—lay behind a thick stand of tall, straight pines.

"What took you so long?" asked Ty Green, seated on the back end of his little pickup. He stood and lifted the tailgate, snapping the latch shut on each side.

With the red farm truck stopped in the gravel road, Artie studied his friend out the driver-side window. "I hope you brought some dairy boots," Artie said, nodding down at the clean pair of white athletic shoes Ty wore. "We had to find an extra pair of boots for Bennie and a couple buckets for the flowers. Why didn't you turn into the driveway and park?"

"I'm not going in there by myself," Ty said. "I've heard scary stories about this place all my life, everything from ghosts to devil worshippers to swamp monsters." He leaned down to look into the cab past Artie. "No offense, Tommy," said Ty, "but I've heard about folks going in there and never coming back out again."

Tommy laughed. "Yeah," he said, "my dad started most of those rumors to keep people from snooping around. But some bad stuff really did go on here. That's why I stayed out of the house as much as I could. Artie, it's okay to park over there next to the house—well, where it *used* to be."

Artie nodded and stepped on the gas pedal enough to ease the red pickup off the service road and onto what had been the house's driveway. Ty got back into *The Luuuvvv Truck* and pulled forward to follow Artie down the drive and into the flat, worn area near the twenty-foot-tall chimney standing like a stone pillar not far from the bank of Cairn Creek.

After reaching into the floorboard for his work boots, Ty sat in the open door of the little truck and pulled on the protective footwear. Lacing the tall boots, he looked up as Artie, Tommy and Bennie clomped over to join him. "They aren't muck boots," Ty said, "but they'll have to do. I wear them out in the woods when Dad and me go hunting. But we try to stay out of the actual swamps."

"If it isn't too grown up," began Tommy, "there's a crooked path through those pine trees to my beeyard. The path follows the higher ground, so you shouldn't have to get your feet wet, Ty—not unless some big trees came down in the storm and are blocking the trail. Come on, guys." Tommy led the way toward the pines, adding, "I mean, I don't like walking in the swamp, either, but mainly it's because of the snakes and leeches."

"Snakes and leeches?" Bennie said, stopping dead in his tracks. He almost dropped the camera slung over his shoulder. "Maybe I'll wait in the truck. Dad didn't say anything about seeing any snakes or leeches when he was here."

Tommy turned around. "So, your dad really did come out here?" he said to Bennie. "I figured he had somebody else check out the place—a surveyor or somebody—so he wouldn't have to come. When did he tell you about buying this farm? How long have you known about it?"

Artie sensed that Tommy's questions were headed in the wrong direction, as far as Bennie was concerned—as if the Presslers had bought the White property for a purpose other than to keep Tommy from losing it, and then had kept the purchase a secret from Tommy alone.

"This farm was sold at public auction just a couple months ago, wasn't it?" Artie noted, not expecting an answer. "The auction wasn't a secret. It had to be advertised in the newspaper, and those auctions are held at the courthouse, aren't they?"

"That's right," said Bennie. "But, Tommy, I didn't find out about it until Thursday night after Dr. Marecek showed you guys the deed and stuff. I asked Mom what the idea was—why they hadn't told you to begin with—and she said they were waiting for the right time to tell you."

"The right time?" Tommy said. "But why now?"

Bennie shrugged. "Dr. Marecek called Mom about what you wrote at the club meeting last Sunday," he said. "I didn't squeal on you to Mom, even though

I was the one who read your paper to everybody. The doc was worried about you—like all of us were."

"He's telling you the truth, Tommy," said Artie. "What you wrote was a red flag. I didn't have any idea you were feeling that way. I thought you'd be on top of the world after wrestling season and now baseball. You're doing great."

"Except for my jailbird parents," Tommy muttered, then added, "but what Minnie showed you and me the other day really did help. It helped *me*, anyway. What about you, cousin Artie?" A sly grin spread across the straw-haired boy's face. "Did that news help *you*?"

Artie grabbed the boy by the arm and shook it playfully. "Has it occurred you, Tommy," he said, "that this is where *my* father—my biological father—grew up, too? And also our grandparents—I mean, the ones on your side? We're just like Bennie and all his grandfathers. *Our* families—whether it's the Bauers or the Whites—go way back, too. You just found out you have a new cousin. Well, I found out the other day that I have a whole new *family*. And I'm happy to say that it includes you, buddy."

Anxious to see what lay behind the trees, Ty Green gave Artie a friendly shove from behind. "Let's get a move on, big guy," he told his pal. "We don't want to keep the snakes and leeches waiting. I'm glad I have these *leather* boots on and not rubber ones like you milk maids."

In single file, the four boys started into the tall pines, entering the shaded grove where a loaf-sized gray boulder sat. "I wonder who put *that* there," said Tommy, still leading the way. "Dad fussed at me once for trying to mark the trail—hit me pretty hard with his belt. He said he didn't want to make it easier for people to sneak up on me. But I think he wanted a good hiding place, too."

None of the other three commented on Tommy's admission. They continued to walk, zigging and zagging through the arrow-straight trees toward a clearing that their confident leader said was at least a football field away. The ground around them was covered with pine straw at least an inch thick. There was no obvious path, but Tommy seemed to have no trouble finding their way, as he followed the contours of the land.

"Do you have a compass in your head?" Bennie asked his foster brother. "There's no way Dad came out here—not through *this* forest. How do you know we're headed in the right direction?"

Tommy stopped again. "Look over there," he said, pointing to a bramble-like shrub growing next to a tree trunk on their left. "That's a swamp rose. I moved it there after Dad gave me that whipping for marking the trail, and I put one everywhere we need to turn. They aren't blooming now, but I recognize the leaves and the thorny branches."

"That's smart," said Ty Green, "but I think somebody else *has* been out here, even if it wasn't Mr. Pressler."

"Why do you say that?" asked Artie.

"Look at that tree we're headed toward—about ten feet up," Ty said, pointing to a pine with a swamp rose growing near its base. "See that splotch of something up there? I'll betcha anything it's paint of some kind." He took out a small flashlight and pointed it at the tree in question. "Yep," he said, "and it's fluorescent paint. See, it glows." The palm-sized splotch shone in the thin beam of light.

"You mean *phosphorescent*," said Artie, with a chuckle. "Remember, *I'm* Yogi. *I'm* the one who's supposed to bungle words. But, yeah, I see what you mean. Have you seen other markers like that?"

"Yep," Ty said, "I started seeing them a couple turns back. So, *somebody* was here not that long ago and marked the way in and out. But, my gosh, I bet that was a job—using a pole or something to get the mark so high up in the trees. Any idea who it was, Tommy?"

Tommy pursed his lips. "It wouldn't have been the teacher who helped me with my bees and flowers," he said. "I showed her how to get in like I'm showing you now, and she wouldn't need glow-in-the-dark paint. She'd only come in the daylight. But, yeah, I have an idea who it might have been. I just don't want to say anything until we see what's in the clearing. Maybe we'll find a clue."

Artie shrugged. "Okay," he said, "but now I wish I'd brought Grandpa's squirrel gun."

"No worries," said Ty Green, reaching behind his own back and pulling what appeared to be a black handgun from his waistband. Pointing it upwards in his cocked arm, he added, "The name's Green. Ty Green."

Artie laughed out loud. "You brought your BB gun?" he said. "Well, it does *look* like a pistol."

"Yeah," said Ty, smiling, "and it stings like the dickens."

Bennie shook his head and turned to follow Tommy deeper into the woods. "Be careful with that thing, Ty," said Bennie. "You could shoot a swamp monster's eye out."

Ten minutes later, they stepped from the darker grove into the full sunlight of an infield-sized clearing that was filled with stands of yellow daffodils, clumps of two-toned irises, and swaths of pink and purple thrift. Bennie Pressler immediately snapped some pictures to record the moment and to give Tommy White something to take with him on his next prison visit. After a minute of taking in the beauty, the boys spread out with their buckets to cut the best specimens of the irises, in particular, but also the prettiest daffodils they could find.

"Hey, Tommy," shouted Bennie, "where were your beehives?"

Tommy pointed toward the back of the clearing. "They're supposed to face southeast," he said. "We put them over there so they'd get the most sun. It also gave the girls plenty of room to go in and out."

"Girls?" said Bennie. "You had *girls* out here?"

Tommy snorted. "No," he said, "I'm talking about the bees. The worker bees are female, every single one of them. They do *everything* for the colony except lay the eggs. The queen bee does that. The workers clean the hive and feed the young bees—the larvae—and hunt for pollen and nectar to make honey and do other stuff for the colony. And, like I said, that one queen bee lays all the eggs."

"Well, what do the boy bees do," asked Bennie.

"The drones?" said Tommy. "They just have one job—to mate with other queens, with *virgin* queens who haven't started laying eggs yet. Other than that, drones just lay around and eat."

Ty Green laughed. "That sounds like my kind of job," he said. "I may have to paint *The Luuuvvv Truck* yellow and call it *The Drone*." He bent down to cut another flower.

Carrying their bucket, Artie Bauer shook his head. "I don't think you'd want to be a drone, pal," said Artie. "After they mate with the queen, they die. Being with her kills them."

"Yeah, I know the feeling," Ty said, guiding a flower stem into the bucket. "Whenever I didn't want to go out—you know, just stay home with Nicie for a quiet night—she'd complain about me not wanting to do anything but lay around and eat. I mean, her mama's a good cook. Mine, too."

Tommy had more bad news for Ty. "The drones that just stay home and eat," Tommy said, "they get kicked out of the hive at the end of the summer, and they starve and die. So, Nicie had the right idea to try and get you out of the house."

Ty shook his head again. "It's a cold, hard world out there, boys," he said, then laughed.

Except for some cinderblocks that Tommy had used to support his wooden hives, there was no evidence that it had been a beeyard. Arranged in two patterns of four, the cement blocks lay toward the back of the clearing and faced southeast, as Tommy had explained. As the boys walked around the spot surrounded by beds of low-growing thrift, Tommy commented that one set of blocks appeared to have sunk deeper into the peaty soil than the other set of four. But his attention quickly turned to something in the trees just beyond the clearing. It was what he had once described as a tree house or hunter's tree stand, where he had often spent nights when bad things were going on in the White farmhouse.

"Set the buckets down—here on the cinderblocks," Tommy told the others. "Let's go check out my tree house. I wanna see if anybody's messed with my stuff."

Six feet square and eight feet off the ground, the wooden platform had been built between four thick pines, with a crude ladder nailed to the first trunk on the back side. A sturdy railing made of sawed pine branches ringed the deck and acted as anchors to hold smaller branches with leaves—now dry and crumbling—that had been used as camouflage on the sides facing the clearing. A dark green, canvas tarp that hung over rotting jute ropes in front and back served as the tree house's roof.

"That's neat," said Bennie. "I've always wanted a tree house. Maybe we can all come here in the summer and camp out for a night or two."

Starting up the ladder, Tommy replied, "You don't want to be here in the summer, Bennie. Trust me. Between the mosquitoes and the ticks—

"And the snakes and leeches," Ty interjected.

"—yeah, and them, too—" continued Tommy, "it gets pretty miserable out here. I used to keep mosquito netting and bug spray in a plastic storage bin in this tree house. I had a sleeping bag and some food, too. By the way, that's not the tarp I used. Mine was light blue—like your truck, Ty. It was cheaper than thick canvas ones or camo tarps like hunters use."

At the top of the ladder, Tommy peeked into the tree house before entering it. "The storage bin is still here," he said. "Actually, there are two containers— the storage bin I had and a long, white cooler like the ones deep-sea fishermen use." He stepped over onto the wooden platform. "Hang on," he said. "Let me make sure the floor's solid." Once assured of its sturdiness, he called for the others to join him.

"Boy, oh, boy," said Ty Green, looking off the deck toward the clearing. "A man could do some good deer hunting from up here. Did you and your dad ever come here to hunt?"

"*He* did," Tommy replied, "but it wasn't deer he was looking to shoot. My flower garden used to be his pot patch. That was back before I was born. He told me he'd sit up here some days and watch out for pot rustlers, sheriff's deputies and DEA agents. If anybody came to steal his pot, he'd shoot at them. If they were lawmen, he'd take off. There's a trail that runs from here back to the swamp. He'd keep a getaway boat on the bank back there."

"Was it a big airboat with a huge fan in back like they use in the Everglades?" Bennie asked. "Or was it a big speedboat like on *Miami Vice*?"

"No," said Tommy, "it was a little canoe—a dugout kind of thing. I think

Dad made it himself, or maybe his older brother did. They were always in the drug business together, even when Dad worked at Pressler's. First it was pot. Then, by the time I was born, it was cocaine and, later on, crack. Mom just kind of got caught in the middle. She knew what was going on, but she didn't have anything to do with their business. And they both made sure I wasn't in the house when the really bad people were there."

"Bad people?" said Artie.

"The smugglers who flew the stuff in," Tommy said. "You know about the forest service airstrip, right? It's only about a mile from here, on down Little Swamp Road. You can even get to it from here by boat—through the swamp, if you know where the channel is."

"Yeah," said Ty, "in fire season, I hear big planes coming in and out all the time. They scoop up water over at Bear Lake to dump on the fires. You know how smoky it gets here in the summertime."

Tommy nodded. He looked down at the white ice chest. "We may as well see what's inside this thing," he said, lifting the lid all the way up. "Let's see, an empty ice bag floating in an inch of water, a moldy—*really* moldy—loaf of white bread, a half-empty jar of peanut butter, some cans of food—pork and beans, beanie weenies, tuna fish, sardines, three beers still in the rings of a six-pack on top of two plastic containers of something I'm not even gonna guess what it is. And I'm definitely not gonna touch it. Oh, yeah. A yucky-looking jar of mayonnaise and an *empty* jar of kosher dills."

"At least the guy had good taste in pickles," said Bennie. "It had to be a guy. No woman would eat this stuff."

Tommy closed the cooler and turned to his old storage container. Lifting the lid and setting it aside, he listed the bin's contents. "A rolled-up sleeping bag—a new one, not mine," he said, "and, yeah, my old mosquito netting folded up." He lifted the square of netting and fell silent.

"What did you find?" asked Artie.

"Come see for yourself," Tommy said, "and, Bennie, how about taking a picture of this before I open it? Maybe you'd better take a bunch of pictures as I go through all this stuff. We might need proof that it was all here."

The other three boys crowded around Tommy and looked down into the plastic container. The netting had covered a thin, square, brown, cardboard box bearing the words *Woody's Surf Shop & Grill* in red script along with a line drawing of a smiling, mustachioed chef tossing a pizza into the air.

"I knew it was him," said Tommy. "I had a feeling this was where Rocket Reep was hiding out, but I didn't want it to be true. Dad said Rocket hung out with him and P.J. when they grew pot." The boy used the netting to lift out the pizza box and lay it on the cooler's top. Moving the box revealed an assortment of pocketknives and slingshots—commercially made and hand-whittled—as well as two more pickle jars, one filled with steel ball bearings, the other with stones of various sizes. Several of the knives were peanut-shaped with identical bone handles, like the ones Artie's grandpa had said Old Man Pressler always gave away at the E-ville store. Other items in the storage bin included a box of .38 Special bullets, a transistor radio, half-empty packages of batteries in two sizes, and a small can of phosphorescent paint. Tommy was careful not to touch anything, instead using a stick to move things around so that Bennie could take pictures.

"Anything in the pizza box?" asked Ty.

Tommy gave him a funny look. "You're kidding," he said. "Didn't you have lunch?"

"No," said Ty, laughing, "I heard a noise when you picked it up a minute ago. I'm not stupid—or hungry enough to eat four-month-old pizza."

Again using the stick, Tommy lifted the box lid. Inside were a small roll of bills—with a ten showing on the outside—two ballpoint pens, both with Sandpiper Realty logos, and a yellow spiral notebook with "Thomas White, Grade 8, Science, Mrs. Harbison" printed by hand on the cover. There were also two simple drawings—of a daisy-like flower with eight petals, and a fat, smiling honey bee with a long stinger.

"I didn't know you were an artist," Artie said to Tommy. "That's pretty good."

Bennie spoke up for his bashful foster brother. "Oh, he's way better than that now," said Bennie. "You should see some of his sketches. He's just too shy to show them off."

Tommy used the stick to flip open the notebook cover. Two papers had been inserted there—a newspaper clipping of the classified advertisement for the White farm's public auction and a white sheet of Sandpiper Realty stationery bearing names, addresses and phone numbers of married couples around the county, most of them within five miles of the White farm. Some of the addresses were in Oakhurst Manor outside Ebenezerville, as well as in the River Bend and Sandpiper Shores developments outside Monk's Landing. Three of the named couples were "Harry and Pearl Bauer," "Russell and Rachel Green," and "John and Elizabeth Russo"—Artie's grandparents, and Ty's and Leah's parents. Someone had put checkmarks in the margin beside those names, as well as next to some others. A phone number with no name was scribbled at the top of the same sheet. Bennie made sure that the number was clear in his viewfinder when he snapped a picture of that page.

The Russos' address wasn't up to date, as three months earlier Leah and her father had moved into the River Bend subdivision outside Monk's Landing. At Christmas, Leah's parents had separated, and Elizabeth Russo had moved back to her hometown in the St. Louis area after two home break-ins and a shooting at the old address listed on the real estate firm's stationery. Both incidents had involved Luther "Rocket" Reep. Shot by an Oleander County sheriff's deputy— though not Deputy Skip Ross, for a change—Rocket Reep had died on the Russos' back porch. The family wasn't home at the time, but the trauma of Reep's violent death in their home while they were still mourning the loss of son Reuben was more than Elizabeth Russo could handle. She left that house never to go back.

"Look," said Bennie Pressler, "I hate to say this, but my mom's gonna start worrying about me soon. I checked, and I don't have a cell phone signal out here, so I can't call her. Maybe we should head on over to Artie's church with the flowers and then go on to E-ville."

The others agreed. They put everything except Tommy's notebook back as they had found it, climbed down, and grabbed the buckets of flowers as they hurried back through the trees to their pickup trucks at the home site. Ty Green hopped back into *The Luuuvvv Truck* and drove home. As the three boys in the red pickup followed Ty past his house and turned onto Shin's Grove Church Road, Artie remembered something he'd wanted to ask Tommy before finding the pizza box in the tree house.

"You told us one time, Tommy, that you slept in the swamp—in the tree house—because your family didn't have a barn," said Artie. "Well, you guys had a barn. We saw its foundation, right?"

Tommy shook his head. "That barn burned down before I was born, Artie," he said. "I can't even tell you what it looked like."

"Really?" said Artie. "Did bad guys burn it down, like they burned down your house after your folks got arrested? Or was it a swamp monster?"

"Yeah," said Tommy, "that was it—a swamp monster—and his name was Bob White. Mom told me that Dad could get really crazy sometimes back in the day. That's something else he won't talk to me about—why he burned down our barn. But who knows? I guess he could've done it for the insurance."

Artie thought for a second. "Well, let's just hope," he said, "that we don't ever have anything like that happen on our farm—not now, not ever. The fire that Josh Stark caused back at Halloween was bad enough."

Tommy nodded. "Yeah, I hope not," he said, "because Bessie and Bossie already don't like me. You know, maybe that's why—because I'm the son of a barn burner. Maybe they think it's in my blood."

"If it's in yours," said Artie, "then it's in mine, too." He glanced at Tommy and on over at Bennie, who was busy looking for a cell signal on his phone to call his mother. "Girls *do* seem to have a sixth sense about trouble," Artie added, "whether they're milk cows or worker bees or worried moms."

CHAPTER 11

SUNDAY DINNER ON THE FARM hadn't been anything special in the months since Pearl Bauer's death—that is, once the sympathy casseroles quit coming in, and Gabby Duran, Ricky's mother, went back to cooking for her own family on weekends. Gabby and Ricardo Duran had pursuits of their own in addition to their duties on the farm; however, they both kept an eye on Grandpa during the week while Artie was at school and on the baseball diamond. The Duran family had attended Solid Rock Christian Church and, after the storm, were involved in both rebuilding the church sanctuary and renewing the congregation's spirit. So, Harry and Artie Bauer, who did not attend church, were for the most part on their own on the weekends. At one time, the Bauers had attended Solid Rock but had quit after feeling out of place. That was after the folks at Shin's Grove Church, where Pearl's family had gone for ages, had gossiped and put down Artie's mother, Ingrid Bauer, for having him out of wedlock. Pearl Bauer had said she would never "darken the door" of Shin's Grove Church again for as long as she lived—an accurate statement, because she didn't return until her own funeral almost eighteen years later.

Grandpa didn't mind cooking for Artie and himself, but Tommy's presence put more pressure on old Harry to come up with a balanced menu for the big meals on weekends. In a pinch, he could prepare meatloaf, mashed potatoes and gravy, and canned vegetables, but even that would get old after a while. Also, Harry didn't like going to that much trouble when a sandwich or scrambled eggs—having breakfast for dinner—would do. Like his grandfather, Artie knew one end of a spatula from the other and could fix eggs in any style. He also didn't mind upping his protein intake with eggs at every meal. Tommy, also an athlete, understood that and didn't complain that first weekend when Artie placed three tall glasses of fresh milk and a big platter of fried eggs, bacon and fried potatoes on the table.

"Artie, my boy, you could work as a short-order cook," said Grandpa, dipping the corner of his toast in his egg yolk. "These are some good eggs—over medium, just the way I like 'em. So, what do you two have on tap for today? Anything exciting?"

The two boys exchanged a worried look. Artie took a deep breath and said, "Grandpa, we found something yesterday out where Tommy used to live. Something big. We need to call the detective I met when that guy, Rocket Reep, was breaking into houses—like when he came out here pretending to be a pizza guy. That detective needs to see what we found."

"Isn't that man dead?" Grandpa asked. "Rocket, I mean. That case is closed, isn't it?"

"Maybe not," said Artie, turning to look at Tommy again. "Tell Grandpa what we found in your tree house—what might reopen the case."

Tommy nodded. "It was an old notebook of mine from school," he said. "I kept all my notes about bees and flowers and things like that in it—everything Mrs. Harbison had taught me and notes about keeping my bees and what flowers they liked and when they bloomed." He frowned. "But I wasn't the only person whose writing we found in it. Rocket Reep had been using the tree house as his hideout. He found my notebook and was using it like a diary or a journal. He wrote down all the meanness he'd done—like, even about beating me up outside Woody's when me and Nicie caught him in the dumpster there." He stopped to take a breath.

Artie picked up the story. "He even wrote about breaking into Leah's house," Artie said. "That was the first time—when she hid under her bed to keep him from finding her." Shaking his head at the memory, Artie continued, "He didn't get a chance to write about the second time he broke into their house. But he pretty much confessed in writing to everything he did up until that last night at the Russos. And there's even some evidence about why he might have been doing everything—that they weren't random break-ins, like everyone thought. That's what we want to show the detective. I still have his phone number." He laid down the lawman's business card where Grandpa could see it.

After squinting at the detective's name for a second, Grandpa looked up and said, "No, boy, you don't need to call that man."

"Why not, Grandpa?" asked Artie.

Harry Bauer picked up his glass, took a swig of cold milk and glanced at the wall clock. "Because he's on his way out here right now," said Grandpa. "I told you yesterday that I had to call a man about a dog. Well, that's who I called—the man whose name is on that card—and he'll be here with his dog in about twenty minutes. That's what I was doing out in the barn this morning—fixing the dog a kennel for when we're working out there. His name is Brody, and he's an old police dog who needs a new home."

Laughing and shaking his head in disbelief, Artie mused, "What're the odds?"

"Of what?" asked Grandpa. "Of me calling the very detective you needed to talk to?"

"No," said Artie, "the odds that you *really were* calling a man about a dog."

* * *

Brody was the most beautiful German Shepherd that Artie Bauer had ever seen—long-haired with black and brown markings and a dark, bear-like face with expressive brown eyes. The dog's long, pink tongue lolled out as he sat panting beside his master, Detective Sgt. Marty Quinn. The young investigator had come out to the farm four months earlier to interview Harry Bauer about Rocket Reep's aborted break-in attempt. Quinn had brought his K-9 partner along that time but had left him in the patrol car while he talked to Grandpa. The conversation had turned to Quinn's experience with Brody, with Grandpa sharing his own love of dogs and familiarity with shepherds, in particular. By the end of that first meeting, Grandpa had invited Quinn to let Brody out of the car for exercise in the yard. Four months later on this second visit, Brody stood on his handler's command and ran straight to Harry Bauer as if they were old friends.

"Thanks, Mr. Bauer, for letting Brody stay with you," said Sgt. Quinn, as he unloaded a cage-like carrier and a dog bed from the back of his SUV. He looked over at Artie and Tommy standing to one side. "Don't worry, boys," the lawman said. "Ol' Brody's more of a lover than a biter—unless you're hurting someone he loves."

"Off," Grandpa said firmly. "Sit." The dog backed off and sat on his haunches, his ears perked up for Grandpa's next command. "Stay."

Quinn smiled. "Brody really took to Harry when we were here before," he said. "It made me kind of jealous. But that's why I figured you'd make him a good foster family—not to mention how great this farm is. There's so much room out here, not like my place in town."

Grandpa held out his hand for the dog to sniff. "Well, Marty, I'm glad you didn't take me at my word Monday when you called," said Harry, "and that you let me change my mind. I talked it over with a good friend, and she said this might be just what I need."

Tommy White spoke up. "Why does he need a foster home?" he asked.

"I'm in the Reserves," said Quinn, "and I got called up. I don't know how long I'll be gone. It's one of those situations." He watched his dog adjusting to a new handler. "I bought him and trained him. He doesn't belong to the department, and I don't want just anyone handling him. They'd turn him over to a patrol deputy. They're the ones who usually have dogs. But Harry will take good care of my boy."

"He will, Sergeant," Artie Bauer said. Then he laughed and added, "Did Grandpa tell you—or did I—that his last dog's name was Sergeant?"

Quinn nodded. "Yes, he did," the detective said, "and I remember what you both told me about that dog being killed years ago, like all those dog killings we had around the county last fall. Hopefully, we're done with that, now that the perp is gone."

"Gone but not forgotten," said Grandpa, still patting the police dog. "Artie was gonna call you today, anyway, before I told him you were coming out. The boys found something over at the old White place that they need to show you."

While Tommy White went inside to retrieve his composition book, Artie Bauer explained to Sgt. Quinn that they had found Rocket Reep's hideout on the farm property that Abe Pressler had bought at public auction on Tommy's behalf. "We tried not to mess up any fingerprints," said Artie, as the screen door from the back porch slammed shut, "and we left things the way we found them."

"Except for this," said Tommy White, continuing down the wooden ramp to where Quinn then stood. "I'd left this notebook in my tree house, and Rocket Reep found it. You'll be able to tell where my notes end and his *confession* starts."

"He confessed?" asked Quinn.

"As good as confessed," Tommy said. "It's more like a list of what he did and when, like he was gonna submit it to his boss so he'd get paid. I read the whole thing last night—so that's why you'll find my fingerprints on those pages."

Artie Bauer added, "And there's a *real* list, too—of people's names and addresses that he got from Sandpiper Realty. We're on that list. So are the Russos. That was where you guys caught Rocket Reep in the act—where he got shot."

To keep from handling the notebook, Tommy had placed it in a plastic bag. He handed the bag to Quinn. "If what you say is true," the detective said, "there's reason to reopen our investigation. But that isn't my decision to make, and I won't even be here after tomorrow. So, someone else will contact you boys for more information, and they'll want you to show them where you found this and everything else. I'm guessing you'll hear something Monday—or Tuesday, at the latest."

"We've got a ball game on Tuesday," said Artie. "We're both on the team, and the game is at Iron Harbor High. Any chance we could meet the other detective there—like you and I did the last time? We could talk during the girls' softball game. I don't think Coach would mind."

Quinn shook his head. "The important thing is to secure the other evidence you found," he said. "Whoever handles this for us might need to get you out of school tomorrow so you can take them to Reep's old hideout. And, of course, we'll need to get a search warrant or the land owner's permission. That would be Mr. Pressler, I take it."

Adjusting the dog's collar, Grandpa answered for the boys. "That's correct," he said, rising to face Quinn. "Mr. Abe Pressler set up a trust for young Tommy here, and Abe is managing the property until Tommy comes of age. I'm sure he would want to be there when you boys search the place. He's already had some run-ins with those Sandpiper Realty folks, especially Mr. Joel Stark, the owner."

Sgt. Quinn studied Harry Bauer's face for a moment and then knelt to say goodbye to his dog. "As much as I'd like to hang around," Quinn said, "I'd better get this evidence up to the sheriff's office. I wasn't planning on making a trip to Iron Harbor on my day off, but this evidence needs to be secured—chain of custody and all, you know?" He patted Brody's head a last time and stood to leave.

* * *

On Sunday evening, the Barf Table gang—including the four new members from Solid Rock—met again at their clubhouse on the farm. Even Julia Safin was there, as her tennis tournament that weekend had been played at Mimosa Beach. Some of the girls—Jamie Foxx and, of course, the Mareceks—had seen her play and win the event. Not wanting to risk distracting his former girlfriend, Artie had stayed away. That night, Minnie Marecek led the meeting whose purpose was for individuals to share their thoughts on therapy projects and to form groups, if possible. After hearing all their ideas, Minnie suggested that they focus on three main areas of expression: dance, music and storytelling. With fifteen friends in the gang, each group had five teens to lead in the particular type of therapy for which they volunteered.

"Remember," said Dr. Marecek, "these are therapies for you to lead at school for any students who are interested in participating. Each one of you can still pursue your other interests outside school, like horse therapy or weight training or surfing or beekeeping. A couple of you also mentioned learning to do first aid and to cook. Maybe we can call in some experts—like Ty's mother and Brett's father—to talk to us here about those things or to meet with interested groups at school."

Minnie added that she had already talked to Principal Church about adding expressive-therapy groups as a way for students affected by the recent tornadoes to deal with anxiety and depression. "Mr. Church liked the basic idea," said Minnie, "and I don't think he'll have a problem with what we've come up with tonight. I'll call him first thing tomorrow morning, but you should probably go ahead and make some plans to introduce your therapy groups to students soon. Your principal said the groups can meet for half of 4th period at least once a week—maybe more often than that, depending on how things go."

She looked around the room. "Let's go ahead and get into our groups," she said, "and I'll get out of the way so you can do your planning. I'll stay over at the house with Mr. Bauer until you let me know you're ready to call it a night." She laughed and then addressed Artie. "I understand that you and your grandpa have a new addition to your family—other than Tommy, that is."

Artie nodded and smiled. "Yeah," he said, "I think Grandpa is really glad to have a dog again. He didn't replace Sergeant, because they were so close. But Brody is making him see what he's been missing all these years. Brody is a great dog."

Minnie left the teens alone. The music-therapy group consisted of Nicie Evans, Bennie Pressler, Brett Woods, Jamie Foxx and Jimmy Gore. While their collective musical talents had the makings of a band, they liked Brett's idea to start a ukulele choir. One problem was finding the financial backing to purchase fifteen to twenty good ukuleles for kids who couldn't afford them.

"I'll go to the music store in E-ville tomorrow after school," said Bennie Pressler. "They haven't reopened yet, but maybe they can put in an order for us. I'm sure my parents will help out with some money for something neat like this."

Brett Woods added, "My dad will, too. I'll bet we could get a good deal on plastic ukes. Mine is wood, but some of the plastic ones are good enough for beginners."

Nicie Evans and Jamie Foxx volunteered to make copies of any sheet music that they might need. "Mom's real estate office has a nice copy machine," said Jamie, "and Nicie works next door at Woody's on the weekends. We could do the copying then."

The two best dancers in the room led the dance-therapy group—Julia Safin, having had formal dance training in Russia, and Ricky Duran, whose moves were self-taught but so impressive that he had been the most sought-after partner at the homecoming dance. Athletes Ty Green and Mike Inouye were interested in dance to improve their coordination, balance and flexibility—and, in Ty's case, to keep ex-girlfriend Nicie from wanting to dance with Ricky so much. The last group member was Jenny Gore, who had always liked dancing but hadn't had that opportunity as a student at Solid Rock Christian Academy. Before the storm, Ricky Duran and his family had attended Solid Rock Christian Church, but its overly conservative stance on entertainment—dancing, listening to certain music, and going to movies—made the church's private academy a bad fit for fun-loving Ricky.

"I can teach some simple ballet moves and tap steps," said Julia Safin. "We will not do anything that requires special shoes or a studio with a barre and mirrors on the wall."

Ricky was excited. "I can't wait," he said. "Also, we will make sure that our dances do not need partners so that everyone can join in. Line dancing will be so much fun."

The third therapy group—with its focus on storytelling—included writers Leah Russo and Wilma Marecek, and artists Kimi Inouye and Tommy White. Artie Bauer, who saw himself as neither writer nor artist, had picked the story group mainly because he had always liked reading and discussing books in school and could churn out well-written, though formulaic, papers on any assigned topic. Also, he did *not* want to be so close to Julia in the dance group. That wouldn't have been good for either of them. And as far as the music group went, Artie couldn't "carry a tune in a bucket"—according to Grandpa Bauer.

Artie would laugh and say that Bessie and Bossie never complained about his singing in the barn.

Artie did have one other reason for being interested in storytelling. "I sure do wish I'd written down some of Grandma's stories," he said. "Maybe Grandpa remembers them, and I can put them down on paper—with some of his stories, too. He has some really good ones." Artie wouldn't admit, though, that since breaking up with Julia Safin, he had also started taking time early in the morning or late at night to write down his thoughts. He figured it would be good practice for the personal essays he would have to include in college applications and entrance exams—and it would help him deal with his scattered feelings.

"Family narratives are important," said Wilma Marecek, whose own immigrant background was filled with stories, "but journal writing—like what we did last Sunday night—can be therapeutic. We saw that, didn't we? But I'm sure we'll be able to do all kinds of writing."

Leah Russo jumped in. "Yeah, and Kimi and Tommy can illustrate what we write," she said, "as well as come up with stories of their own." The two shy teens merely nodded, though their bright eyes showed that they, too, were eager to take their talents to a different, more public level.

CHAPTER 12

A SMILE LIT UP JERRY CHURCH'S FACE on Monday as he walked into the cafeteria and headed straight for the Barf Table. He even waved to Jug Johnson and Joe Carson already kicked back in their recliners at the "faculty table." It was a Meatless Monday, and tomato soup was the entrée. The students in the lunchroom were behaving themselves and didn't seem to be planning any hijinks for the minutes prior to the upperclassmen's release bell halfway through the hour-long period. The older Barf Tablers were seated; the young ones who didn't pack their own lunches were in line, waiting to get their soup and to pay cashier Frankie Hughes. Principal Church even walked over to Frankie and complimented him on his T-shirt choice, and continued into the serving area to commend the cook and server on that day's fare. His uncharacteristic positivity confused the teens seated at the double Barf Table and reminded them of what they had forgotten to discuss at the previous night's meeting.

"Hey, Jamie Foxx," called Leah Russo. "Come over here." Hearing Leah's summons, Artie was tempted to join the pair, but he stayed put, not wanting to attract more attention than necessary.

Jamie laid down her sandwich and scooted around the table to kneel next to Leah. "What's up?" Jamie asked. "We aren't having a prank today, are we?"

"Not unless Lurch is the one pranking us," replied Leah. "What did you say to him last week that made him back down with the coaches? I meant to ask you last night, but I forgot with everything else going on."

Jamie shook her head, but smiled knowingly. "Not now," she said. "I'll tell you at practice." She looked over at Artie and winked. Then she moved back to her chair before Church turned his attention from the cafeteria workers to the Barf Table gang. The underclassmen had finally gotten through the lunch line and had taken their seats.

Principal Church cleared his throat to get the group's attention. "I want to thank all of you in person," Church said. "I just got off the phone with Dr. Marecek. She updated me on the therapy projects that you'll be leading here at school during 4th period. I think it's a wonderful idea. It has so much potential to help your schoolmates, especially the new students from Solid Rock. And I love the slogan you came up with for the uniform patches and for the T-shirts we'll all be wearing soon—*We Are Solid Rock Strong*. That's wonderful."

"When can we start?" Wilma asked the principal. "With the therapy sessions, I mean."

Church nodded. "We'll make announcements on the school intercom this afternoon and tomorrow morning," he said, "and then you can hold organizational meetings on Wednesday during the last half of 4th period. How's that?"

"Great," said Wilma Marecek. "Can we also set up an information table here in the lunchroom tomorrow? And Wednesday, too? Then the kids can see what we're offering."

"Oh, certainly," Church said, "that's another great idea." He smiled broadly, adding, "The other three schools will be so jealous. They're doing nothing like this, not even at Iron Harbor High."

Artie Bauer raised his hand. "Mr. Church?" he said. "Maybe we could share what we're doing, not just with the other high schools, but with the elementary schools, too. Little kids would love what we're planning—the ukuleles and the line dancing and the storytelling."

Church was quiet for a second, as if he were considering Artie's suggestion. "Well, maybe," the principal said, suddenly becoming serious. "Artie, I need a private word with you—and with Tommy. It's about another call I received this morning. Let's step outside for a minute."

The two boys rose and followed Church outside to the breezeway. As they had expected, he told them about a call from the Oleander County Sheriff's

Department, and he said they should expect a visit from an officer right after lunch. "You don't need to report to 4th period," Church said. "Just come to my office—or to Miss Hopper's office, that might be better—when you leave here. The sheriff said he didn't know how long you'll be gone this afternoon, so you should also inform Coach Johnson that you might not be at practice until late, if at all. Any questions?" When there were none, Church turned and headed back to the school office.

As the boys returned to their seats, Artie stopped and told Jug Johnson what was going on and why they might miss practice that afternoon. Artie also whispered in Bennie Pressler's ear, asking about the pictures he had shot Saturday on the White farm, especially the ones of the evidence that they had found in Tommy's tree house. Nodding, Bennie reached down into his book bag and withdrew a packet of photos that he handed to Artie.

"Wait a second," said Bennie. "Let me call that phone number again—you know, the one on the cover of Tommy's notebook. Mom picked up the photos for me yesterday at QuikyPics, and she had this extra set of prints made. You can keep this packet. I have the one with the negatives."

Artie opened the photo packet and started flipping through the prints. "When did you call the number?" he asked. "Did anybody answer?"

"I didn't have the pictures last night until after our meeting," said Bennie, "so I called the number from home. I got an answering machine."

"You didn't leave a message, did you?" asked Artie.

"Of course not," Bennie said. "I couldn't tell whose phone it was from the message. It sounded like an office, though. Maybe they're open now."

Artie handed the picture of the yellow notebook cover to Bennie so that the 9th grader could dial the number on his cell phone. Even with the noise in the cafeteria, Artie could hear each time the phone rang and then when a man's gruff voice answered, "Permits. How may I help you?" Bennie started to hand the phone to Artie, but the big guy shook his head and mouthed the words, *Hang up*.

"I guess we could call back and ask who's speaking," said Artie, "but I'd rather let the sheriff's department do that. Whoever that guy is, we don't want to make him suspicious. Right, Tommy?"

Tommy agreed. "No, we don't want to tip him off," he said, "not somebody who talks like that. He sounds like a rough character."

When the last lunch bell rang, Artie and Tommy left the lunchroom, stowed their books in their lockers, and headed to the guidance counselor's office. They weren't worried about seeing Vicki Duke, as they already knew she hadn't come to school that day. Coach Carson had told the softball girls at the Barf Table that Vicki wouldn't be pitching on Tuesday at Iron Harbor, maybe not even on Friday at Mimosa Beach because of the injury she had suffered the previous Friday at Woody's Grill.

It hadn't been a good Friday night for the Arbor guidance office—neither for Vicki Duke, nor for Thelma Hopper. Unlike her sheriff's deputy boyfriend, perky Miss Hopper had needed only emergency room treatment after the car crash involving Josh Stark, but the pretty counselor's face was so bruised that she wore more makeup than usual and sunglasses to hide two black eyes. She was on the phone at Vicki's usual station in the outer office when the two boys walked in the door.

". . . glad she's feeling better," said Miss Hopper, her head turning to acknowledge the boys. She covered the mouthpiece and said, "You two have a seat. I'll be right with you." She continued her chat with the person on the phone, saying, "Now, Victor, you tell our girl to take just as long as she needs to get well. We can handle everything here. Do you know if she wants me to send home her assignments?"

Miss Hopper listened for a few seconds to the man's long-winded reply. She frowned and then moved the handset a few inches away from her ear to spare her hearing. The man's voice was so loud that Artie and Tommy could hear it where they sat. They exchanged a startled look.

"Well, thank you, Victor," Miss Hopper said. "Give Vicki a big hug for me when you get home from work tonight. I'll check in on her again tomorrow. Bye-bye, now." She hung up the phone and checked her makeup in the mirror that her guidance office assistants kept at that work station, all of them being

Arbor cheerleaders.

Standing up, she turned to face Artie and Tommy. "Now, what can I do for you two boys?" she asked. "Arthur Bauer, while I'm thinking of it, you need to get your Ebenezer essay turned in soon. You wouldn't want to be overlooked for something as important as that endowment, now would you?"

"No, ma'am, I'll do that tonight," Artie said. He explained that he and Tommy were waiting for someone to pick them up at the start of 4th period. "Was that Vicki Duke's father on the phone? Where does Mr. Duke work?"

Miss Hopper trained the dark lenses of her sunglasses on Artie for a moment before answering. "He does something at the county health department," she said. "I'm not exactly sure what he handles."

"*Permits*, maybe?" asked Artie, nudging Tommy with his elbow.

"I think that *was* what he said when I called a minute ago," Miss Hopper replied. "Frankly, I was surprised that the health department didn't have a good receptionist answering his phone, but that was the only work number Vicki gave me for her parents. I didn't want to call and upset her at home. We all know how sensitive she is."

Miss Hopper paused for a second. "I am so glad she wasn't badly hurt the other night," she continued. "Victor said she has a slight concussion from that bump on the head at Woody's, but she certainly would have been hurt much worse—*seriously* hurt—if she had left the restaurant with that boyfriend of hers. Did you hear what happened to the passenger side of Josh Stark's car?"

"Yes, ma'am," said Artie. "I heard that side of the car was smashed up pretty bad and that Josh was lucky to get out with just minor injuries. By the way, I hope *you're* feeling okay—and that Deputy Ross is getting better. We're all worried about him. He's a good guy."

"I am just fine," she said. "I called the hospital to check on Skip before I called Mr. Duke, and I was told that Skip *is* improving. Thank you for asking, Arthur. You're quite the gentleman."

The dark lenses moved from Artie to Tommy. "And I am so proud of you, too, Thomas," she said. "Your grades have improved so much this year."

"Thanks," said Tommy, looking down as his face started to flush.

A car horn sounded outside. It was an Oleander County Sheriff's Department cruiser. The officer at the wheel could see the boys through the two sets of plate-glass windows between them. Artie threw up his hand to the lawman to indicate that he and Tommy would be right out. The officer climbed out of the car and opened a back door for the boys, instructing them to sit there behind the screen dividing the front and back seats. Ready to slam the door shut, the man appeared angry and kept one hand on the black, semi-automatic pistol holstered on his hip. Tommy hesitated, but the deputy ordered for him to hurry up and get in. Once everyone was in the cruiser and it was moving, Artie tapped on the divider to get the officer to open the small sliding window.

"Do we need to give you directions?" Artie asked.

"No," the deputy said. "I know where to go." He turned onto the highway toward Ebenezerville.

"Oh, okay," said Artie. "By the way, I'm Artie Bauer, and this is Tommy White."

The man looked up into his rear-view mirror. The dark pupils of his deep-set, steely eyes were as small as BBs. "I know who you are," he said. "Just sit tight."

"Oh, okay," Artie said again. "Thank you, sir." Then he thought to ask, "Excuse me, sir, but are we in some kind of trouble?"

The deputy's eyes narrowed. He said, "Why do you ask that?"

"Your gun," Artie replied. "You kept your hand on your gun back there. Did you think you were gonna have to use it?" The look that Artie now saw in the mirror was one of amusement, even though his question had been serious.

"On you two?" the cop said. "Give me a break." The man must have known that things weren't going the way he wanted. "You know much about guns, kid?" he said. "You know what a gun like this would do to somebody?"

Artie shook his head and asked, "No, what caliber is it?"

"Forty caliber," the deputy replied, "and it can blow your head clean off. I used to carry a forty-four magnum, a revolver—you know, like in the movies. It did even more damage."

"Why don't you carry it now?" asked Artie, glancing over at Tommy to see how he was taking all this talk about guns. When Artie raised his eyebrows, Tommy just shrugged.

"It was stolen," said the lawman. In the mirror, his hard eyes squinted up at Tommy's reflection. "You know all about that kind of stuff, don't you, White?"

Still, Tommy said nothing. He clenched his jaw and shook his head. Instead, Artie spoke up for them both, saying, "Excuse me, sir, but will you tell us *your* name? Sgt. Quinn didn't say who would be picking us up today. Aren't you supposed to identify yourself?"

The man snorted. "You aren't being arrested," he said, brushing his closely-cropped hair with its reddish tint. "And I won't be reading you your rights, either—even though I've done that for just about everyone in *that* boy's family at one time or another." He raised his thin eyebrows at Tommy's image in the mirror again, but the boy still remained silent.

Artie had heard enough. "I don't like this, sir," he said. "You need to take us back to the school. I insist. We aren't going *anywhere* with you."

"You're not?" the deputy said, more as a dare than as a question.

"No, sir, we're not," said Artie. "As a matter of fact, you can let us out of the car right here. We'll walk back to the school. It isn't that far."

"Suit yourself," the deputy said. He stopped the car on the shoulder and popped the door locks so that the boys could get out.

"Thank you, sir," Artie said again, after Tommy had slid out on the same side. But before Artie could close the car door, the deputy stepped on the gas. The door slammed shut on its own, as the car's rear wheels spun up dirt and grass on the shoulder.

Artie looked over at Tommy to see his young friend's response to what they had experienced. But Tommy was chuckling and shaking his head. "What?" asked Artie, confused at the boy's reaction.

"I *thought* I recognized that guy," said Tommy. "I remember Dad saying there was a bad cop in the sheriff's department that had red hair and evil-looking eyes, and that he was bad news."

Artie looked back up the highway in the direction they'd be walking. The high school was not in sight. "No kidding," he said. "Then what's so funny?"

"Nothing really," replied Tommy. Then he added, "Well, just that you *are* quite the gentleman, Arthur Bauer—even with the crookedest cop in Oleander County. You called him sir twenty times."

Artie frowned and shot back, "Oh, be quiet . . . Thomas."

Before Artie and Tommy had walked ten yards, a brown, four-door sedan speeding toward them braked and veered onto the shoulder just past them. It was Principal Church. He leaned out his window and yelled to them. "I'm glad I caught you," he shouted. "Come get in. Quick."

Church was dialing his cell phone as they got into the car. Artie sat up front with the principal; Tommy, in back. Artie wondered what Church had meant by *I caught you,* but he didn't ask while the man waited for his call to connect.

"Is this Abe Pressler?" said Church into the phone. "Yes, this is Jerry Church at Arbor High. . . . No, sir. No, Bennie is just fine. This is about your foster son, Tommy White. I also have Artie Bauer here with me. . . . No, they're both fine, too. It's just that we have a situation here that you should be aware of. And we don't have much time, from what I understand."

The principal listened for a moment. "I'm glad I caught you, sir. You don't want to be out there with this particular deputy. Let's just say, I've heard bad things about him. I mean, he didn't even check the boys out of school properly. That's what alerted me. I don't know how they got out of his car, but I have them with me now, and we'll be headed back to the school building in just a minute."

Artie could hear snatches of Abe Pressler's voice through the phone pressed to Church's ear, but it was too garbled to understand. Church replied, "That's right, sir. You do not want to be alone with this man. . . . Yes, I plan to call the sheriff and talk to him about this situation after I talk to the boys. . . . Okay, yes, I understand. I'll wait to hear from you, and I'll send the boys on to their classes after we talk. I'm sure they'll be fine. . . . Thank you, Mr. Pressler. Goodbye."

Church snapped his phone shut and put it back inside his jacket. Turning to

Artie first and then looking back at Tommy, the principal said, "Mr. Pressler is calling the sheriff himself right now to head that deputy off. And don't worry, Tommy. Abe is *not* going out there alone. I watched you guys getting into the patrol car, and I could tell that you didn't want to go with him, Tommy. That's also why I came after you. So, when we get back to my office, you can tell me what happened with the deputy, and then I'll call the sheriff myself. I'm just glad you're both safe."

* * *

When practice finally ended Monday evening—the next day's road game was against the Iron Harbor Gray Dukes, after all—the Barf Table's baseball boys were surprised to see that the gang's softball girls were waiting for them in the parking lot. Leaning up against Artie Bauer's old red pickup and Ty Green's *Luuuvvv Truck*, the girls looked primed for an impromptu club meeting.

"What happened to you guys 4th period?" Leah Russo asked Artie. "All sorts of stories are going around school. Somebody said you two got busted. Bennie said you were kidnapped, but he was getting on the bus and couldn't tell me anything else."

Artie gave her a wry look. "Well, you *are* in the story group," he said, "but neither one is true—not entirely. We didn't get busted. You know that wouldn't be possible. And we weren't kidnapped, although we might have been headed in that direction. The cop stopped the car and let us out when I told him to."

"*Told* him?" said Tommy White, stowing his gear in the truck cab. "You *asked* him, politely, and even said *please* and *thank you*. You sounded like Mr. Church talking to Mr. Pressler on the phone later." Tommy shrugged. "But, hey, I didn't say *anything*, so I'm glad you did. That guy really was bad news."

"Well, you know who he is, don't you?" asked Leah. "Red hair? Mean-looking eyes? That's Red Dedmon—some name, huh? He's the deputy who shot Rocket Reep at my house. The pizza guy's body was gone when we got home that night, but Dedmon was still there answering questions. He acted like it was no big deal that he'd just killed a guy—even told Mom that cold water would get the blood out of the rug on the porch. He gave me the creeps."

By then, all the club members except Bennie Pressler and Julia Safin had assembled around the two trucks. Kimi Inouye was even there, waiting to ride home with her mother and brother. Artie Bauer explained what had happened to him and Tommy White that afternoon. From their discussions Sunday night, the teenagers already knew about Tommy's tree house and what the boys had found there, like the pizza box and its contents—mainly the composition book and the cash—the bullets, the jars of ball bearings and rocks, and the other odd items. They also knew that someone from the sheriff's office would be coming to talk to the boys and to take them back out to the tree house to recover the new evidence. But none of the other students at Arbor High knew any of that information. They had only seen Artie and Tommy being loaded into the back of a patrol car and driven off. An ounce of truth turning into a wild tale was understandable. All their lives, Artie and Tommy had been forced to live with rumor and innuendo because of their parents.

"So, then we were getting ready to walk back to school," Artie Bauer said, "and that was when Mr. Church came flying down the road. I didn't know that brown car would travel that fast."

Ty Green yelped, "Ol' Lurch Church came through for you, didn't he? You two would've worn yourselves out walking back to school."

"It was more than that, Ty," said Tommy White. "Mr. Church knew something was wrong with that crazy cop, and he was coming to help us. He didn't know we'd be standing on the side of the road. He thought he'd have to drive all the way out to the farm."

"Yeah," Artie said, "so you won't hear me calling him *Lurch* ever again."

Ty laughed. "You don't call him that *now*," he said. "You don't call *anybody* names, not even Jug Johnson—and that's what *everyone* calls him, even his wife."

With a sly smile, Tommy White added, "That's because, according to Miss Hopper, Artie is *quite the gentleman*."

Artie blushed, but he turned to Leah Russo and asked, "How does the real story compare to the rumors? Will the kids buy what really happened?"

Leah shook her head. "Nope," she said, with a grin. "Not that Mr. Church is actually a hero—not after what Jamie told us about him today."

Now Artie was confused, as were the other boys. Leah glanced back at Jamie and got a nod, and then continued, "Well, you know that Jamie's mom and Mr. Church work together at Sandpiper Realty—some nights and weekends, anyway. She said they have a hard time scheduling open houses, especially after it rains, because the houses smell bad. Anyway, it seems that Ms. Foxx was riding back to the real estate office with him real late one night. This was after an open house in Sandpiper Shores—you know, way over there on the river—and they were in that brown car of his. So, guess what happened." She gave them a second, then said, "He *ran out of gas!*" There were titters from the girls.

"My man!" said Ty Green. "I'll have to loan him *The Luuuvvv Truck* some evening—with the gas can that Donnell threw in."

"Oh, come on," Artie said, with a laugh. He turned to Jamie Foxx and asked, "He didn't actually do that, did he? Mr. Church is smarter than that."

"No, you don't understand," Jamie said. "He *actually* ran out of gas. Mom teased him about it. She told him that if he wanted to spend that much time alone with her, they'd have a lot more fun at the beach. And he is kind of sweet on her. But it embarrassed him. He wanted her to promise not to tell anybody, but she told him he was just being silly."

"So, what did you say to him that day at lunch?" asked Artie.

"Nothing much," said Jamie. "Just that if he wants to date my mom, all he has to do is ask her. She thinks he's the sweetest guy—that's what she said. I didn't say one word about him running out of gas, whether I believed him or not."

Quiet until then, Nicie Evans said, "Well, you know, Jamie, sometimes running out of gas is the best thing that can happen to a couple. Then you really get to know each other." She looked over at Ty Green and smiled, and Artie noticed that his best friend Ty was smiling back. Artie wondered, though, if Nicie meant "running out of gas" in more ways than one.

CHAPTER 13

THE *SOLID ROCK* PATCHES, sewn on by Arbor High home economics classes, looked sharp Tuesday on the Bruins' and Bruinettes' uniforms, adorning their off-hand sleeves with the simple statement of county-wide solidarity. The Iron Harbor High teams had received their patches, but hadn't sewn them on yet, still sporting a black square of tape on their sleeves, as Arbor's players had done the previous week. These games had originally been scheduled to be played in Monk's Landing; however, they were moved to the Iron Harbor stadium complex, which had escaped the extensive damage that Arbor's ball fields had sustained in the Good Friday Storm. Being the largest school in the largest town in Oleander County, Iron Harbor High's Gray Dukes and Lady Gray Dukes had the largest and best athletic facilities, whatever the sport, and usually fielded the largest and strongest teams—except in baseball and softball, for some reason. This time around, the Iron Harbor squads didn't even get the advantage of being the "home team," and so they became the "visitors" on their own home fields and scoreboards. Also, on this day, the Arbor High players' sharper look exemplified the way they played.

"We didn't just look good out there," said Nicie Evans, as the victorious Bruinettes dashed off their field and piled into the baseball bleachers, "we played good! C'mon, Artie! C'mon, Ty! Show 'em who's boss!"

Throwing his final warm-up pitches on the mound, Ty Green looked strong. Artie's mitt popped as each fastball zipped from Ty's hand to the plate. The blue-clad umpire took his place behind Artie and waved the Gray Dukes leadoff batter over from the on-deck circle. "Play ball!" the ump shouted. He was the same umpire that had made the questionable call at home plate in the teams' last meeting—a call that had given Iron Harbor the walk-off win. It was Arbor's only Suncoast Conference loss.

The first two Iron Harbor batters struck out swinging on only four pitches apiece. Neither batter even fouled off a ball, as Ty Green used his screwball—which broke inside on the right-handed batters—to set up his rising fastball for the strikeouts. The third batter, another righty, leaned into Ty's first pitch and took a screwball off the elbow guard on his left arm. Even though the boy had made no effort at all to avoid the pitch and, in fact, had stepped into it, the umpire awarded him first base. Artie looked over at the "home" dugout—the Arbor bench—to see if Coach Johnson was going to come out and argue the call, but Jug just shook his head, not wanting to antagonize this umpire so early in the game.

Batting cleanup for the Gray Dukes was Louis Hines, who, like the Bruins' Jimmy Gore, was one of the best football players in the state and had also signed to play football at State College. In addition, the gargantuan defensive lineman shared the state heavyweight wrestling championship that year with none other than Artie Bauer. Hines stood just outside the batter's box to Artie's right and took a couple of extra practice cuts. He looked out to left field where Jimmy Gore stood.

"You and Jimmy okay?" Hines asked. "Last time we played Solid Rock, he dogged it at third."

Artie took a new ball from the ump and tossed it to Ty on the mound. "Doing good, Louis," said Artie. "He's great in left. You gonna put one out there to test him?"

Amused, Hines grunted, "*Hmph.* You know I'm a pull hitter, Artie." He took a few lazy practice swings in the box, and added, "Better tell Smitty to back up in right."

Sure enough, the big lefty batter waited for Ty's fastball and, on an 2-1 pitch, made solid contact and lifted the ball high to right field. Shielding his eyes from the late-day sun, Johnny Smith drifted back and toward the right-field corner. He turned and watched the baseball sail over the outfield fence—just to the right of the tall, yellow foul pole.

"Nice one, Lou," said Artie, throwing Ty another ball. "You got all of that one."

"*Hmph*," Hines grunted again. He tapped the plate with his bat and took his practice swings, as Ty looked in for Artie's sign and nodded.

The 2-2 pitch was another screwball, this one breaking away from the left-handed batting Hines. He committed to the ball just as it broke, having to extend his arms simply to make contact. That was all he could do with the pitch—Ty's best screwball of the inning—and Hines popped the ball weakly toward shallow left field, high enough to give Jimmy Gore plenty of time to run in and make the catch to end the top of the 1st inning.

"Yeah," Artie said, passing the slugger as they jogged toward their respective dugouts, "Jimmy's lookin' good in left."

Hines nodded. "Ty is, too—on the mound," he said. "That pitch was ugly."

The top of the Bruins order—little Ricky Duran leading off, followed by Manny Freeman, and designated hitter Mike Inouye in the three slot—put three runs on the board with a walk and stolen base; a single and run batted in; and a two-run homer. Batting cleanup, Jimmy Gore took advantage of the Iron Harbor pitcher's shakiness to draw another walk, but was picked off at first base when Artie Bauer popped up with a hit-and-run play on. Jimmy had seen Coach Johnson signal the special play and had taken off like a shot as the pitcher delivered the ball to the plate. But the popup had forced him to scramble back toward first base where he was easily caught off the bag and put out. A perfect hit-and-run play would have sent Jimmy to third base and Artie to first. Instead, there were two outs, with the bases empty. Next up, Ty Green hit a line drive off the left-field fence for the Bruins' second extra-base hit of the inning, summoning the Gray Dukes coach to the mound for a pitching conference. The talk turned out to be ineffective as both Johnny Smith and Brett Woods walked to load the bases, bringing number-nine hitter Tommy White to the plate.

Iron Harbor's coach, however, had seen enough. He called timeout and returned to the mound, taking the ball from his starting pitcher and handing it to his top reliever, a gangly boy with shaggy blond hair. In the Bruins' dugout, Jug Johnson knew what was coming from this pitcher, and he called Tommy over for instructions. Artie joined them at the dugout fence.

"Tommy boy," said Jug, "you know how I always tell you guys to take the first pitch? Well, this feller starts off every batter he faces with a fastball, right down the middle. Isn't that right, Yogi?"

"Yes, sir," said Artie, "and then that's the only good ball you'll get to swing at, Tommy. All he has is that good fastball, but he'll work the corners of the plate and move his pitches from low and away, to high and tight. You need to swing at that first ball and not give him an easy first strike."

Tommy White nodded, turned and trudged to the plate, as if he were mounting the gallows. It was his first time at bat with the bases loaded and his first time being told to swing at the initial offering. Tapping the front, back and both sides of the plate as he had seen Jimmy Gore always do, Tommy took his practice swings and tried not to give away that he wouldn't be taking the reliever's first pitch.

From the stretch, the Gray Dukes pitcher hurled the ball toward home. Tommy started his swing and tried to keep it as level as he could, following the ball into his bat as he had been taught by his coach and older teammates. He kept his head down, stepped into the pitch and drove the baseball toward the deepest part of center field, where the white dot rose and rose against the backdrop of evergreen trees beyond the fence before disappearing behind them. Though elated, Tommy was careful not to flip his bat or sling it too hard toward the dugout.

"You're out!" shouted the umpire. "You stepped on the plate. Third out, inning over."

That call got Jug Johnson out of the dugout. "He didn't step on it!" Jug screamed, looking down at the white slab of hard rubber at their feet. "Look here! You brushed it off not two minutes ago when the boy came up to bat and there *still* isn't any dirt on it! He didn't step on it! That's a grand slam, blue!"

The umpire shook his head stubbornly and turned away. When Jug continued to argue, the ump pointed toward the Arbor dugout. "You either go sit down, Jug," the man said, "or I'll let you cool off out in your bus for the rest of the night. He was out. No more argument. And don't bother appealing to Fred out there at second. He was watching the baserunners."

Still shaking his head, Jug Johnson went to Tommy White and patted the tall boy on the back as they returned to the dugout together—Tommy to retrieve his first-baseman's mitt, Jug to sit and stew over the four stolen runs.

"That was one heckuva shot, son," said Jug. "You did exactly what you were supposed to do, and anywhere but here that was a grand-slam home run. We can't ask you to do anymore than that. You oughta be proud of yourself, Tommy."

* * *

The crooked ump's horrendous call to end the 1st inning lit a fire under the Arbor High ballplayers. As the tenderness of Artie Bauer's glove hand could attest, Ty Green's pitches got harder and nastier as the innings rolled on. Ty attacked every Gray Dukes batter that came to the plate, allowing only one runner on base over the next five innings—that runner on a bobbled squibber in front of third base. Even that batter would have been called out if the game had been played at Arbor High with different umpires, as Brett Woods's hurried throw across the diamond to Tommy White appeared to beat the runner. Bruins closer Phil Waters—rested from not having to play in the field—shut down Iron Harbor in the 7th inning, preserving the 9-0 Arbor win, as well as his and Ty Green's combined one-hit shutout.

At bat for the Bruins, Mike Inouye was 4-for-4, with a homer, a double and two singles; Jimmy Gore, 2-for-3, with a pair of doubles; Ty Green, 3-for-5, with a double and two singles; and Artie Bauer, 1-for-2, with a homer and three walks. Every other Arbor batter reached base once or twice, on singles, walks and fielding errors. Also, speedsters Ricky Duran and Manny Freeman distinguished themselves with three stolen bases apiece. With Mike and Jimmy leading the way on offense, the Bruins certainly were Solid Rock Strong that night in Iron Harbor.

On the bus ride back to Monk's Landing, the chatter wasn't just about the teams' big road wins over Iron Harbor High (whether Arbor High was called the "home team" or not). Jamie Foxx had spotted two college coaches—assistants from Iron Harbor A&M and State College—and a pro scout in the stands during that night's baseball game. She recognized all three because her father, Jimmy Foxx, had been an assistant baseball coach the previous year at Mimosa Beach High and had tried to schmooze all three of those guys prior to several Waverunners baseball games that Jamie had attended at her old school. This year, after moving to Arbor High for a new basketball coaching job and being fired at mid-season, Jimmy Foxx was back at Mimosa Beach as their varsity baseball coach. Jamie Foxx and exchange student Julia Safin came to Arbor when Jimmy Foxx got the job there, and they stayed after he lost it.

"Hey, big guy," said Jamie Foxx, twisting in her seat to address Artie Bauer sitting behind her. "Do you know if Ty's thinking college or pro ball? That old guy—the scout—comes to a lot of games in this part of the state, but he doesn't sign all that many players. Most of the players come from Capital City—after a year or two at the university. He signed one pitcher last year straight out of high school."

Artie shrugged. "I don't know," he said, looking up from the composition book in his lap. "Why don't you walk back there and ask him?" Artie and Ty usually sat together, but on this night the big farm boy was trying to finish the rough draft of his Ebenezer Endowment essay for Miss Hopper, the essay he'd promised to write the previous day but hadn't.

Wilma Marecek, who was sharing a bench seat with Jamie, also turned to look at Artie, but with a different kind of question. "You haven't turned that in yet?" she asked. "The deadline is tomorrow."

He looked up again. "That's why I'm writing it *now*," he said. "When did you turn yours in?"

She shook her head and said, "It's not important—when I turned mine in, I mean. Do you need any help, Artie? I'm pretty good at those things."

"No, it's almost done," he said. Then he remembered why he was interrupted to begin with. "I don't know what Ty's thinking now, Jamie, not since he broke up with Nicie. When they were together, he told me he wanted to stay pretty close to home—you know, since she'll probably hang around here for at least a year or two."

"Yeah," said Jamie, "as good as she is in basketball, it's a shame no college coaches will take a chance on her—thanks to my hateful dad. And there's no future in beach volleyball, not around here, anyway. I hope she goes to community college and gets into a nursing program. That's what she really wants now—to help people like she did Vicki the other night. She could even be an EMT or paramedic."

Artie laughed. "Maybe *you* better help me finish this essay," he said. "The topic is, *How have you contributed to your community, and how do you hope to contribute to it in the future?* But you're making Nicie's answer sound better than mine. Maybe you should be in the story-therapy group instead of me."

Wilma Marecek turned around again and hooked her arm over the back of her seat. "Oh, come on, Artie," she said. "If I were you, I'd write about the Barf Table. You've done more over the past four years to help the kids who sit there—including me—than you realize. Look at Leah. Look at Bennie. And Ricky and Tommy. Even Ty and Nicie. And that's just *this* year."

The big girl held his gaze and didn't look away. Artie saw then that Wilma was more insightful than he'd ever be, and that realization scared him.

CHAPTER 14

AS THEY HAD DONE THE DAY BEFORE, the Barf Table friends set up and worked information tables in the lunchroom in advance of Wednesday's 4th-period organizational meetings. The students' response on Tuesday had been lukewarm at best, and so the gang took different approaches on Wednesday in the cafeteria. Julia Safin and Ricky Duran demonstrated simple line-dance steps next to their table. Brett Woods brought his ukulele to show how easy the instrument was to play. Kimi Inouye set up an easel and sketched model Tommy White as a comic-book superhero.

At his request, she drew him as *The Drone Ranger* riding a big, yellow-and-black honey bee. "*Hi-yo, Stinger!*" appeared in the speech bubble above the Ranger's head. Kimi shrugged and motioned for Tommy to move along when he pointed out that drones don't have stingers. "You aren't riding a drone," she said. "That's a worker bee—I looked it up, freshman." They both laughed.

The lines of students at each table kept the Barf Table gang busy the entire lunch hour, barely giving them time to eat. The two old coaches even climbed out of their recliners to observe the fun—until Julia Safin tried to coax Jug Johnson and Joe Carson into joining the line dance. Joe was game, but Jug claimed his trick knee was acting up and sat back down.

Later, all three therapy groups held their organizational meetings in the cafeteria during the latter half of 4th period. With help from Artie Bauer and the boys, cashier Frankie Hughes had cleaned the entire lunchroom and rearranged the tables so that Dr. Minnie Marecek could speak to the whole gathering before the groups were left alone to discuss their separate types of therapy. As Minnie had hoped, many of the students were transfers from Solid Rock, as well as Arbor students from rural areas near Ebenezerville. Each group attracted twenty-some participants, not counting the Barf Table members—a better turnout than anyone had expected. It was a surprise to Minnie and the gang that two of the Solid Rock transfers were deaf students—one joining the dance group, the other choosing the storytellers.

Five minutes before the 4th-period release bell rang, Minnie Marecek got everyone's attention again and gave them their first assignment for the following week's meeting. "Whatever your group is," she said, "I want you to be prepared to answer this two-part question: What was most important to you *before* the Good Friday Storm, and what is most important to you *now*?" She repeated the question and explained that the students could answer it any way they wished—by writing their answer down in any form; by drawing any kind of picture; by sharing something, like a magazine photo or a favorite song or an object with special meaning; or just by stating the answer out loud. Minnie also pointed out that the question and her suggestions for answers were admittedly vague, but she reminded them that the Barf Table group leaders were there every day at lunch to assist them, if anyone needed help.

As the therapy groups disbanded and the sixty-odd students left for the school's extracurricular 5th period, Miss Thelma Hopper entered the cafeteria and headed for where Minnie Marecek and Artie Bauer were standing. Artie had stayed behind to thank Minnie again for advising his grandfather to take in Detective Marty Quinn's police dog.

"Brody is the best thing that's happened to Grandpa in a long time," Artie told Minnie. "That dog exercises Grandpa more than the other way around. By the time I get home, he's worn out—but happy." They both laughed, as they turned to face the incoming guidance counselor bearing an uncharacteristic frown. She still wore the dark glasses.

"Arthur Bauer," fussed Miss Hopper, "you are putting me in a very bad spot. Why haven't you turned in your Ebenezer Endowment essay? Everyone else has turned theirs in, including the transfer students who will be considered for Solid

Rock's scholarship. You aren't *that* busy, are you?"

Artie glanced at Minnie before answering Miss Hopper. "I talked to somebody about my essay last night," he told the guidance counselor. "They showed me that what I had written was way off base. I don't think I deserve the Ebenezer—not as much as another person I know."

"That's silly," said Miss Hopper. "You are one of the top seniors here at Arbor, and you should at least be in the running for such a prestigious award. I mean, look at what you've done this year—captain of our football and baseball teams, all-conference in football and more than likely in baseball, too, and a state wrestling champion."

"*Co*-champion," Artie corrected. "Yeah, those things give people something to cheer about for a little while, but they aren't all that important in the long run. Besides, that's what athletic scholarships are for. The Ebenezer should go to somebody who's gonna make a real difference in whatever they do in life—not to someone like me who's just good at playing games."

At that, Miss Hopper's mouth dropped open, but no words came out for a few seconds. "Well, young man," she insisted, "I *need* your essay before school starts tomorrow morning. That's when I'll be leaving to deliver all of the essays to the central office in Iron Harbor. Don't let me down, Arthur." She left as quickly as she'd come, her heels clicking furiously on the tiled floor.

Minnie Marecek leaned her head toward the big farm boy and said quietly, "I know what you're doing, Artie, and you don't need to do that—sabotaging your own chances for someone else. Trust me, Wilma *will* go to college next year, with or without that endowment, and without having to enlist in the military. I'll see to it."

Artie shook his head. "That isn't it, Minnie," he said. "She's smarter than I am, and she doesn't get the attention she deserves, just because she isn't . . ." His voice trailed off.

"Isn't what?" Minnie said, frowning. "*Pretty*? Or *perky*, like Thelma Hopper?"

"No," said Artie, shaking his head. "Because she isn't a *guy*. That's all

I meant." He was afraid that he had lost a friend for both himself and his grandfather, but he was relieved to see Minnie's hazel eyes relax as her familiar smile returned.

Minnie Marecek nodded across the cafeteria toward her niece, who was happily talking to a cluster of students who had stayed behind. "Look at her, Artie," said Minnie. "I agree with you—she's really something, and she's going to make her own mark in this world." She paused. "But she wouldn't want you to hand it to her on a silver platter. She'd want you to do your best—just like when you two were competing for the same spot on the wrestling team. She made you *earn* the top spot."

Artie thought about that for a moment. "Yeah, you're right," he said. "When we were freshmen, Wilma was better than me. She'd been wrestling longer. And she helped Tommy like that this year, too. She made him work hard in practice."

Minnie placed her hand on Artie's shoulder. "Go home tonight, and write that essay," she said. "Maybe Harry and Brody will *both* be tired out, and you'll be able to write the best essay you've ever written. Maybe Tommy can milk the cows for you."

"No such luck," said Artie, chuckling. "Those two girls out in the barn *still* don't like him. I don't know why."

* * *

Getting home from practice that night around dusk, Artie Bauer told Tommy White to take his shower first while Artie milked the cows and Grandpa put the finishing touches on the evening meal. Grandpa wasn't a great cook like his wife had been, but he could handle a can opener, stovetop and microwave oven. By the time Artie himself had showered and dressed for dinner, Grandpa and Tommy were sitting on the back porch with Brody lying in the new dog bed that Grandpa had bought for him. Brody's food bowl at the back door was empty. Steam no longer rose from the bowls of people food on the kitchen table, with its three empty plates and three sweating glasses of ice water.

Artie stuck his head out the door to the porch. "Hey, Grandpa," he said, "should I put the food back in the microwave for a minute?"

"No, don't bother," said Harry Bauer. "Come out here a second. We got a phone call while you were in the shower. We need to talk."

Taking a seat next to Tommy on the old sofa, Artie said, "What's up?" He knew that Grandpa wasn't usually one to brace a person for bad news. Harry also didn't delay a meal any longer than was necessary. Artie feared the worst.

"When we didn't hear nothing from nobody," said Grandpa, "I went ahead and called ol' Sheriff Logan myself this morning. He said he knew all about that mess Monday with Red Dedmon and you boys, but that he would personally look into the investigation and see where it stands. I wondered at the time—this morning, I mean—if he was talking about what happened Monday or about something else. But something changed between my call this morning and his call a few minutes ago. That was him getting back to me. I guess he was calling from home, as late as it is."

Grandpa looked over at the big German Shepherd and sighed. "I sure have enjoyed having this big boy here on the farm these past few days," he said, "but he does bring back some sad memories—like years ago when your mama took off for good. She left about the same time that worthless, no-good Rocket Reep killed my last German Shepherd, ol' Sergeant. And that's kinda what the sheriff called me about tonight—not just about the way Red Dedmon did you boys the other day."

Artie shook his head. "I don't understand, Grandpa," he said. "What do my mother and your old dog have to do with Red Dedmon?"

Grandpa explained, "Sheriff Logan had read Marty Quinn's report from Sunday about what all you boys had found in that tree house out at the White place—the pizza box, the slingshots, the cash, *everything*. But the sheriff said Red Dedmon went on out there Monday after that mess with you two, and he didn't find anything like what was in Marty's report. I asked about that yellow composition book we gave Marty, and Sheriff Logan said nothing like that had been entered into evidence—or if it had been, it wasn't there now."

"I *still* don't get it," said Artie. "Where does my mother fit into this? And the dog?"

Grandpa cleared his throat and continued, "This is the same thing that happened when Ingrid disappeared—when you were just a baby. We tried to file a missing-persons report—to get the law to investigate—but the sheriff back then wouldn't let us. He tried to tell us Ingrid just ran off with that no-good boyfriend of hers—yeah, the very man we know now was your daddy, ol' P.J. White." He glanced at Tommy, then looked back at Artie. "Back in those days, anytime I saw P.J. White—or *Bob* White, for that matter—that worthless Rocket Reep was right there with them, just like in that prom picture that I took of your mama and Tommy's folks right out there in the yard next to that rosebush." He pointed out the porch's screen door.

"Just like seventeen years ago, the sheriff—a different one, but still the sheriff—just now told me that his department is *finished* looking into the matter," said Grandpa. "The investigation is *closed*. According to him, there's no evidence and no reason to waste his officers' valuable time. He also said that Red told him we have the department's *canine* out here on the farm—that was the word he used, *canine*—and that he wants him back. That was when I put my foot down and told Sheriff Logan he didn't know what he was talking about. This dog is Marty Quinn's personal property—his *pet*—and Marty asked me to keep Brody here until he gets back from his military assignment, whenever that is. Brody ain't going nowhere—and *that* matter is closed, by gosh."

Artie finally understood Grandpa's frame of mind. "You're right," said Artie. "There's something fishy going on—just like Monday when Red Dedmon picked us up. What they don't know and what they aren't gonna find out just yet is that we have *photos* of everything—the stuff in the tree house and part of that composition book, too. I was planning to give them to Dedmon the other day, but everything fell apart so quick that I wasn't about to say anything about that packet of pictures. Now I'm glad I didn't."

"Where are those pictures now?" asked Grandpa.

"Upstairs in my book bag," said Artie. "I'll go get them."

"No," Grandpa said, "leave them wherever they are right now—just in case Red Dedmon or the crooked sheriff comes calling tonight. But if they don't, you just make sure to put them somewhere safe once you go upstairs to bed. You can tell Tommy and me, but don't tell anybody else."

For the first time in their conversation, Artie managed a soft laugh. "I'd better go do that now, Grandpa," he said, "because I'm gonna be down here for a good long while tonight after dinner. I have an essay to write, and it's due first thing tomorrow morning."

* * *

It was midnight before Artie could clear his head enough to settle on the opening paragraph of his essay for the Ebenezer Endowment. He sat alone at the kitchen table, now cleared of the plates and bowls and all but one glass of water. Tommy White was asleep upstairs in his own bedroom. Grandpa, with the sheriff's words fresh on his mind, had moved Brody's dog bed into his bedroom off the kitchen so that his new best friend would be safe. Every few minutes, Artie heard Grandpa's mattress springs creak as the old man tossed and turned. *He can't get to sleep*, Artie thought. *He's worried, just like me.*

Artie must have read the writing prompt a hundred times that night: *How have you contributed to your community, and how do you hope to contribute to it in the future?* He thought about what Wilma Marecek had told him on the bus coming home from Iron Harbor—that he should write about sitting at the Barf Table and being a friend to students who had no choice about where they could sit and where they would be accepted. As a 9th grader, he had been one of them. But as he had distinguished himself in sports, he had chosen to keep his seat at the round table near the tray-return window and trash bins, instead of sitting with the athletes and other popular kids elsewhere in the lunchroom. Now, as a senior, Artie knew that he had made the right choice all along, and that Arbor High students now looked to him and his tablemates for leadership, and not just on the field or court or mat or diamond.

Also, he thought about prominent community members—like Abe and Deborah Pressler, Woody Woods and Minnie Marecek—who were always donating time, money and expertise to help fill voids in the various communities they served. Artie couldn't see himself as that kind of contributor, not with all the obstacles he would have to overcome just to hang onto his family's small farm. But maybe a person didn't have to be wealthy or well-educated to make a difference. Ricardo and Gabby Duran selflessly donated labor and resources almost beyond their means. And then Artie thought about the adults just at Arbor High who had contributed to his own success—Coach Johnson, Coach Carson, Miss Hopper, his teachers, and even Frankie Hughes, the death-metal cashier and bus driver. And for as willfully ignorant of sticky situations as Artie had always considered Principal Church to be, the man *had* been prepared to put himself in danger that week to save Artie and Tommy from Red Dedmon. Church had come after the boys when he realized who they were with and what could go wrong.

Still unsure of how to start the essay, Artie looked up *Ebenezer* in his dictionary and saw that, in addition to its biblical significance, the word meant "stone of help." Then Artie thought about the patch on the left sleeve of his baseball uniform—*We Are Solid Rock Strong*—and he considered whether or not he could actually be someone's *solid rock* in their time of need. Maybe that was what he had been for his friends through his four years at the Barf Table—their *rock*, their *stone of help*. And maybe that was what his best friend Ty Green and others—like Leah Russo's late brother Reuben—had always been for him. It was about being a good friend, being a good neighbor, and, on whatever stage or field of play, win or lose, being a good teammate and good competitor.

We Are Solid Rock Strong, Artie Bauer said to himself. Then he knew he was ready to write.

CHAPTER 15

AT THE BARF TABLE ON THURSDAY, Wilma Marecek was quick to ask Artie Bauer if he had turned in his essay. He simply nodded, tired from writing until two o'clock in the morning and then rising at the usual time to do the milking before school. Bessie and Bossie's milk production was falling off because neither cow had calved since the previous spring, but the amount they did produce was more than enough for Artie and Grandpa, and milking them twice a day kept the big farm boy busy. However, they had little milk left to sell to friends and neighbors, as they always did when Grandma Bauer was alive.

"Good deal," said Wilma, about her friend's essay, "and good luck, Artie." She took a small sip of chocolate milk from her tiny carton. "I wish both of us could get the Ebenezer. But, who knows, neither one of us might win. The scholarship committee could pick someone else—like, oh, I don't know, maybe even Vicki Duke. I heard she applied."

Artie nodded again, wondering if he should thank Wilma for giving him his essay topic or just be quiet and eat. As for his essay, he also owed little Ricky Duran gratitude for inspiring the slogan that had taken the county by storm, literally. Credit also was due everyone whose good example had motivated Artie to produce what he felt to be his best composition ever. *Maybe I* do *belong in the story group,* he thought—*or maybe I just need a lot of writing therapy myself.*

"I wrote about the Barf Table," Artie told Wilma, keeping his voice down, "like you suggested on the bus. Thanks, Wilma." Then he had a worrisome thought and said, "You didn't write about it, too, did you? They'll think I copied you."

"No," she replied, "I wouldn't do that to you, buddy." Then she grinned. "I did mention you, though—in a good way. I wrote about *duty*."

Confused, Artie looked up from his plate of food. "You wrote about *what*?" he asked. "*Doody*? You mean, like cleaning out the stalls?"

Wilma laughed. "No," she said, "like having a sense of D-U-T-Y. *Duty*. How late did you stay up last night, Artie?"

He shook his head and held up two fingers. "What did you write about *me*?" he asked. "I mean, if you don't mind telling me."

"I don't," she said, looking around the table to see who else might be listening. "I've just noticed how we all do things out of a sense of obligation—a sense of duty. You're a good example of that, Artie, in the way you are with your grandfather and the farm. Julia? She played basketball to honor her father, and she dances to be like her mother. And then look at *me*. I wrestled on the boys' team for three years to honor my Czech grandfather—even though people made fun of me—and now I'm learning all about equine therapy to help Aunt Minnie. And my father? He expects me to go into the military straight out of high school—just like he did—if for no other reason than to pay for my college education. But I don't want to do that—always being held back by my sense of duty, or by someone else's. I want to finally do something for me."

Artie laid down his spork and pushed the tray away. "What is it you want to do, Wilma?" asked Artie. "Be a writer? Is that why you picked the story group?"

"I don't know," she said. "Maybe. But maybe I want to sing, too, or dance— or *be* a therapist, I don't know. As far as *that* goes, how can I help other people live their lives when I haven't lived my own yet? And why do I have to map out my entire life right now? Why can't I take a little time—like four or five years, maybe—to live my life and find out who I really am? Does that make sense, Artie?"

"Yeah," he said, "but is that what you wrote?"

"Yes, I did," said Wilma, "in so many words. And, no, I wasn't trying to blow up my chances of winning. I was just being honest. I'm good at a lot of things, and I want to give all those versions of me a chance—like Henry David

Thoreau. Remember when we read about him last year in English class? I want to live my life *deliberately*, not by accident."

"I see what you mean," Artie said. "I want to save our farm, not sell it when Grandpa's gone, like what happens to so many other family farms. I don't want it to be turned into a housing development like Oakhurst Manor or a golf course community like Sandpiper Shores. I can remember when that was a beautiful farm along the river. Now look at it." He looked around the twin tables at their friends. "But I don't want to be the same kind of farmer that Grandpa has been all these years, or that his father was, and on up the line. Times are changing fast, and we're gonna have to change with them to survive—with all due respect to Henry David Thoreau."

Just then, the three freshmen—Bennie Pressler, Tommy White and Ricky Duran—approached with their lunch trays. Artie Bauer and Wilma Marecek fell silent and waited for the boys to pass as they headed for their seats at the other round table.

"Hey, you two," said Bennie. "Keep whispering back and forth like that, and people are gonna start talking. And who is this Henry David guy who's so *thorough*? Sounds like one of *my* people." He winked at them and continued to his chair.

Bennie's offhand remark about their private conversation embarrassed Artie but sent Wilma in another direction. "Hey, speaking of couples," said Wilma, "where are Ty and Nicie today? They're both usually here by now. I know why Julia isn't here. She's always having to make up tests from all the days she misses for tennis. But I know I saw Ty and Nicie this morning—not together, but around school."

"Yeah, they're here," Artie said. "Ty has some news that I'm guessing he's sharing with Nicie—*big* news. He told me he got a call last night, but I'll let him tell you about it. It isn't my place to speak for him. I'm not his agent—yet." He grinned.

"Really?" said Wilma, growing excited. "Was it one of the college coaches or the pro scout from the other night?" When Artie just shook his head and zipped his lips, she continued, "Wow, that's great, Artie. I'm happy for him, whatever his good news is. I hope Nicie is just as happy."

* * *

Before the Arbor High teams' practices Thursday afternoon, the Barf Table friends got together for a few minutes to compare notes on the previous day's information meetings and on their plans for the days to come. Neither Julia Safin nor Bennie Pressler was present—Julia, at her regular tennis practice; Bennie, in Ebenezerville, still helping his parents. Kimi Inouye was on hand, though she was not a softball player herself. She was simply waiting for a ride home with her mother, the teacher, and her twin brother, the baseball star. Sitting in the new set of bleachers overlooking the softball infield, Wilma Marecek asked Ricky Duran, Leah Russo and Brett Woods to tell everyone how the meetings went for their respective groups. All three had positive reports about the interest of so many Arbor students.

"Bennie told me today his mother ordered our ukuleles," said Brett Woods. "They should get here in a few days. Isn't that great?"

"It is," Wilma Marecek said. "Now—here's something to think about for our meeting this Sunday night: Whatever else our school groups do individually, we need to come up with one thing—one really big, cohesive thing—that we can all do together. Any ideas?"

Leah Russo spoke up. "A play, maybe—like a ballet or musical?" she said. "Our group could write it, and Brett's group could provide the music, and Ricky's group could do the dance numbers."

"Yeah," said Wilma, "that's a good idea. Anybody else?"

"What about something for our last ball game?" suggested Jamie Foxx. "We can't do anything tomorrow because the game is at Mimosa Beach, but what about the Hawthorn game next week? It's gonna be special, anyway—because we'll finally be back home in our own ballparks."

"What would we do at the game?" asked Artie Bauer. "It's this coming Tuesday, and our groups won't meet again until Wednesday. So, if anybody does anything, it'll have to be us. Is there anything we can work up that quick?"

Jamie Foxx shrugged. "I don't know," she said. "The National Anthem? On ukulele?"

"But you can't dance to The Star-Spangled Banner," said Artie, "and what would the story group do?" He frowned at the idea of having another pressing assignment so soon, especially a task that might distract him and his teammates from their upcoming battle with Hawthorn Military and Josh Stark.

Ty Green saved the day. "Look," Ty said, "we don't have to decide anything right now, do we? Let's just take one game at a time—tomorrow's game at Mimosa Beach—and then start worrying about the Hawthorn game. We're gonna have our hands full with *both* teams."

"You're right, Ty," said Wilma Marecek. "Everybody just think about what we've talked about today, and we'll discuss it again Sunday night at the clubhouse. I mean, next Tuesday's game will also be Senior Day—since it's the last home game—and that'll be special, too. Like Ty said, *one game at a time.*"

* * *

Late Thursday evening, the telephone on the kitchen wall of the Bauer farmhouse rang. Grandpa Bauer was asleep in his recliner on the back porch, with Brody lying on the floor next to him. Artie had done the milking and his other chores, and was getting out of the shower upstairs. He knew that Tommy White was doing homework in his bedroom, and he heard the boy dash up the hallway and down the stairs to answer the phone.

Toweling himself dry, Artie listened. "*Hey, Artie!*" shouted Tommy from downstairs. "*It's for you! Brett says it's important!*"

Artie cracked open the bathroom door and yelled back, "Tell him to hold his horses. Let me put something on. I'll be right down."

But when Artie made it to the kitchen, Tommy had put the phone back on the hook and was sitting at the long table next to Grandpa. Both of them were petting Brody and giving him treats.

"Why'd you hang up, Tommy?" asked Artie. "Didn't you say it was important?"

Tommy nodded. "It is," he replied, "but Brett said it would be better if we both went over there tonight, because he has something we need to look at. He's still at Woody's—with Jamie."

"Jamie Foxx?" said Artie. "Did he tell you what it is—this thing we need to see?"

"Well, not specifically," Tommy said. "He had to get off the phone real quick. He said it might be something he heard us talking about the other day—after our little run-in with that sheriff's deputy. And if it is, we're gonna want it."

"What does Jamie Foxx have to do with it?" Artie asked.

Tommy shrugged. "I don't know," he said. "Brett didn't say. Can we go, then?" Both he and Artie looked at Grandpa.

"I'll be fine," said Harry Bauer. "I've got Brody and my squirrel gun if anybody decides to come around here and cause trouble. You boys just give me a call when you're ready to start back home—so I don't sic Brody on you or put some buckshot in the side of my own truck."

Despite the tenseness caused by Brett's call, Artie smiled at his grandfather's warning. "How about if you call Ricardo, too?" said Artie. "He and Ricky could keep their eyes peeled while we're gone and make sure nobody turns off the highway onto the farm road—especially a sheriff's department car. We don't want them coming for Brody when you're here by yourself."

Grandpa nodded. "I'll call the Durans," he said, "but don't you worry, son—me and Brody can take care of ourselves."

* * *

Thirty minutes later, Artie Bauer and Tommy White were seated at the counter of Woody's Grill, along with Jamie Foxx and Brett Woods. On the floor behind the counter sat the storage bin that Tommy had kept in the tree house on the White farm—the plastic tub that didn't exist, according to Deputy Red Dedmon and the county sheriff.

"Where'd you find it?" asked Tommy.

Brett handed Tommy a folded piece of paper bearing the words, *Check the dumpster for storage container. Check tonight!* Tommy read the note and said, "Who wrote this?"

"Jerry Church," replied Jamie Foxx. "He said to give it to Brett. That was right before he and my mom left to show a house together—or that's what they said they were doing. They still aren't back, and I want to go home." She went on to explain that she and Brett had looked in the dumpster together and had pulled out the trunk-sized storage bin. "We lifted the lid just enough to see inside," she added. "We didn't want to touch anything. All we saw was the sleeping bag and mosquito netting folded up on top."

Tommy rose from his stool and headed around the counter. "Well, let's see if the stuff we saw before is here," he said, bending down to unhook the lid and remove the bundle of netting. The pizza box was, in fact, still there.

But as Tommy reached into the container to take hold of the flat cardboard box, Woody Woods came out the kitchen door. "Whoa, there," said Woody. "Put these gloves on—just to be safe." He held out a pair of disposable gloves from the kitchen.

Tommy nodded and donned the gloves. Everything that the boys had seen when they'd visited the tree house Saturday was there, except for the box of bullets, the roll of cash and Tommy's yellow spiral notebook. The pocketknives, slingshots, pickle jars of ball bearings and rocks, ballpoint pens and everything else remained.

Leaning by his elbows on the counter, Woody looked down at the storage tub. "You guys will never guess who I saw hauling that into Sandpiper Realty this afternoon," Woody said, with a wry smile. "Here are some hints: red hair, beady eyes, a gun and a badge."

"That would be the cop who picked us up Monday," said Artie. "Deputy Red Dedmon. So, who was he bringing the tub to? Have any idea?"

Woody nodded. "It must have been Joel Stark," he said. "He and Jamie's mother were the only people left in the building after regular office hours. Jerry Church came in to work about thirty minutes later, and Stark left sometime after that. I got busy in the kitchen and lost track of what was going on."

"I'll ask Mom later," said Jamie, "but I don't think that cop brought it to *her*. It had to be for Joel Stark. And I'm betting Joel made Jerry—I mean, Mr.

Church—take it out to the dumpster. Mom says Joel is always bossing Jerry around—you know, just to prove he can. He can be a real jerk sometimes."

"Mr. Church?" asked Tommy.

"No," said Jamie. "Joel Stark. It figures that he and my dad are friends. That's how Mom got her job—because Joel and Dad are golfing buddies at Sandpiper Shores. She doesn't like working there, but she needs the job. *We* need the job."

The boys explained the storage bin's significance to Woody and asked for his advice on what to do with it. "Well, you can't give it to the sheriff," said Woody. "It sounds like he's on the take, too—or just plain gullible. This is how things were in Oleander County back when I was in high school—and when both of your mothers were in school, too, guys. We never knew who we could trust. As a matter of fact, that was when Red Dedmon was hired at the sheriff's department. Everybody said he was crooked back then, but nobody could get anything on him."

"That's what Grandpa said," Artie noted, pointing out that the tables might have turned in that regard. "Yeah, this proves that Red, at least, tampered with evidence, maybe Sheriff Logan, too. Should we get this stuff to somebody up in Capital City? Or to some federal agency, like the FBI?"

Woody shook his head. "No," he said, "for right now, just get it out of sight and out of the dining room here. And don't say a word about it to anyone—not even to your mom, Jamie. I don't want my business to mysteriously catch fire one night because Joel Stark or Red Dedmon or the sheriff thinks I have evidence against them." He told Brett to carry the tub up to the store's storage space in the attic and to hide it behind surfboards and big boxes of surfing equipment.

"I'll have a little talk with Jerry Church," Woody continued. "We've been friends for years, and he won't say anything about this. As a matter of fact, I'm guessing he went out on a limb by writing that note today. So, when the time comes that you need that stuff, just say the word, and we'll haul it back down here. It can stay up there for as long as it needs to."

Artie Bauer used the grill's phone to call his grandfather and let him know that he and Tommy White were headed back home. Grandpa told him that all was quiet on the farm. As the boys prepared to leave, Tommy thanked Woody, Brett and Jamie for their help. "I hope nothing bad happens because of this," said Tommy, "but sometimes I think my family's cursed."

Artie held the door open for Tommy to step out onto the deck. "I hope not, buddy," said Artie, without reminding his young friend that he, too, was family, and that he'd had the very same thought.

As the red pickup headed down Ebenezerville Road toward the Bauer farm, Tommy stared out the passenger window. "Are we doing the right thing, Artie?" he asked. "I mean, what difference does it make whether we save that stuff or it all just disappears? Rocket Reep is dead—has been for months—and everybody knows what he did."

Artie was quiet for a few seconds. "This isn't about *what* Rocket Reep did," he said. "Well, not exactly. This is about *why* he did it, and *who* put him up to it." He paused for a moment. "I want to know why *our* names—why Grandpa's and the Greens' and the Russos' names—were on the list that Reep got from Sandpiper Realty, and why Rocket was harassing some, if not all, of those people."

Tommy looked over at Artie. "Yeah, you're right," said Tommy, nodding. "That guy hurt an awful lot of people last fall—broke into their houses, stole their stuff, killed their dogs. We thought everything he did was kind of hit and miss, but . . ."

"But after finding that list and what he wrote in your notebook," said Artie, "that crime spree of his wasn't random—that's for sure. It was planned out, and Sandpiper Realty was behind it, along with the Oleander County Sheriff's Department, or, at least, that one crooked deputy."

Tommy peered into the darkness beyond the headlight beams. "Yeah," he said, "we're gonna have to watch our step. This is how my folks got into so much trouble—according to my mom, anyway. They got involved with the wrong people, and then they made the mistake of going to the law for help. They thought that would solve all their problems, but it just made matters worse."

CHAPTER 16

IT WAS A BEAUTIFUL APRIL FRIDAY in Oleander County. The sun's rays pierced the plate-glass windows of the cafeteria. The spring weather was so nice that coaches Jug Johnson and Joe Carson took a chance on abandoning their recliners to stand outside in the breezeway while students filed into the lunchroom. The oniony scent of freshly mown grass competed with the smells of fish sticks, crinkle-cut fries, broccoli with cheese and yeast rolls. On the wall behind the coaches' recliners was a wide banner: *BEAT MIMOSA BEACH! WIPE OUT WAVERUNNERS!* Also, if not for the Good Friday Storm two weeks earlier, this would have been the start of prom weekend at Arbor High. But prom would have to wait.

Julia Safin was the only member of the Barf Table gang who appeared the least bit subdued that day, as she had withdrawn from that weekend's out-of-town tennis tournament. The Russian exchange student had made the decision a month earlier, before the tornadoes, so that she could go to the junior-senior prom, though not as Artie Bauer's exclusive date. The couple had already broken up by then, but were "still friends," to star-crossed Artie's mixed feelings.

To accommodate the Solid Rock Christian Academy transfers, the Arbor prom committee had decided to postpone the formal affair for a month and add a catered banquet to be held immediately prior to the dance. The event would still be held at Sandpiper Shores Golf & Country Club—the meal, with entertainment, in the large dining room; the dance, in the big ballroom. Arbor's 11th-grade class was responsible for planning and putting on the event. Barf Table juniors Jamie Foxx and Mike Inouye served on the prom committee, with

Mike having been added to represent Solid Rock students.

"Hey, Kimi Inouye," called Nicie Evans, across the twin Barf Tables, "do you think your mom will let you stay for the dance on prom night?" Nicie was asking for fellow senior Jimmy Gore, seated nearby. Everyone knew that Kimi's folks were still opposed to her dating Jimmy, or anyone else.

Mike Inouye, sitting at the same table with Nicie and Jimmy, spoke up for his twin sister so that she wouldn't have to yell back with her answer. "Our parents don't mind if we go to the dance with our friends," said Mike. "They just don't want us to go on a *date* with one person—or go somewhere *after* the prom that isn't chaperoned. After our junior-senior banquets at Solid Rock, the church would hold a late-night thing called *The Vigil* that juniors would put on for the seniors. It had music, and it had little skits making fun of teachers and popular kids—but nothing bad. I was looking forward to doing that."

"You still can," called Jamie Foxx, from the other table. "Wilma wanted us to come up with a way for our therapy groups to work together on one big project—right, Wilma? Well, what if our groups provide the entertainment for the banquet on prom night? That would give us a month to get ready."

Wilma smiled and nodded. "That sounds great!" she said. "And, like Mike said, we can all go as friends so that he and Kimi can stay for the dance. We'll work all that out at our club meeting on Sunday night, okay?" Wilma looked at Artie Bauer, then at Julia Safin, and noted that neither was smiling, nor were they looking at each other. Both appeared intent on eating their lunches.

Bennie Pressler was particularly happy because he would get to attend that day's softball and baseball games at Mimosa Beach. "Dad and Mom are driving down there this afternoon to check on some things at the mall store," he said, "and they're looking forward to seeing Tommy play again. Me, too. Besides, I need to prepare for next Tuesday's home game when I'm the *Voice of the Bruins.*"

He was referring to his job as Arbor High's public-address announcer, a task that he had been forced to put on hold but would resume Tuesday against Hawthorn Military Academy.

Bennie wasn't the only member of the Barf Table gang who now had the chance to reprise an old role. "Hey, Julia," called Bennie, "since you're in town this weekend, why don't you come be Bruno at the ballgame? It'll be fun, and I'm sure Coach Foxx will get a kick out of it."

His sarcasm was hard to miss. During basketball season, Bennie Pressler and Julia Safin had taken turns performing with the cheerleading squad as the Arbor mascot, wearing a cartoonish brown bear costume with an oversized head and padded body. Jimmy Foxx, who had been the Arbor boys' basketball coach, however briefly, had lost his job at Arbor High due to one particular on-court run-in with Bruno.

"I like that idea," said Jamie Foxx. "Dad will be so annoyed when he sees Bruno that he won't be able to think straight. He won't be expecting it."

Artie Bauer looked up from his food tray. "Neither will *our* coaches," he said. "You'd better go ask them about it. It could be a big distraction—and not just for Coach Foxx." In fact, Artie wasn't sure that he himself liked the idea of his ex-girlfriend prancing around on the visitors' dugout in a bear suit.

Before Artie could object further, Jamie jumped up and pulled Julia out of her chair at the senior table. The pair hurried outside where Joe Carson and Jug Johnson stood, and asked them about having a mascot that day in Mimosa Beach. Artie twisted his head to see the coaches' reaction and was surprised when both men broke into belly laughs. The happy girls returned to their seats.

"They just *love* it!" said Jamie. "And so will Dad." Her impish grin disappeared when she noticed that Artie wasn't as amused.

"How about you, Ty?" asked Artie, turning to his friend. "Do you mind having Bruno there? Will it be a distraction—since she hasn't been to any games yet this season?"

Ty Green laughed. "Nope, not one bit," he said. "Matter of fact, it'll take my mind off who else is coming to the game—that pro scout and his big boss. And when we win and those guys offer me a pro contract, I'm gonna dance on the dugout, too—*with* Bruno. Isn't that right, Julia." He winked at his best buddy's old girlfriend.

"I will hold you to that promise, Ty," said Julia. "I am so happy that your dream is coming true. I hope that I can be as fortunate." She turned to her former sweetheart. "Arthur, do not worry," she said. "I will behave while you and Ty are on the field. I understand. And perhaps you will dance with us, too?"

Artie snorted. "I don't care anything about dancing," he said, but added with a sly smile, "I'm a writer, not a dancer."

* * *

As it turned out, the distraction at the Arbor/Mimosa Beach game didn't involve anything happening atop the visitors' dugout; it happened, first, in the grandstand—of the softball game. Having attended Mimosa Beach High before transferring to Arbor High, both Nicie Evans and Jamie Foxx were jeered by their former schoolmates. Nicie, in particular, was loudly booed when she came to bat in the top of the 1st inning. That didn't stop her, however, from rapping a single into right field and then taking second base on a wild pitch. She scored the Bruinettes' first run on a line-drive single by Jamie two batters later. The Mimosa Beach crowd went easier on Jamie—the catcalls were scattered—only because her father was the current Waverunners baseball coach, and also because both Jimmy Foxx and his estranged wife Louise were in the stands, though sitting separately. That wasn't the distraction, though, not in and of itself. What set the stadium abuzz was Louise's choice of escort to the game—Arbor High principal Jerry Church. They even arrived early and, therefore, were easy to spot as they leaned toward one another in the golden afternoon sun, chatted amicably and laughed often.

Bruinette Leah Russo, playing shortstop this game so that Jamie Foxx could pitch, peered around the dugout entrance at the happy couple on one side of the grandstand and the disgruntled husband on the other side. "Jeepers," said Leah, "this could get ugly. Coach Foxx looks like he could spit nails." Like watching a tennis match, she looked back and forth from one section of stands to the other, adding, "I sure am glad I loaned my camera to Kimi to take some pictures. This could be big for the school paper—*and* for the yearbook."

The Lady Waverunners' best player was no stranger to the Arbor nine and their coach. The tall, strong girl had been a standout on the hardwood for the Mimosa Beach basketball team, as well as in the soft, sugar sands of the actual beach strand. According to Nicie Evans, the girl was "the best center in the conference and the second-best beach volleyball player in Oleander County." She was also Nicie's beach volleyball partner, making the duo unbeatable. On this day, the tall girl played first base, whereas she had pitched and won both earlier games against the Bruinettes that season.

When Nicie reached first base again on her second at-bat, this time by beating out an infield hit, the imposing Lady Waverunner greeted her old friend and teammate. "You know we've already won the conference, right?" the girl asked, taking the optic-yellow ball from her mitt. "Why are you girls playing like this game matters?" She tossed the ball back to her pitcher.

Still breathing hard from her sprint to first, Nicie said, "We win today, we won't have a losing season. Just one game left." Right then, the Bruinettes' overall record stood at 7-7.

Nicie took a short lead off first but returned to the bag when the first pitch to the next batter was a ball. She did the same for the next two pitches and was actually glad to see the Mimosa Beach coach call time and come out of the dugout with the count 3-0, to confer with his second-best pitcher. Behind Nicie, the Arbor boys leaned up against the chain-link fence that separated the softball diamond from the wide walkway between ball fields. She turned and saw that Artie Bauer and Ty Green were standing close enough that they could probably hear her conversation with the big girl. Nicie smiled and waved to them, and brushed some imaginary sweat from her brow, as if the run to first had been hard.

"You need to tell Ty Green to watch his back," said the Lady Waverunner. She pounded her fist into the long webbing of her first-base glove.

"Tell him yourself," said Nicie. "He's standing right over there with Artie Bauer." She pointed back at her two friends and tablemates.

The big girl shook her head and said, "I shouldn't be saying anything, but our boys are out for blood today. No kidding. There's a bounty on your guy—for whoever can put him out of the game."

"We aren't dating now," said Nicie, "but thanks for telling me. I'll pass the word along. But why Ty? He hasn't done anything to any of your guys."

"You didn't hear *me* say this," the big girl replied, "but the idea didn't come from the guys. From what I heard, it came straight from the coach. Foxx said Ty Green needs to be put in his place."

Nicie did a slow burn as she watched the Mimosa Beach coach leave the mound for the home dugout. "Yeah," said Nicie, "Ty quit the basketball team because of the way Foxx did me. The man fixed it so I can't get a college scholarship. But that chump did *himself* in—like he's fixing to do right now with Ms. Foxx and Jamie."

Nicie pointed toward the grandstand, where Jimmy Foxx had risen and was making his way over to where Louise Foxx and Jerry Church sat. The Lady Waverunners pitcher slung the ball toward home plate. The umpire shouted, "Ball four! Take your base." Nicie headed on to second, thanking her old teammate for the head's up as they parted for the time being.

Behind the chain-link fence, Artie Bauer nudged Ty Green. "Look, up in the stands," hissed Artie. "You think Mr. Church might need some backup?"

Turning his attention away from the field to see what was going on, Ty shook his head. "Nah," he said, "Lurch can take care of himself. But it won't get that far. Foxx is just a lot of talk."

Sure enough, before Foxx reached the couple's seats, the Mimosa Beach PA announcer called out Jamie Foxx's name as the batter coming to the plate. That froze Jimmy Foxx in place. Then he simply turned and sat in the first empty space he could find to watch his daughter bat.

"C'mon, Jamie!" Nicie shouted from second base. "Knock me in, babe!"

Jamie took the first two pitches—both of them balls—and then jacked the third pitch clean out of the park, giving the Bruinettes a 3-0 lead that they would not relinquish. Louise Foxx and Jerry Church jumped to their feet to cheer Jamie's home-run trot around the bases. Jimmy Foxx sat and clapped to acknowledge his daughter's feat, which also resulted in a pitching change. He used the break in action to climb down out of the grandstand and to skulk over to the fence beyond the home dugout on the third-base side. He stood there for the next few minutes until it was time to meet with his baseball team on the other side of the athletic complex.

As Foxx left the softball facility, Bruno the Arbor Bruins mascot passed him on the wide walkway between fields. In character, Bruno—whoever played the part—never spoke out loud; they only made gestures with the costume's padded arms and oven mitt-like paws. On this late afternoon, when Bruno recognized the former Arbor basketball coach and current Mimosa Beach baseball coach, the bear threw up one paw in greeting. Foxx angrily slapped the extended mitt down and stomped on toward his team's dressing room in the two-story brick building that also housed the concession stand and press box.

Still watching from their post along the softball fence, Artie Bauer and Ty Green laughed when they saw Bruno the Bruin spin around at the coach's slight and put up both dukes for a play fight—an invitation that the angry coach did not accept in any fashion, whether he saw it or not. Jimmy Foxx had gotten fired from his Arbor High job for knocking down the mascot in a fit of anger one night when the costume was being worn by Bennie Pressler. Foxx couldn't have known that Julia Safin was performing as the bear on this day. But then, he probably didn't care one way or the other after having seen his wife with another man. Jerry Church would be lucky if Jimmy Foxx could control his infamous temper for the remainder of the evening.

* * *

The Mimosa Beach baseball coach waited until his own game's 5th inning to blow his top. He might have done so earlier, except that he was distracted with locating his estranged wife and her new boyfriend in the larger grandstand on the baseball side of the complex. Facing away from the beach strand three blocks away, the baseball field's power alleys were 320 feet to left field and 315 to right, with the high green fence in center beyond most high school batters' best swing at 400. However, with the onshore winds, good power hitters—like Mike Inouye, Jimmy Gore and Artie Bauer—could stroke balls out of Mimosa Beach Memorial Field with regularity. That was the case on this Friday, leading to Jimmy Foxx's downfall.

Coach Jug Johnson's plan was for Ty Green to start the game on the mound and to pitch no more than four innings before handing the ball to reliever Johnny Smith. Ideally, Smitty would handle the 5th and 6th innings, and then let Phil Waters close out the game in the 7th. The main problem with Jug's pitching plan was that the Waverunners were playing rough with barely legal tactics—and not just against Ty Green—injuring Smitty in a collision at second base in the top of the 4th inning. Sliding headfirst into the bag on a steal attempt, the Bruins right fielder and number-two pitcher took a hard tag to the head and, at first, appeared to be okay despite being called out. But upon getting up and trying to jog back to the dugout, Smitty stumbled and then collapsed on the infield dirt before reaching the 3rd-base foul line. He said he wasn't hurt, just dizzy. He let Artie and Ty help him to his feet, but Coach Johnson scratched Smitty's name from the lineup card and sent Phil Waters to right field for the bottom of the 4th. That forced Ty Green to pitch more innings than planned—a situation that the pro scouts in the stands didn't mind one bit. One scout pointed a radar gun at Ty to measure the speed of every pitch; the other man held a big notebook with a team logo on the cover. He charted balls and strikes, locations of pitches, and whether they were fastballs, changeups or, in Ty's case, screwballs. Now the scouts could measure his durability.

In the grandstand, the crowd sat largely divided, with Mimosa Beach fans on the 1st-base side next to the home dugout and the Arbor faithful on the 3rd-base side next to the visitors' dugout. Louise Foxx and Jerry Church sat together down low on the Arbor half so that the principal could get up from his seat and supervise students, if necessary. Having won their game and guaranteed themselves no less than a .500 season, the Bruinettes had showered and dressed, and had spent the early innings of the boys' game celebrating in the concession area behind the grandstand. In pairs and groups, they made their way into the seats where they could watch the last half of the baseball game and cheer along with Bruno's antics atop the visitors' dugout between innings. The mascot was in rare form, pirouetting and leaping and gesticulating to the music that blared over the stadium speakers on changeovers. Even the Mimosa Beach fans got involved in the group cheers, as Bruno led the Chicken Dance, boogied to the Twist and spelled out Y.M.C.A. with padded mascot arms. Everyone seemed to be having a good time—except for Coach Jimmy Foxx, mainly because his wife was obviously enjoying herself with Jerry Church. Foxx couldn't have been too upset by the score, as his team trailed 2-0 on a pair of hard-earned runs.

Then came the 5th inning. Mike Inouye led off for the Bruins. The first pitch was a high, hard fastball that made him jump backwards to keep from being hit. Already out of the batter's box, Mike gathered himself, took two practice swings and stepped back up to the plate. The next pitch brushed him back again, this time sending him to the ground. Mike shook the dirt from his gray pants legs, the cuffs gathered like pajama bottoms around his black-leather baseball spikes. Again, he went through his usual at-bat ritual before and after stepping back into the box. The third pitch was another fastball, low and away, but called a strike by the umpire. The count stood at 2 balls, 1 strike. Keeping one foot in the box, Mike stepped back and looked over at Jug Johnson coaching at third base. From the top step of the dugout, Artie saw that Jug was giving Mike the sign to swing away—proof that the coach already trusted the Solid Rock transfer to look for a good pitch in what wasn't an ideal hitter's count. With no one on base, the pitcher went into his windup and hurled the ball toward the plate. Mike swung and connected. With a jolting ping, the ball rocketed straight-away toward the deepest part of center field and was still rising as it sailed over the green fence. Arbor 4, Mimosa Beach 0.

The majestic home run appeared to infuriate the Waverunners hurler, even though Mike's no-nonsense home-run trot should not have been offensive, even to the most sensitive opponent. But this pitcher's pride was bruised, maybe from his coach's angry reaction in the home dugout. The pinstripe-clad youth bounced the dusty resin bag on his right hand distractedly and slammed it to the ground at the back of the mound as right-handed batter Jimmy Gore walked from the on-deck circle toward the catcher and umpire standing at home. Righty on righty, some inside pitches were expected. But every pitch that Jimmy saw moved him away from the plate until the count was 3-2, thanks to the umpire's generous strike zone. Kneeling on deck, Artie Bauer heard Bennie Pressler in the stands mimicking his favorite major-league play-by-play announcer on the last brush-back pitch: "That was *ju-u-u-ust* a bit inside." Bennie's call was followed by laughter from the Arbor fans. Whether that frivolity affected the next throw or not, the payoff pitch whizzed down the middle of the strike zone, belt-high. Jimmy Gore, the Bruins' best hitter, turned on the pitch and sent it over the left-field fence. Arbor 5, Mimosa Beach 0.

Now it was Artie Bauer's turn at the plate, with Ty Green on deck. There were no outs. After a heated conference on the mound, Coach Jimmy Foxx returned to his dugout and motioned for another right-handed pitcher to start warming up in the Mimosa Beach bullpen. The mistake Foxx made was not switching pitchers right then, because the starter felt the pressure of throwing a strike and grooved his first pitch to Artie. Not usually a first-ball hitter, the big farm boy reacted to protect the strike zone and swung an instant late, but made good contact and sent the ball on a lazy, slicing arc to right field. Artie tossed his bat aside and started down the first-base line, keeping his eyes on the fly ball to see if it left the field. It did, but just foul.

Retrieving his bat and returning to home plate, Artie checked the flag flapping on the pole beyond the center-field fence and saw that the wind was gusting from left to right, hardly the best conditions for an opposite-field homer. The count was 0-and-1. Artie wondered what Jimmy Foxx was waiting on—why he didn't go ahead and bring in the relief pitcher—but that was the hot-headed coach's business, Artie figured. He stepped back into the batter's box and took his practice swings. The pitcher wound up and fired another fastball down the middle, and Artie again swung late, sending the ball toward the right-field foul pole once more. This blow, however, was more of a line drive than the previous foul ball. The Waverunners outfielder ran full speed toward the right corner and leapt for the ball at the top of the green fence. He crashed into the eight-foot-high barrier but appeared to have made the spectacular catch. Artie was halfway to first base when he saw the right fielder pick himself up, look into his glove for the ball, and then throw the empty glove to the green turf. No ball was visible near the fielder, as he had dumped it over the fence. Arbor 6, Mimosa Beach 0.

Half of the crowd roared at the apparent catch, followed by the other half at the unlikely homer. But so did Coach Jimmy Foxx—roar, that is—when he realized what had actually happened and saw the ump circling his index finger in the air to signal another round-tripper. Before Artie reached second base on his home run trot, he saw the irate Mimosa Beach coach rush the plate and scream, "He caught the ball! He caught the ball!" Foxx claimed that the catch was an out, even if slamming into the fence had caused his outfielder to drop the ball on the other side. The umpire rightly disagreed, pointed for Foxx to return to his dugout, and motioned for Ty Green to step up as the next batter. Ty met Artie there as the big boy stepped on the plate to make the home run official.

Still, Jimmy Foxx did not make the pitching change. It didn't take long for the boys in Arbor gray to understand why not. On the first pitch to Ty Green, the disgruntled Waverunners pitcher—having just given up three straight home runs—nailed Ty in the back with his fastball. Ty couldn't avoid being hit, as the pitcher had hurled the fastball behind him, knowing he'd instinctively step backwards into the pitch. The umpire checked to make sure Ty was okay and then told him to take first base. The man also issued a stern warning—to the pitcher and to both coaches—that throwing at batters would not be tolerated and would result in ejections. Jimmy Foxx ignored the plate ump as he stomped to the mound to make the pitching change. Still coaching at third base, Jug Johnson nodded to the man in blue and tipped the bill of his cap, glad that his star pitcher hadn't been hurt. Artie Bauer looked up into the stands and saw that the two pro scouts were talking and shaking their heads.

But the Waverunners weren't done with Ty Green. With Phil Waters batting in place of injured Johnny Smith, the new pitcher threw over to first base every time Ty tried to take even a short lead. He made it back to the base well ahead of the pickoff throw, but the first baseman never failed to smack Ty with the ball in the webbing of his large mitt. After three hard blows like that—to different parts of the Bruins pitcher's anatomy—Ty had enough. With the count 2-0 to the batter, Ty took no lead this time and waited for the pitcher to get set. Coach Jug Johnson had not signaled for either a steal or a hit-and-run play; however, when the pitcher went into his stretch and stepped toward the plate, Ty took off for second base like a gray streak with green-and-gold trim. Phil Waters saw Ty make his move and tried to help out by swinging at the overdue pitch, careful that if he made contact, his swing would keep the ball on the ground, not pop it up so that Ty could be doubled off 1st. But Phil whiffed the pitch, and the catcher jumped up to make the throw to 2nd. What had happened on Johnny Smith's steal attempt the previous inning must have been fresh on Ty's mind, because he chose not slide headfirst into the bag. Instead, he did a hook slide that should have kept his body outside the second baseman's reach. Extending his left hand to touch and then grab the base on the wide slide, Ty beat the throw and was called safe by the infield ump. That didn't stop the Waverunners shortstop covering 2nd from putting down a hard tag on Ty's hand clutching the base. The fielder also came down heavily on Ty's left forearm with his knee after making the failed tag.

Grasping one hand with the other, Ty Green sat in the red clay at second base and waited for the pain in his throbbing fingers and bruised arm to ease. Both Jug Johnson and Artie Bauer ran out to him, to see if he needed assistance. Artie imagined that his best friend's back still smarted, too, from being hit while at bat minutes earlier.

"I'm not coming out, Coach," said Ty. "These jerks aren't gonna win."

Jug took the boy's hand and pressed each finger enough to see if any were broken. "He got the knuckle of your index finger," Jug said, "but it isn't broke—just sprained, I guess. And there's no blood. That's good. C'mon, we'll tape up your hand in the dugout."

"No," said Ty, "I'm not going anywhere—except home when Big Phil gets a hit. *Then* Artie can tape up my hand. He knows how to do it." He rose and dusted himself off, wincing at the sore knuckle that had taken the brunt of the shortstop's punishing tag. "If I leave the game," he added, "even for a courtesy runner, they'll think they won. The heck with them."

The old coach studied the young man's face for a moment before nodding. "Okay, son," Jug said, "we'll do it your way. But they ain't gonna win nothing today." He looked at Artie. "Right, Yogi?"

Artie Bauer smiled and patted his friend on the back as Ty stepped up onto the base. "Well, at least put your batting gloves back on," Artie said, nodding at the pair hanging from Ty's back pocket. "I tell you what, buddy. I'm just glad you slid with your left hand and not your right."

"Yeah-boy," Jug Johnson said, "that's like throwing punches when you're a pitcher. Never throw one with your pitching hand. But I hope it doesn't come to that today. We'll see." He headed back to third base, and Artie returned to the dugout, where he started putting on his catcher's gear.

When play resumed, Big Phil Waters did get a hit—a hot grounder down the 1st-base line that got past the fielder and rolled all the way to the fence. Ty rounded 3rd with Jug waving him home, and before the half inning's first out was recorded, the score was Arbor 7, Mimosa Beach 0.

Now Jimmy Foxx decided to pull his pitcher and send in a lefty to face the bottom of the Bruins order—Brett Woods and Tommy White, both left-handed batters. During the reliever's on-field warmup, Bruno the Bruin climbed atop the visitors' dugout to lead a cheer—actually, another impromptu dance number based on the PA announcer's music choice. The ill-timed song happened to be "Wipe Out" by the Surfaris. In seconds, the entire crowd—fans from both schools—came to their feet to fake surf and let Bruno lead them in '60s dance moves like the Swim, the Watusi and, in Jimmy Foxx's honor, the Jerk.

Acting like the song was a comment on the game score, Coach Foxx went ballistic. He stormed across the diamond and shouted at Bruno to stop dancing and come down from the flat dugout roof. Bruno either didn't see and hear the coach because of the costume's huge head and crowd noise, or simply ignored him. Either way, Foxx's face grew redder and redder, and he screamed profanities until he looked ready to explode. By then, Principal Church and the Mimosa Beach principal had made their separate ways from the stands to the dugout area, and each man took Jimmy Foxx by an elbow to lead him away.

Foxx struggled at first but calmed down when his own principal said something in his ear. By then, they stood outside the fencing that separated the baseball field and the stands. The coach nodded and started to head back inside to the diamond, but the unsmiling Mimosa Beach administrator shook his head and pointed toward the parking lot. Jimmy Foxx was ejected from the game, and the principal took the coach's place in the home dugout. The home-plate umpire motioned for Brett to step up to bat and for the relief pitcher to start pitching. The game resumed.

Being rid of Jimmy Foxx seemed to help the Waverunners. With their principal at the helm, the Mimosa Beach nine could concentrate on playing good, solid ball instead of being distracted by Foxx's gamesmanship and dirty tricks. At the same time, Ty Green's effectiveness began to wane, after getting banged up and having to pitch more than planned. If Ty had known he would have to pitch more than four innings, he could have paced himself better. But as it was, he lost some zip on his fastball and its pinpoint accuracy. Also, he hung more screwballs—that is, they didn't break—than he usually did. He gave up two runs in the bottom of the 5th and loaded the bases in the bottom of the 6th, before being relieved by lefty Phil Waters. Needing one out to end the inning, Phil got the only Waverunners batter he faced to hit a soft grounder to Ricky Duran for an easy out at first base. On the other side, the Mimosa Beach left-hander dug deep and found his best stuff, and kept the potent Bruins offensive attack at bay.

Heading into the bottom of the 7th inning, the score was Arbor 7, Mimosa Beach 2. Suddenly, Phil Waters couldn't find the strike zone, and he walked a pair of Waverunners on eight straight pitches before getting a batter to ground into another fielder's choice. With one out and runners at the corners, Phil failed to regain his control with the next batter and had to groove a 3-0 pitch to keep from loading the bases. Instead, the batter drilled a long fly ball to Ty Green in right field and sacrificed home the Waverunner on 3rd. Arbor now led 7-3, with a runner on first base and two outs in the bottom of the 7th and final inning.

Eight pitches later, the bases were loaded, and Coach Jug Johnson called for a meeting on the mound. As the fates might allow, the Mimosa Beach batter coming to the plate—with a chance to tie the game on a grand-slam homer—was their best long-ball hitter.

Jug didn't ask Phil for the ball—because there were no other regular pitchers to call on—but he did ask the big guy if he might find the strike zone anytime soon. "Now, Phil," said Jug, "we can walk this boy and walk in a run, and we'll still be okay. But you're gonna have to start finding the plate. Ain't that right, Yogi?"

Holding his facemask under one arm, Artie Bauer nodded. "Yes sir, Coach," he said. Then he looked at Phil. "You can do this, buddy. Just keep the balls down in the strike zone so they'll hit it on the ground, and be ready to cover home if a ball gets past me."

Big Phil Waters did walk the next batter—the home-run threat—but he promptly gave up a two-run single to the next hitter, making the score Arbor 7, Mimosa Beach 6. Now it was the bottom of the 7th inning, two outs, with the tying run on second base, the winning run on 1st, and a good hitter at bat.

Again, Jug Johnson called timeout and walked to the mound, this time asking Phil for the ball and patting him on the shoulder. "Keep your head up, big fella," said Jug. "You know how it is—some days are diamonds, and some days are stone. Well, you take a seat and don't worry, Phil. We're gonna rock this next boy's world."

Standing next to his coach, Artie Bauer almost laughed. "What?" asked Artie. "Who's coming in to pitch, Coach? Manny? He can get the ball across the plate, but he doesn't have much of a fastball." Artie was referring to center fielder Manny Freeman, the team's utility player who *had* pitched once earlier in the season in a mop-up appearance, but had given up several hits—including a home run—in a runaway win for the Bruins. Arbor couldn't afford to give up a homer or extra-base hit now.

When Artie turned to go back to home plate, he saw coming from the dugout the pitcher that Jug Johnson had referred to—former Solid Rock pitching phenom Mike Inouye. "But Coach," said Artie, "he's hurt, isn't he? I mean, as far as pitching goes. But you asked him to pitch, anyway?"

Jug headed back toward third base. "Not my idea, Yogi," said the coach. "He told *me* to put him in—that he could get the last out for us."

Artie took his place behind the plate and watched Mike stride to the mound. For a moment, the lean, dark-haired boy in Arbor gray stood tall and peered at his target sixty feet, six inches away. Artie tossed him the ball. Mike threw four easy pitches to locate the strike zone, four medium-speed pitches to loosen up his strong right arm, and four harder pitches whose heat Artie could feel as they smacked into the pocket of his leather catcher's mitt. He took the last pitch more in the padded glove's thinner palm and knew that Mike was ready to throw for real.

The last Mimosa Beach batter went down swinging on three pitches. Game over. Arbor won its last regular-season conference game 7-6, improving their records to 11-1 in the Oleander Conference as regular-season champs, and 13-2 overall with one non-conference game left to play. That last game—on Tuesday against Hawthorn Military Academy—would be a tune-up for the state playoffs. It would also be Senior Day and the team's return to their home field.

On the bus ride home from Mimosa Beach that Friday night, the mood was joyous. The softball girls had played a good game. The baseball boys had saved a close one in a total team effort—with *wa*, as Mike Inouye pointed out. Jimmy Foxx had knocked *himself* out of the game without any of his players claiming the bounty on Ty Green. The pro scouts had seen Ty tough out a bad situation and get a win. And, after getting on the bus, both teams and their coaches had voted Bruno the Bruin the day's MVP—Most Valuable Performer. Without Julia Safin's participation, Jimmy Foxx might not have lost his temper and gotten ejected, and Julia might not have gotten an offer from the head pro scout.

"Did you hear?" Leah Russo asked Artie Bauer on the bus. "Those scouts told Julia that she's the best mascot they've ever seen. They want her to contact their home office about a tryout."

"Really?" said Artie. He turned and looked toward the middle of the bus where Julia sat near Jamie Foxx and Wilma Marecek. "Well, that's great—I guess. But she's a tennis player."

Leah shrugged. "It's always good to have a backup plan," she said, trying to keep her voice down now. "So, did you hear what the Mimosa Beach principal said to Coach Foxx? He said, *Go home, Jimmy—well, you don't have to go home, but you can't stay here.*"

"Did Kimi get any pictures of that?" asked Artie softly, so that Jamie Foxx wouldn't hear him.

Leah nodded. "Sure did," she said, grinning. "And now we know what dance we're gonna brush up on for the Prom—*the Jerk.*"

No sooner than the word was out of Leah's mouth, Jamie Foxx rose from her seat and stood in the bus aisle to face Leah and Artie. "I heard that," said Jamie, with an exaggerated frown. But then she smiled and, when she drew closer, said, "Don't worry about it. It's the truth. You know it. I know it. And, best of all, Mom knows it, finally. She just needed to be around a guy who *isn't* a jerk. That's what made *me* happy—to see Mom have so much fun with Jerry, even with Dad acting up today. I mean, Jerry's a good man—even if he *is* the principal."

After what Jerry Church had done earlier in the week involving Deputy Red Dedmon, Artie Bauer had to agree that the principal's heart seemed to be in the right place.

CHAPTER 17

SATURDAY MORNING ON THE BAUER FARM, Leah Russo and Bennie Pressler showed up early for their weekly horse-therapy sessions. What had been twice per week was now once on Saturday, at a time that allowed both teens to pursue other responsibilities—Leah, working her part-time job at Woody's Surf Shop & Grill; Bennie, helping his parents in Ebenezerville as they rebuilt their family business from the Good Friday Storm. Dr. Minnie Marecek's therapy practice through the week was starting to pick up again, but she and her niece, Wilma Marecek, knew that Saturdays would be busiest with school-aged clients who didn't want to drive out to the farm for an evening session on a weekday. Saturday sessions also gave Tommy White a chance to earn some extra cash as Dr. Marecek's second assistant. The added hustle and bustle on the small farm was welcome. Harry Bauer's farm had seen less and less activity through the years as he had grown older and become less able to run the operation by himself. But now with the hardworking Duran family living in the old homeplace near the highway and grandson Artie Bauer coming of age, the farm's future seemed more hopeful than it had since Harry's accident in the late summer and his wife Pearl's unexpected death in the fall. Grandpa Bauer was finding comfort, not just because he had such a good grandson in Artie, but also because he was surrounded by friends who cared about his health and welfare. And because he now had, at least for the time being, a good dog to keep him company—Brody, the long-haired German Shepherd.

With the morning milking done, Artie Bauer joined his grandfather and Brody on the clubhouse deck to watch Leah Russo and Bennie Pressler finish their riding sessions in the corral. The teenagers no longer needed their horses to be led—Micki and Belle were both gentle mares—but therapy assistants Wilma Marecek and Tommy White stayed close at hand. Dr. Marecek stood near the closed corral gate and directed the activities. Sometimes she turned and addressed Grandpa on the deck, having not yet convinced him to mount a horse himself in her presence.

"When was the last time you went riding, Harry?" asked Minnie. "I've never even seen a picture of you on a horse."

Grandpa laughed. "That's because Tom and Dick are workhorses," he said. "They *pull* things—plows, hay wagons, harrows, manure spreaders. They *work* for a living."

Minnie checked to make sure her clients were okay and looked back at Grandpa. "Well, Harry, you must have ridden them before," she said, smiling. "Those big boys may work hard, but they run and jump in their hearts, I'm sure—just like you." She winked at her friend.

"I have, I have," Harry confessed. "Me and Pearl used to go for long rides of a Sunday afternoon. But that was ages ago, and that wasn't on Tom and Dick. I had some pretty horses for riding when Pearl first came to live here on the farm. It was something we loved to do together."

Artie Bauer couldn't help but correct his grandfather. "Hold on, Grandpa," said Artie. "You and I rode Tom and Dick not that long ago, remember? And Grandma got upset about it. She was afraid you'd fall off and get hurt. We were riding them over to the homeplace to plow that field out back. You said I needed to learn the old-fashioned way of doing things."

Grandpa scoffed. "I remember," he said, "but your grandma was looking out for *you*. She wasn't worried about *me* falling off old Tom. She knew good and well I could ride. Still can—when I want to."

Turning to face the deck again, Minnie pointed at Harry. "I *thought* so," she said. "Well, buddy, you and I are going for a ride one of these days, and I won't take *no* for an answer." She smiled and went back to supervising the sessions.

"You know, Grandpa," said Artie, "riding has really helped Bennie. It's hard to believe he started the school year in a wheelchair, and now look at him. He gets around really well. And Leah—she's doing so much better now than when I met her the first day of school. She's still sad about losing Reuben—you know, like we are about Grandma—but she's learning to live again."

"Son, you don't have to sell me on riding horses," said Harry Bauer. "It's just that I'm still a little bit shaky—about getting on and off a horse, and *also* about people getting the wrong idea about me and Miss Minnie. She's my friend, and I don't want people talking about her—how it's too soon and all. You know how they are—how they talked about your mama and ran her off."

Artie was quiet for a moment. "I know you loved Grandma," said Artie, "and I know that you and Minnie are good friends now. There's nothing wrong with that. The more friends we have, the better off we are. Nobody will say one word about you and Minnie going riding together—or nobody who matters, anyway." Artie looked down at the dog lying on the deck next to Harry's chair and added, "And just think how much Brody will enjoy a ride in the country. Shoot, I'll go, too—if I can find a saddle big enough for Tom or Dick."

Grandpa laughed. "Yep," he said, "it'll take a plow horse to carry a big fella like you—but you're welcome to come along. The more, the merrier."

Artie knew his grandfather was just teasing him, but he couldn't help noticing that they had expressed the same basic idea in their separate ways. Life was hard enough without suffering alone.

* * *

Bennie Pressler had to wait around for his ride to Ebenezerville after finishing his therapy session. His parents always worked long hours, but they had gone that Saturday morning to a breakfast meeting on recovery efforts, and it was running longer than expected. Being more centrally located than county seat Iron Harbor, Monk's Landing—or, specifically, Woody's Grill at Sandpiper Beach—was the meeting place, at Abe and Deborah Pressler's suggestion. Among the attendees, according to Bennie, were Sheriff Jesse Logan and other local, state and federal officials. Jerry Church represented the county school board, and Woody Woods attended as a business and tourism leader, along with real estate and golf resort developer Joel Stark. Woody had banned the son, not the father, from his grill.

"Mom and Dad had a blast seeing Tommy play last night," Bennie said, "even though they got to the game late. They talked about him all the way home—how playing sports has been so good for him."

"Yeah," said Artie, "I don't know what I would've done if I hadn't been able to play ball. Tommy is just like me—well, not as big as I was, but just as shy."

Artie and Bennie sat alone on the clubhouse deck and watched Minnie and Wilma with another client in the corral. Grandpa and Tommy had taken Brody for a walk in the grassy field where the young beekeeper had set up his new hives that spring. Leah was already gone, as her father had driven out to the farm to take her back home to shower and dress for work at Woody's that afternoon and evening.

"Artie, what happened with that stuff we found at Tommy's tree house?" asked Bennie. "Did the cops ever find it? Did you show them the pictures I took?"

"I was getting ready to," Artie said, "but now we don't know who we can trust—if anyone. We did find the stuff—or most of it—and it's safe. The less you know, the better. And don't tell anyone that we found it or even that we have pictures of everything, not your parents and not the cops if they ask you about it. *They're* the ones we don't trust."

"My parents?" asked Bennie, confused. "You don't trust my parents?"

"No, the cops," said Artie, "and somehow Joel Stark is mixed up in this mess. So that's why we need to keep your folks—and even my grandpa—out of the loop for right now. The fewer people who know about what we've learned, the safer it'll be for all of us in the long run."

Bennie nodded. "I understand," he said. "Dad's upset with the sheriff's department right now, anyway. Remember the safe you helped move from the old store? Remember I told you that Dad was acting weird about it? Well, he finally told me that he tried to report a theft, and now he's getting the runaround from the sheriff."

"Really?" said Artie. "What was stolen?"

"I still don't know that," Bennie replied, "and neither does Dad. Whatever it was, it disappeared years ago, sometime after my great-grandfather Noah Pressler quit running the company full-time. Dad was just out of college by then and was managing the new mall store in Mimosa Beach. His father—my grandfather Elisha—was running the big store in Iron Harbor, and so when Noah named Elisha company president, they moved the corporate headquarters to Iron Harbor. But Noah stayed there in E-ville and ran the old store for a few more years, and the old safe stayed there with him. Are you following me?"

"I guess so," said Artie, with a chuckle, "but will I be tested on this?"

Bennie rolled his eyes. "Don't be a wise guy," he said. "Besides, that's my line. Anyway, Grandfather told Dad once that the old safe had a false bottom, and that it held something that his father—Noah Pressler—had brought here from Bavaria, something *precious*, he said, that shouldn't be sold or even taken out of the old safe except in the direst emergency—like what's happening now, I guess. But Grandfather wouldn't tell Dad what the thing was, just that old Noah Pressler had sealed it inside another box for safekeeping—like a safe inside a safe. It never had to be opened, because business was always good."

"Wow," Artie said, "and your dad really doesn't know what the thing was? If it had been me, I would've peeked inside that box. How many years has it been since anyone looked?"

"Maybe sixty years," said Bennie. "That was when Noah Pressler originally opened the E-ville store and bought that old safe. It was about twenty years ago when he turned the business over to Grandfather Elisha, and, according to Dad, the wooden box was in the safe then and hadn't been opened. Grandfather told Dad that he and Noah had checked on it when the corporate office was moved. The false bottom was intact, and the box was still sealed. That was all they cared about—"

Artie started to ask another question, but Bennie cut him off. "No, hold on," Bennie said. "A few years later the old store got robbed. Some burglars broke into the office one night and cracked that old safe. It was like something out of a movie. Dad said they got away with money and other stuff, but Noah said they did not find the safe's false bottom or the box hidden inside it. He checked to be sure the box was still there before he reported the robbery, and it was. But evidently he didn't take the box out and inspect it to make sure it hadn't been opened. Dad wishes he had now."

"Yeah," Artie said, "you have to wonder what this mysterious treasure is."

"Dad asked Grandfather," said Bennie, "but he told Dad the same thing that you told me about Tommy's stuff a minute ago—the less Dad knew, the better." Bennie shrugged. "We figure it must have been some kind of jewelry that Noah smuggled out of Bavaria after World War I, something the German government would have tried to confiscate. There was even an old German newspaper—from Munich—still in the safe. That's our best guess now."

Now Artie was confused, and he asked, "So, how did your dad report something stolen that he didn't know existed for sure? I mean, other than what your grandfathers told him."

Bennie tapped the tip of his own nose. "Bingo," he said. "That's what the sheriff told Dad. But everything else about the story checked out. After you helped us move the safe, Dad opened it and found the false bottom. He also found a heavy wooden box with an old-fashioned, red, wax seal—just like Noah claimed. But Dad looked really close, and he could see that the seal had been tampered with. He opened the box, and there was nothing in it. Who knows when the treasure disappeared?"

"What are you gonna do?" said Artie. "File an insurance claim? Take it off your taxes?"

Bennie shook his head. "There's not much we *can* do," he said. "It wasn't on our inventory for insurance or tax purposes. We can't do anything until we figure out who found the wooden box and stole whatever was in it. It still bothers Dad that the other robbery—the one where the robbers cracked the safe—that it was never solved. That was kinda weird in a small town like E-ville, where everybody knows everybody else. But Dad's trying to solve all those mysteries, as if he doesn't have enough on his plate already. He's making a list of everyone who's ever worked in the E-ville office."

"Is your grandfather still around?" asked Artie. "Still alive, I mean."

"No, he died about five years ago," said Bennie, "and that's another complication to this story. Great-grandfather Noah had serious memory problems, but he lived to a ripe old age. My grandfather Elisha was as sharp as a tack until the day he died, but he died unexpectedly and at a relatively young age. What's worse, he died before he got around to telling Dad the big family secret." He sighed. "It's such a good secret that even we don't know what it is. He didn't even tell Grandmother."

Just then, the sound of a vehicle approaching on the farm lane caught the boys' attention, and they saw that it was Bennie's parents come to pick him up. "I like your new SUV," said Artie. "It beats that handicapped van your dad always drove when you were in the wheelchair."

"Yeah," Bennie said, "it isn't *Moby* or *The Luuuvvv Truck*, but it's nice and roomy. I actually kind of miss the old van, though. When I get my license next year, I might ask Mom and Dad to buy me one."

"Not a Corvette or a Ferrari?" teased Artie.

Bennie shook his head and said, "Nope. I need something that I can haul my sound equipment and other electronics around in. I want something that doesn't call attention to what my family has." He waited to see Artie's reaction and added, "I like to joke around, but I'm not a jerk—like my old surfing buddy Josh Stark has turned out to be."

Artie nodded. "Or like Coach Foxx was at our games yesterday?" he said. "Wouldn't the world be a better place without guys like that?"

Bennie nodded. "What is it that Coach Johnson always says?" he asked. "*From your lips to God's ears*? Sometimes I wish it worked the other way around, but I figure some people still wouldn't listen."

* * *

Minnie and Wilma Marecek were still busy with clients Saturday afternoon when Grandpa Bauer asked if Tommy White minded if the three of them— Grandpa, Tommy and Artie—went out to the White farm to gather more flowers. In fact, Tommy was happy to show Grandpa the property so that the old farmer could give him advice on how to begin rebuilding.

"I'm going to get the beeyard going first," said Tommy, after they had piled into the red pickup, "but after that, I'm not sure what to do. Lease out the fields? Build back the barn? Build a house?"

Grandpa nodded. "Yes, son," he said, "it can be right daunting—all the decisions a farmer has to make. But, you know, the county can be a big help, too. Maybe if you call the county ag agent to come out and look at the soil and to test the water. He can tell you what other farmers would do with land like what you got, so close to the swamp."

"The ag agent now is a lady, Grandpa," said Artie, braking the pickup to a stop at the farm lane's intersection with Ebenezerville Road. "She comes out to the high school all the time." He looked both ways and turned right, pulling out slowly to keep from jostling Brody in the truck bed.

"How's he doing back there?" Artie asked his passengers.

Grandpa twisted his head to check on the long-haired dog. "That boy loves going for rides," said Grandpa, "but this is his first time in a convertible. You take it slow now. That wire cage he's in doesn't break the wind like a regular crate would."

Artie shot a look at Tommy, and they decided to let Grandpa's comment about "breaking wind" pass. "Mr. Bauer, did you ever come out to the farm when my grandparents had it?" asked Tommy. "I mean, do you remember when it looked nice? I've seen pictures, but even those old photo albums are gone now—after the fire."

"That's *Grandpa*, son," said Harry Bauer. "Yes, when me and Pearl went to Shin's Grove Church back in the day, we knew your granddaddy and grandmother White. They were good folks. But we never went over to their house. Me and Ned White would stand out in the churchyard and smoke cigarettes between Sunday school and preachin', and that's about all the socializing we did—solved all the world's problems over two Camel Filters." He laughed and smacked his lips, adding, "Hazel White, though, could make the best Japanese fruitcakes I've ever tasted. She brought one to every dinner-on-the-grounds the church had—

probably why nobody would lay out on those Sundays. It was always packed."

Artie enjoyed listening to his grandfather's stories. *Maybe I* will *write the best ones down so that they aren't lost*, thought Artie. He turned left onto Little Swamp Road.

"What's a Japanese fruitcake?" asked Tommy White. "My mother never made one for us that I can remember. She always fixed us stuff to eat out of the microwave."

"It's the closest thing to heaven you'll ever taste," Grandpa said, with a smile, "or, at least, the ones your grandmother made were. Pearl tried her best to copy them, but Hazel White wouldn't let go of her exact ingredients. Her recipe was a family secret, she always said."

Tommy shook his head. "Well, Grandma White must not have written the recipe down," he said. "Maybe she wanted to make sure that nobody married Dad after she was gone just to get that Japanese fruitcake recipe." He laughed. "But I don't think Mom married Dad for *any* kind of recipe."

"Your mother was a good girl," said Harry Bauer. "Connie Henderson—Connie *White*—was our Ingrid's best friend. When Ingrid took off—for whatever reason—and we put out that missing-person report, Connie called Pearl once and just cried and cried on the phone about Ingrid being gone. But she never came over to the house again after that. No offense, Tommy, but that was a mighty rough crowd that started hanging around the White place after Ned and then Hazel passed away. And there wasn't any smoking Camel cigarettes in the churchyard with those boys—they smoked something else. Besides, we quit that church ourselves around that time—when Artie was a baby."

When they arrived at the White property, Artie parked the truck next to where the barn used to be. Grandpa went around back and dropped the tailgate. He opened the wire door of the carrier so that Brody could scramble out and jump down to the ground. The German Shepherd was excited about being out of the cage, but obeyed Grandpa's commands to sit and stay while he looked around and waited for Artie and Tommy to give them directions to the old beeyard.

"This looks like about the only place you *could* build a house, Tommy," said

Grandpa, "but you'll still need to get somebody from the county out here to see if it *percs*."

Tommy furrowed his brow. "What does *that* mean?" he asked. "Percs? Like coffee?"

"No, son," said Grandpa. "It's called a percolation test—a *perc* test—to see if the ground drains fast enough for the house to have a septic tank. If the drainage isn't good, that means the water table is too high to be pumping sewage into the ground. Nowadays that means no septic tank, and—out here in the country—no house. You don't want your wastewater and your *drinking* water—you know, from your well—mixing together, right?"

Now Tommy scrunched up his face. "*Eewww*," he said. "No, you don't."

Artie Bauer bent down to pet Brody's head. "That's how it is all over Oleander County, isn't it, Grandpa?" said Artie. "I mean, since we're close to the ocean and have so much swampland."

"Not in the big towns like Iron Harbor and Mimosa Beach—the ones with sewer systems," said Harry Bauer. "But, yeah, everywhere else it's septic tanks, even in those fancy golf course developments they're trying to build now." He chuckled. "I knew one boy from the church that built his house on his parents' farm, over where that Sandpiper golf course is now. The water table was so high that he dug his well by pounding one six-foot length of pipe into the ground. Needless to say, your grandma and I would *not* accept that family's invitations to Sunday dinner. Of course, they ran their septic into the swamp."

This time Artie said, "*Eewww*," but he thought to add, "Not even if the fellow's wife could make a good Japanese fruitcake?"

"No, sir," said Grandpa. "That's a good way to get sick. But that kind of thing used to happen all the time here in Oleander County, and it still happens now—even with the county health department doing those perc tests and issuing county permits and such." He took Brody's leash from his coat pocket and snapped it onto the dog's collar. "Which way we going, boys?" he asked.

"Behind where the barn was," said Tommy White, "and through that stand of trees back there. Brody will be okay off the leash, Mr. . . . uh, Grandpa."

"Well, we'll see," said Harry Bauer. "Let's just be on the safe side since this is mine and Brody's first time out here. Don't want to step into an old well or something. You lead the way, Tom."

With Tommy in front and Artie at the rear, the procession entered the woods where someone, presumably Rocket Reep, had placed the gray stone, and zigzagged through the trees wherever Tommy had planted the thorny swamp roses, still not in bloom. It was another sunny spring day, and the open field where the beeyard had stood was literally buzzing with activity from all the flowers blossoming as before. Grandpa Bauer surveyed the sun-drenched clearing to make sure it appeared safe, and stooped to unhook Brody's leash. The dog put his nose to the ground and seemed to follow the boys' tracks from their earlier visit. Brody went straight to the back of the clearing where Tommy's beehives had stood. He sniffed the sets of cinderblocks that the young beekeeper had used to support his now-missing wooden hives, and, without being prompted, sat stock-still next to one grouping of four, as if he were waiting for Grandpa's next command.

"What's he doing?" asked Artie.

Tommy shook his head. "He's just sitting there," he said. "Maybe he smells the honey that used to be in my hives. Maybe it seeped into the ground."

"Grandpa, did Sgt. Quinn say what Brody was trained to do?" said Artie. "Maybe he smells the pot plants that grew here. Maybe that's where they stored them—near the beehives. I wouldn't mess with a bale of pot near a beehive."

"No, he didn't say," Harry Bauer replied, "just that Brody would protect his master. That's all I needed to hear about what he can and can't do." He laughed and called the dog over for a treat. "Good dog," he said. "Let's go see what we can find at that tree house over there."

Grandpa reattached the leash and walked with Brody over to the makeshift structure eight feet off the ground. Tommy and Artie climbed the ladder into the tree house and looked around the covered platform while Grandpa let the dog sniff the ground underneath. All that was left from before was the white cooler full of canned goods and ruined food. Brody tugged Grandpa here and there in the shadow of the tree house, but did not bark, scratch or do anything else to indicate that he had found something of interest.

"I'll have to ask Marty about Brody the next time he calls," Grandpa said, as he and the German Shepherd waited for the boys to descend the ladder. "Let's go find the prettiest flowers in that field and then head on over to the church, boys. I'll hold onto Brody until we get back in the clearing, in case he wants to go jump in the swamp and take a swim."

They all laughed and walked back out of the trees into the old beeyard. Grandpa turned Brody loose again and watched the dog wander toward a different section of the clearing, to another patch of colorful thrift on the edge of the treeline but away from the trail back to the truck.

"He really likes that thrift," shouted Tommy across the clearing. "Look, old Brody's sitting there just staring at it, like it's the prettiest thing he's ever seen." He held a bunch of daffodils and irises in the crook of one arm, and waved for the others to follow him back through the woods on the crooked path.

Likewise, Artie Bauer had found some beautiful flowers, mainly the special, two-toned irises whose bulbs his grandmother had shared with Connie White. "Yeah, come on, Grandpa," called Artie. "We need to go on over to the church and then get back to the farm—to *our* farm—so Tommy and I can get ready to go out tonight. We're going to Woody's—after I do the milking."

Grandpa nodded, gave Brody another treat and rejoined the boys in the woods. Soon, they were in the red pickup—with the dog back in his cage— headed for Shin's Grove Church. Rather than park in the graveled church lot, Artie pulled off the paved road past the white-steepled building but next to the cemetery, stopping near the wide granite gravestone bearing the name *BAUER* in capital letters.

Before they all got out, Grandpa had a request. "You boys stay here with the flowers and with Brody," he said, "and give me a minute alone with Pearl. Okay?" His steel-blue eyes suddenly looked tired, as if he were carrying the weight of the world, or at least his corner of it.

"Sure, Grandpa," said Artie Bauer. "You take as long as you want. Just give us a wave, and we'll bring the flowers. Should I leave Brody in the back?"

"No, no, you bring him, too," Harry Bauer said, with a hint of a smile. "I want to introduce my new best buddy to Pearl. After ol' Sergeant died, she always told me I needed to get me another dog, but I wouldn't have it. I wish I'd listened to her. I almost hate telling her she was right."

Tommy let Grandpa out of the truck and waited while the old man picked a single, perfect iris from the bunch that the big boy held. The old man stepped across a drainage ditch that separated the shoulder of the road from the cemetery grounds and then made his way across an empty expanse of lush grass to his wife's grave, the closest one to the paved road. Artie was happy to give Grandpa some quiet time there, as much as he needed. Like Harry Bauer, Artie didn't enjoy seeing his grandfather's name—and his own, *Harold Arthur Bauer*—chiseled in the gray stone, but that was the price of paying respect to the most important woman in their lives.

After a few minutes at the grave—the lines dividing the squares of turf no longer visible, as they had been for weeks after the funeral—Harry Bauer, his head down, lifted his hand and motioned for the boys and dog to join him. Artie got Brody out of the cage and put him on his leash, and followed Tommy across the thick grass to where Grandpa stood. The old man turned and held out his hand for the strap, but there was no need to restrain the dog, as Brody sniffed around Harry's shoes and then sat calmly at his feet. Without budging, the German Shepherd watched intently as Grandpa divided the flowers that Tommy carried and placed them in two bunches in the stone vases at either end of the tombstone. It was as if the dog didn't want to distract his master during this quiet moment at the graveside.

"Good boy," Harry Bauer said again, giving the dog another treat from his pocket. "Okay, stand, Brody. Stand. Now, heel." The big dog rose and walked at Grandpa's left side, close enough to keep the leash loose as the four friends made their way back to the red pickup truck.

* * *

Artie Bauer's red pickup and Ty Green's baby-blue *Luuuvvv Truck* pulled into the lot at Woody's Grill one in front of the other. Tommy White rode with Artie, and Ricky Duran rode with Ty in order to give them all more leg room on the ride to Sandpiper Beach. Also, having two vehicles gave them more flexibility about leaving at the end of the night. Even though Ty hadn't admitted that he and Nicie Evans might be back together, Artie had a feeling the couple would reconnect soon. If that happened on this particular Saturday night, then Ty would have his truck, and Ricky would still have a ride home with Artie.

With Arbor High's softball and baseball Senior Day coming up, the Barf Table crew decided to have a Senior *Night* beforehand at Woody's. It was also their chance to try out some of the ideas that the different therapy groups were considering for the regular season-ending ballgames on Tuesday and for the junior-senior banquet and prom in May. Brett Woods would debut some songs on ukulele; Julia Safin would demonstrate a dance routine for a couple of Brett's songs; and Kimi Inouye would snap additional photos to illustrate the story, "We Are Solid Rock Strong."

As usual, Brett Woods, Leah Russo and Nicie Evans were working their regular Saturday night shifts, with Brett in the kitchen and the girls out front. But Woody Woods promised to cut them some slack when business slowed down after the dinner rush. He would still need Brett to deliver a pizza now and then in *The Woody Wagon,* but the teen wouldn't have to work in the kitchen all night.

With Bennie Pressler's help as soundman, Brett set up a small stage in one corner of the dining room, with a wooden stool and a microphone plugged into the grill's sound system and wall speakers. Brett climbed onto the stool, adjusted the mic stand, and plucked the strings to make sure his uke was in tune.

"Hi, guys," Brett said, leaning toward the microphone. "Gotta admit I'm kinda nervous, but here goes." He started to strum the tiny instrument with his right thumb, creating a regular rhythm down-up-down, down-up-down, and changing the chord with his left hand on the uke's slim neck every two beats or so. His head was down to make sure his fingers hit the right strings, and he strummed once through the tune before beginning to sing, "Some . . . where . . . over the rainbow . . . ."

Seated together at one table, Bennie Pressler leaned over to Artie Bauer. "We heard this version in Hawaii," whispered Bennie. "The singer was great."

Wanting to listen, Artie simply nodded without taking his eyes off their uke-playing friend. Artie and the gang had already heard a boatload of stories from Bennie and Brett about their winter of surfing the North Shore of Oahu, but few of the tales involved the boys' activities off the beach. How Brett had learned to play the ukulele and to sing so well in such a short time was a mystery.

As Brett Woods finished his first number and checked the ukulele's tuning again, Nicie Evans came to the table with four tall glasses of soda. "What did *you* learn how to play, Bennie?" Nicie asked, as she slid a glass to the boy.

"In Hawaii?" Bennie said. "Well, I learned how to play *Hukilau*." He took a sip of his drink.

"Hooky-lau?" said Nicie, laughing as she reached to set down the other sodas. "Yeah, I'll say you did. You skipped a whole month of school."

Bennie shook his head. "Not *hooky*," he said, "*Hukilau*. It's a song about going fishing with your friends and then having a big party—like what we're doing right now." He frowned. "Besides, it isn't playing hooky if you have to do schoolwork."

Nicie stared down at him. "Oh, be quiet and drink your soda, hooky boy," she said, with a grin. "Brett's starting his next song. The pizza will be out in a minute." She looked around the table and dared freshmen Bennie, Tommy and Ricky to say anything else.

When she walked away, Bennie shook his head and said, "I sure did miss that in Hawaii. Nicie and Leah both know how to keep a guy humble."

Artie started to say how lucky Woody Woods was to have the two girls working weekends, but he held back to hear Brett's next song—one that Woody himself had requested about having troubles and needing a good friend's help. As Artie listened to the familiar tune, he glanced around the table and then around the room at all his friends enjoying themselves on this perfect evening. Brett's voice was soothing as he sang the words they all knew by heart, and soon they were all singing along.

Like a hula girl but in khaki shorts and a loose T-shirt, Julia Safin got up and stood next to Brett Woods. In seconds, she was dancing—almost signing—the reassuring lyrics. In the background, the deep but muffled percussion of waves on the cold, dark beach at low tide provided an odd counterpoint to this easygoing song and pop classic.

Brett sang the last phrase and held the last word, while Julia stood like a statue to end their performance. Their friends clapped and whistled. Woody came out of the kitchen and spun a white hand-towel in the air to show how much he'd liked the song. But before Brett and Julia could stand and take a bow, the door to the patio flew open, and into the grill stepped two of Oleander County's most despised figures—Mimosa Beach baseball coach Jimmy Foxx and Sandpiper Realty developer Joel Stark. The two men headed for a booth in back—appropriately enough, the same one that Josh Stark and Vicki Duke had occupied a week earlier.

Without missing a beat, Brett started strumming two chords—a half tone apart—over and over to mimic the soundtrack of a movie shark attack. Duhhh-*dup*. Duhhh-*dup*. Then faster and faster, until Jimmy Foxx and Joel Stark figured out what the musician was doing and scowled at the laughter from many of the teenagers. Every so often, Kimi Inouye's camera flash lit up even the darkest corners of the room. Woody Woods smiled and threw up his hand to the pair, indicating he'd wait on them himself in just a minute. Neither Nicie Evans nor Leah Russo was about to take orders from those two men.

Artie Bauer leaned over to Jamie Foxx at an adjacent table. "We can find you a ride home if you need one," Artie said. "Your dad doesn't need to wait."

"I don't live with him," said Jamie, frowning. "Mom's coming to get me after her date tonight."

"With Mr. Church?" asked Artie. "Maybe that's why your dad's here—to spy on your mom."

Jamie nodded. "Maybe," she said. "But that's not why he's here with Joel Stark. Mom said he's offering Dad a new job—managing the golf club at Sandpiper Shores."

Artie's eyebrows rose. "Did he get fired last night?" he asked. "That was quick."

"No," said Jamie, "but it's just a matter of time. A bunch of people complained. They said he was drunk. He wasn't, but he acted like it. That was pure temper. Believe me, I've seen it before."

Artie nodded and turned around to see how Woody was handling his two new customers. On stage, Brett had quit playing the *Jaws* theme and switched to an old ukulele number about having to choose between serving the devil and being cast into the deep, blue sea, like in the story of Jonah and the whale. Ty Green, sitting at the counter so that he could talk to Nicie, nudged Jimmy Gore and Mike Inouye on either side of him. This was a song that Ty had suggested to Brett after hearing Coach Jug Johnson say the phrase when players put him in a bad spot. Artie turned again toward the back booth.

"What'll it be, gents?" asked Woody Woods, not needing an order pad and pencil.

With a sly smile, Joel Stark replied, "Where's your wait staff, Woods? Business that bad these days?" He cut his eyes at Jimmy Foxx across the table.

Woody took a step back from the booth. "Why so dressed up, Joel?" he asked, looking down. "I see you're wearing socks with your penny loafers." Woody continued, "No, the girls are busy with their friends. I told them I'd wait on the riffraff." He paused again. "Just kidding, fellas. What'll you have?"

Jimmy Foxx didn't appear amused. "Do you have pitchers?" he grunted.

"Yeah," said Woody, "we got two of the best in the state sitting at the counter . . . but I think you've had enough of them, after yesterday. . . . Sorry, too soon?"

Joel Stark jumped in. "Come on, Woody," he said, smiling blankly. "You know Jimmy means a pitcher of *beer*. We can get along here, can't we? We're adults."

Woody smiled. "Yeah, we can get along," he said, "as long as you two behave yourselves. And, no, we don't serve beer here. You should know that, being our neighbors here on the beach."

"Are you saying you don't want our business?" asked Stark. "We just want to have a little drink to celebrate ol' Jimmy, here, coming to work for me. He's gonna manage our golf club. C'mon, Woody. A couple of beers with our pizza won't hurt anything. I'll even run and grab them out of my office fridge."

"Look," said Woody, "there are plenty of bars down in Mimosa Beach or up in Iron Harbor—or, hey, here's an idea—at your own golf club, if you boys need to whet your whistles that bad. I'm here for the kids—and for families."

When Artie heard Woody say that, he glanced over at Jamie Foxx again and hoped that neither she nor her father made a scene. Even stone-cold sober, Jimmy Foxx's temper tantrum on the baseball diamond Friday had been enough trouble for everybody. Up front, Brett and Julia started into another song, this one a country tune about good days being like diamonds and bad days being like stone—another one of Coach Jug Johnson's favorite lines.

Woody continued, "Yeah, Joel, the kids are calling this their *Senior Night*— you know, ahead of Tuesday's game when the ball teams recognize our seniors." He pointed around the room. "That would be Artie and Ty and Jimmy, and, let's see, Phil and Smitty over there. And, of course, there's Nicie and Wilma and Mel. Brett's gonna miss them at school. They're all such great kids."

The developer didn't acknowledge Woody's observation—and the implication that Brett *didn't* miss his former friend, Josh Stark, who had attended both Arbor High and Solid Rock Academy earlier in the school year. "Speaking of us being neighbors, Woods," said Joel Stark, "we need to sit down soon and discuss our little parking problem here on the beach. I thought we could talk about it tonight and come to terms, but this isn't the right time to talk—too much *noise* in here."

Woody ignored the "noise" remark. "What parking problem?" he asked. "My parking lot is on the opposite side of the building from your office."

Stark's eyes narrowed. "The alleyway," Stark said. "And the dumpster. The kids coming in here—whether it's to your surf shop during the day or to eat here at night—they pull in and block the alley. It needs to stay open for the garbage truck, especially on big beach days, like at Easter and the Fourth of July—and over Memorial Day weekend coming up."

"We share that dumpster," said Woody, "and all I see parked around it anymore are work vans and septic-company trucks there to see you. Besides, the scheduled garbage pickups are on Mondays and Thursdays, in the mornings before we open. You know that."

Stark slid his legs around to rise from the booth. "Yeah, I do," he said, motioning for Jimmy Foxx to follow him out, "but there's a town ordinance—and a new 'No Parking' sign next to the dumpster—that says to keep personal vehicles out of that alley. I talked to a sheriff's deputy just this afternoon—Red Dedmon, you know him, right?—well, he said all I have to do is call him, and he'll come ticket cars that are illegally parked and have them towed." Stark smiled again.

Woody let the threat sink in before responding. At first, he just shook his head and flipped the white towel onto his shoulder. Then he said, "Well, you fellas have a good evening. And, don't worry, I'll keep an eye on that dumpster for you."

As Woody Woods watched the two men leave, he caught Artie Bauer's gaze and gave the big farm boy a wink and a nod to let him know he hadn't forgotten about the storage container in the grill's attic—the disappearing tub of evidence that Joel Stark had tried to throw away.

The patio door finally pulled shut on its pneumatic spring just as Brett Woods and Julia Safin concluded their last song with, ". . . and some days are stone." Everyone in the grill cheered, and then someone—maybe it was Jamie Foxx, maybe it was Jenny Gore—began the chant, "We Are Solid Rock, Solid Rock Strong" above the rumble of the distant surf. It was dead low tide right then, but soon the tide would begin to rise.

CHAPTER 18

AT SUNDAY NIGHT'S CLUB MEETING on the Bauer farm, the Barf Table friends finalized their plans for Tuesday's Senior Day games against the Hawthorn Blackhawks and arch rival Josh Stark. In addition to regular ballgame songs, the music- and dance-therapy groups had worked up a rendition of the National Anthem that would be performed before the softball game. Both Arbor High coaches had given all their players permission to participate in the performance, which involved the "dancers" signing the anthem. Ricky Duran had arranged for the director of Solid Rock Christian Church's deaf ministry— who had also transferred to Arbor High as an interpreter for one of the Solid Rock deaf students—to come to the club meeting and teach the song to the dance group. Bennie Pressler, the music group's sound man, handed out three of the ukuleles that his parents had ordered for them; and Brett Woods passed out copies of "The Star-Spangled Banner" sheet music for ukes so that they could practice.

The third therapy group—the storytellers—finished work on a handout for Tuesday's games that included information about each senior and their plans for the future. The non-seniors in the group—Leah Russo, Kimi Inouye and Tommy White—had done interviews and taken pictures for the program that would be printed out and copied at school on Monday. Seniors Artie Bauer and Wilma Marecek did most of the writing. That was when Artie learned that his best friend Ty Green wasn't ready to announce whether he would play college baseball or sign with the pros. The Arbor pitching ace's future remained a mystery, except to Ty Green himself and perhaps to former girlfriend Nicie Evans.

After the club meeting, Ty left his *Luuuvvv Truck* parked near the barn and walked with Artie to the farmhouse, giving the two pals time to talk privately. Tommy White and Ricky Duran had hung back in the clubhouse to study for a test, as both had the same 9th-grade English class.

"So, are you and Nicie back together again?" asked Artie. "I hope you don't mind me asking."

"We are, but we aren't—if that makes any sense," said Ty. "We're going to the prom together, but after that . . . who knows? As far as us being a couple, we aren't looking any farther down the road than that."

"Why not?" Artie said. "Are you waiting for a pro team to make you an offer? Or to hear from another college?"

"I just don't know what to do," said Ty. "The scout *made* me an offer, but I'd have to report to their rookie-league team the Monday after graduation." He shrugged. "And the State College coach got word to me that they're interested. You know I've always wanted to go there—if I go anywhere."

Artie looked up ahead and saw that his grandfather had turned on the back porch light. "What do your folks say?" Artie asked. "Are they pushing you one way or the other?"

"No, they're being good about it," said Ty. "They say it's *my* decision to make, but I know they'll back me one hundred percent no matter what." He was quiet for a moment. "This is the biggest decision I've ever had to make. I sure hope I don't screw up."

The two friends cut across the yard toward the back porch. "Ty, you aren't going to screw up," Artie said. "Besides, you can do both, can't you? Didn't you say Mike Marshall did that—play minor-league ball and go to college at the same time? He's still your guy, isn't he?"

Ty nodded. "Yeah," he said, "but I don't think I'm smart enough to do like Iron Mike did. I mean, he even got a PhD in kinesiology later on. Me? I'm lucky to make B's and C's in *high school* classes—and I can't even spell *kinesiology.* I'm not like you, big guy."

"What's Nicie gonna do after graduation?" asked Artie. "Will that affect *your* decision?"

"Maybe," Ty said, with a shrug, "but she won't even talk about that—what *she's* gonna do—because she doesn't want it to influence what *I* do."

Now Artie was shaking *his* head. "Yeah," he said, "I've heard *that* line before. Sounds like Nicie and Julia got together at the end of basketball season and compared notes." He pulled the door open for his friend to step inside the back porch where Harry Bauer sat waiting for them. At Grandpa's feet, Brody perked up when the screen door creaked.

"What are you boys talking about?" Grandpa asked, folding the Iron Harbor newspaper and laying it on the table beside his recliner. The table lamp shone on him from the chest down, his face in shadows, as if he were a cop leading an interrogation. "What in the world did you boys do to run those two sweet girls off in the first place?"

Taking a seat next to Ty on the porch sofa, Artie laughed. "What did *we* do?" said the big farm boy. "They dumped *us*. Right, Ty?" When his friend didn't speak up, Artie repeated, "Right . . . Ty?"

There was enough light on the porch to see the sheepish look on Ty Green's face. "Well . . . ," Ty began, "maybe I did do a *little* something I shouldn't have."

"Oh, Lord," said Grandpa, "what did you do? Run out of gas with some other little girl?"

Ty shook his head. "No, Grandpa," he said. "It wasn't anything like that. All I did was tell Nicie to go ahead and apply to Iron Harbor A&M—that the athletic director there had told me he could get Nicie a free ride, too, if I'd play both football and baseball for them. And she got mad about that."

"About you playing two sports?" asked Artie Bauer, hearing this for the first time.

"No," replied Ty, "she said she didn't want a scholarship *that* way—under the table. The A.D. said he could give me *two* scholarships for the two sports, and that I could give one scholarship to my girlfriend, even though it's a recruiting violation. He didn't know I was dating Nicie. He didn't care who she was or that she's a great athlete on her own."

Grandpa nodded. "Well, I don't blame her," he said. "That's a slap in the face—like she doesn't deserve any consideration other than being your girl. And what if you two broke up? Then where would she be? I guess you could take that *free ride* away from her and give it to somebody else."

Artie laughed. "Yeah," he said, "even though Nicie's dad is giving *you* a free ride right now—at least until he gets *The Whale* fixed for you." He patted Brody's head and added, "Besides, Ty, you've never wanted to go to A&M— and especially not now with State interested in you. But that doesn't solve your problem choosing between college and the pros."

"No, it doesn't," said Ty, "but since we're playing *True Confessions*, Artie, how about telling us why a nice girl like Julia dumped you. Wouldn't you like to know that, Grandpa?"

"Indeed I would," Harry Bauer said. "I really like that girl. She's a lot like my Pearl was back when we were courting—speaks her mind and doesn't put up with any guff. So, let's hear your story, son."

Artie shifted his position on the sofa so that he could look out the row of porch windows toward the highway in the distance. Every so often a pair of headlights would glide in one direction or the other along Ebenezerville Road just below the dark, tree-lined horizon. "It's like I said," Artie replied. "I didn't do anything. I mean, I . . ."

"Well, maybe that's why she broke up with you, buddy," said Ty, trying not to laugh. "Maybe she *wanted* you to do something. I could've loaned you *The Whale* if that old red pickup was the problem."

"Hey," said Grandpa, "that's my pickup truck you're talking about. Ain't nothing wrong with her. Drove that baby right off the showroom floor at E-ville Motors eighteen years ago this July, and she still runs like a top—as long as you don't let her run out of gas." He winked at his grandson.

"Eighteen years ago?" Artie asked. "So, that was the summer after I was born, right? And when my mother was still around?"

"It was," said Grandpa, nodding. "We were celebrating new additions to the family. Yep, things were going good—you were a big, healthy baby; and I had me a nice, new truck." Then he slapped his knee and added, "Of course, I never would've guessed I'd still be driving the old girl now and that she might even end up being your graduation present—if you play your cards right."

Artie smiled. "And if you can find yourself something new to drive, huh?" he said. "Hey, maybe *The Luuuvvv Truck* will be available then, after Ty's back to driving *The Whale*—or when he signs a big contract and buys himself a fancy sports car."

"Nice try, pal," said Ty, "but let's get back to the original question: Why did a pretty Russian girl like Julia Safin dump a nice guy like you, Artie Bauer? Huh?"

Looking back out into the darkness, Artie was quiet for a few seconds. He caught sight of a blue light moving at high speed on the highway toward Ebenezerville. The cruiser's siren was barely audible with the windows closed to the chilly night air. "The question should be: Why did she ever start dating somebody like me to begin with?" said Artie, smiling sadly. "Nah, it happened after the Friday we played Solid Rock in E-ville—our first conference game, remember?"

"Yeah," said Ty, growing animated. "We were really excited about going up against Mike after everything we'd heard about him, and I was pumped about facing Jimmy again this season." Ty smacked a fist into his palm, adding, "And when we beat them, I *knew* we could win the conference."

"Well, that was the weekend of Julia's first big tennis tournament," explained Artie. "It was in Capital City, and she wanted me to drive up on Saturday, to spend the whole day up there watching her play—maybe even spend the night and go—"

"See there," said Ty. "I *told* you she want—"

Artie shook his head. "No, no, no," he said, glancing over at Grandpa. "That wasn't the plan. She just wanted me to be there . . . and I couldn't be there. I had too much work to do here, and you guys on the team wanted to get together at Woody's that Saturday night to celebrate. Remember?"

Now Harry Bauer spoke up. "Come on now, son," said Grandpa. "All you had to do was ask me and Ricardo and little Ricky to cover for you that day, or even the whole weekend. Everybody deserves some time off now and then, and the good Lord knows you've earned it."

"Well, I didn't feel comfortable doing that, Grandpa," said Artie, "and when Julia and I talked on the phone that Friday night—after the game—I told her so. I also said I felt funny about driving our truck up there to that fancy tennis center and sitting there in the stands with all those rich folks—me, a big fat hick who didn't belong there. What was I gonna wear? My Sunday overalls and plaid shirt?" He couldn't help but smile at the mental image.

"You have nice clothes, boy," said Grandpa, growing irritated. "Me and Pearl have seen to that ever since you were a tyke."

"You're right, Grandpa, and I'm sorry," Artie said, "but if I had stayed all day and then spent the night, where would I have slept? In the truck? I couldn't have afforded even a cheap motel, and Wilma Marecek's mom shares a room with Julia as her chaperone. That would've been . . . embarrassing."

Artie could feel his face grow hot from having to explain his awkwardness with beautiful Julia, his first real girlfriend. "Not to mention," Artie added, looking at his best friend and teammate, "I really did want to celebrate with you guys. I mean, you and I are team captains. We've played ball together since we were kids. How would it have looked if I hadn't been at Woody's with everybody that night."

Shaking his head, Ty reached out and patted his friend's shoulder. "I understand, bud," Ty said, "but we're gonna have to work on your confidence— with girls, anyway—before you go off to college in the fall. Right, Grandpa?"

"Darn tootin'," the old man said. "I bet you hurt that sweet girl's feelings, not giving her the attention she deserved. Sounds like having you there at that tennis thing was important to her."

"It was," said Artie, "and later on, she told me that I really *had* hurt her. She said being away so much is lonely for her, always having to travel to tournaments. Still, that's her goal—to be a professional tennis player—and she has to give it her best shot. I understand that because I have a goal, too—to help you make this farm more profitable, Grandpa. But Julia said our goals are pulling us apart, at least for the time being. That's why we're just friends now."

Right then, the screen door came open, and Tommy White stepped inside the back porch. "Did you guys hear the siren a few minutes ago?" he asked. "It was a sheriff's car flying up the highway. Me and Ricky went outside to check, and I think they turned onto Little Swamp Road—sounded like they headed in that direction, anyway. I wonder where they were going."

Tommy's information bothered Ty Green, as he lived near there. He stood to leave and held up his hand to Artie and Grandpa. "I'd better get going," Ty said. "If I find out what's going on, I'll give you guys a call. If I don't call, everything's okay."

"No news is good news," said Grandpa. He motioned for Ty to hold on for one second. "Before I forget, I want all three of you boys to hear this," he said. "Speaking of getting phone calls, I got one this afternoon from Marty Quinn. I don't know where he was calling from, 'cause he said it was already night there. He said he was just thinking about ol' Brody here, wondering how his good boy's doing being a farm dog." Brody's ears perked up at the mention of his name.

"I hope you boys don't mind me doing this," continued Grandpa, "but I asked Marty what he did with Tommy's notebook that Sunday after he was here. I told him that the sheriff claims it never got to Iron Harbor. Well, Marty said that's a lie. He turned it in and did the paperwork himself. So, something fishy is going on, but he said to hold off on doing anything until he gets back home— whenever that is."

Harry Bauer reached down and rubbed Brody's back, smoothing down his thick coat. "I had one other question for Marty," said Grandpa. "I asked him what kind of dog ol' Brody is. Now, I didn't mean a German Shepherd; I meant what's he trained to do—sniff out drugs or bombs or guns, or attack bad guys, or what?" He stopped for a second and petted the dog's head.

"Marty said this boy is trained to find people," Grandpa continued, "not as a regular tracking dog, like a bloodhound, but one they use to find lost folks, like after tornadoes and hurricanes and earthquakes. The last time Marty used him was doing search and rescue after the Good Friday Storm. Marty also said Brody *isn't* an attack dog, but he'll protect you if need be—like any German Shepherd worth his keep would."

Again, Ty said his goodbyes and promised to call if the blue light and siren turned out to be anything important. As they watched him jog down the sidewalk and then toward the barn where his little truck was parked, Tommy said what was on Artie's mind. "Darn it," said Tommy. "I was hoping Brody could help us find any drug stashes Dad could have hidden out there—not to go into business ourselves, but to get rid of it."

"Where would he have hidden something?" asked Artie Bauer. "I mean, unless it's hidden in that chimney or maybe in a foundation of the house or barn, it would've burned up in the fires, right?"

Grandpa Bauer laughed. "You'd be surprised where folks can hide things out in these swamps," he said. "I knew one old fellow who didn't trust the savings and loan in town—called it the Jesse James Bank. He'd get his and his old wife's monthly checks cashed, and then he'd stick the money in a Mason jar and keep it under their mattress until the jar was full. Then he'd bury it somewhere on his farm—but without telling his wife where it was buried."

He chuckled again. "Things went on like that for a few years," Grandpa continued, "and the old guy would dig up a jar now and then if they needed money to buy something. Then, wouldn't you know it, he got forgetful—senile, we used to call it—and he couldn't remember where a single jar was buried to save his life. They couldn't pay their light bill or buy food, and the sheriff was about to haul them off to the poor house when a big storm came. It rained for three days and two nights. And durned if Mason jars didn't start popping up all over that old man's farm—everywhere he'd buried them over the years."

"Why's that, Grandpa?" asked Tommy White. "Why would the jars pop up like that?"

"High water table," Grandpa said. "Like I told you yesterday, the ground out near the swamps is so saturated—the water is so close to the top of the ground—

that things that are buried will pop up, like septic tanks in yards and coffins in cemeteries and, yeah, Mason jars full of money on a senile old man's farm. It was like an Easter egg hunt for that poor fellow's old wife, finding all those jars of cash sticking up out of the ground—or maybe it was like Christmas morning. He died not long after that."

They had a good laugh and got up from their seats on the porch to get ready for bed. No phone calls came, whether from Ty Green or anyone else with news of any sort. Artie was glad that the sheriff's cruiser he had seen wasn't responding to anything directly involving his best friend, but still he feared that—like in Grandpa's story of the Mason jars—something long hidden from sight might soon pop up and surprise everyone.

CHAPTER 19

THE BARF TABLE TEENS TOOK TURNS working a special booth in the cafeteria on Monday, selling the *We Are Solid Rock Strong* T-shirts that Deborah Pressler had ordered for all four high schools. Like the uniform patches worn after the Good Friday Storm, the shirts bore the storm-recovery logo and motto created by Ricky Duran, Kimi Inouye and Tommy White. Arbor's T-shirts were green with gold trim, just as Iron Harbor, Port Oleander and Mimosa Beach sold shirts in their own school colors to raise as much money as possible for recovery efforts. When head cheerleader Vicki Duke saw the T-shirt booth, she suggested that the school call the next day's games "Senior Green-Out Day," and she offered to have her squad sell shirts in the stands to parents and other supporters in attendance.

Vicki still hadn't fully recovered from the concussion she had suffered just over a week earlier at Woody's Grill. Still, she couldn't help but do little jumps and squeals when Artie Bauer invited her to take the last empty chair at the Barf Table, no longer the place for misfits. Even Nicie Evans laughed and told Vicki to come sit next to her, Wilma Marecek and Julia Safin, who were the other senior girls seated there. Taking her own turn in the booth that Monday, Vicki sold T-shirts to all her cheerleaders, Miss Thelma Hopper, Principal Jerry Church, coaches Jug Johnson and Joe Carson, and—to the toughest customer of all—the cafeteria's death-metal cashier, Frankie Hughes. Artie Bauer quickly saw how much better it was to have Vicki Duke working *for* the Barf Table than against it.

"Girl, you need to do that for a living," Nicie said, as the cheerleader came back to her seat.

"What?" said Vicki, looking happy but confused. "Sell T-shirts?"

Nicie smiled. "No, just sales, in general," she said. "You're a natural salesperson. If you worked at the surf shop with us, you'd have everybody on Sandpiper Beach wearing Woody's T-shirts and caps in a week."

"I wish I could get a fun job like that," said Vicki. "This will be the first year I'll be able to work a good job all summer long, because I won't have to go to any cheerleading camps."

Wilma Marecek leaned forward to look past Nicie. "Aren't you going to cheer in college, Vicki?" asked Wilma. "A&M—that's where I'm going—they have a great cheerleading squad."

Vicki shook her head. "No," she said. "Miss Hopper says I should go to community college first and get an associate's degree. That may be all I need, to do what I want to do."

"What's that?" asked Nicie Evans.

"Fixing hair and doing makeup," Vicki said. "I'm already pretty good at it. I do all my girls' hair and makeup when we go to cheerleading competitions. It makes a big difference, you know. When you look good, you feel good about yourself. You're more confident."

Artie Bauer agreed with self-assured Vicki Duke, but didn't say so out loud. Through their senior year, Artie had watched the popular, pretty girl grow from being a shallow gold-digger to being a kinder, more empathetic classmate. Her growth had suffered setbacks—mainly due to the bad influence of old boyfriend Josh Stark—but she was always a leader on the school campus for better or worse. That's why Artie was willing to bet that making Vicki one of the gang would pay off sooner or later. *Maybe her self-confidence will rub off on me*, he thought.

"You could even have your own business," Artie told Vicki. "That's what I want to do, too."

She looked confused again. "You, Artie?" she said. "You're interested in cosmetology?"

He laughed. "No," he said, "but I *would* like to run my own business. It's called agri-business and agri-tourism, actually—you know, out on my grandpa's farm."

"With all that pretty land," said Vicki, "you could be a developer like Mr. Stark, Josh's dad. I bet your farm would make a pretty golf course. That's what Mr. Stark does. He turns old farms into nice golf courses and big housing developments. He's a good businessman and makes a lot of money."

She seemed sincere, so Artie didn't snap at her. "If I played golf, it might be different," he said, "but Grandpa and I are into cows and chickens and corn and hay—*that* kind of farm business."

"And horses," added Wilma Marecek. "Don't forget the horses out there, Artie Bauer. That's *my* family's business—or my aunt's, anyway."

Nicie Evans laughed. "Then I guess *my* family's business is cars," she said, "even though Daddy's the only one who messes with them. All I do is drive the fun ones." She looked over at Ty Green, who was working in the T-shirt booth right then. "I may keep *The Luuuvvv Truck* for myself after Daddy gets Ty's old car fixed up. It's the perfect size for a girl—the pickup truck, not *The White Whale*."

Artie considered asking Nicie if she and Ty were back in the *luuuvvv* business for keeps, but he decided not to chance messing things up for his best friend. Instead, he turned back to Vicki. "I was just wondering," he said, "what exactly does your father do for the health department, Vicki? I mean, what's *your* family's business?"

She giggled and said, "You know how you guys were always calling me *Digger*? Digger Duke?" Artie's face flushed, but he kept quiet. She went on, "Well, that's what my father does—he digs holes. They even call him *Digger Duke* at the county office. He handles permits, and that's how he knows who gets a permit and who doesn't. He digs holes on somebody's land. He fills the holes with water. And then he sees how long it takes for the water to drain out of the holes."

"Does he like doing that?" asked Artie. He noticed that she hadn't used the terms "septic tank" or "perc tests" to describe the type of permits that her father issued and the work he did.

"He must," she said, "because that's all he's ever done—for as long as I can remember, anyway. And Daddy's the head of his division. Well, he's the *only* person who works out of his office, but he likes it that way. He says he doesn't like people looking over his shoulder—unless it's me cutting his hair." She giggled again.

"About that, Vicki," said Wilma Marecek. "Did Miss Hopper really advise you *not* to apply to a four-year college? You could get a cheerleading scholarship somewhere and major in business."

Vicki nodded. "I know," she said, "but if I get my cosmetology license first, then I can work my way through college and major in anything I'm interested in—business or even education. Then I could *teach* cosmetology in a high school or at a community college, and run my own beauty salon at the same time." Wilma and Artie exchanged a surprised look.

"That's really smart, Vicki," said Artie. "Miss Hopper gave you some good advice. Maybe I *should* talk to her about my college plans."

"Oh," Vicki said, "she's the best, but she's under a lot of stress right now—after the car crash at the beach. I'm just glad I wasn't with Josh when he ran that stop sign in front of them." The girl's frown turned into a smile. "Did you hear?" she asked. "Skip Ross is out of the hospital now. He's doing so well. Miss Hopper says she might even bring him to our Senior Day tomorrow, if he's up to it. They make such a cute couple, don't they?"

Nicie Evans spoke up. "I think it's nice that Miss Hopper has someone," she said. "I remember when she first met Skip. It was at our homecoming dance last fall, wasn't it? Didn't he arrest—"

"So, Nicie," interrupted Artie, "I hear you and Ty are going to the prom together. Will your dad have *The Whale* ready by then?" He didn't want Nicie's reminder about the homecoming dance fiasco to become the topic of conversation and embarrass Vicki on her first day at the Barf Table.

"Huh?" Nicie said, looking daggers at Artie for a second. Then she must have realized why he had changed the subject. "Yeah, we're going together," she said, "but, no, Daddy's gonna find us a nice car to take. I told Ty Green that I'm not going to my senior prom in something called *The Luuuvvv Truck* or *The White Whale*. I want to go in style."

Vicki had a suggestion. "Maybe all of us seniors can go together," she said, "and rent us one of those stretch limos like they have down in Mimosa Beach."

Just then, Ty Green and Jimmy Gore walked up after finishing their shift at the T-shirt table. "I *like* that idea," said Jimmy Gore. "Then me and Kimi can ride together, and her parents won't be upset about it. That solves one problem."

Not seated yet, Ty Green scrunched up his face. "Yeah, but that brings up a different problem," he said, nodding at Vicki. "Who are *you* going to the prom with? Your *real* date, not your *pretend* date, like Brett Woods was at homecoming. You aren't bringing Josh Stark to our prom, are you?"

Now Vicki Duke was embarrassed, and she almost started to cry. "I told you I was sorry about that," she said. "And, no, I would never bring Josh to the prom—not after he did that at the dance last fall and then left me on the floor at Woody's the other night. He doesn't care about me. I'm done with him." She sniffed and dabbed her eyes with a cafeteria napkin.

"*Ty Green*," said Nicie Evans, her eyes blazing, "would you please sit down and be quiet. Vicki knows better than to bring that boy around here again. He's nothing but trouble."

"You're right about that," Ty said, heading toward his chair, "about the trouble part, anyway. And I'm afraid we're gonna find out tomorrow exactly how much trouble he can be. Right, Artie?"

The big farm boy nodded and looked down at the empty soup bowl and almost-eaten grilled-cheese sandwich on his tray. Before taking the last bite, he said, "But if he tries to cause us trouble on our own diamond, Josh Stark is gonna find out what we mean by *Solid Rock Strong*."

* * *

Before softball and baseball practice that Monday afternoon, the Barf Table gang gathered in the newly constructed stands to touch base on final plans for Senior Day. They passed around copies of the special program that the storytellers group had prepared. On the front cover was the *We Are Solid Rock Strong* design; on the back, half-page advertisements for Woody's Surf Shops and Pressler's Department Stores, featuring pictures of the two teams. The pages inside contained action photos and casual pictures that Kimi Inouye had taken at recent ballgames, as well as detailed write-ups on each Arbor High senior team member. Coaches Jug Johnson and Joe Carson both had nice spreads that recognized their long coaching careers and their impending retirements—Jug, at the end of the state playoffs for the Bruins; and Joe, with Tuesday's game, since the Bruinettes softball season would end then.

"The stadium looks great, doesn't it?" Artie Bauer said to the group. "Mr. Church told me he had to get an electrician to come out here Saturday to fix the scoreboards. Now everything is back the way it was before the storm, if not better."

Leah Russo spoke up. "Bennie told me last night that he and his dad came over here yesterday afternoon and tested the PA system," she said. "He told me it was working great but that he had *a little surprise* for us. He wouldn't say what it was." She gave them an ominous look. "So, do you think I should find out before tomorrow?"

Artie laughed. "Yeah, maybe so," he said, "but if you think it's harmless, just let us be surprised. We trust your judgment, Leah. Right, guys?" Everyone agreed, though Leah's announcement did inject some unease, as Bennie Pressler's sense of humor sometimes rankled. At Arbor's last football game the previous fall, Bennie had played a certain sound clip over the PA that had so infuriated Joel Stark that he ran onto the field and disrupted the final minutes of the contest. That was also when Solid Rock football star Jimmy Gore had tackled the angry real estate developer to keep him from blindsiding Josh Stark, his own son, on the gridiron.

"Okay, well, does anyone else have anything to report?" Artie asked. "Music group . . . Brett? Are you guys all set for the National Anthem?"

Brett Woods stood up. "Yep," he said, "we sound good—on the anthem and on everything else, even though we'll be switching off between games."

"Great!" said Artie. "Dance group . . . Ricky? You're it, since Julia's at tennis practice."

On the bottom bleacher, Ricky Duran leapt to his feet and, before reporting, did a tight little spin like a pop singer. "We are ready to go!" the energetic boy announced. "Everyone has a handout to study tonight. It will be a surprise when we sign the National Anthem. My church is bringing a van with people from our deaf ministry. They will sign 'God Bless America' for our game. I can't wait!"

"Well, I'm excited," said Artie, "but kind of sad, too. This will be the last time all of us—I mean, guys and girls both—will have games together out here on these fields." He got quiet for a moment as he saw the others' smiles disappear. "Hey, I didn't mean to do that," he said, trying to find Vicki Duke among the softball girls. "Hey, Vicki, stand up a second. I have a question."

The pretty cheerleader and senior softballer popped up from behind big Wilma Marecek and waved at Artie. "Here I am," Vicki said. "What do you want to know, Artie?"

"Will you be pitching tomorrow?" he asked. "Are you well enough to play?"

She beamed. "Yes, I am!" she declared. "Coach Carson said he will start me in the circle, and he's gonna leave me in as long as I feel okay—and keep getting outs." She shrugged and laughed. "I don't blame him," she added. "We want to win! Right, girls?"

As one, the other Bruinettes shouted, "That's right!" Jamie Foxx and Leah Russo—the team's other regular pitchers—smiled at Vicki's enthusiasm.

"Okay, then," said Artie, preparing to end the meeting, "does anybody else have something to say? We're selling T-shirts again tomorrow at lunch, so this might be our last chance for all of us to talk before the games."

Jamie Foxx raised her hand and stood. "This is something on down the road," she began, "but last night when I got home, Mom told me about another fundraiser being planned—one we might be able to do something with. It's a benefit golf tournament at Sandpiper Shores. She heard about it the other day when Dad met with Joel Stark at the office. It was Dad's idea, believe it or not."

"What can we do?" asked Leah Russo. "None of us play golf."

Jamie shook her head. "I don't know," she said. "Sell T-shirts? Have a bake sale in the parking lot? From what Mom said, everybody who's anybody is gonna be there. It's a couple weeks off."

Artie nodded. "Thanks, Jamie," he said. "Everybody keep it in mind, and we'll come up with something to do there later—maybe at Sunday night's meeting. Okay? Let's have good practices and finish out this season right—I mean, finish the *regular* season right."

The big guy wondered if he had just jinxed the Bruins' chances in the state playoffs. But when no one else seemed to notice his slip of the tongue, he smiled and motioned for the others to go on to their separate clubhouses and get ready for their last regular-season practices with their beloved old coaches. Artie knew that Jug Johnson and Joe Carson were standing behind the Quonset hut-like batting cage, though not strategizing new plays or reordering their batting lineups to prepare for Hawthorn Military Academy the following day. Jug and Joe were undoubtedly getting in one last dip of smokeless tobacco and one last cigarette before their practices began. The two old friends could still enjoy each other's company after they retired, but it would always be off the field and away from the action—which would never again be the same.

* * *

After letting Ricky Duran out at the old homeplace after practice that night, Artie Bauer and Tommy White rode on down the lane to the farmhouse, where Minnie Marecek's white pickup was parked. As the boys strode up the sidewalk, they saw that Minnie sat alone on the back porch. Grandpa Bauer's old recliner was empty. Likewise, Brody was nowhere to be seen right then. But Artie opened the screen door and heard Grandpa's gruff voice coming from the kitchen. The big farm boy nodded to Minnie and started to say hello, but she held up her hand for him to be quiet.

"That's what my friend thought he was doing," said Grandpa, standing at the telephone in the kitchen. *"He did it twice at the cemetery—once at my wife's resting place and once at that scoundrel's grave in back—and he did it two more*

times on the old White farm." Artie peered through the kitchen door and saw that Brody sat at Grandpa's feet. The old man's brow was furrowed as he studied the drugstore calendar on the wall next to the phone and listened for several seconds.

"*No, sir, we haven't told anyone yet,*" Grandpa replied. "*The boys just drove up, and I'll tell them, of course, but I promise not to tell another soul—well, except for Abe Pressler, since he does own that property and he is the boy's guardian.*" He was quiet again. "*Okay, then. I'll ask Abe to wait until we hear back from you. Thank you for taking my call. This whole situation has us all worried. Goodbye, sir.*"

Artie and Tommy took seats on the porch sofa and waited for Grandpa to return to his recliner, but the old man and his dog headed into the bedroom off the kitchen first. "So, you and Grandpa went for a ride today?" Artie Bauer asked Minnie Marecek. "In your truck?"

"No," said Minnie, "on horseback, believe it or not. And, Artie, your grandfather did really well. He acted fifty years younger and was cutting up like a teenager—until we got to the church. Then Brody had a little surprise for us."

"What happened?" asked Tommy White, looking up as Grandpa Bauer opened the kitchen door and let Brody go to his spot on the rug next to the recliner.

Minnie replied, "That's what the phone call was about. I'll let Harry tell you." She got quiet and bent down to pet Brody while Grandpa got settled in his chair.

Harry Bauer scratched his head and took his time choosing the right words. "I'm not rightly sure how to say this, Tommy, but . . . ," said Grandpa, "we may have us a bit of a situation over on your old farm. That was Marty Quinn on the phone. I had a time reaching him, but we finally got a call through—wherever he is. Me and Minnie had another question about Brody here, and Marty just answered it."

Grandpa explained that he, Minnie and Brody had visited the Shin's Grove Church cemetery that afternoon, and that Brody had again sat up straight at the foot of Pearl Bauer's grave without being commanded to do so. "Minnie commented on it, just like we did the other day," said Grandpa, "but me and her didn't really think anymore about it until he did it again at *another* grave. I was taking Brody to the woods to do his business, when he just stopped, pretty as you please, and sat at attention again."

Harry noted that the second grave lay by itself toward the back of the cemetery and was basically unmarked, with only a temporary nameplate and spike from the funeral home at its head. The glass on the nameplate was cracked, he said, and the name and dates on the paper underneath had become illegible from rain and sun. "I used Minnie's phone and called the preacher," Grandpa went on. "He said *Luther Reep* was buried back there last December. That's right—our old friend, Rocket Reep."

Shifting position in the big chair, Grandpa continued, "Minnie said she seemed to remember that some dogs *alert* like that—by sitting up without being commanded to. That was when I put my first call in to the base up at Iron Harbor, to try and talk to Marty again about Brody—about what kind of lost people they used him to find." Grandpa's eyes got big. "Yep, Marty just now told me that Brody is what's called a *cadaver dog*. He finds *dead* people—like those poor folks who got killed near E-ville in the Good Friday Storm."

Grandpa let that information sink in for a moment, and then said, "So, this boy alerted for our sweet Pearl and then for mean ol' Rocket Reep." He smiled a bit. "I guess Brody doesn't judge 'em; he just finds 'em." He added that Marty Quinn had kept that bit of info from them earlier, because people often treated Brody differently once they heard the word *cadaver*.

"Harry had told me about Brody doing the same thing the other day at Tommy's beeyard," said Minnie Marecek. "I hope you don't mind, Tommy, but I suggested we ride over there and see how Brody acted today—if he'd do the same thing in the same places. And sure enough, he did." She didn't have to say anything else. All four of them now suspected that drugs and arson weren't the only illegal activities that had been covered up at the old White place.

"Now, Tom," said Grandpa, "we know you didn't have anything to do with what all went on over there back in the day, and maybe your mama and daddy didn't either. We don't know who's buried in that old beeyard or who put them there, and that's why we've got to be careful right now. Like your daddy said, asking too many questions of the wrong people can be dangerous. Do you understand?"

"That isn't what he said," Tommy replied, "but I understand, Grandpa. I was afraid of something like this coming up. Dad looked awful scared when he told me that—and not just for me, but for himself. I don't know if that means *he* killed somebody and he doesn't want to be charged with murder, or if he's afraid the killer might be after him, too."

Something occurred to Artie Bauer. "So, do you think Rocket Reep was the killer?" Artie asked. "I mean, other than killing dogs. You read what he wrote in your notebook, Tommy. Did he say anything about stuff that happened a long time ago?"

Tommy shook his head. "Not *that* long ago," he said, "but I wish we still had my old notebook. Knowing what I know now, some of the stuff he *did* write might make more sense. Any idea where it is?"

No one knew, but Grandpa volunteered, "That's something else Marty mentioned on the phone tonight. He'd made a couple calls this morning before we talked, and he tried to find out what happened to that notebook without making a big deal about it. He said, yep, it's gone—like he never took it up to Iron Harbor to begin with. That's another reason he says we need to watch our step. There's quicksand all around us—at least until we can find someone in law enforcement we can trust, like our friend Marty Quinn." Grandpa's steely eyes bespoke the seriousness of the situation.

The old man went on, "You boys need to keep this quiet. Not a word to your friends, no matter how much we trust them. Minnie isn't even gonna tell Wilma, so don't assume she knows anything at all about this. Like I told Marty, there's only one other person I'm gonna tell, and that's Abe Pressler. He's responsible for you, Tommy, and he's a good man who knows how to get things done the right way. He will know exactly what to do when the time comes to do it."

CHAPTER 20

ABE AND DEBORAH PRESSLER WERE BUSY helping the Barf Table gang and cheerleaders set up before Tuesday afternoon's games at the rebuilt Arbor High ball fields. While Bennie Pressler tested the public-address system by playing every baseball-themed song in his extensive collection of tapes and compact discs, his parents unloaded boxes of *We Are Solid Rock Strong* T-shirts from their SUV—green shirts for the Arbor faithful and neutral white ones for any sympathetic visitors from Hawthorn Military Academy. A good number of Blackhawks fans were expected for the doubleheader—if not for the softball game at five o'clock, then for the baseball game to begin around seven, about an hour before sunset. Mr. and Mrs. Joel Stark would be on hand to witness son Josh's personal homecoming at Arbor High, six months after their boy, acting like a drunken monkey, had ruined the high school's actual homecoming dance, as well as homecoming queen Vicki Duke's reputation.

As for the Arbor crowd, baseball parents—like the Durans, Greens, Inouyes, Woodses and Harry Bauer—arrived early for the softball game, to support the Bruinettes, too. Jimmy and Jenny Gore's mother, father and both sets of grandparents were there. Of course, the Dukes, Evanses, Foxxes—though sitting in separate sections—Minnie and Lena Marecek, and John Russo came to support their girls, but they planned to stay for the baseball game as well. Even Brody the German Shepherd was there, though his presence forced Grandpa Bauer and Minnie Marecek to sit in lawn chairs away from the stands. That was planned so that Grandpa could talk in private to Abe Pressler during the softball game. Later, that privacy was convenient for another guest of honor.

That guest was Oleander County Sheriff's Deputy Skip Ross. It was Senior Day, but the players who were to be honored and the Barf Table mates who were handling the entertainment all decided to share the spotlight with Deputy Ross, whose contributions to Arbor High's cultural life—at least where Josh Stark had been concerned—had been tremendous. The previous fall Ross had been the officer on duty at the ill-fated Arbor homecoming dance and the contentious Solid Rock-Arbor football game, and, in the interim, had responded to the Halloween night vandalism and assaults at the Bauer farm. Spoiled rich boy Josh Stark had been the main culprit in all three incidents, aided and abetted by his father. Skip Ross had learned the hard way not to give either Stark an inch of slack, as both father and son were used to grabbing the whole rope and hanging someone else with it. At the dance, the deputy had let higher ups talk him into going easy on the boy. At the football game—the last of the trio of events—Ross had taken both Starks into custody on the gridiron and escorted them both out of the stadium to gleeful chants from the Arbor crowd. From that night on, Thelma Hopper's soon-to-be boyfriend was a hero at Arbor High School.

On this April afternoon, Skip Ross was not in uniform, as he was still on leave from the sheriff's department. Ross wore a light-blue, button-down shirt, open at the neck, with nice khaki slacks. He also sported a black sling for his injured shoulder, held a cane in the opposite hand, and wore a bulky brace around his cracked ribs. Still, in perky Miss Hopper's eyes, her beau might as well have been a knight in gleaming armor. In fact, she was perkier and happier than Artie Bauer had ever seen her.

"Skip and I can't wait to see you all perform the National Anthem," Miss Hopper told Artie and the other Barf Table teens. They had gathered behind the metal batting cage for a last run-through, and the guidance counselor had hunted them down. "I just want to make sure that Bennie doesn't use that ghastly *Barf Table* name when he introduces you to the crowd," she continued. "He should call you our *expressive arts group leaders*. Artie, will you tell Bennie for me so that Skip and I can find our seats?"

Artie nodded. "Sure, Miss Hopper," he said. "I'll do that right now. Bennie's up in the press box." He gave the deputy a wave and added, "Good to see you here, Officer Ross."

"Thanks, Artie," said the officer. "I'm glad to be here." He reached out to shake Artie's hand. "By the way, is your grandfather coming tonight? I need to talk to him about something important that just came to my attention."

"Yes, sir, he is," Artie said. "Grandpa and Minnie Marecek are sitting in lawn chairs over in the grass between the diamonds." He felt he needed to explain. "Grandpa brought his dog," he continued. "He figured Brody might scare some people if they sat in the stands."

"That's what I need to speak with Harry about," said Ross. "No, I'm not on duty. This is personal. My friend Marty Quinn called me last night." The deputy checked to make sure that no one, not even his girlfriend, was listening in. She had turned to encourage the other teens. Still, the injured man leaned on his cane closer to Artie and said, "It's about Brody—what he can do—and about a missing notebook. You know what I'm talking about, right?"

Again, Artie nodded. "I do," he said, "and, Officer Ross, you can talk in front of Miss Minnie—I mean, Dr. Marecek. Grandpa and her are friends, and she saw Brody, uh, do what he did. You know?"

"Yes," Ross said, "Marty told me that Dr. Marecek noticed the behavior." He glanced at Thelma Hopper and saw that she was paying attention to him again. "So, okay then, good luck on the diamond tonight. Go, Bruins!" He tried to raise his free arm to cheer, but the cane got in the way.

"Thanks, Officer Ross," said Artie. "I need all the luck I can get—especially singing the National Anthem in a few minutes. I hope I don't run off too many spectators." Artie grinned and said, "Speaking of running, I'd better run and deliver Miss Hopper's message to Bennie. Now, you two enjoy yourselves." The farm boy—already wearing his Arbor Bruins home pinstripes—waved again and took off toward the press box.

* * *

The National Anthem went off without a hitch prior to the softball game. Like an old-time string band, the Barf Table ukulele players—Brett Woods, Nicie

Evans, Jimmy Gore and Jamie Foxx—stood in a semi-circle behind two mic stands that Bennie Pressler had set up between home plate and the backstop. The gang's storytellers, including Artie Bauer, stood behind the uke players to help sing. The dancers spread out on each side of the musicians to sign "The Star-Spangled Banner." Julia Safin, outfitted as Bruno the mascot, stood behind them in the pitcher's circle and held Old Glory high to let the red, white and blue banner wave in the late April breeze and sunshine. The song's final strains faded into the capacity crowd's show of appreciation, not only for America but for these future leaders. The smiling fans took their seats, and the Barf Table teens hurried off the field to get ready for the next part of the pregame festivities.

"Welcome back, fans, to Arbor High's newly renovated softball and baseball fields," announced Bennie Pressler, his voice echoing throughout the athletic complex. *"Before we introduce our seniors—on both the softball and baseball teams—we want to take a minute to recognize the newest members of our Arbor Charter High School family—our sisters and brothers, parents and friends from Ebenezerville's Solid Rock Christian Academy. Harvesters, please stand so that we Bruins may acknowledge your recent loss and yet express our joy that you have become a part of our Arbor High community."* Bennie paused for effect, then said, *"Truly, on these diamonds today, we are Solid Rock strong."* The crowd's response began as polite clapping, but quickly grew in intensity as young Harvesters and Bruins alike—all wearing Arbor green—cheered as one body.

When the applause began to subside, Bennie recognized the *"expressive arts group leaders,"* as Miss Hopper had recommended. *"Weren't they great?"* said Bennie. *"And they'll be performing for us all evening, so get ready for more great entertainment. And remember—Arbor High students—that our new support groups meet every Wednesday afternoon during 4th period. We hope to see you there!"*

On behalf of the Arbor High administration, Bennie went on to thank members of both schools and communities that had helped repair the stadium's storm damage or in some other way had made the hundred-plus Solid Rock students' transition to Arbor as smooth as possible. Then he introduced the Bruinettes and Bruins, as well as their retiring coaches. Joe Carson and his softball girls assembled from home plate up the line to third base; Jug Johnson and his baseball boys lined up from home to first. One by one, each senior honoree stepped forward as Bennie read an abbreviated version of their profile from the special game program. Some of them dabbed their eyes—Jug Johnson certainly did when his boys' turns came—as their parents and classmates heard about each player's plans for the future. Again, there were scattered shouts from the stands when Bennie read that Bruins pitcher Ty Green had not yet decided whether to attend college or play pro ball. Artie Bauer knew that his best friend was still waiting to hear something definite from State College. Artie couldn't imagine what the college was waiting on.

Before the players left the field, Bennie Pressler announced, *"Today, the administration of Arbor Charter High School recognizes the distinguished careers of two very special coaches—Bruinettes softball and basketball coach Joseph Carson, and Bruins baseball, wrestling and football coach, the one and only, Arky 'Jug' Johnson. Let's give them both a round of applause."* Doffing their ball caps to the crowd, the two old coaches stepped forward at home plate.

Artie noticed the two friends turn and look at each other as if neither man had an idea of what was coming next. *"Joe and Jug,"* continued Bennie Pressler, *"in honor of your many years of dedication and service to the young people of Oleander County, Arbor High School hereby renames this diamond as Joe Carson Field and, next to us on the baseball side, Jug Johnson Field. Our sincere thanks, coaches, for everything you've done for us."* Artie smiled as Jug took out a folded handkerchief to dry his eyes.

But Bennie wasn't done. *"And today, folks, we have one more special person to recognize—our guest of honor, Oleander County Sheriff's Deputy Skip Ross. As we all know, Officer Ross was injured in an automobile accident. . . ."* Bennie's pause for polite applause gave Artie a few moments to scan the stands, but he couldn't find Joel Stark and his wife seated there. Artie did know that Hawthorn Military's baseball team and their star pitcher, Josh Stark, hadn't arrived yet, so he assumed that Josh's parents weren't there, either.

Bennie Pressler continued, "*. . . and we're fortunate to have this fine public servant here with us today. This year, in particular, Officer Ross has helped make Arbor High School a better and safer place for everyone, and for that we say a huge thank you.*"

When the applause faded, Bennie invited the deputy, with Miss Hopper's help, to come onto the field to address the crowd. Artie Bauer was pleased but confused when the couple were met on-field at the mic stands by Brett Woods and Bruno—Julia Safin, in costume—especially when the mascot lowered one of the mics to about three feet. Brett, still holding his ukulele from his group's earlier performance, readjusted the other microphone so that he could play and sing into it. But then he stepped aside to let Skip Ross speak.

"*Can everybody hear me?*" the deputy asked, his lips almost touching the mic. "*Good. Thank you for this honor—to be able to share this big day for the seniors here on the field with Thelma and me. It has been my pleasure to watch them grow as leaders this year. So let's give them all a big hand again.*"

Skip stopped for a few seconds while people clapped, though he himself couldn't because of his sling and cane. "*There* is *one favor I'd like to ask, if you'll indulge me for a minute longer,*" he continued, "*but I'll need a little help from my good buddy Brett Woods and then from our favorite bear, Bruno the Bruin.*" Using his cane to steady himself, the deputy moved a couple of steps away. Miss Hopper started to follow him, but Bruno held out one mitten-like paw to stop her. The mascot motioned with its other paw for the guidance counselor to turn toward Brett, as he began plucking the strings of his ukulele.

It took fewer than six notes of the familiar introduction for folks in the stands to know what was coming and to cheer in anticipation. As Brett Woods sang the opening words—"*I've got sunshine*"—Ty Green, Ricky Duran and Mike Inouye, all members of the dance group, took positions behind him. Brett played and sang the beach music classic, while his teammates danced and sang "*hey, hey, hey*" and "*my girl*" in all the right places. By the end of the tune, Bruno had danced solo all the way around the group and now stood at Skip Ross's side as

Brett Woods strummed the song's closing chords and crooned its last, staccato *"my girl."* Beginning to see the light, Artie Bauer was glad that he hadn't joined the dance-therapy group. If he had, Miss Hopper might never have forgiven him.

With Bruno's help, Skip Ross got down on one knee and knelt in front of Thelma Hopper. *"I love you, Thelma,"* he said, into the lowered mic, letting everyone in the complex hear his proposal. *"Will you marry me—and be* my girl *forever?"*

An impromptu chorus of squeals and *awwww*'s came from the girls along the third-base line. The boys on the first-base side—even Artie—stood in shocked silence, but then they all *whoop*'d and clapped with the rest of the crowd when Thelma Hopper said, *"Oh, yes, Skip—with all my heart. Yes."* Artie Bauer turned to say something to his coach, but said nothing when he saw that old Jug Johnson's ruddy face was buried in his handkerchief once again.

* * *

The Arbor Bruinettes—with an 8-7 overall record going into Tuesday's game—played their hearts out and beat the Hawthorn Lady Blackhawks. As good as his word, Coach Joe Carson started senior Vicki Duke at pitcher, and, surprisingly, she hurled—but in a good way—her best game of the season despite giving up a run in the third inning. When Carson went to the pitcher's circle to calm Vicki down, she mentioned that she'd been seeing double for the last few batters. He immediately pulled her for his number-one pitcher, Jamie Foxx. Instead of simply turning Vicki over to her family, Joe called Dr. Kato Inouye down from the stands to look at the girl—a measure that eased her parents' worries. On the doctor's advice, anxious Victor Duke agreed to drive Vicki to the emergency room in Ebenezerville for tests and, if necessary, treatment. Duke and his pretty wife—a full-figured version of their daughter—helped Vicki from the stadium to an ovation from the crowd.

When the game resumed, Jamie Foxx pitched one-hit ball for the next three innings, striking out five Lady Blackhawks batters. Leah Russo, the team's youngest and third-best pitcher, relieved Jamie in the seventh inning and closed out the game to ensure both another victory and a winning season for the

Bruinettes in the last game of their beloved coach's career. The final score was 4-1, with seniors Nicie Evans, Mel Grayson and Wilma Marecek, and junior Jamie Foxx scoring the team's runs. As if the Arbor softballers had won the conference championship instead of finishing with a 9-7 record, the Bruinettes carried Joe Carson off the field, with the three seniors doing most of the heavy lifting—something not even they could have done if he were as big as his buddy Jug Johnson. Carson had to be proud not only of his girls' late-season winning streak, but also of the way they had improved throughout the spring.

While the two schools' baseball teams warmed up with infield and batting practice on the other diamond, most of the fans milled about in the concession area between the separate fields. Once when Artie Bauer was getting ready to take his practice turn at the plate, he glanced over and saw that Minnie Marecek was walking Brody on a short leash while Skip Ross sat in her lawn chair and talked to Harry Bauer. During the earlier softball game, Artie had noticed Grandpa and Minnie talking privately to Abe Pressler, with all three of them petting the dog at times throughout their conversation. Artie looked forward to finding out what Abe and Skip thought about Brody alerting at the two spots in Tommy's old beeyard. But right then, the Bruins' upcoming battle with Hawthorn Military and Josh Stark came first.

As arranged by the Durans, members of the deaf ministry at Solid Rock Christian Church signed "America the Beautiful" while the Barf Table girls sang it before the two baseball teams' starting lineups were introduced. Led by music group members Nicie Evans and Jamie Foxx, the other singers were Leah Russo, Wilma Marecek, Kimi Inouye and Jenny Gore. Exchange student Julia Safin stayed in costume as Bruno the flag-bearing Bruin.

"For the first time ever, folks," announced Bennie Pressler from the press box, *"welcome to Jug Johnson Field for tonight's game between the Hawthorn Military Academy Blackhawks . . . ."*—with a long pause to acknowledge some polite applause but also scattered boos—*". . . and your very own Arbor High Bruins, champions of the Suncoast Conference!"* He stopped as the home fans stood and cheered.

"Here are tonight's starting lineups," Bennie continued. *"First, for the visiting Blackhawks . . . ."* He ran down the Hawthorn batting order, noting that starting pitcher Josh Stark would bat for himself in the leadoff spot. Putting on his catcher's gear in the home dugout, Artie Bauer heard more jeering when the former Arbor and Solid Rock athlete was announced, but the catcalls subsided when Bennie went on with the visiting lineup, which would come to bat first.

"Starting in the field for the home-standing Bruins," said Bennie, *"at catcher, senior co-captain Artie 'Yogi' Bauer."* The farm boy winced as he left the dugout and jogged toward the umpire in blue at home plate. Coach Johnson must have gotten to Bennie before the game and told him to use players' nicknames in the pregame introductions, Artie figured. But, no, this turned out to be Bennie's *real* surprise that Leah had hinted about Monday afternoon. She hadn't said anything else about it to Artie, though.

For whatever reason, Bennie Pressler had decided unilaterally to use nicknames for every player in the Bruins lineup. Later, Bennie claimed that he hadn't done it to cause trouble, and he added that he *had* told Leah Russo about his plans that morning. After *co-captain Artie "Yogi" Bauer*, there was *Tommy "The Drone Ranger" White (or "Buzz," for short)* at first base; *Ricky "The Shooter" Duran* at second; *Brett "The Pele of the Ukulele" Woods* at third; *Ozzie "The Wizard" Maye* at shortstop; *Jimmy Gore, "The Solid Rock Sledgehammer,"* in left field, *"or anywhere he darn well wants to play,"* Bennie added; also, *Manny "The Man" Freeman* in center, and *Mike "The Missile" Inouye* in right, starting for injured senior *Johnny "Smitty" Smith. . . .*

That left only the starting pitcher to be introduced, and this was where Bennie Pressler made his big mistake. The outfielders were still headed toward their positions when, in Bennie's best PA voice, he came out with, *". . . and on the mound tonight, the Bruins' all-time winningest pitcher, senior co-captain Ty 'The Luuuvvv Machine' Green."*

As soon as those words boomed over the loudspeakers, Artie Bauer removed his facemask and headed straight for the mound to intercept his best friend. Ty was already fuming as he approached. He reached the pitching rubber and kicked it twice even though there was no dirt on it. Artie said, "That wasn't me. I didn't tell *anyone* what you told me. Bennie is just trying to be funny."

Ty took off his cap and turned his back to the crowd, as if he were trying to locate the resin bag. "Well, if you didn't tell him," said Ty, into his cap, "I know who did. It was either Nicie or another one of those girls." He shook his head and muttered, "Makes me sound like an idiot." He put his cap back on.

"Come on now," Artie said. "We've got a game to play. And Josh Stark is up first." Artie turned and saw the umpire on his way to the mound, as if he were breaking up an in-game conference. "Let it slide, Ty," said Artie, starting to head back to the plate. "Bennie didn't mean anything by it. He looks up to you. You know that." Ty continued to mutter as Artie walked away.

The big catcher hoped that his battery mate would settle down during his ten to twelve warmup pitches, but the first one was as hard as the last, and not a single one was in the strike zone. Artie Bauer knew that was a bad sign—that Ty Green wasn't focused and didn't have his usual control. Artie was afraid that Ty wasn't thinking about facing Josh Stark and the Blackhawks, but instead about losing face with girlfriend Nicie Evans, her parents and her friends. Some fans had, in fact, laughed at Bennie's introduction of *The Luuuvvv Machine*; however, Artie had also heard a chorus of *oooooo*'s from the section of stands where the softball girls, including Nicie, sat. When he turned to watch Josh Stark walk from the on-deck circle to the plate, Artie glanced into the stands and saw that Nicie was smiling and seemed to be having fun with her teammates, as if Bennie's use of the couple's pet name for Ty hadn't bothered her a bit. Artie wondered if perhaps she *had* given Bennie the nickname on purpose—to declare their renewed love in front of her parents and friends.

"Ready to get your butt kicked, fat boy?" said Josh Stark, as he stepped into the batter's box on the right side of the plate. After adjusting his batting gloves and helmet, he dug footholds in the red clay with his cleats and swung his bat in lazy loops until Ty Green nodded and set himself to pitch. "The Love Machine better bring some heat," said Josh, "or I'm taking him yard."

"You mean like Jimmy did you at Solid Rock?" Artie shot back, careful to quit talking when Ty went into his windup. He didn't want the umpire to call him for distracting the batter, even though a catcher chattering behind the plate during an at-bat wasn't against the rules. Artie was afraid that this ump might try to enforce some unwritten code of his own. He was hoping that, if anything, his buddy's first pitch would be as wild as his warm-up throws had been, and brush big-mouthed Josh Stark back.

But that first pitch was a run-of-the-mill fastball right down the middle, as if Ty Green had hoped to improve his accuracy by backing off his velocity. *I should've called a screwball*, thought Artie Bauer, as Josh Stark uncorked a line drive that rose and rose toward Mike Inouye in right field. Tracking the ball, Mike backed up until he reached the dirt warning track, and there he turned to watch the white sphere sail into the green trees standing between the outfield fence and the highway to Ebenezerville. Three little boys playing outside the fence chased after the ball.

Josh had stopped a couple of steps from the batter's box to watch his home run leave the ballpark. Then, flipping his bat, he looked back at Artie and sneered. "Yeah, just like that," Josh said, pointing with both hands across the diamond at his Hawthorn teammates in the visiting dugout as he hopped into low gear and began a slow, home-run trot around the bases. Later, Artie learned that Josh had shared choice words with every Bruins infielder he passed. When Josh finished his trek, he jumped with both feet on home plate like a child splashing in a mud puddle, and then he stopped and bowed at the waist to Artie and the ump.

"That's enough," the man in blue said to Josh. "You're holding up the game." The umpire had already handed Artie a new ball, but the Bruins catcher had held it until Josh was off the base paths. He tossed the ball to his pitcher and tried not to watch Josh anymore as the showboat skipped toward the Blackhawks celebrating in their dugout. One pitch into the game, the score was Hawthorn 1, Arbor 0.

The next batter was the Blackhawks shortstop, a short, wiry boy whose batting average was twenty points higher than Josh Stark's and whose speed made him a stolen-base threat in any league. Annoyed over having given up the leadoff home run, Ty Green threw the shortstop three straight balls and got more upset with himself. Artie motioned for Ty to calm down and just get the 3-and-0 pitch across the plate to stay alive in the count. That would have been a good plan, except that the Hawthorn batter swung away instead of taking the pitch, as most batters would do early in a game with no runners on base. Without Josh Stark's size and strength, the righty-batting shortstop pulled the ball toward left field, bouncing it to the corner where Jimmy Gore had a hard time running it down before the speedy batter reached third base.

"Time out," Artie called. He looked toward the home dugout and saw that Jug Johnson also was headed toward the mound. Jug, though, waved for the infielders to stay put instead of coming in to hear what he would say to the flustered pitcher. Artie knew this would not be a strategy meeting.

Ty Green's head was down, as the catcher and coach arrived on the hill. "I know, I know," said Ty. "I'm thinking too much. But I threw a fastball. That was the sign."

Artie could have come back with, But it wasn't a very *good* fastball; however, he knew to let Coach Johnson do the talking. "That's right, son," said Jug, "and any other batter would've taken that pitch for a first strike. And, yeah, you *are* thinking too much—about the wrong stuff. Get your head in the game, son. Don't worry about that college coach up in the stands." That was a surprise to both Ty and Artie—that State College's baseball coach was in attendance.

Lifting his head to look Jug Johnson in the eyes, Ty Green didn't have to say anything to express his frustration with the situation. Jug continued, "Don't give me that look. For four years now, I've heard you talk about that hero of yours—ol' Iron Mike, isn't it?—how *he said this* and *he said that* about how to exercise and how to throw screwballs and what's important out here on the diamond. Well, didn't he also say that what's *most* important is playing your best? Didn't he say that?"

Ty nodded, but dropped his head again. "Well, then, son," said Coach Johnson, "I just have one question for you, and then we'll get this show back on the road." Jug paused. "But look up here at me—hurry, the ump's headed this way."

The young pitcher raised his head, glancing at the approaching ump first, then at his best friend, Artie, and finally at his old coach. Jug studied the tall, strong boy's expression for a moment, then asked, "Are you ready to start playing your best now? I've got all the confidence in the world in you, Ty Green, and so does Yogi here." A mischievous grin creeped across the old man's face. "And, evi-*dang*-dently, so does that pretty girl sitting up there in the stands. I heard her say, 'That's right. That's my man,' when you was introduced. So, how about showing us some of what you learned from ol' Iron Mike? What do you say?" He waited for an answer.

Artie Bauer noticed a flicker in his best friend's eyes and the hint of a smile. "That was *three* questions, Coach," said Ty Green, "but we'll be okay. Right, Artie?" He looked at his catcher, as if he needed that extra bit of affirmation.

"You know it," said Artie, with a nod, just as the umpire reached the mound to break up the meeting. Following the ump back to the plate, Artie called over to Jug, who was plodding toward the home dugout, "We've got this, Coach. No more cheap runs for them—not on *your* diamond. That's a promise."

Glancing over at the big catcher, Jug Johnson smiled and reset the green-and-gold Bruins cap on his balding head. "From your lips to God's ears, Yogi," said Jug, taking care not to step on the first-base foul line as he crossed it, "but don't jinx us, bud—not unless you can carve that promise in stone."

* * *

Coach Jug Johnson shouldn't have worried. The baseball gods heard catcher Artie Bauer's pledge about "no more cheap runs" and backed his guarantee, at least until the 5th inning. As far as *carving* went, the pitches that Ty Green served up from the third Blackhawks batter on—mostly fastballs and screwballs—sliced off the corners of the plate and swerved into right-handed batters who dared to crowd the dish. Artie was surprised to realize that Ty was mixing *cut* fastballs—or *cutters*—into his offerings whenever Artie asked for fastballs to lefty hitters. He knew Ty had been experimenting with cutters—which broke late into left-handed batters—but Ty hadn't said he was ready to use the pitch in an actual game, much less in this particular outing. Then it occurred to Artie that maybe those wild warm-up pitches had been cutters, with Ty getting ready to face lefty-batting Josh Stark. And maybe Artie's rebuke for Ty to focus on Josh coming to bat in the lead-off spot had been unnecessary.

Between strikeouts and weak groundouts, Ty Green and his infielders retired twelve of the next thirteen Hawthorn batters over the next four innings. The fast Blackhawks shortstop, who had been left stranded at third base in the top of the 1st inning, leaned into one of Ty's better screwballs in the top of the 3rd and was hit by the pitch. His time on base, however, was short-lived when Artie Bauer called for a pitch-out and hung the shortstop up between first and second base. The ensuing rundown involved all four infielders, with Artie and Ty backing them up. Third baseman Brett Woods won the dubious honor of tagging the Blackhawks speedster out at second after an entertaining back-and-forth chase—*dubious* because the runner finally decided to crash into Brett and try to knock the ball from the third baseman's glove. Brett Woods held onto the ball to get the third out of the half inning, but for standing his ground, he also got a bloodied nose and split lip that pulled Dr. Inouye from the stands once again. After getting Brett into the dugout with the rest of the Bruins for the bottom of the 3rd, the doctor tried his best to stop Brett's nosebleed, but all he could do was plug both nostrils.

"We should get this young man to the emergency room as well," Dr. Inouye told Jug Johnson. "He can breathe through his mouth, but his nose appears to be broken and should be set."

By then, someone had called Woody Woods to the dugout from the concession stand where he had been volunteering. Woody took a seat on the bench beside Artie Bauer, who was still busy removing his catcher's gear. "He's not coming out, is he?" Woody asked Artie. "It's just a busted nose, right?"

Artie shook his head that he didn't know. "It was a pretty big hit," said Artie, "I mean, as hard as in football—but without a helmet and pads. You need to ask Doc Inouye."

Woody did just that, at the same time letting Brett know he'd do whatever

Dr. Inouye advised. Like his father, Brett didn't want to leave the game. "Can you set my nose here, Doc—in the dugout?" Brett asked, in obvious pain. "I wanna stay and play. I can take it."

Inouye smiled. "Yes, I'm sure you can," he said, "but I'm not sure everyone else in the stadium who hears you scream can." He glanced up at Woody now standing next to them. "Mr. Woods," said Inouye, "anesthetic and a sterile environment—which this dugout is *not*—would be preferable in your son's case. I also have instruments at the hospital that would make my job easier and my insurance company happier. Please consider transporting your son to the hospital. You do not need to rush—it is not that kind of an emergency—but the sooner he receives treatment, the better for him and his nose."

"But, Coach," said Brett Woods, turning to look up at Jug Johnson, "who's gonna play third? We're only up by a run." The boy's face was blood-streaked; his eyes, red and watery.

The Bruins had tied the game with a hard-earned run by Ricky Duran in the bottom of the 1st and had gone ahead with a solo homer by Tommy White in the 2nd, his dinger traveling even farther than Josh Stark's game-opening round-tripper had. This time, the umpire didn't claim that Tommy had stepped on home plate during his at-bat. Josh Stark, who had handled the Bruins' big bats well enough to that point, had never given Tommy White or Ricky Duran the respect the two boys deserved, neither as athletes nor as schoolmates. Josh was plainly irritated that those two 9th graders, in particular, had gotten the better of him. During his weeks at Arbor High early in the year, Josh Stark had made the two Barf Table boys' lunchtimes and after-school hours miserable. But on this April afternoon, Tommy and Ricky had turned the tables on Josh Stark.

Down the bench, Jimmy Gore heard Brett Woods ask Coach Johnson who would take his place at third base for the rest of the game. The senior left fielder and former Solid Rock third baseman stood and said clearly, "I'll play third, Coach. I can handle the hot corner." Big Phil Waters—the team's usual closer—volunteered to come into the game as a fielder, but he asked to play right field, where he was more comfortable. The coach agreed and moved Mike Inouye to left.

Seated next to Artie, Mike nudged the big catcher. "This is what wa is all about in Japan, Artie," said Mike, nodding. "First Brett and Jimmy. Now Phil. This is true team spirit, my friend—team before self, even if it hurts."

"You were first, buddy," said Artie, "getting the win for us Friday night at Mimosa Beach. I guess you're rubbing off on us." Artie laid his shin guards on the bench.

Mike smiled and said, "In baseball, one does not want to be the nail that sticks out—like Josh Stark. I have a score to settle with him from our game at Solid Rock. Jimmy handled him. Jimmy always handles things. But Josh made me look bad."

Holding up his hand, Artie stopped him. "You don't have to tell me about it," he said, "because it doesn't matter now." Then he added, "But if Josh wants to be a loose nail on the mound, we'll just have to do some hammering—like Hammerin' Hank Aaron, right?"

"Or like the great Sadaharu Oh," said Mike, rising to find his favorite bat in the bin. "I just missed his curveball my first time up. I won't miss it this time." With the shiny, jet-black bat under his arm, he put on his batting gloves as he walked to the on-deck circle for three practice swings. Then he adjusted his gloves and his helmet, and he strode on to the plate, where he led off the bottom of the 3rd for the heart of the Bruins batting order—first Mike, then Jimmy, then Artie, and then Ty, if anyone got on base.

Josh Stark's first pitch was a low fastball that Mike Inouye, batting left, took for strike one. Mike stepped back with one foot still in the batter's box and adjusted his grip on the big bat's tapered handle. The second pitch was a curve that broke inside. Mike tried to hold back, but went around far enough for the infield ump to call it a swinging strike. It was no balls, two strikes—a pitcher's count. This time Mike stepped out of the box entirely, turned toward the home dugout, and took a vicious cut in the air. He stood in again, took three practice swings and waited for the next pitch.

From the dugout, Artie Bauer looked from Mike Inouye at the plate to Josh

Stark on the mound, and saw the Blackhawks pitcher shake off his catcher's initial sign before nodding that they now agreed on what was coming next. Artie knew that most catchers would call for their pitcher to waste the next ball—ask him to throw a breaking pitch low and inside, or a fastball so far outside that the batter would make contact near the tip of the bat, if at all, and foul the ball off. But, as usual, Josh Stark wanted to go his own way and do his own thing. When the ball left Josh's hand, Artie could tell that it was going to be trouble. The high and tight fastball was what old-timers called "chin music"—so far inside that it would have smashed into the earpiece of Mike's batting helmet, if he hadn't jumped back out of the way. One ball, two strikes.

Again, Mike stepped out of the batter's box to gather himself. Artie saw him take a deep breath and step back up to the plate for his three practice swings. This time, Josh Stark uncorked the curveball that he probably should have tried to throw one pitch earlier. Mike was ready for it. Josh's intent must have been for the off-speed pitch to break across the inside corner of the strike zone, but it didn't break soon enough in what those same old-timers called a "hanging curveball." Mike launched it over the flag poles beyond the center-field fence. Arbor 3, Hawthorn 1.

Rather than face slugger Jimmy Gore—who had a homer off Josh Stark that season, though in a different uniform—the Blackhawks coach called for Josh to put Jimmy on base with an intentional walk. When the Hawthorn catcher held his mitt out wide to signal the first of four wide pitches, Josh nodded and then proceeded to nail Jimmy in the shoulder. The brash pitcher feigned innocence, indicating that the pitch had "slipped" out of his hand, but everyone—including the umpires—knew better. The home-plate ump issued a warning to Josh and to the Blackhawks bench.

Josh Stark's first pitch to Artie Bauer was a fastball that was belt high but too far inside for the big guy to turn on. The count was 1-and-0. The next ball was high and away, with the Hawthorn catcher having to come out of his crouch and jump for the ball to keep it from flying to the backstop. 2-and-0. Ball three came next. Artie stepped back to look at Jug Johnson in the third-base coaching box and saw him give the sign to take the next pitch.

Artie took a couple of half-hearted practice swings and then held his stance. With the bat barely off his shoulder, he waited for Josh to throw a fastball down the middle. Instead, a high and tight heater sent Artie to the deck to keep from being hit. But it was ball four, anyway, so he dusted himself off and took his base. Jimmy Gore trotted to second. Coaching at third, Jug Johnson was red-faced about what was developing on the diamond, but the umpires didn't issue another warning because the last pitch hadn't been an actual beanball.

Now it was *The Luuuvvv Machine*'s second time at bat. As Bennie Pressler announced Ty Green's name and that he was 0-for-1 at the plate so far that night, an audible *click* sounded over the PA system. A fast, twangy, bass-guitar intro and a guttural "*Oo-oo-ooo yeah*" from a low-voiced singer accompanied Ty's walk from the on-deck circle to the plate. In the stands, the Bruinettes rose to their feet, their hands waving, as they sang along with the music. Nicie Evans laughed and danced happily with Bruno the Bruin on the concrete in front of the softball team's section. Standing at first base, Artie Bauer held his breath.

Then Ty Green threw back his head and laughed. He pointed up at Bennie in the press box and gave him a thumbs-up. And Artie knew then that his buddy would be all right. Ty turned on Josh Stark's first-pitch fastball and pulled it over the left-field fence for a three-run homer. Arbor 6, Hawthorn 1.

* * *

The Bruins held the Blackhawks scoreless again in the top of the 4th, before adding five more runs in the home half of the inning. To his obvious chagrin, Josh Stark was pulled for a lanky, redheaded left-hander. But in a double substitution, Josh stayed in the game by moving to left field. Trailing 11-1 going into the 5th, Hawthorn had to score at least one run to avoid a mercy-rule stoppage; therefore, Josh Stark's big bat—coming up third in their half inning—was still needed. If Josh and his mates put a run on the board, the game continued. If they didn't, the game was over. It was that simple. Or was it?

Ty Green still had good command and control of his pitches, and the velocity of his fastballs—two-seamers, four-seamers and cutters—was still impressive after four full innings on the mound. His pitch count also was relatively low for that point in the game. The first two Blackhawks batters went down swinging on no more than five pitches apiece. So, with two outs and nobody on base, Josh Stark came to the plate as Hawthorn's last chance to keep the game going.

Knowing that Josh Stark was a first-ball hitter—that day, at least—Artie Bauer put down two fingers and waggled them to call for a screwball. Ty Green nodded, got set and went into his windup, but before he released the ball, the batter held up his hand and stepped out of the box. Unable to stop mid-motion, Ty went ahead and threw the off-speed breaking pitch. "*Hmm,*" murmured Josh Stark, loudly enough for Artie to hear. "What a screwball—your pal, that is."

Artie tossed the ball back to Ty on the mound and then settled into his crouch to call the next pitch. Even though the count was still no balls and no strikes, Artie heard the ballpark's PA system click on again, and then the loudspeakers came alive with a staticky "*Finish him!*" sound clip from Bennie Pressler's favorite video game. Artie smiled to himself and put down one finger, then patted the inside of his right thigh, calling for an inside fastball to lefty-batting Josh. Again, Ty nodded, got set, went into his windup, and this time fired a cut fastball at the inner half of the plate. Its movement took it even closer to the batter but was still only inches out of the strike zone.

Josh Stark could have easily stepped away from the pitch, which Artie Bauer would have caught without coming out of his crouch. Instead, Josh stepped *into* the pitch and took it squarely on his right elbow, protected by a thick guard that looked like armadillo scales. "Hit by pitch," announced the ump. "Batter, take your base." Jug Johnson came out of the dugout to object—maintaining that Josh hadn't tried to avoid the inside pitch—but the umpire just shook his head and would not relent, especially after everyone had heard the "*Finish him!*" clip on the PA. In the visiting stands, there was a commotion. Artie glanced that way and saw that Joel Stark was standing at his seat halfway up and was shouting down at Coach Johnson across the diamond. Artie couldn't hear exactly what the rich real estate developer was yelling, but other fans appeared to be upset about his outburst.

Jug Johnson called timeout but was in no hurry to reach the mound, waving in all the fielders—infielders and outfielders—to this team meeting with Ty and Artie. "What was he yelling?" Artie asked the coach about Joel Stark's shouting fit.

"Not a clue, Yogi," said Coach Johnson. "I don't think he's forgot football season yet." Jug looked at Jimmy Gore. "Hey, Jimbo," said Jug, with a wink, "you have my full permission to tackle that fool again if he runs out on the field after one of us—or after his own kid." He thought for a second before adding, "Then again, maybe you'd better just hold him for Skip Ross to come down and arrest, even though he's off duty. We wouldn't want to hurt ol' Joel's feelings too bad." Jimmy Gore nodded.

Jug Johnson continued, "One out—that's all we need—and it don't matter how we get it. But, heck, even if they make us come to bat again, we can still end the game this inning. All you boys have played some great ball today—in the field and at the plate—and we're gonna win this thing. I promise." Now he looked at Artie Bauer and winked. "This is *my* diamond, and I'm carving that promise in stone."

Maybe Jug shouldn't have tempted the baseball gods. Batting behind Josh Stark, the speedy Hawthorn shortstop waited for the right pitch and rapped the ball sharply down the line past Tommy White at first base. As Phil Waters hurried over to cut the bounding ball off before it reached the right-field corner, Josh Stark rounded second base and headed toward third, where Jimmy Gore awaited him. Phil caught up with the ball, spun around, and heaved his throw toward the infield. Barely in the outfield grass, Ricky Duran took the throw from the corner and relayed it straight at Jimmy Gore standing behind the bag at third base.

Ricky's throw was on target—*too* on target, it turned out, striking the runner in the helmet as he slid feet-first, spikes-up into third. The baseball caromed into left field, where it was immediately picked up by Mike Inouye and fired toward Artie Bauer, who had moved back to cover home plate.

If Josh Stark hadn't tried to spike Jimmy Gore at third, the runner might have been able to rise quickly and run for home. But Josh had slid wide of the bag in an attempt to cut Jimmy's legs out from under him and had gotten tangled up just long enough to give Mike a shot at throwing him out. Still, the Blackhawks coach in the third-base box, spun his arm like a windmill and sent Josh home, prompting the other Hawthorn runner to round second and head toward third. That put Josh Stark in no-man's land as a runner. He had no choice but to try to score. He could not retreat to third base.

With Ty Green backing him up in case he muffed the catch, Artie Bauer was careful not to block the plate. Mike's strong, low throw bounced once in the infield grass about fifteen feet from home and bounded straight at Artie. The big catcher squeezed the ball in his outstretched mitt and dove to tag Josh Stark as the runner slid headfirst this time, both boys' arms fully extended. Artie's mitt stopped Josh's white-gloved hands inches before they touched the plate, but now the play depended on the umpire's call—whether or not the man in blue had seen the tag underneath the big catcher and through the dust that the slide and collision had kicked up.

"You're out!" the umpire shouted, pulling back with his right fist and then punching the air. Then he proclaimed, "That's it. Game over." Whether or not the man had seen the tag clearly, he had made the right call. Artie was positive that he had tagged Josh out.

Josh Stark and his father, on the other hand, were livid. But the Hawthorn coach hurried from his post at third and pushed his hot-headed player away from Artie and the umpire. An enraged Joel Stark stumbled and staggered his way down out of the packed stands—accidentally tripped by several joyous Arbor fans, it was later claimed—and the umpires had left by the time Stark reached the field. He wasn't interested in high-fiving Bruno the Bruin, and so he stormed off toward the parking lot.

Celebratory funk music blared from the PA speakers as Bennie Pressler shouted into the microphone, *"Final score: Arbor High 11, Hawthorn Military Academy 1. Haaaaaavvve mercy!"*

CHAPTER 21

AT THE BREAKFAST TABLE ON WEDNESDAY, Harry Bauer told his grandson and their house guest about his separate talks at the ballpark with Abe Pressler and Skip Ross. After pouring a big scoop of kibble into Brody's bowl next to the kitchen door, Grandpa straightened up by bracing himself on the free-standing lavatory, and, while there, he paused to glance at his bristled chin in the mirror on the wall.

"Miss Minnie says I'd look good with a beard," said Grandpa. "What do you boys think?" He ran a thumb along his jawbone. "Pearl wouldn't let me grow one, not even a mustache—said it tickled her."

Seated at the other end of the table, Artie Bauer raised his eyebrows at the old man's question. "Well, it *would* make your face look fuller, Grandpa," said Artie. "You lost an awful lot of weight after the tractor accident." Artie looked over at Tommy White and added, "What do you think . . . Buzz?"

Tommy almost spat out the milk he'd just sipped. Setting down the glass and wiping his mouth, he said, "I think you'd look real sharp, Grandpa. I might grow one myself—as soon as I start shaving." He smacked Artie's hand away when the big guy reached out to feel his cheek.

Grandpa sat down and scooted his chair up to the table. "Well, I just don't know," he said. "Miss Minnie is a good friend, but I don't know if I'm ready to change my looks for her—not just yet, anyway."

Surprised by Grandpa's confession, Artie figured a change of subject was in order. "So, Grandpa, what did Skip tell you yesterday?" he asked. "I mean, about Brody and about Tommy's old notebook?"

Taking up a piece of toast, Harry Bauer cut two pats off the stick in the butter dish and slapped them on his still-warm bread. "You did a fine job with these eggs, Tommy," said Grandpa, looking down at his plate. "I like to dip my toast in a runny yoke, but the white needs to be good and solid. Yep, *over medium* is the only way to fry an egg. Pearl always scrambled them."

"Well, then, Tommy's just gonna have to stay here with us," said Artie. "I can milk the cows and slop the hogs, but I don't like messing with chickens— or honey bees. They *both* get after me too much." They laughed. "No, really, Grandpa," he said, "what did Skip Ross and Abe Pressler say yesterday?"

"Let me tell you this first—since you just mentioned it," Grandpa said. "Abe asked how the three of us are getting along—if we need to make any changes, now that baseball season is just about over, or if we want to keep things the way they are, at least until the State Playoff Series is done. I told him that we're just one big, happy family." He looked Tommy square in the eye. "And I meant that, Tom, my boy. Me and Artie both like having you here. But how about it? Do you feel like you belong now?"

Tommy White shrugged. "Well, yes and no," he said. "I feel the same way about you and Artie, and I like staying here on the farm better than anywhere else I've been—even better than at the beach. I'm not a water person like Bennie and Brett. I'm like you guys. I like growing things and taking care of animals— my honey bees, especially. And I've been able to do that here. But this is *your* family's farm, not mine."

Grandpa nodded that he understood. "Yes," he said, "you always hear that blood's thicker than water, and there's some truth to that. But what about the stuff over at your old homeplace? I'm talking about the drugs, the fires, and whatever that no-good Rocket Reep was into—not to mention whatever or *whoever* it is that Brody found over there the other day. Does any of that make a difference?"

"Yes, sir, that *does* change things," said Tommy. "It reminds me of how scared I always got when bad guys would come to our farm, and I'd have to go hide in my tree house. I always thought I was safe in my beeyard, but maybe I was in danger even there. Staying at the Presslers' house on the beach and now here on the farm with you guys has helped me see how bad things were for me when I was living with Mom and Dad. I don't want to go back to that."

"You don't have to," Grandpa replied. "Abe said again yesterday that there's always a place for you as part of their family. Same goes with us here. So, there ain't no big rush to change anything—and that's what I told Abe. We're just fine keeping things the way they are."

Artie Bauer laughed and said, "Besides, Tommy, you may know how to fry an egg, but you're still in training with Bessie and Bossie. I may need you to sub for me when I go off to college, depending on where I go. Grandpa, here, is getting spoiled, sleeping late every day. I think he's forgotten what it's like to do the milking at zero dark-thirty."

"Hold on now," said Grandpa, acting offended. "I milked the cows on this farm every day for at least forty years before you were born, young fellow. And we had a lot more than two milk cows back then, because selling milk—and eggs—was a big part of how we made our living. That was our kind of—what d'ya call it?—*agribusiness*."

Tommy White raised his hand like a Boy Scout making a pledge. "I *am* gonna learn how to milk a cow," he said, "even if I move back in with Bennie and his folks. But I *do* want to stay here—at least until baseball is done." With a glint in his eye, he added, "Tell me again how the playoffs work . . . Yogi."

"We're one of the top sixteen teams in the state," Artie explained, ignoring Tommy's teasing. "It's kind of like the College World Series. All sixteen teams play this Thursday afternoon and evening at different locations around Capital City—just one and done—and that narrows the draw down to eight. Those teams play best-of-three series at Capital City High and Saint Corbinian's on Friday and Saturday, to get it down to the final four. That's *this* weekend. *Next* weekend, the four teams play semi-final series on Thursday and Friday at those same two schools. And then the championship series is on Saturday and Sunday at State College—best of three, again."

Tommy whistled. "That's a lot of baseball to play in not much time," he said. "How do you play a best-of-three series in two days? Doubleheaders?"

Artie nodded. "Yep, you got it," he replied. "It's grueling for any team—up to six games in four days—and it's especially tough on pitchers. I sure do hope Smitty is able to play. Phil can do more than just close. And maybe Mike can step up again and pitch a few innings for us—if his father will let him."

"How did we do last year?" asked Tommy. "Pretty good?"

Artie shook his head. "Last year was horrible," he said. "We won the conference but lost in the first round at Capital City. We were supposed to do better, but we'd lost Reuben Russo—you know, in the car wreck—and we just didn't want it bad enough in the playoffs, I guess. Reuben Russo—man, oh, man, he was Mr. All-Everything—he'd played third for us other years and led in batting. He would have been team captain his senior year. So, we lost our main guy, our rock, our leader out on the diamond."

Neither boy had anything to say for a few seconds. Harry Bauer broke the silence. "Well, now, let me tell you what else I learned yesterday," Grandpa said. "Skip Ross told me Marty Quinn called him and said Skip should be our one and only contact at the sheriff's department, at least until Marty gets back from his military service. While Skip's out on leave, he's gonna look into some things for us. He can go wherever and do whatever he wants without having to report to anybody. We don't know who all is mixed up in this—other than Red Dedmon and maybe the sheriff himself. So mum's still the word."

Tommy nodded. "But what about my notebook?" he asked. "Skip told Artie he was gonna talk to you about that, too. What did he say?"

"He said not to worry too much about it," Grandpa replied. "Having the original notebook would be the best evidence, but Marty xeroxed every page from cover to cover. He hid the copies somewhere they'd be safe—away from the sheriff's office—just in case something happened to that notebook while he was overseas. Good thing he did that."

"And the bodies?" asked Artie. "What did Abe Pressler say about that little surprise?"

Grandpa pursed his lips for a second. "Well, let's put it this way," he said. "It was quite a shock—but it wasn't the first one poor Abe's had to deal with lately."

Grandpa fiddled with the wedding band on his bony ring finger. "Do you boys remember helping Abe with that old safe after the tornado? Turns out something important was missing from it—stolen from it, in fact. He didn't tell me what was gone or when it was taken, just that it was a family heirloom worth a lot of money. *Priceless* was what he said."

Artie had heard most of this story before—from Bennie Pressler—but he let Grandpa continue. "When I told Abe about Brody finding two old graves out at the White place," Harry Bauer went on, "he got a funny look on his face. Then he reminded me about something that happened at the old Pressler's store in E-ville years ago. He's wondering if they might be connected. I remember reading about it in the paper and hearing the story on the radio. It was the talk of the town for a good long while."

The old man let that sink in, then went on, "There was a big robbery—a burglary, actually, on Christmas Eve fifteen or sixteen years ago. Somebody—at least two people, they figure—broke into the store after closing time and got into that old safe. They made off with the cash and checks from all the shopping on Christmas Eve *and* with all the jewelry—mostly wedding bands and diamond engagement rings—the valuables that old man Noah Pressler always put in the safe overnight. None of it—none of the money and none of the jewelry—ever turned up anywhere, and nobody was ever arrested, even though there was some talk about, well, about certain people being involved."

Grandpa glanced at Tommy White. "Well, I'll go ahead and say it," said Harry Bauer. "This was back when your mama and daddy both worked at Pressler's, Tom, and when they were living together but not married yet. Connie worked in the office, and Bob was a maintenance man. Of course, this was before you were born, young man—not even a spark in your daddy's eye. Still, word got around that Connie and Bob were involved in the burglary somehow, and they were even questioned by the sheriff's department—not arrested, mind you, just questioned. I bet you can't guess who the investigating officer was." He nodded. "Yep, Officer Red Dedmon—just a few years into his long and checkered career in local law enforcement." Tommy shook his head, as if he wasn't surprised.

"Anyway," Grandpa continued, "that's something else Abe's gonna get Skip Ross to check out—maybe even drive up to Capital City and talk to your folks again, Tommy. Ol' Bob might have more to say now. Or maybe Skip can make them some kind of a deal—that is, if one or the other does happen to know something that will help us." There was pity in Grandpa's blue eyes. "I'm sorry, son. But like I said before, none of this is your fault. We've just got to make sure it doesn't come back to bite us."

Artie Bauer rose from the table and motioned for Tommy White to follow him. "We'd better get going, bud," said the older boy. "This is gonna be a big day. We have the therapy groups 4th period and baseball practice after school, and then we need to get things ready here on the farm so we can be gone for at least two days. I would say *all weekend*, but Coach Johnson would get me for jinxing us."

As Artie had done, Tommy got up and took his plate and glass to the sink to be washed. "I'll get those dishes for you, boys," said Harry Bauer. "You two go on to school. Me and Brody will hold down the fort here until you get back tonight. And I'll make a few calls to the neighbors to see if they can help us with the milking this weekend—*all* this weekend and all *next* weekend, too."

Grandpa grinned. "And, Artie," he said, "you tell ol' Jug Johnson that there ain't no such thing as a jinx. Whatever happens—good or bad—is what's meant to be."

* * *

At lunch that day, the whole Barf Table gang—not just the 9th and 10th graders—hung around after the 11th- and 12th-grade release bells to talk about that afternoon's group meetings. With the junior-senior banquet and prom three-and-a-half weeks away, they needed to finish planning how each therapy group would participate in the banquet, in particular. As usual with school dances, the prom would be mainly in Bennie Pressler's hands as Arbor High's resident disc jockey and electronics geek. They also needed to start the process of mixing and matching couples so that even the freshmen and sophomores could participate in an event ordinarily restricted to upperclassmen.

The first order of business was to come up with a new banquet and prom motif. The old theme—when the affair was a formal dance—had been *License to Thrill* and had revolved around spy movies. The décor had featured stylized images of shadowy men in black tuxedos, silhouettes of shapely women wearing diamond jewelry, foreign sports cars and gun-barrel spirals. But all of that was too racy for the Solid Rock crowd—for their straight-laced parents, anyway—and the new banquet/prom committee was stumped on how to salvage the night.

"We worked hard on that theme," protested Jamie Foxx. "I still think we should use *some* of the stuff, but Mike says none of it will fly with the E-ville church people. Right, Mike?"

Mike Inouye nodded, but laughed at her reference to the Solid Rock faithful. "Ricky knows what we're up against," he said, pointing to the diminutive 9th grader at the adjoining table. "Kimi and I can't watch those movies on TV, much less at the movie theater. And renting tapes of them at the video store is out, too. Mother says they're wicked."

"Man," said Bennie Pressler, "I'm glad your mom isn't an English teacher. We'd never get to see anything in class other than *The Wizard of Oz*." He snapped his fingers. "Hey! What about that—'Somewhere Over the Rainbow' or 'We Aren't in Solid Rock Anymore'? We could invite Josh Stark to come and be a flying monkey!" Vicki Duke, sitting at the senior Barf Table, coughed weakly as she set down her carton of chocolate milk.

Artie Bauer shook his head at the 9th-grade comedian. "I'm glad you have your sense of humor back, Bennie," said Artie, with a wink, "but we need to work on your timing a bit—like last night with the nicknames. That came close to backfiring big-time."

Bennie shrugged. "Yeah, well . . . ," he said, looking across the tables at Ty Green and Vicki Duke, to see if they were angry with him. "Sorry about that, guys. I guess I'm just out of practice." Both seniors nodded and smiled.

"That's okay, Bennie," said Vicki Duke, "but how many times do I have to promise not to bring Josh Stark back here. I told you, I'm done with him. But about your idea—*The Wizard of Oz*? Every high school in America has done that at one time or another."

Nicie Evans spoke up. "I like it!" she said. "Rainbows and cyclones and the yellow-brick road! Friends holding hands and skipping toward the future!"

"Wow," said Vicki Duke, "that gave me a chill, Nicie—especially because we had a *cyclone* here, just like in the story. And now we're all working together to fix things."

Wilma Marecek smiled and said, "Yes, I think it's a great idea. Let's do that. Jamie? Mike? Can you guys get the committee to go along with it? Mike, will the Solid Rock folks support this theme?"

"Probably," said Mike Inouye, "as long as we don't over-emphasize the supernatural elements—you know, the wizard and the witches, in particular."

"Why?" Leah Russo said. "It's all just a dream. The wizard and witches aren't real."

"Not in the book," replied Kimi Inouye. "*The Wonderful Wizard of Oz* is a scary story, and that goes for more than the wicked witch and winged monkeys. Mike and I have both read it. In our family, when we aren't allowed to watch the movie, we read the book." She smiled. "But I love that story."

"Have you read *Jaws*?" asked Ty Green. "You know it's a modern version of *Moby-Dick*, right?"

Nicie Evans popped him. "Oh, be quiet," she said. "You and your fish stories—like *The Old Man and the Sea*. That's the most boring book I've ever been assigned. Good thing it's short. I still think the title should be *Catch the Fish, Already!*"

"But it's about baseball, too," he said. "Joe DiMaggio and my Yankees are in it."

"To you, *everything* is about baseball—and fish," said Nicie. "By the way, Ty, I forgot to tell you. Dad says he's almost finished with your car. So, you can drive us and one other couple to the prom."

"We could do that now," said Ty, "but they'd have to ride in the bed of *The Luuuvvv Truck*." He took another big bite of his PB&J sandwich.

Vicki Duke chirped, "I thought we were going to rent a limo."

"Yeah," said Jimmy Gore, "so Kimi and me can ride together—with everybody else. A limo is the way to go. All of us are going, aren't we?" He looked around the two tables.

Everyone but Julia Safin—who was scheduled to play in a tennis tournament that weekend—confirmed that they could attend the event. The only problem was that some of them were too young to attend on their own. That included 9th graders Leah Russo, Tommy White and Ricky Duran, and 10th graders Jenny Gore and Brett Woods. Master of ceremonies and disc jockey Bennie Pressler always got a free pass to banquets and dances, so he could go stag, if he wished, as could juniors Jamie Foxx and the Inouye twins. So, in the same way that Artie Bauer and Tommy White's parents had done nineteen years earlier, the group decided that their seniors would pair up with the freshmen and sophomores to get them into the banquet and prom—Artie with Leah, Wilma with Tommy, Nicie with Ricky, Ty with Jenny, and, finally, Vicki with Brett, in a do-over from the previous fall's homecoming dance.

* * *

The group meetings at school went well on Wednesday afternoon. The new group members—especially the freshmen and sophomores from Solid Rock— were excited about getting to participate in the junior-senior events, and they enjoyed helping develop the leaders' ideas. At baseball practice, Coach Johnson let the boys know that they were seeded third in the playoffs but that Iron Harbor High had been placed in their quarter of the tournament draw. In other words, Arbor would probably have to beat Iron Harbor again that Friday and Saturday in the quarterfinals, to make the final four teams. Jug also informed them that they would play their first-round, "one-off" game Thursday afternoon against the Oakmont Owls on the campus of Saint Corbinian's Catholic School near Capital City. On a neutral field this time, the playoff game would be a rematch of Arbor's season opener, an 8-2 win at home.

The coach warned his boys not to take wins "for granite" on the diamond. "Winning ain't etched in stone," said Jug Johnson. "We need to focus on Oakmont Prep tomorrow and nobody else. Then we won't jinx ourselves looking past them."

Brett Woods, with his broken nose, had attended practice but wasn't able to drive yet, so Artie Bauer agreed to give him a lift to Woody's Grill if Ricky Duran could catch a ride home with Ty Green. Ty was still driving *The Luuuvvv Truck*, even though Donnell Evans had confirmed that *The White Whale* was fixed and waiting for its owner to pick it up—something Ty had mixed feelings about doing too soon. *The Luuuvvv Truck* made him *The Luuuvvv Machine* in Nicie Evans's eyes. What was he in *The Whale*, besides the teenage owner of a big, old, white car that was always running out of gas? Was he Ahab? Or was he Ishmael? And did he really need a bigger car? At the wheel of the red farm truck, Artie Bauer laughed as he told Tommy White and Brett Woods about his best friend's musings, as they crossed the bridge onto Sandpiper Beach.

"I'll be glad when I get a car of my own," said Brett Woods, adjusting the plastic nose-guard on his face. "I'm getting tired of sharing *The Woody Wagon* with Dad. And he won't let me drive *his* car. He says I'm too messy—you know, with sand and my surfboards and all."

Sitting in the middle of the wide bench seat, Tommy White stared at the half mask. "I can paint that for you," said Tommy. "You'll look like a superhero tomorrow when we play Oakmont."

Artie laughed again. "Or like a professional wrestler," he said. "*The Masked Third Baseman*! I can't believe you're gonna play tomorrow."

"Are you kidding?" said Brett. "I appreciate Jimmy covering third for me yesterday, but now it's *my* turn to do that *wa* thing—you know, what Mike's always talking about." Then he grinned. "Besides, if I don't go with the team to Cap City tomorrow, I'll have to take a big test in Mrs. Inouye's math class."

All three laughed. "What kind of car do you want?" asked Tommy White. Artie was wondering that, too, because the Woodses had enough money to buy Brett any vehicle he desired within reason.

"I don't really care," Brett said. "Anything that gets me and my surfboard where we want to go will be fine." He cocked his head in thought. "Actually, I wouldn't mind having a *Thing*—you know, a VW *Thing*? A yellow one. Dad said he'll try to find one for me, if he can paint *Woody's Surf Shop & Grill* on both sides. I wouldn't care."

Artie parked in the lot at Woody's, and the three boys went inside together. The restaurant was empty, except for a couple paying their bill at the cash register up front. Woody counted out the man's change and thanked them for dining there. "You come back, now," he said, smiling at the young woman and nodding to the young man as they turned to leave. He closed the register and greeted the boys. "Hi, guys. How was practice?"

"Boring," said Brett Woods. "I wanted to get out there and play, but Coach wouldn't let me. He wouldn't even let me take batting practice."

"No, that's a good thing," Woody said. "I'd be kinda worried if Jug Johnson pushed you to play this soon. You'll be in good shape tomorrow after the rest of the swelling goes down." He motioned toward the empty seats at the counter. "You boys want something to eat? Can you stay a minute? I've got some fries left in the basket over the deep fryer."

Artie pushed Tommy toward a stool. "We *always* have time for your fries," said Artie. "Woody's fries are the best! Right, Tommy?"

Tommy spun around on his stool and caught the counter before making a second revolution. "I could eat those fries three meals a day," Tommy said. "I wish I could make them like that at home."

"Funny you should say that, Tommy," said Woody, wiping down the counter with a dish towel. "Turns out I'm gonna need an extra fry cook in a couple weeks to help with a big catering job. Think you might be interested? Baseball will be over, and this job coming up is on a Saturday."

"Sure," Tommy said, "if Artie and Grandpa don't need me on the farm. I don't think Miss Minnie will need me all day. What's going on?"

Woody went to the kitchen and brought out three baskets of fries, one for each boy. "It's that big golf tournament at Sandpiper Shores," Woody said. "Jimmy Foxx came by this afternoon and asked if I could handle the food concessions out on the course—drink carts, a sandwich stand on the back nine, a barbecue and shrimparoo at the awards ceremony. I said I could, if I can get some help."

Artie Bauer raised his hand. "Excuse me, Woody," said Artie. "Did you just say *shrimparoo*? Our boy Tommy, here, has always wanted to learn how to fix good shrimp, too. If you'll teach him, then me and Grandpa would be *more than happy* to let him practice making fries and shrimp for us."

"We could use you, too," Woody said, with a laugh. "I figure Leah and Nicie can drive the drink carts around, and Brett can handle our food trailer if Tommy helps him. But I'll still need somebody to man a sandwich stand—maybe two people—and somebody to run barbecue over to the golf course from here, where I'll be. Do you think Ty and Ricky would be interested? And Bennie? I'll give him a call myself. I know he's been busy helping his parents. The tournament is two weeks from this Saturday."

Artie nodded. "We'll check with Grandpa," said Artie, "but I'm pretty sure me and Tommy can work for you that day, and I'll ask the other guys tomorrow on the bus. It'll be fun—and Ty can use all the money he can get to pay Nicie's dad for fixing *The Whale*."

As the boys ate their fries, Woody Woods mentioned the storage tub from Tommy White's tree house that they had hidden away upstairs—the square, plastic container holding mainly belongings that the late Rocket Reep had left behind. "Our little, uh, *package* up in the attic is still out of sight," Woody said, "but not out of mind, it seems. I've had a visitor in here every day this week, and he's been asking questions about the dumpster—like, how often we put stuff in it, and if we have a problem with people dumpster diving. I think the questions have to do with that tub."

"Who's your visitor?" asked Artie Bauer. "Joel Stark?"

"No," Woody replied. "Red Dedmon. Joel is too good to park his car in the alley and open the dumpster to look inside. Red has been doing that all week so far, morning and evening."

Tommy White wiped his mouth with a napkin. "What's that creep looking for?" he asked. "Do you think he knows we got the tub out of the dumpster?"

Woody shook his head and said, "No, but he remembers how Rocket Reep liked to dumpster dive, and he's wondering if Rocket left that job to some other bum in his last will and testament." He laughed, adding, "That's what graduating seniors would do back when I was in high school—you know, write their *class will* and leave crazy stuff to younger kids. Are you guys doing that?" He looked at Artie.

"Not yet," said Artie, "but I heard Vicki Duke and Miss Hopper talking about us doing that one day before the junior-senior." He grinned. "What did you leave, Woody?"

"Oh, nothing important," Woody said, with a chuckle. "Just my girlfriend. She was a 10th grader. I left her to my buddy, who was a junior. Funny thing was, they ended up getting married before she got out of school. Named their kid Woodrow after me—Woodrow Harmon. Then they had twins a few years later—Clara and Sara, you know, on the basketball and softball teams? Aren't they juniors?"

"Yeah, they're good girls," said Artie. Then a thought occurred to him. "That was Mimosa Beach High, right? I wish my mother hadn't dropped out. Of course, if she had stayed, maybe she would've dated that Harmon boy, and I'd have twin sisters." He shook his head but smiled.

Tommy White objected. "But then we wouldn't be cousins, Artie," said Tommy, "not unless that Harmon guy had a brother for *my* mom to date."

"Yeah," said Woody Woods, "those two girls—Connie Henderson and Ingrid Bauer—they were like sisters that one year they were together at Mimosa Beach. Ingrid and I were freshmen, and Connie was a sophomore, but it didn't matter— those girls were like two peas in a pod." He grew wistful. "I've gotta tell ya, Artie. I always thought your mother was the prettiest little girl at school—even though she wouldn't give me the time of day, not even in grade school."

Woody patted the counter in front of Tommy. "And *your* mother," Woody continued, "was a pretty girl *and* a good student—well, she was after she settled down. I always thought she'd go off to college, and we'd never see her again in Oleander County. As I recall, she took all the business classes—I took typing with her when I was a junior—and she won a prize in a business contest her senior year."

"You can type?" Brett Woods asked. "Dad, you've been holding out on me. You could've typed all my homework papers for me when we were in Hawaii last winter."

The man laughed. "I can do a lot of things you don't know about," he said, snapping the dish towel at his son. "I'll have you know I'm more than the chief cook and bottle washer here. I also know how to balance the business's books. I do all the landscaping work outside. I wheel and deal with sales reps who come in here trying to sell me things. I even fix the toilets when they're out of order, which seems to happen at the worst time—like this morning when Red Dedmon was here. He said it must be *him*, because toilets overflow everywhere he goes now. He wasn't kidding, either. They must be having trouble next door at the real estate office, too, because I keep seeing plumbing vans and honey wagons coming and going over there all the time."

"Honey wagons?" asked Tommy.

"Don't get your stinger bent out of shape, Buzz," said Artie. "As Coach Johnson would say, that's one of those *euphoniums* for trucks that pump out septic tanks." They all laughed again. "But seriously, Woody," continued Artie, "do you think Red Dedmon might figure out that we have Rocket's storage tub after all? Do we need to move it?"

Woody's smile faded, and his eyes narrowed. "I don't know," he said. "My guess is that Red didn't want them to throw it away in the first place, and now he's making doubly sure it's gone—that some beach bum didn't pull it out of the dumpster before the trash truck hauled it off. I imagine Red's already been to the landfill looking for the tub."

Brett Woods—who along with Jamie Foxx had actually retrieved the tub the previous week—feigned indignation. "Hey now, Dad," said Brett, tugging at his facemask again, "you say *beach bum* like there's something wrong with being one. This is a surf shop, you know. Beach bums keep us in business. *I'm* a beach bum—*the Pele of the Ukulele*, remember?"

Woody's smile lit up his face again. "You guys, get on out of here," the man said, gently fussing at them. "Go on home and get some rest. You, too, Zorro.

You can take my car. You don't need to hang around and wait on me. I'll get Mom to come get me later. Besides, don't you have some *typing* to do?"

"No," said Brett, "it's math, actually. So, what kind of grades did you make in geometry, Dad? If we win tomorrow in Cap City, maybe I can talk my teacher into giving me a take-home test. What do you think, guys?" He winked at his two teammates.

"With Mike and Kimi's mom?" Artie said. "Not a chance. They may believe in that *wa* thing when it comes to baseball, but in her math class . . . it's all you, buddy. You'd better study, or else *waaa* will be what you're crying after you fail that test."

CHAPTER 22

THE OAKMONT OWLS 'DIDN'T GIVE A HOOT' about winning in the "one-off" first round of the State Playoffs Series on Thursday evening. That's what Jug Johnson told his victorious Arbor Bruins late that night when they got to their motel on the outskirts of Capital City. According to Coach Johnson, the difference between winning and losing was more than *wa*—just those two little letters—it was "*wa*-nt to." Jug added that whoever scheduled Oakmont Prep's prom for that weekend also hadn't done the baseball team a favor, according to the Owls coach. "Those boys were thinking more about circling the dance floor with their gals at the prom," said Jug, "than circling the bases on that diamond. You've got to want to win, boys. Don't forget that tomorrow against Iron Harbor." The Gray Dukes had also won Thursday night, but on a different high school ball field nearby.

The Bruins' motel—a cheap motor lodge whose only amenities were clean sheets and plenty of towels—was located at the far end of a busy commercial strip leading into the state capital. Only a mile from Saint Corbinian's Catholic School, where Arbor's best-of-three, quarterfinal series with Iron Harbor would be played on Friday and Saturday, the humble Cardinals Tourist Court wasn't good enough for the Gray Dukes. They were booked downtown at the high-rise Capital City Inn & Suites, within easy walking distance of the capitol building, the state museum, and The Rumpus Room, the best sports bar in town.

With Johnny Smith on the mound, Arbor won Friday afternoon's game 5-3. Smitty, back from being hurt, got off to a rocky start in the 1st inning, giving up two quick runs on a long homer by senior slugger Louis Hines. Over their high school careers, Louis Hines and Artie Bauer had become friendly competitors from facing each other on the football field, on the wrestling mat—where that winter the two heavyweights had shared the state title—and on the baseball diamond. Brawny, bearded Lou—a State College football recruit—also had the distinction of being the Suncoast Conference's fiercest and most menacing athlete. That, however, didn't keep Smitty Smith from finally settling down on the hill and his teammates' bats from coming alive at the plate.

The Bruins didn't trail after the 3rd inning, but also never quite caught fire on offense to put the Gray Dukes away. Coach Johnson let Ty Green's arm rest after his outings on Tuesday and Thursday of that week, and called on Phil Waters to pitch more innings than usual in relief. Playing right field for Smitty, Ty Green got the rest he needed and also contributed at bat by knocking in four of the Bruins' five runs. Mike Inouye closed out Arbor's scoring with a solo homer in the 6th inning.

On Friday evening after the game, Jug Johnson insisted on walking the team from the motel up the strip past three car dealerships to a hole-in-the-wall joint called simply Sal's Italian. They didn't take the bus, because Jug had agreed to give driver Frankie Hughes time off to attend a death-metal concert that night at a biker club across town. Sal's—which had formerly housed either a fast-food restaurant or a gas station—needed a coat of paint and bulbs to replace the burnt-out, initial S in the sign across the front. "Sal's by day, Al's by night, I guess," said Jug Johnson. "Don't matter. This is the best spaghetti in town, boys. Trust me." Jug patted his belly and held the front door open for his hungry players. When Sal himself came out of the kitchen, he and Jug embraced like the old friends they were. The coach said he and his Bruins would be "carb loading" that night with Sal's famous spaghetti and meat sauce. "And gelato for dessert!" said smiling Sal. "For good luck!"

And on Saturday morning the Arbor Bruins ran the Iron Harbor Gray Dukes off the field, making a third game that afternoon unnecessary. Arbor would get to play in Capital City the next week as a final-four team in the State Championship Series. Their opponents would not be determined until that afternoon, although top-seeded Capital City High was favored to repeat as state champs. The Red Caps' stunning loss that Saturday morning to the Craventon Ravens had been their first of the season.

On the ride back to Monk's Landing Saturday afternoon, Ty Green held court in the back of the activity bus. "Next weekend," Ty began, loudly enough for Jug Johnson to hear up front, "we're staying somewhere *nice*—not at that same old no-tell motel. We had to get breakfast out of the snack machine. And the ice maker was broken when we got there."

"Where do you think we should stay?" asked Artie Bauer. "That fancy hotel where Iron Harbor stayed?" He laughed. "You know, that's probably why they lost."

Ty snorted. "How do you figure that?" he said. "Do you think they slept *too well* last night?"

"Not hardly," said Artie, shaking his head. "Louis told me after the game that a few of their guys didn't sleep at all. He went to bed pretty early, but three other boys snuck out and went to The Rumpus Room. They didn't get caught, but that's why they couldn't hit anything you threw at them this morning. I heard one of them say it looked like you were throwing *two* balls at him. He was seeing double."

Ty lifted a finger to his lips. "*Shhh!*" he said. "That's my secret weapon—the old double-rumpus ball." He grinned. "But seriously, Artie, we need to stay at an actual hotel—with a pool and an exercise room and a big breakfast buffet and movie channels in the room. I mean, it's our last chance to win the state championship. We've never stayed anywhere nice. We need to have some fun."

"What about respecting the streak?" asked Artie. "When the team wins, you aren't supposed to change anything until the streak's over."

Ty thought for a second. "Okay, how about this?" he said, loudly again. "We stay in town at the Capital City Inn, but we drive out to Sal's for all our meals—Thursday, Friday, Saturday and Sunday after we win the whole thing. How's *that* for a streak?"

Up front, Jug Johnson rose and stood in the aisle, holding onto the chrome-plated pole behind the driver's seat for support. "Ty Green," said Jug, "what have I told you boys about jinxing yourselves? I don't know *where* we're gonna stay yet, but it may very well be that high-rise hotel downtown. We're gonna have a bunch of parents coming to next weekend's games—and, by the way, that ain't counting our chickens too soon, because we *will* be playing at least two games for sure. Hopefully, we won't lose them both, and we'll get to eat more than one meal at my buddy Sal's place. I like that part of your plan. We'll see about the hotel, but if we *do* stay in town, I better not hear about anybody sneaking off to The Rumpus Room—not unless you take me and Frankie, here, with you." He nodded and sat back down.

* * *

It was a quiet Sunday morning in Oleander County—a welcome change after lines of storms had blown through the area on Saturday night. One thunderstorm right after sunset was so severe that it triggered tornado watches in one community after another from west to east, but conditions never merited an actual warning, as no funnel clouds were spotted by weather watchers. Still, for over an hour, the night sky lit up every other minute with jagged lightning strikes as the storm barrel-rolled its way across the county. Rainfall from the squalls left water standing in ditches and other low-lying spots on the Bauer farm, and the gusty winds managed to take down the broken tree limbs that hadn't fallen in the Good Friday Storm. But the sight of Venus in the clear sky greeted Artie Bauer and Tommy White as they walked to the barn just before sunrise Sunday to do the day's first milking. The morning star—a crescent-shaped diamond of sparkling facets—reminded Artie that beauty and love and light shine even after the darkest night.

"I hope the rest of this week can be like this," said Tommy White, "but I have a feeling it's gonna be more like last night." He pushed the barn door open enough for the boys to enter and reached inside for the light switch. A small barn cat—jet black, like a lump of coal with four legs and a tail—shot outside in front of Tommy's feet, tripping him up.

"You're not superstitious, are you?" asked Artie Bauer. "I mean, if you are, we can walk around the barn and come in the back door." He winked. "But you know Cat isn't bad luck—not unless you're a mouse. She'll be back in a minute for some milk. Make sure you save her some."

Tommy shook his head. "I'm no more superstitious than you are," he said, "but the coach's talk about jinxes is making me jumpy. He's got me afraid to step on the foul lines—even though I play first base—and now I worry about doing something different after I have *good* luck. I'm starting to think we need to stay at the Cardinal again this weekend, just to keep our good-luck streak alive."

Artie took down a three-legged stool from a peg on the wall in the milking parlor next to Bessie and Bossie's stalls. "Tommy, if you'll go to the creamery and get us a clean pail," Artie said, "I'll bring one of the girls in here and get her cleaned up for you. Just don't grab a thirteen-quart pail."

"Why not?" said Tommy. "Bad luck?"

Artie laughed and said, "Well, it is if each girl gives her usual two gallons and your bucket isn't big enough to hold all that milk. Then Cat will get more than she needs."

While Tommy was gone, Artie cleaned up Bessie and then waited for his partner's return. "Yeah, that's a good size," Artie said. "But about being superstitious? All that stuff's just in your head. It's like Grandpa said the other day—whatever's gonna happen, will happen. It won't matter where we stay, as long as we get some sleep and don't sneak off in the middle of the night to some sports bar."

"Like The Rumpus Room?" asked Tommy, taking a seat on the stool next to Bessie.

"You got it," Artie said. "Okay, are you ready? Did you remember to wash and dry your hands while you were in the creamery?"

Tommy nodded. "I did," he said. "I remember you saying how important that was—that our girls like clean hands and a warm heart." He looked confused and added, "Or *warm* hands and a *clean* heart."

"Well, in Bessie's case," said Artie, with a laugh, "your hands need to be clean *and* warm. As far as your heart goes, just be gentle with her, or else you'll find out what bad luck really is. Now, watch out for her tail. And don't let her kick the bucket."

"Kick the bucket?" Tommy said. "For real?"

Artie shook his head. "Let's hope not, smart guy," he said. "Sorry, I should have said, 'kick the *milk* bucket.' If she tries to, just block her leg with your left forearm—you know, like in wrestling. Don't worry, Tommy. You'll do fine."

And he did.

* * *

Late that afternoon, a gray sedan turned off the highway and rolled down the farm lane past the barn and toward the house, where Artie and Tommy rested on the back porch with Grandpa and Brody. The boys had spent the day picking up limbs and storm debris from all over the farm and making a huge pile to be burned another day. Even on a farm the size of theirs, dense smoke on a Sunday afternoon would have upset many of their neighbors, and so they decided the fire could wait until another day when the ground was still saturated from rainfall. The nondescript car pulled onto the gravel near the sidewalk and stopped—the two front-seat occupants sitting and talking for a few seconds before getting out. Artie was surprised to see Thelma Hopper, the driver, jump out and hurry around to help her new fiancé, Skip Ross, climb out on the passenger side. Both were dressed as if they had been to church—Thelma, in a breezy, floral-print dress; Skip, in a tan suit, white shirt and paisley tie. He still wore the arm sling outside his jacket. But where they had been that day, they had seen more sinners than saints.

Opening the screen door and stepping outside, Artie Bauer greeted the visitors. "Miss Hopper! Skip!" he called. "Come on in! We're all out here on the porch—even Brody." When he saw the guidance counselor hesitate and look down at her nice dress, Artie added, "Don't worry. He won't jump on you."

"Oh, I know," said Thelma, "but Skip needs to talk to you privately. I'll just go back and sit in the car. It's a rental, by the way. I'll be glad when I can get a new minivan."

Officer Ross blushed a bit. "Yes," he said, "and you can be sure I won't be driving it—not after what happened the last time I took the wheel. That's what I get for not letting Thelma drive us on our date. My old car was in the shop, and I was too proud to ride shotgun."

Artie laughed and waved the deputy up the handicap ramp to the back door. "Well, come on in, and pull up a chair, Skip," said Artie. "Miss Hopper, you don't have to wait in the car. Minnie and Wilma Marecek are in their office over near the barn—the doublewide trailer there. You might enjoy talking to Miss Minnie about her horse-therapy practice."

Thelma Hopper beamed. "Oh, my, yes!" she said. "I am *so* interested in equine therapy. I've seen how much it helps youngsters with so many problems, and I have so many questions. Thank you for suggesting that, Arthur. You're *so* thoughtful." She patted Skip on the shoulder as he continued up the ramp, and she turned to walk back toward the barn.

On the enclosed porch, Officer Ross shook Grandpa's hand, nodded to Tommy, and took a seat next to Artie on the old couch. "Thanks again for the other night," he told Artie, "for sharing your Senior Night with us. That made it even more special. Thelma thinks so much of her students, like you're all her children—even the new kids from Solid Rock."

"We were glad to do that for you," Artie said. "You and Miss Hopper have both done a lot for us this year—in and out of school." He looked at Grandpa and Tommy, and added, "Isn't that right?"

Harry Bauer leaned forward to make sure Brody was comfortable. "It sure is," Grandpa agreed. He sat back up, turned to Skip Ross, and said, "We couldn't have made it without you at our Halloween festival, what with all the trouble that Stark boy and his friends caused. So, what brings you out our way this afternoon?"

Skip Ross explained that he and Miss Hopper had driven up to Capital City that morning so that they would blend in with the regular visitors at the separate men's and women's prisons where Tommy White's parents were inmates. "Being a Sunday, it was pretty crowded," Skip said, "but I didn't want to attract attention—not from the other prisoners *or* from the guards. We can't be too careful, considering who all is involved in this."

The deputy said there were two questions he had wanted to ask Connie White before talking to her husband: what she remembered about the Christmas Eve burglary years earlier when she worked in the office at the Pressler's store in Ebenezerville; and what she knew, if anything, about a person who had been buried on the White property. "I didn't tell her that Brody alerted on *two* graves," he said, "and I didn't tell her where they were on the farm. I wanted to see what she came up with, and then I was going to compare it with what Bob said later."

Skip chose his words carefully. "At first, she seemed . . . confused," he began. "She said there wasn't a family graveyard out there, as far as she knew. But then she got this sick look on her face, and she told me about a few of the drug deals that Bob did later on, some of the close calls he had with drug runners. But she didn't know about anyone dying and being buried out there."

"What did she say about the store robbery?" asked Tommy. "It happened before I was born, but they *never* talked about it around me. I would remember if they ever mentioned it. Mom always spoke highly of the Presslers. That's why she went along with them being my guardians when she and Dad got caught in that drug sting and went to prison."

Skip paused to gather his thoughts. "Well, this isn't the same thing your father told me," the deputy replied to Tommy, "but your mother said she found out Christmas morning that Bob's brother—Peter Jacob White, or P.J., as she called him—had committed the robbery the night before. Con—"

"Hold on!" interrupted Grandpa Bauer, suddenly animated. "P.J. White? He was back here in Oleander County that Christmas? So, did Connie say anything about our daughter Ingrid—Ingrid Bauer? Was she here with P.J.? They'd run off together, you know."

"No, sir," said Skip. "I mean, no, your daughter wasn't here in the county with him—so, on the bright side, she wasn't involved in that robbery. But Connie *did* mention her in our conversation, and I'll get to that in just a second." Grandpa nodded apologetically and leaned back again.

"Anyway," Skip said, "Connie claimed that she and Bob had nothing to do with robbing the Pressler's store, and that, in fact, they both loved working there. According to Connie, an old friend of theirs, Rocket Reep, helped P.J. get into the store's office area somehow, and then Rocket drove P.J. back to the White farm after the robbery. Other than that, P.J. planned and executed the whole thing. He was the mastermind."

Artie, not Tommy, put his hand to his face in dismay, wondering how many of P.J. White's traits he had inherited. But Tommy gave the big guy a reassuring pat on the arm. "Don't worry, cuz," said the straw-haired boy. "It gets easier."

The deputy gave the boys a confused look, but went on, "According to Connie, on Christmas Day not long after lunch, Bob got called in to work by one of the Presslers. They needed him to fix something up on the roof. Connie didn't know exactly what it was—a door, a window, something like that—but she said that after Bob left, she and P.J. got into a big fight. He had started drinking, and he started bragging about what he'd done—about the robbery." Skip stopped to go easy on Tommy, not knowing that this info also embarrassed, even angered, Artie as well.

"Connie said what made her so mad," Skip continued, "was that P.J. laughed at her and said he wouldn't have known how to rob the store and wouldn't have gotten away with so much if they hadn't been so stupid and run their mouths about working at Pressler's, like their jobs were so great. Connie said that was when she slapped him, and she said, 'No wonder Ingrid left you.' Well, that infuriated him, she said, and that was when he beat her up—so bad, in fact, that she ended up in the ER. When she got home from the hospital, P.J. had taken off, she said. He just disappeared like before, and he hasn't come back or been in touch with them all these years."

Grandpa leaned forward again. "Ingrid *left* him?" he asked. "Did Connie explain that? Did she say anything else about our girl?"

"I asked her who Ingrid was," Skip replied. "She said Ingrid was her best friend, and she did say that Ingrid and P.J. had run off together a few years earlier. But Connie hadn't heard anything from her and didn't know where she was or where she'd been, just that she'd *left* P.J. at some point."

"Why didn't she report all that to begin with?" Grandpa asked. "Maybe we could've found Ingrid if we'd known P.J. had come back here. When Connie and Bob was questioned, neither one of them said a word about P.J. or about him beating on her."

Raising his eyebrows, Skip nodded. "She said she *did* report it," he replied, "but I've never seen any paperwork other than the original robbery report and transcripts—if you can call them that—of Red Dedmon's interviews with store employees." He paused. "But no transcripts with Bob and Connie White. Their interviews—if they did happen—weren't in the folder."

"How does *that* come about?" said Grandpa, as if he couldn't guess.

"The same way a yellow notebook—Tommy's notebook—disappears from the evidence room," Skip said. "But after talking to Bob today, I doubt that Red Dedmon even wrote up what he learned from them. Bob wouldn't say much, but I suspect that before P.J. left town, Red confronted him and got a cut of what P.J. stole—money or jewelry or whatever—to keep quiet. I'm sorry to admit, that's how some of the older guys in the department do things, when they can get away with it."

Tommy's face was red. "What exactly did Dad say?" he asked. "Did he back Mom up at all?"

"No, not really," replied Skip Ross, "but I could tell he was nervous, and he said I'd better watch my back if word gets out that I'm investigating that robbery. He said P.J. had *connections*—that was the word he used—connections that I don't want to mess with. I guess he was talking about his brother's *drug* connections. I'll have to check with my DEA source about that."

Then Skip laughed nervously. "Sorry, but that was when Bob told me I should let sleeping dogs lie," he said, "and I hadn't even told him about Brody here." At hearing his name, Brody lifted his head and yawned. "And like I'd done with Connie," Skip went on, "I didn't explain to Bob why I was asking him about graves out there. But when I brought it up, Bob thought for a minute, and then he distinctly said *those two graves*—yeah, he referred to *two* graves—that they were probably the graves of an old Indian couple that lived in the swamp back when the Whites first bought the property. I asked him what their names were—the old Indian couple's—and he said he had no idea, that it was just an old family story."

Skip looked at Tommy again and asked, "Have *you* ever heard that story?"

"Nope," said Tommy. "It's news to me, and I would've liked hearing that story. But maybe they didn't want to scare me, with my tree house and bees in that clearing. I spent a lot of time out there—a bunch of nights, even—and they might have figured I wouldn't leave the farmhouse if I was too afraid of seeing old Indian ghosts. It wouldn't have scared me, though. What was happening in the house when I was there was a lot worse than ghosts haunting a clearing in the woods."

"Really?" Skip said. "Do you mind telling me? It could have a bearing on our case here."

Tommy shrugged. "I don't know," he said. "Mom would run me out of the house when the bad people were coming around. I'd stay in my tree house until they were gone, but sometimes I heard a lot of yelling. Once I heard gunshots—or maybe they were just firecrackers—and another time I got back to the house and saw Mom cleaning up what looked like blood on the floor. She said it was wine somebody had spilled, but it sure did look like blood to me."

"Where was your father in all this?" asked Skip.

"Well, that night," said Tommy, "he was headed out the door as I was going in. And he didn't come back for a long time, not while I was still up, anyway. That was when he was still growing some pot in the clearing near my tree house—not much, but a little—so maybe he was out there. He was mainly into cocaine and other stuff then. But I don't know what happened—just that I was scared all the time."

* * *

"How did everything go with Miss Hopper this afternoon," Artie Bauer asked Wilma Marecek, as they waited for the Barf Table's regular Sunday night meeting to start. The two friends—also rivals for the Ebenezer Endowment—

were sitting on the deck, watching as the other gang members shot hoops on the goal at the barn and walked the horses in the corral. The meeting would start when Minnie Marecek got back from the farmhouse, where she had gone to talk to Harry Bauer about his earlier visit from Skip Ross. Artie wondered how much Grandpa would tell Minnie about what Skip had learned in Capital City.

"It went great," Wilma said. "Miss Hopper told me that you and I are still neck and neck, as far as our grades go. If we end up with the same GPA, she'll use our Ebenezer Endowment essays to decide who's valedictorian and who's salutatorian."

"Well, that won't be necessary," said Artie, remembering his difficulty with the essay. "You deserve to be valedictorian—and probably get the Ebenezer, too. This has been a bad year for me."

Wilma shook her head. "Oh, right," she said sarcastically. "You win the state heavyweight championship, and it's a *bad* year. What would a *good* year be like for you, Artie?"

He turned his head away to look off toward the farmhouse, where he could see Harry Bauer and Minnie Marecek standing and talking at the back door. "Grandma wouldn't have died," Artie said, "and Grandpa wouldn't have had that tractor accident. That almost ruined us. We could've lost the farm." He swallowed hard. "And that was just the worst of it."

"I'm sorry, Artie," said Wilma. "I wasn't thinking. But haven't you gotten *any* scholarship offers? You're a great football player, even though the team didn't go anywhere this year. You're a wrestling champion—well, *co*-champion. And you're the catcher on one of the best baseball teams in the state."

"And I'm catching the best pitcher in the state," said Artie, turning back to face her. "But none of that really helps me. In fact, some of it *hurt* me, as far as colleges go."

Wilma frowned. "What are you talking about?" she said. "How could any of that possibly hurt you? Is it because being an offensive lineman or being a catcher isn't as showy as being the quarterback or the pitcher on a team? Coaches know everybody can't be the star player."

"No," said Artie, shaking his head. "It's because one man—one *coach*—whose opinion counts more than anyone else's has decided that I don't have the *heart* to be a college athlete."

"Jimmy Foxx?" asked Wilma. "That jerk ruined Nicie's chances for a scholarship, too."

"No, not him," Artie said, "and not Coach Johnson, either. He's my hero—even though he calls me *Yogi* all the time. I owe him everything. To most folks, I was just a tubby 9th-grade farm boy, but not to Coach Johnson." Artie dropped his eyes. "No, I'm talking about Coach Landis at State College."

Wilma looked surprised. "The football coach?"

Artie nodded. "Remember?" he said. "Coach Landis was at the wrestling finals when I went up against Louis Hines, his star football recruit. He was afraid I might hurt Louis. But now Coach Landis says I'm not tough enough to play football for him—or on any *other* team at State. Why? Because I wasn't willing to finish Louis off in that one match, he said, even though I really *could* have hurt him. He said I don't have the killer instinct he wants in his players. Ironic, huh?"

"Yeah," said Wilma, "but when did Coach Landis say that? I saw you and Ty and Jimmy talking to him at Capital City High a few weeks ago. And the next day at lunch, I heard what Jimmy told Jug about him—how Landis had messed with his head. Was that when he said it—about you not having heart?"

"Yes, and I didn't disagree with him," Artie said. "He'd just insulted Ty, too, and we *both* stood there and took it. He said if Ty was set on being a Cardinal, it would have to be on the baseball diamond, because his list of football recruits was set in stone. He said he'd heard Ty was a quitter, and he wasn't gonna waste a scholarship on somebody he couldn't count on. And *that* . . . that was why Ty got off to such a bad start that day against Capital City."

Wilma shook her head and asked, "Now, why in the world didn't you guys tell Coach Johnson about that the next day at lunch, like Jimmy did?"

"Because I was embarrassed," Artie said, "and because Ty didn't want Nicie to feel like she was responsible for ruining his dream. He quit basketball because of how Coach Foxx had treated Nicie and then had bad-mouthed her in front of Ty. Besides, Coach Johnson couldn't have done anything about it."

"Well," said Wilma, "that makes me glad I'm going to A&M, with or without the Ebenezer. It would be nice if I could go without having to join the military afterwards. But you know, Artie, I think my father is rooting for me to *lose* the endowment so I have to join ROTC. How's that for ironic?"

Minnie Marecek walked up just as *The Woody Wagon* pulled around the barn and parked beside the doublewide, where *Moby* and *The Luuuvvv Truck* sat. Brett Woods, Leah Russo, Bennie Pressler and Nicie Evans piled out of the station wagon and hurried onto the deck behind Dr. Marecek. She called for the other teens to follow her to the clubhouse side of the trailer. Ty Green, Jimmy Gore and Mike Inouye were already inside lifting weights. Once again, Julia Safin was the only club member not present.

When they were all seated, Minnie Marecek called the meeting to order. "Tonight, you all can work in your groups," she said. "The junior-senior is three weeks away. I know that sounds like forever to you young folks, but—take it from me—it isn't much time at all. And we want to do our very best with the banquet part of the program, in particular, and involve as many students as we can. We're leaders, too, not just the stars of the show. We need to be inclusive, not exclusive."

As they sat together in the storytellers' group, Artie Bauer could tell that Leah Russo was about to burst with news about something—what, he was afraid to guess. Artie wondered if Brett had spilled the beans to Leah about the storage container that had been found in the tree house on the White farm, recovered from the dumpster outside Woody's Grill, and hidden in the attic there.

"You seem excited," Artie said to Leah. "What's going on?"

"I had boat trouble on my way to work this afternoon," said Leah, "and I saw something that was absolutely disgusting—and I *smelled* it, too. It was when I ran aground on the river near Sandpiper Shores. I wish I'd had my camera in the skiff, but I had enough trouble getting off that sandbar."

Relieved, Artie said, "What was it? Did something die and wash up on shore?"

"Not hardly," said Leah. "Have you seen all the septic-waste trucks over on the beach? Well, this was one of those big pumper trucks with all the hoses. The driver had pulled off a maintenance road at the back of the golf course and was pumping the contents of the truck's tank into the river. That can't be legal, and I'm gonna get whoever owns that waste company. I see trucks there all the time, but I had no idea that's what they were doing."

At the next table, Vicki Duke leaned back in her chair toward Leah and Artie. "Forgive me for eavesdropping, guys," Vicki said, "but when I heard you say *septic*, Leah, I thought you were talking about my daddy." She seemed eager to help her new friends. "He works with all those companies. If you saw the name on the truck, I can tell Daddy, and he can look into it, because you're right—they aren't supposed to do gross things like that."

Leah stared at Vicki for a second, as if she were trying to decide whether or not to accept her help. "It was Tri-W Services—whatever that means," Leah said finally. "Thanks, Vicki."

The head cheerleader and homecoming queen smiled. "You're welcome," she chirped. "I hope they don't do that when the cheerleaders are there selling T-shirts at the golf tournament. I'm gonna tell Miss Hopper, too. That's just . . . *icky* . . . and I should know. It would make me throw up."

Vicki Duke initially blushed at her own mention of the embarrassment she had suffered at that year's Arbor High homecoming dance—shame caused largely by Josh Stark. Then she giggled. Leah Russo and Artie Bauer responded only with polite smiles, as neither chose to add to their new friend's pain by acknowledging her references, whether ironic or not, to *Icky Vicki* and *Pukey Dukey*.

CHAPTER 23

THAT WEEK DURING LUNCH PERIOD, the main order of business for Vicki Duke and the other senior cheerleaders who worked in Thelma Hopper's guidance office was gathering last wills and testaments. The guidance assistants set up a table on the cafeteria's upper level and passed out forms beginning Monday for all the seniors to fill out and return by Friday. Knowing that six other seniors—three of them baseball players—sat with her at the expanded Barf Table, Vicki grabbed a handful of forms and took them down to her friends.

"You boys need to turn yours in by Wednesday," the head cheerleader reminded Artie Bauer, Ty Green and Jimmy Gore. "We're getting buses for Sunday's games—like we did for wrestling—and I don't want to worry about your forms in Capital City. I'm going to be cheering! Go Bruins!"

The three boys laughed and promised to get their Class Will entries back to Vicki by the end of lunch that day. The form was simple, with a single, typed line at the top of a blank sheet of paper so that each senior could write as much or as little as they pleased: "I, _____, do hereby leave _____ to _____. My advice for _____ is _____."

"Mine's easy," said Jimmy Gore. "I'm leaving all my love to Kimi Inouye. My advice is for Jenny to stay here at Arbor next year, even if Solid Rock reopens. It's gonna take a long time for them to get back what they had." Jimmy's sister, who had finished the season on the Bruinettes softball team, had made more friends at Arbor than Jimmy himself had.

Ty Green snorted. "Well, I can't do mine that way," said Ty, "because my girlfriend is graduating, too, and I don't have a little sister." He thought for a second. "Okay, I've got it. I'll leave my ability to run out of gas on a date to—let's see—to Ricky Duran, as if the little Casanova needed any help in that department. Bennie should have introduced Ricky as *The Dancing Machine* the other night."

"And what about the testament part?" Artie said. "Are you going to advise Ricky to start keeping a little black book so he doesn't run out of gas with the same girl—or with her best friend?"

Ty eyed Artie suspiciously. "Did I tell you about that?" Ty said, cocking his head to one side. "No, my advice is for Mike Inouye—that he should play his own game and not let college coaches or scouts or anybody else mess with his head. I don't know who's gonna coach Arbor—or Solid Rock—next year, but Mike and his dad have done a good job on their own. I wish my dad could have helped me more with my pitching, but he's too busy making a living for us. And Coach Johnson always does what's right for me."

When Artie didn't speak up and reveal his own last will and testament, Ty said, "Come on, now, big guy. Vicki's waiting for our forms." He pointed toward the gaggle of cheerleaders at their table near the senior section. "Look at her up there. Maybe I should have left my running-out-of-gas superpower to Brett, for him to use after prom in a couple weeks—if we weren't renting a limo."

Artie smiled, but shook his head and scolded, "I don't think Leah Russo would like that one bit. But, yeah, you're right—Vicki's a good-looking girl. And now she's trying to be a good person. I'm glad we were patient with her." He glanced over at Leah, who sat with the underclassmen at the other round table.

"I'm gonna leave my seat here at the head of the Barf Table to Leah," said Artie, "and my advice is for Tommy, my cousin, to make friends with as many good people as he can find, even if it takes a little patience to see the good in them—within reason, of course. The more friends you make, the more help you'll get when times get tough, like this year has been for me."

* * *

At Nicie Evans's insistence, Ty Green relinquished the keys to *The Luuuvvv*

Truck at lunch on Tuesday. Nicie had driven Ty's old car, *The White Whale*, to school that morning in order to trade vehicles with her boyfriend, but even then Ty was hesitant to take back his old Ford LTD that had been smashed by a light pole in the Good Friday Storm. He didn't have the money to pay Donnell Evans for fixing the car's extensive damage, and he didn't want to ask his hard-working parents for a loan. Also, he had gotten used to tooling around in the little blue pickup truck and had even grown to like it, particularly after Artie Bauer had remarked that girls would think the vehicle was cute and enjoy riding in it with him.

So, with a measure of optimism, Ty invited his best buddy and two other teammates—Tommy White and Ricky Duran—to pile into *The Whale* after baseball practice to cruise over to Sandpiper Beach and back before they went home. Ty hoped to regain some of the pride and joy he had once felt behind the wheel of the old car that had carried him and Artie everywhere they had needed to go, not to mention Ty and all his girlfriends, including Nicie. When his father had given it to him for his sixteenth birthday, older kids at Arbor had laughed and called it a hooptie, but the freedom that it represented to Ty—and to Artie— had been life-changing for them both.

Sitting together in a booth at Woody's Grill, Ty Green looked around the table at his buddies and lifted his soda glass. "Yep, she handles better than before," Ty said, toasting his car. "Donnell did a great job, don't you think?"

"He did," said Artie. "So, how much did the repairs end up costing? The bill for all the body work alone must be more than *The Whale*'s worth."

Ty screwed up his face. "Excuse me?" he said. "I'll have you know *The Whale* is priceless." He laughed. "No, you're right. Donnell gave me the labor as my graduation present, but I have to pay for the parts he scrounged from junk yards and the new paint job. Nicie said not to worry—that he'd put me on an easy payment plan. But maybe I can get a job this summer and pay it off."

"What?" asked Tommy. "Pay it off before you leave for school? I want a summer job like that."

"I didn't say anything about going to school right away," Ty said. "I may go pro after all—if the signing bonus is right—and at least give the minors my best shot. There's a rookie-league team over in New Salem near Craventon—the Sunfish. That's probably where they'd send me to begin with."

This was the first definite "maybe" that Artie had heard about his best friend's future. "I thought your big dream was to go to State College," said Artie. "Aren't they still interested in you for baseball? I'm sure their baseball coach will be at the final four this weekend. I just hope Coach Landis stays away and doesn't mess with Jimmy's head again."

"Or with mine, either," Ty agreed. "That's why I said I *may* go pro. State is dragging their feet for whatever reason, but if they offer me and you *both* something this weekend—because we're a matched set—I'll go there. If not, I'll sign with the big boys and see how things go. I can always go to school later."

"But not on an athletic scholarship," said Artie. "Playing pro ball would mess up your college eligibility. You wouldn't be an amateur anymore."

Ty shrugged. "There's more than one way to get a college education," he said. "I can start out going to community college—like Nicie's gonna do—and get myself certified in physical therapy. Then I can transfer to a four-year school and finish up my degree. I could even work my way through school."

"You've thought about this, huh?" said Artie.

"I have," Ty replied, with a confident nod. "Me and Nicie have talked it over a lot. I even sat down with Miss Hopper one day and listened to what she had to say. She said it sounded like a good strategy to her, because she's big on *fall-back plans*. That's what she calls them."

Ricky Duran raised his soda in another toast. "Here is to the best pitcher in the state," said Ricky, "that he does not need a fall-back plan after this weekend in Capital City."

The four teammates clinked their glasses—figuratively, at least—and drank to Ty's success, as the door to the beach deck swung open, and Jamie Foxx stepped inside. "Hey, Jamie!" called Artie. "Over here. We ordered a pizza. You wanna join us?"

A smile crossed the tomboyish girl's face. "Sure!" she said. "I was getting bored over there by myself. I'm waiting on Mom and Jerry to get back from another open house in Sandpiper Shores. They had that same old *problem*."

"What?" Tommy piped up. "Did Mr. Church run out of gas again?" They all laughed.

"No," said Jamie, "but I don't want to ruin your appetites. It's that *smelly* problem that's been popping up so much lately, literally *popping* up—in bathrooms, in yards, in all sorts of surprising places, even over at the golf course. I heard that their bar and grill—the 19th Hole—is closed."

"It is," said Brett Woods, crossing the dining room with plates and utensils for the boys. "That's why we're catering the golf tournament next weekend. Let's just say they have *sanitation* problems. The guy at the health department who does restaurant inspections isn't the same one who issues septic-tank permits. That's what Dad told me."

Artie glanced toward the kitchen. "Where is he right now—your dad?" asked Artie. "Can you fix a pizza as good as he can?"

"All I have to do is pull it out of the oven," Brett said. "Dad's in the office right now with Bennie Pressler. He's helping Dad install a fax modem on the store's computer. I told him I could handle things here for a few minutes." He laid down the plates and asked Jamie if she wanted something to drink.

"I can't stay long," said Jamie. "I need to get back to the real estate office in case Mom calls. I've been there by myself ever since the receptionist got tired of waiting and went home an hour ago. Mom figured this might happen, so she left me her key. Don't tell anybody. I just hope Dad doesn't call before Mom does. I don't want to tell him that Mom's with Jerry again—even though it's business."

"Is it a master key?" asked Artie. "Will it get you into Joel Stark's office?"

"No such luck," Jamie replied. "I've already tried. It just opens the front door. Mom's work area doesn't lock. Neither does Jerry's. After Olivia gave up and left, I tried every door in the building to see what I could get into. It wouldn't even open the door to Joel's private bathroom."

"Did you have to go *that* bad?" Ty Green asked. "Or were you looking for something? Reading material, maybe?" He smiled, as if he were joking, but

Jamie didn't laugh.

"Yeah," she said, "I was looking for any of the stuff that was missing from the . . ." She fell silent, apparently suspecting that not everyone at the booth—notably Ty Green and Ricky Duran—knew all the information that she, Artie Bauer, Tommy White and Brett Woods had shared and sworn not to tell. So she stated simply, "I was looking for a notebook."

When none of the three boys in the know responded, she bid the group farewell. "Look," she said, "the other reason I came in was to warn you guys about Red Dedmon. Olivia told me that he's been cruising the beach all afternoon and pulling cars that park near the real estate office. I think *The Whale* is okay where it is there in the lot." She gave a little salute. "All right then. See you tomorrow at school."

Jamie Foxx was out the door before Brett Woods went to get the boys' pizza from the oven. Wearing an oven mitt as he came out the kitchen's swinging door, Brett balanced the hot pan on his right hand and carried the steaming pie to them. "I cut it into eight slices," he said, with a straight face. "I didn't think you guys were hungry enough to eat twelve."

"You're kidding, right?" said Artie. "By the way, Brett, how'd you do on that math test for Mrs. Inouye? Did you pass it?"

Brett laughed as he flipped a dish towel over his shoulder like his father always did and headed back toward the kitchen. "I aced it, brother," he said, pumping his mitt-covered fist in the air. "Hey, I'll run into the store and see if Bennie's still helping Dad. They might want to know you're here."

It turned out that Bennie Pressler did, in fact, have some news for the boys about that weekend, information that was of special interest to Tommy White. Bennie explained, "My father is doing the TV thing again—you know, making arrangements for our ballgames to be televised, like he did last winter for the state wrestling tournament. But this time it isn't just on a local-access cable channel. He's getting Channel 37 to carry our games, and that means people here can watch them! They won't have to drive all the way up to Capital City to root for us!"

"Well, that's great!" said Artie. "So, my grandpa can watch the semi-final series in his recliner and then ride up to State College with Ricardo and Gabby for the championship series on Sunday—the last two games, anyway . . . if we make it that far."

"Yeah," Tommy White chimed in, "and my folks can watch from, well, from where they're staying, too. And Sunday is Mother's Day. I'll be sure and send Mom a card so she knows to watch our games and pull for us."

"What about your dad?" asked Artie.

Tommy's joy faded fast. "What about him?" he said. "He didn't care about watching me wrestle last winter. I doubt if he'll care about watching me play baseball now. It's like he doesn't claim me as his own son anymore. Mom can send him word—if he even bothers wishing her a Happy Mother's Day."

* * *

On Wednesday evening after baseball practice, Artie Bauer dropped Ricky Duran off at the old Bauer homeplace near the highway. Artie made sure that Ricky's parents—Ricardo and Gabby—knew about the weekend games being televised, and he thanked them for covering his farm chores the previous week and for agreeing to do them again in the days ahead. Ricardo pointed out that a neighboring farmer, as well as his young son and daughter, would again milk the cows and collect eggs on Sunday morning, at least, so Artie might want to do something special for them in return.

"Grandpa called Fritz on Monday to thank him," said Artie. "What do you think? Should I take them a fruit basket or something? Maybe some cupcakes?"

Ricardo smiled. "No," he said. "I think that you should win the state championship for them—and for us all. That would be the greatest gift."

As Artie steered the old red pickup truck down the farm lane past the barn, he was surprised to see that the Mareceks' white Suburban, *Moby*, was parked out back at the clubhouse and that a horse-therapy session was underway in the corral. Wilma Marecek was working by herself with two familiar clients—Bennie Pressler and Leah Russo. For whatever reason, neither friend had mentioned that they planned to resume their twice-a-week sessions that night. Still, Artie was glad that they were there and that life on the farm was getting back to normal, as sports seasons and school schedules wound down, and as storm recovery, except in Ebenezerville, felt much less desperate. There, it would take months or even years of rebuilding to revitalize the devastated downtown area, in particular.

Though Artie's family—he and his grandparents, that is—had left Solid Rock Christian Church under strained circumstances when he was a boy, the present congregation had reached out to the Bauers the previous fall after Harry Bauer's near-fatal tractor accident. Maybe that was because their friends, the Durans—Ricardo, Gabby and Little Ricky—had faithfully attended Solid Rock until the storm. Nevertheless, Artie hoped he could continue to help members of the Solid Rock congregation and school community in their own recoveries. If the Good Friday Storm had a silver lining, it was that Solid Rock Christian Academy, Arbor Charter High School and the county's three public secondary schools had grown together to become Solid Rock strong.

The horse-therapy session wasn't Artie's only surprise that evening. When he and Tommy White reached the farmhouse, they saw that the Presslers' new SUV was parked at the edge of the yard. And when the boys walked into the kitchen from the back porch, they found Harry Bauer seated at the head of the long table, with Minnie Marecek and Abe Pressler sitting on either side of him. Brody lay on the floor next to his bowl. He looked up at Artie and Tommy as they entered.

"Come on in, boys," said Grandpa. "Take a seat. Abe has some news for us. We've been waiting for you two to get home."

Artie pulled out a chair next to Minnie. "Sorry, Grandpa," said Artie, scooting up to the table. "We stopped at the Durans' for a minute. I thanked Ricardo for helping us last weekend." Grandpa nodded and motioned for Abe to speak.

Still dressed in a gray suit and tie from his workday at the company office, Abe Pressler looked the part of a successful businessman. His dark, wavy hair was neatly cut, and his lean, tanned cheeks appeared so smooth that Artie wondered how many times the man shaved each day, but the big farm boy said nothing. On more familiar terms with his foster dad, Tommy White lifted his nose into the air and exclaimed, "I love that smell, Abe! You just came from the barber, right?"

Abe eyed Tommy's unruly, blond hair and said, "Don't you think it's about time for another haircut yourself? How long has it been since your last one? Four months? Five months?"

Tommy laughed. "That wasn't a haircut," he said. "They *scalped* me at the hospital after Rocket Reep clobbered me with that pipe from the dumpster. I didn't mind short hair when I was wrestling, but the babes at Arbor like the shaggy, surfer look. Don't they, Artie?"

"Don't ask me," said well-groomed Artie, with a chuckle. "Long or short—it doesn't matter. I just want to still have hair, like Grandpa, when I'm his age. I hope I take after his side of the family."

Abe Pressler smiled. "Well, surfer boy," he said to Tommy, "I'm going to get appointments with my barber for both you and Bennie before prom, so don't get too attached to that shaggy head of hair, no matter how much the girls like it." He reached over to pat Tommy's arm.

"I thought about calling with this information earlier today," Abe continued, "but then I remembered Bennie's session tonight, and I figured it would be better to tell you boys this in person instead of getting it second-hand. Right, Harry?"

"Right," said Grandpa, "and you being here now—with your boy out in the corral—doesn't set off any alarms." When Artie made a face at Grandpa's choice of words, the old man explained, "We've been having a regular parade of sheriff's cars out on the highway and even over on Little Swamp Road today. I called Russell Green at noon and caught him in the house. He said they're up to something over toward the old White place, but he didn't know what it was."

Abe nodded. "It must have to do with what I'm about to tell you," he said. "Skip Ross called me at work this morning. He'd just heard from his contact at the DEA that their regional office in Capital City is reopening a cold case that involves the disappearance of three drug dealers. The investigation ran into a dead end ten years ago or so. But here's why it matters now: Two of the drug dealers were pilots who regularly landed their cargo plane at the forest service airstrip not that far from here. The landing strip is off Little Swamp Road, and according to Skip, it's near the opposite bank of Cairn Creek—well, across the swamp, really—from the White farm." He studied Tommy's face for a moment before continuing.

"The third drug dealer—and that's what Skip called him—was a local man," said Abe Pressler, pausing again to look this time at Artie Bauer. "His name was Peter Jacob White—P.J. White. Skip told me they just received new information concerning the missing men's possible whereabouts. A recent aerial photograph shows what appears to be the wreckage of a cargo plane in the swamp."

"They're just now seeing it?" asked Artie. "It would have been out there for, what, up to fifteen years if that's how P.J. White disappeared—you know, when he took off after the robbery. Wouldn't a plane wreck have shown up in an aerial photo—or even in a satellite photo—before now?"

Abe shook his head. "Maybe not," he said. "That swamp can swallow something like a plane or a boat, and cover it in vegetation in no time. According to Skip, this wreckage was uncovered when one of the tornadoes on Good Friday cut through the swamp there. FEMA flew over the whole county and took new aerial photographs to help with damage assessments after the storm. A technician in that office spotted the plane's outline in the swamp and sent prints to the FAA, and then they sent them to the DEA. So this is old news when you get right down to it."

"How is our sheriff's department involved in the DEA's investigation?" asked Minnie Marecek. "The feds don't usually like to work with local law enforcement on something this big—a plane crash, three missing drug dealers, two of them probably Colombians or Panamanians."

"P.J.'s the local connection," Abe Pressler said. "For a while, he and Bob White—Tommy's father—would meet the planes at the airstrip and help unload whatever was going to be distributed from Oleander County—whole planeloads of cocaine, Skip said. P.J. and Bob would take the pilots back to their house for a meal and to rest up before they took off again, and over the next couple of days, lower-level dealers would come to the White farm and get the coke they were going to distribute wherever."

Tommy looked confused. "I don't remember big cargo planes flying in and out when I lived out there," he said, "unless there was a forest fire. The only business I remember Dad doing was small-time. I saw single-engine and twin-engine planes flying around that airstrip, but if they were drug smugglers, they were doing business with somebody else, not Dad."

"No, Tommy," said Abe, "the *big-time* drug operations at the White farm were over by the time you came along. That was all P.J. White's doings. Later on, I'd like to think Bob made more money working for me at the store than he did selling drugs, or at least I hope he did. No offense, but he started using almost as much of his stuff as he sold. It was too bad that your mother got dragged into his mess, but at least she protected you." The boy was quiet.

Minnie Marecek lifted her hand. "Hold on," she said. "Did Skip say how the DEA found out about all this? I don't mean spotting the plane wreckage. I'm talking about them knowing the in's and out's of P.J. White's drug dealings."

"Skip said they had a confidential informant—someone on the inside," Abe replied. "He didn't know their identify—and, yes, I did ask if he knew who it was and if he'd tell me their name. He refused because he wasn't sure if the informant was an *undercover cop* or just a regular *snitch*—or both. Again, his words, not mine."

Grandpa shook his head and said, "Well, I still don't understand what those sheriff's deputies were looking for on *this* side of the swamp all day long. Has anybody gone out to the wreckage yet? Have they found any bodies? And why would that rascal P.J. White waste his time breaking into Pressler's Department Store if he was a big-time drug kingpin? Did Skip have answers for all that?"

"As a matter of fact, he did," Abe said. "Well, not about what the deputies here are doing. I figure they heard about the plane in the swamp, and they're covering their, well, their *bases*." He looked at the two baseball players and shrugged. "Skip said the DEA or the FAA or the NTSB—take your pick—that somebody's going out tomorrow to hunt for the wreckage. So, no, there aren't any bodies yet. Also, as to why our store was robbed, the snitch told the DEA that P.J. had come up short on money to pay his drug suppliers, and that was why he broke in on Christmas Eve—because the safe was full of money."

Abe continued, "Grandfather Noah and my father discovered the burglary Christmas morning when they went in to count the cash and checks, and then take the deposit to the bank's drop box. I don't know why they didn't do that the night before. But they saw that the safe had been broken into, and they found a trap door to the roof forced open. That was how P.J. got out of the building without setting off the alarms downstairs. The trap door was at the top of a back staircase to the office area. It was a private stairway that the general public didn't use or even know about. Rocket Reep had caused a distraction in the store near closing time—he knocked over a display up front—and that allowed P.J. to slip into the stairwell without being seen."

"So," said Grandpa Bauer, "I can see why they suspected Connie and Bob of being involved in that. But Connie did say that P.J. laughed about her and Bob telling him how to rob the store without even knowing what they were doing. Yeah, that boy was sneaky, but he sure was smart."

Artie Bauer had nothing to share with the others about his grandfather's observations, but the farm boy couldn't help but wonder if intelligence was a characteristic that he had inherited from P.J. White, since his mother hadn't stayed in school long enough to distinguish herself in the classroom. All of the stories were that Ingrid Bauer had dropped out of school during her 10th-grade year at Mimosa Beach High, and that she had sneaked off with P.J. White that summer. That didn't sound smart to Artie, but maybe he had gotten from his parents a double dose of sneakiness that hadn't shown itself yet.

"One last thing," Abe Pressler said. "Skip didn't tell the DEA about the graves, or whatever they are that Brody found near Tommy's tree house. He suggested that we wait until the wrecked plane has been found and thoroughly searched before we tell anybody official about those graves—whether they hold the bodies of Colombian drug dealers or poor Native Americans. After we find out what secrets the drug plane holds, we'll decide where to go from there."

CHAPTER 24

THE ARBOR BRUINS' WINNING STREAK continued that week in Capital City, as the boys from Monk's Landing upset the second-seeded Fairfield Falcons in two games on Thursday and Friday. As the tournament's third seed, Arbor beat Fairfield 4-2 in the opener at Saint Corbinian's, with Ty Green going six innings for the win. The Bruins' runs came on a pair of two-run homers by Jimmy Gore and Artie Bauer. Arbor closed out the best-of-three series on Friday morning with an offensive barrage that ended Game Two early. Starter Johnny Smith gave up four runs in two innings before being relieved by righty Mike Inouye, whose cut fastball shut down the Falcons in their last three innings at bat. Mike also delivered the *coup de grace* on offense, hitting a grand-slam home run in the top of the 5th inning that gave the Bruins a 14-4 lead. The Arbor hitting attack was once again led by Jimmy Gore, with two homers and eight total runs batted in. Going into Saturday and Sunday's championship series, Arbor High had won nine straight games. Their opponent—decided in a hard-fought three-game series—would be top-seeded Capital City High.

Dining at Sal's Italian on Friday evening, Coach Jug Johnson reminded the players that the meal wasn't a celebration. Likewise, in order to respect their win streak, the team was staying at the Cardinal Tourist Court again, but Jug warned them about sneaking out and taking a bus or cab downtown to The Rumpus Room just to spite him.

"That's what fixed Iron Harbor's little red wagon last weekend," said the coach. "So, pound that pasta, boys. We have two more days of hard work, and then we'll think about taking it easy. That's right, fellas. Yogi, show 'em how to do it. Load up on those carbs, boys, because you're gonna need 'em." And he was right.

* * *

Led by co-captains Artie Bauer and Ty Green, the Arbor seniors did, in fact, sneak away from the Cardinal Tourist Court on Friday night, but not to The Rumpus Room—instead, back to Sal's Italian. With a disposable camera that Artie had thought to pack, the senior boys posed out front of the restaurant with white-aproned Sal, each of them holding up an index finger to predict— and, later, to hopefully celebrate—what would be the greatest win of their old coach's long career. Artie and Ty certainly didn't tell Jug what they planned to do, because they were sure he would call it a jinx. But the two friends were just as confident in their own abilities on the diamond and in the whole team's resolve to compete at its highest possible level, even against an opponent that had embarrassed them earlier in the season—or, rather, that had let Artie Bauer, Ty Green and Jimmy Gore embarrass themselves. But that would not happen this time, whether famous college coaches or pro scouts were in the stands at these games or not. That determination was set in stone.

As an example of the team's special kind of *wa*, third baseman Brett Woods admitted to Coach Johnson on Saturday morning at breakfast that the protective mask he wore over his broken nose made playing the hot corner much more difficult for him. "I can't see anything that isn't in front of me," Brett confessed, touching the half mask. "This thing keeps me from seeing anything to either side. I had to turn my head this way and that way all the time. I looked stupid— like I was watching a tennis match."

"Yeah, you were a sight yesterday," said Jug, blowing on his coffee. "But if your parenthetical vision's messed up, maybe we need to do something about it—like, I don't know, maybe carve out those eyeholes bigger—but then you *would* look like Zorro." He squinted at Brett's mask for a second and then checked nearby place settings for a steak knife.

Jimmy Gore spoke up from the next booth. "Or Brett and I could switch places again, Coach," said Jimmy. "I don't mind playing third, not anymore."

So, thanks to the senior from Solid Rock, Brett's unsightly problem with *parenthetical* vision was solved.

* * *

State College's baseball stadium was the biggest ballpark that Arbor High had played in all season, more imposing than the facilities at either Iron Harbor High or A&M. Attendance had been sparse Thursday and Friday for the semi-finals at Saint Corbinian's. Capital City High had enjoyed home-field advantage in their semi-final series. For the championship series beginning Saturday afternoon, fans for both Capital City and Arbor streamed into the stands as soon as the stadium gates opened thirty minutes prior to the one o'clock start. Atop the three-story press box, Channel 37's home-plate camera and operator stood out like an automobile hood ornament against the southeastern horizon. Another camera outpost sat on a metal scaffold in center above the six-foot-high, ivy-covered outfield wall. The UHF station's lone sportscaster looked down on the field from the press box's third level, through gleaming plate-glass windows that he could slide open if the weather allowed. It was a better setup than he'd had the previous two days at Saint Corbinian's. On this Saturday afternoon in early May, puffy white clouds dotted the blue sky, a mild breeze ruffled the trio of flags in center field, and the air was warm enough for short sleeves, though the forecast indicated that a light jacket might be needed by day's end. In right field, the huge scoreboard spelled out *WELCOME BRUINS, RED CAPS!* in bright, three-foot-high letters on a black background next to the blank, seven-inning line score showing third-seeded Arbor as the visitors and top-seeded Capital City as the home team.

"I'm glad Nicie was able to come with Mom and Dad," said Ty Green to Artie Bauer, as the two walked back to the visitors' dugout from the bullpen down the first-base line. "Leah's covering for her tonight at Woody's. Speaking of that, I saw the Durans—over there on the third-base side—but I haven't seen Grandpa yet. Is he here?"

Artie shook his head. "Nope," he said. "Ricardo called me and Tommy over to the screen while you were taking your cuts in the batting cage. He said something came up on the farm this morning, and Grandpa had to stay home. But Ricardo said not to worry—that Grandpa and Brody are okay. Grandpa will be here tomorrow morning if he can hitch a ride with Minnie and Wilma and Leah."

"He could ride the school bus with the other kids," said Ty, with a smile. "I'd almost pay money to see that." They both laughed.

"Ricardo also asked if Tommy had seen his mother yet," Artie said, "but he didn't mean she was here at the game, just that he figured Tommy would go visit her before Mother's Day tomorrow."

"How did Tommy take that?" Ty asked. "Is he okay?"

Artie shrugged. "I don't know," he replied. "He had a funny look on his face, but all he said was that it wouldn't look good."

"What?" said Ty, with a grin. "Our team bus parked outside Women's Prison? Yeah, it wouldn't be good for *The Luuuvvv Machine* to be so close to all those desperate women. It might cause a prison break." He snorted.

Artie was glad that his best friend seemed relaxed and ready to pitch, though he knew Ty's focus right then was on offense—hoping the Bruins got off to a good start in the top of the 1st inning and gave him a lead to defend. But depending on how the top of the Arbor batting order did, neither Artie nor Ty might come to bat before they had to play in the field. Bruins batters—Artie and Ty included—had been ineffective in their regular-season matchup with Capital City, with one exception. In his first-ever outing in a Bruins uniform, Jimmy Gore had come close to hitting for the cycle—that is, hitting a single, double, triple and home run in the same game. All Jimmy had lacked was the triple. Still, his homer was the only run scored by his new team in the 11-1 loss, shortened to only four-and-a-half innings. Even though Jimmy had batted well against the Red Caps ace—a gangly lefty with a wicked slider—he had failed his team by playing tentative defense at third base, not diving for hot shots down the line or chasing pop-ups into foul territory. In fact, his timid play had contributed to a five-run first inning that had been all the scoring the home team had needed to win.

As Artie Bauer and Ty Green waited in the dugout for the player introductions, Artie mentioned that McIntosh, the best Red Caps pitcher, was sitting this game out. "Yeah," said Artie, "Mac has to rest today. He pitched his ten innings in their three games Thursday and Friday. He can't pitch again until tomorrow."

Ty nodded. "That should help us today—not having to face him right off the bat," he said, "but I wish a guy could pitch more than ten innings on consecutive days, especially in a series like this. And if you throw one ball to one batter, that counts as an inning. That's not right."

The Bruins starters stayed in their dugout as the public-address announcer spieled off the Arbor batting order, while the home team's number-two pitcher was already on the mound, snapping warm-up throws to the Red Caps catcher. The PA announcer then ran down the Cap City starting lineup, calling the red-clad infielders and outfielders, in order, out of the home dugout on the third-base side to their positions. The Arbor players and coaches—including Joe Carson, who had driven up to lend a hand—wore their traveling grays. As far as home and away designations were concerned, Arbor would be the home team on Sunday morning and visitor again on Sunday afternoon, if a third game were necessary.

In the top of the 1st inning, Arbor manufactured their only runs of the game against the Capital City pitcher, a righty who was better than the top hurler on most other teams. Little Ricky Duran led off with an infield hit. He promptly stole second and then advanced to third on a fielder's choice by Manny Freeman. With one out, designated hitter Mike Inouye—batting for shortstop Ozzie Maye—launched a long fly ball to deep center. Tracking down the shot on the red-clay warning track, the Red Caps center fielder caught the ball, turned and flung it toward the plate as Ricky tagged at third and sped home to put the Bruins on the board. Next up, Jimmy Gore walked. Artie singled to right. Ty Green walked to load the bases. With two outs, right fielder Johnny Smith—also the Bruins number-two pitcher—smacked an opposite-field line drive into the gap in right, a double that scored both Jimmy and slower-footed Artie. Brett Woods grounded out to end the half inning, but Arbor led 3-0—definitely a better start than in their regular-season meeting with Capital City.

"Way to go, boys," said Jug Johnson, clapping as he walked back to the bench from his coaching spot at third. "That's the way to start a game."

Joe Carson, who had coached at first, waited for his old buddy at the dugout railing and waved him down the two steps to where Artie sat putting on his catcher's gear. "That's the fastest I have ever seen Bauer run," Joe said to Jug, with a laugh. "He looked like something was chasing him." The big boy pretended not to hear and focused on tightening his shin-guard straps.

"I heard somebody up in the stands ringing a cowbell," said Jug. "Ol' Yogi, here, must've thought he was late for dinner at home plate." When Artie winced, the coach added, "I'm just teasing you, son. You know I'm proud of you."

But those were the only runs Arbor scored that day. Chastened, the Red Caps pitcher found his rhythm and shut down the Bruins the rest of the way. He gave up a couple of walks and the occasional hit, but he managed to pitch himself out of every jam without allowing another run. In the top of the 5th inning, Artie heard Jug and Joe speculating in the dugout as to why the Capital City coach was leaving his starting pitcher in the game for so long, because his pitch count was getting high. The main reason might have been that Mac, the Red Caps ace, had to sit out the game, according to state rules. But Joe wondered if Cap City had any other strong hurlers on their bench. Jug said probably so, but he pointed out that both teams would be in a pitching bind if the series went three games. As for Arbor, pitchers Johnny Smith, Phil Waters and Mike Inouye were eligible to pitch as much as they were needed on Saturday, but Jug wanted to have his entire pitching staff—including Ty Green—available for Sunday's potential doubleheader. The only other "pitcher" on the team was center fielder Manny Freeman, who had one reliable pitch—a fair to middling fastball—and had thrown only in preseason scrimmage games and batting practice.

On Saturday, pitching wasn't the Bruins' defensive problem. Ty Green came close to throwing a perfect game, allowing no baserunners until the bottom of the 5th inning. After Ty's third flawless inning, Artie had been amused in the dugout to see his best friend seated alone at the end of the bench, as his teammates and coaches ignored him, according to baseball tradition. Artie was sure that Ty knew what was going on—that no one wanted to do anything in the dugout that might break Ty's focus—but *The Luuuvvv Machine* did look awfully sad and lonely sitting by himself hugging his glove. Ty seemed to perk up after the Bruins allowed a first Red Caps batter to reach base, though the same play made one other Bruin feel worse.

Facing the Capital City center fielder—who, in his first at-bat, had grounded out to third and just missed getting an infield hit—Ty Green went into his windup and saw the left-handed batter square up to bunt. The speedy player caught Ty's pitch on the barrel of his bat, dragging it behind him as he turned to dash up the base path. At first base, Tommy White saw the drag bunt laid down and rushed forward to field the slow-rolling ball. Ty sprinted behind Tommy to cover first base and to take the younger boy's throw. Although Tommy fielded the bunt cleanly and turned to flip the ball to first, he didn't lead Ty to the bag and, instead, threw well behind his teammate, who got his glove on the ball but couldn't haul it in before the runner crossed the base. After discussion in the press box, the official scorer gave Tommy an error for his bad throw, ending Ty's bid for a perfect game but preserving his no-hitter.

Jug Johnson called timeout and waved everyone to the mound for a meeting. Before Jug arrived from the dugout, Tommy blurted out, "I'm sorry, Ty. I ruined your perfect game."

Ty Green looked relieved. "No, you didn't," he replied. "We're still up 3-zip, and we're gonna sit the next three guys down in order." For whatever reason, neither Ty nor any teammate mentioned that he still hadn't given up a hit.

When Jug arrived on the hill, he complimented Tommy on his quick reaction to the bunt and on his fielding, but he did say, "I'm not gonna fuss at you, boy. You know what you did wrong, and you ain't gonna do it again. That right?"

Tommy nodded, and the meeting was over. Still, the young first baseman apologized again to Ty and then jogged with his head down back to first. He took his position behind the baserunner but didn't talk to him, as Tommy knew to watch for pickoff throws, whether from Ty on the mound or from Artie at the plate. Ty's earlier prediction about retiring the next three Red Caps was inaccurate. He faced only two of them, because one hit into a double play that Tommy took pleasure in completing—the ball going from shortstop to second to first. The straw-haired boy snatched the ball out of his mitt and flipped the white pill toward the mound as he turned and trotted back to the bench with his teammates.

The 6th inning was uneventful, except that Ty Green retired all three Cap City batters in order.

In the bottom of the 7th inning, Ty was still on the mound, with Arbor's 3-0 lead intact. So was Ty's no-hitter, as Capital City's only baserunner had reached on an error. After two strikeouts—down to the Red Caps' last out—Ty walked the batter on a 3-2 pitch that could have been called either way. It was one of Ty's better screwballs, breaking toward the right-handed batter, who flinched unnecessarily and drew the bad call from the umpire. Ty and Artie knew not to argue balls and strikes—that it could result in an ejection—and so they shook off the walk and looked to end the game on the next batter.

Pitching from the stretch—an abbreviated windup used when a runner was on base—Ty saw the baserunner take off toward second, but he couldn't hold up his throw to the plate. The batter swung and missed; however, the swinging strike kept Artie from coming out of his crouch fast enough to gun down the runner at second. Two outs, with a runner on second, in scoring position. That was when Jug Johnson decided to call time again.

"Now, look here, boys," Jug said on the mound. "We're okay. We're up 3-to-nothing. We got two outs on 'em. And we got the best pitcher in the state up here on the bump. If this next boy puts the ball on the ground, just take it to first and this one's in the books. Don't worry about that boy at second. All right? All right." He clapped his hands and headed back to the bench.

The Capital City coach must have told his player to be patient—that Ty had to be tired and might miss again—because the boy refused to swing until he had taken two balls and another strike. With the count even at 2-2, Artie called for another screwball, Ty's favorite pitch. This time, the ball broke sharply *away* from the left-handed batter, who was fooled and swung to protect the plate. It was strike three—but the sinking ball, just above the ground, hit the heel of Artie's big mitt and dribbled away, allowing the batter to take off toward first on the dropped third strike. Artie pounced on the ball, spun and threw down the first-base line at Tommy, but pulled him off the bag just enough for the runner to be safe. On his toes mentally as well, Tommy fired the ball right back to Artie, to hold the lead runner on third.

Bottom of the 7th . . . Bruins still up 3-0 . . . Red Caps runners on 1st and 3rd. Ty Green's no-hit shutout was in jeopardy, but of greater concern was that the next two Cap City hitters were the heart of the home team's batting order. Either slugger could knock the ball out of the park and tie or win the game. Artie wanted to kick himself for dropping that last third strike and giving Capital City four outs in the inning, not the standard three. It was another lousy error—this one chalked up to Artie as a passed ball—but it wasn't a hit, at least. Artie just hoped that after such an impressive outing, his friend Ty didn't lose the game by giving up only one hit. The big catcher turned and checked to see if his coach wanted them to walk the next hitter intentionally to load the bases so that a force out could be had at any base. But Jug clapped his hands twice, touched the bill of his cap and then clapped again once, his sign that no special play was on—for Artie to call the next pitch, as usual.

It was a fastball, and the Red Caps batter, a lefty, turned on it and lifted a long fly ball toward the right-field foul pole. Knowing they couldn't be doubled off their bases, the runners took off—one toward home, the other toward second. Johnny Smith dashed diagonally across the warning track and toward the right-field corner, where the ivy-covered wall met a lower, chain-link fence that separated the playing field from the visiting bullpen. The arc of the ball was a few feet inside the yellow foul pole. Smitty leapt as high as he could, his body making contact with the wall just as the ball settled in the webbing of his glove. He crashed into the ivy and fell to the ground on the warning track. The collision shocked the crowd into silence . . . until Johnny's left arm popped up, the white ball still held like a scoop of vanilla ice cream in a big, brown waffle cone. The fans from Arbor High exploded with joy at the win.

* * *

The bad news for the Bruins came a couple of hours later at Sal's Italian when Joe Carson and Johnny Smith rejoined the team at dinner. Having driven himself to Capital City that morning, Joe volunteered to take Johnny to the nearest ER to be checked out, so that Jug Johnson could take the boys back to the Cardinal for showers and then to Sal's. The black sling that stabilized Smitty's throwing arm was all his teammates needed to see, to know that Saturday's hero wouldn't be playing in Sunday's doubleheader. Mike Inouye, who had suffered a similar shoulder trauma a month earlier, got up from the booth where he sat with Jimmy Gore, Ty Green and Artie Bauer, and offered his place to the injured senior hurler. As Smitty sat down, he looked up at the talented junior and said, "Thanks, Mike. You need to get us a win tomorrow morning. Mac's good . . . but you're better." Mike nodded quietly and turned to look for a new seat in the dining room, finding one in the next booth with the three younger Barf Table boys.

Most of the fans who had driven up from Oleander County that day for the championship series had checked into the Cardinal or nearby motels. The Greens, the Durans, the Gores and the Inouyes, as well as other players' parents, wanted to stay as close to their boys as possible without interfering too much with team dynamics. Nicie Evans, Kimi Inouye, Jenny Gore and Jamie Foxx—there to "chaperone" her mother and Principal Jerry Church on their first out-of-town date—shared a room at the slightly less seedy Sunset Travel Lodge next to the Cardinal. On the other hand, Louise Foxx and Jerry Church stayed in separate hotel rooms downtown at the Capital City Inn & Suites, the principal's rationale being that after dinner he and Louise would spend the evening at The Rumpus Room to make sure no ballplayers sneaked into the establishment and got into trouble. Team bus driver and death-metal cashier Frankie Hughes offered to go to the sports bar with the principal and his date; however, Jerry Church suggested that having the Arbor activity bus parked in The Rumpus Room lot might not project the right image for the school and its student-athletes. Principal Church and Mrs. Foxx—now legally separated from Jamie's father, Jimmy—didn't want to stir up too much gossip themselves, but they also wanted to get a good night's sleep away from all the teenagers at the motels. The couple did join the team at Sal's Italian for dinner and even bought gelatos for everyone at meal's end. For his part, Frankie Hughes fed coins into Sal's jukebox all evening to let the boys pick whatever type of music they preferred, as long as they didn't pick "That's Amore," which Sal himself sang as his staff served the boys their plates of spaghetti.

Midway through the meal, Artie Bauer turned to Tommy White in the next booth. "I need to go call Grandpa now, Tommy," said Artie. "He should be finished with the milking and back in the house. Is there anything you want me to ask him?"

Tommy thought for a second. "Yeah, there is," he said. "Ask if he's planning to bring Brody with him tomorrow. It might be too hard for him to take Brody in and out of the ballpark for exercise and to do his business—not unless he turns him loose in the outfield."

Artie grinned and rose to head for the pay phone in the hallway outside the restrooms. "Don't anybody eat my breadsticks—Ty Green," he warned. "I've counted them." Ty waved him off, but cut his eyes toward the big guy's half-eaten plate of pasta.

In the dark hallway, Artie dialed *0* and the farmhouse's phone number to place a collect call. When the automated voice asked for his name, he said, "Artie Bauer—I'm fine, Grandpa," and waited for the call to connect. Since his grandmother's death, Artie always made sure that he didn't worry his grandfather by calling collect. Older folks—like Harry Bauer and maybe even Minnie Marecek—were accustomed to receiving telephone calls with the long-distance charges reversed only when a tragedy had occurred to a family member or close friend.

Grandpa accepted the charges and answered, *"Artie, boy, I'm glad you called. I sure am sorry I couldn't be there today, but I watched the game on TV—the last part of it, anyways. I hope your friend Johnny is okay. That was some kind of catch!"*

"Yeah, Smitty hurt his arm, but not too bad," said Artie. "So, what's going on there, Grandpa?" Artie kept his head down to keep the phone conversation as private as possible, as restaurant patrons walked in and out of the two restrooms.

"Well . . . this isn't something I like saying over the phone," Harry Bauer began, *"but Abe Pressler called me this morning and said the plane in the swamp was empty—no bodies anywhere—and so Skip Ross told the feds about the graves at the White place. We've all been out there today—I took Brody to show them the spots he found—and they started digging."* He stopped, as if he weren't sure whether he should tell what else he knew.

Artie's heart began to race. "What did they find, Grandpa?" he asked.

Again, the old man hesitated. *"Well . . . they found the two pilots,"* he said, *"or who they think are the pilots—from the clothes on them. They sent the bodies to the state coroner's office up there in Capital City. It'll be a few days before they know for sure."*

"So, they didn't find P.J. White, then?" said Artie. "One of the bodies couldn't be him?"

Grandpa cleared his throat. *"No, son,"* he said. *"Skip Ross—he was there, too—he told me both men were too short to be him. Matter of fact, Skip took me aside and told me—just between him and me—that P.J. and Bob White are the prime suspects in those two murders. He wouldn't tell me how the pilots died, but he said it didn't appear they were killed in the plane crash. He said he and that little gal of his were gonna be up there tomorrow to see you boys play, anyway, so he might as well run over to the prison and talk to Bob again—if the FBI allows it."*

Now Artie was the one who didn't know what to say. "I don't know, Grandpa," said Artie. "In a strange sort of way, it's almost a relief to hear it was those pilots buried in that clearing. It might shake Tommy up, but—"

"Don't say a word about this to Tommy, son," interrupted Grandpa. *"Not one word. He might call his mama or his daddy and say something to mess up the FBI's interview tomorrow."*

"Yeah, you're right," Artie said. "Besides, I could tell something was bothering him today. I think it's that tomorrow is Mother's Day, and he's thinking about his mom." Neither spoke for a moment. "So, are you riding up with Minnie tomorrow? I was wondering if Wilma and Leah will ride with her, too, or if they'll come on one of the buses from school. And, before I forget, are you bringing Brody? Tommy said it might be hard to find some grass for Brody around the stadium—you know?"

Harry Bauer cleared his throat again. "*That's something else, Artie,*" he said. "*Skip Ross wasn't the only local cop at the White place today. Marty Quinn showed up there this afternoon—said his hitch in the reserves is done, and he'll be going back to work for the sheriff's department on Monday. He took Brody home with him—just now left after getting his box and bedding—but Marty said he'd bring the ol' boy back for a visit now and then. Jeepers, I miss him already.*"

"I'm sorry, Grandpa," said Artie. "I'm gonna miss Brody, too. He's a part of the family now. So, you'll be okay there by yourself tonight?"

The noise that the old man made at first was hard to identify. "*Son, I didn't answer those other questions you had,*" said Grandpa. "*The girls—Wilma and Leah—they want to ride the bus up the road with the other youngsters tomorrow morning, and John Russo is gonna haul them over to the school around sunup. Wilma is gonna spend the night with the little Russo girl.*" He hesitated again.

"Where's Minnie gonna be?" asked Artie, knowing the answer before he asked the question.

"*She's right here now,*" Grandpa said, "*but before you get the wrong idea, she's gonna sleep in her office out in the trailer. She was doing paperwork out there when I got home and told her about the goings-on at the White place, and she said it might not be a good idea for me to stay alone here on the farm tonight, what with so many things—evidence and such—disappearing right and left.*"

"I'm sorry, Grandpa," said Artie again. "I didn't mean to butt in. You always do what's right, but I sure do wish I was there with you right now."

"*I do, too, son,*" Harry Bauer said, his voice cracking. In the awkward silence that followed, Artie sensed that his grandfather had something else to say but couldn't.

"Well, I'd better hang up," said Artie. "This call's gonna cost a fortune. See you tomorrow. I love you, Grandpa. You and Minnie drive careful."

"*We will, son,*" Grandpa replied. "*I'm proud of you, boy. Don't you ever forget that.*"

Back at the senior players' booth, Artie Bauer looked down at his nearly empty plate, then at his best friend. "Really?" asked Artie. "You ate my spaghetti?"

"Hey, man," replied Ty Green, "Coach said to pound that pasta. . . . And you said not to eat your *breadsticks*. I didn't. I even left you a little spaghetti sauce to dip them in."

Artie gave a tired laugh. "Thanks, Ty," he said. "It's nice to know you're always thinking of me."

CHAPTER 25

LIKE A CONVOY OF TRUCKS HAULING HOPE, four packed buses from Oleander County pulled into the stadium parking lot at nine o'clock Sunday morning, a full hour before Game Two's first pitch. Three were yellow Arbor High school buses being pressed into weekend duty. The fourth was a battered but repaired Solid Rock Christian Church bus that had survived the Good Friday Storm. Artie found out later that the Solid Rock church group had held a worship service—complete with a printed bulletin, hymns, offering and rousing sermon—in their bus on the way up the road that morning. They had also handed out red rosebuds to people whose mothers were still alive; white rosebuds, to those whose mothers had passed on. Many pinned the flowers on their shirts, making it easy to identify which fans were Solid Rock church members.

A line of smaller vehicles—cars, trucks, vans, SUVs, *Moby* and *The Woody Wagon*—followed the buses and filled over half the huge lot with family, friends and students from both Arbor and Solid Rock. Watching the fans file into the ballpark, Artie Bauer, Ty Green and Jimmy Gore stood behind the batting cage while Tommy White took his practice swings, and they marveled that everyone arriving wore a green-and-gold *We Are Solid Rock Strong* T-shirt, some with rosebuds, some without.

"Man, oh, man," Artie Bauer said, "Vicki and Miss Hopper outdid themselves with the shirts. They must have sold one to everybody. But it looks great!"

"Yep," said Jimmy Gore, "and I see Solid Rock kids who transferred to the other schools, not just to Arbor—to Mimosa Beach and Port Oleander and Iron Harbor. They're *all* here for us."

A minute later, the boys spotted Harry Bauer and Minnie Marecek sitting high in the grandstand, in the first row of red seats below the lowest level of the press box. They waved to the players. Next to them were Abe and Deborah Pressler, Donnell and Alicia Evans, then Skip Ross and Thelma Hopper, and Woody and Hannah Woods on down the line. In the second row were the Greens, the Durans and the Gores, as well as Jerry Church and Louise Foxx, all of whom had attended Saturday's game. If Jimmy Foxx was there, he didn't show himself. The Inouyes' seats were low in the stands behind the Bruins dugout on the first-base side. That was also the section where most of the Arbor High students saved seats for each other before dashing off to the concession area for hot dogs, popcorn and sodas.

What surprised Artie even more was that Solid Rock Church brought many of the youth, adults and translators from their deaf ministry, also attired in the green-and-gold tees. They sat in the section next to the students, but appeared to enjoy the energy of the excited fans from home. Artie recognized the nice lady who had taught the Barf Table gang how to sign the patriotic songs for Senior Day, and he pointed her out to Jimmy and Ty. She was smiling and signing to the young folks and older adults around her, and some of them were signing back.

"Dang, everybody *is* here," said Ty. "We can't let them down, guys. We gotta win this thing." He took up his bat and walked around the side of the cage to take Tommy White's place inside.

Catching sight of the crowd from home, Tommy likewise was taken aback. "Whoa," he said to Artie and Jimmy, "I sure didn't think so many people would come, not with the game on TV."

"And with it being Mother's Day," Jimmy added. That reminder appeared to dampen Tommy's spirit, and he turned toward the dugout with his head down.

Jimmy shook his head and asked, "What did I say, Artie? Mother's Day?"

"Yeah," said Artie, "it's his first Mother's Day without his mom. You know about her, right?" Jimmy nodded contritely and started to speak, but Artie looked past him and said, "Hold on a second. Football coach at twelve o'clock."

"Huh?" said Jimmy. "It isn't even *ten* o'clock yet." But when he turned to see where Artie was looking, Jimmy recognized State College football's Coach Landis and another man in a red Cardinals jacket and baseball cap headed toward them. "Uh-oh," Jimmy said, "this doesn't look good at all. Coach Carson is trying to head them off."

The boys turned to watch as Carson hurried to keep Landis and the college's baseball coach from reaching the batting cage. But Landis shook his head in annoyance and came close to pushing the Arbor assistant coach aside. That was when Jug Johnson stormed out of the dugout. "Who in the Sam Hill do you think you are?" Jug howled at Landis, ignoring the other State coach for the moment. "Stay away from my boys until after the game—when the series is over. Got it?"

Landis, turning to face Arbor's head coach at the top of the dugout steps, shot a string of words back at him that the boys couldn't make out. Jug Johnson had no problem understanding this important man who was used to getting his way even if it meant breaking the rules. "No, sir, I didn't jinx a dadgum thing!" Jug yelled. "Get off the field and get back in the stands where you belong! Both of you. You aren't allowed to talk to anybody right now. Football don't start until baseball's over, Landis."

Jug's red-faced tirade stopped the college coaches in their tracks, but the looks they gave Jimmy and Artie before returning to their seats could have wilted the Mother's Day rosebuds worn by the Solid Rock folks in the stands.

As the home team that morning, the Bruins would take the field on defense first. In the dugout before the National Anthem, Jug Johnson looked up and down the bench at his boys, knowing that Mike Inouye would be heading to the mound and Artie Bauer to the plate for warm-ups. Then, minutes later, the other players would be heading out to their positions as they were introduced.

"Some of you probably heard what I said to Coach Landis," Jug began, "I mean, about the series being over after this game. Tell you the truth, that's what I believe—I do. Boys, we're gonna take care of business this morning, and we're gonna make all these folks wearing green and gold proud."

The coach was quiet for a second. "Now, I *do* need to say one thing about our pitching situation before we get going," he said. "Mike, here, is starting for us today. I sincerely believe Mike Inouye and Ty Green are the two best high school pitchers in this entire state, bar none. But, boys—and this goes for everybody in this dugout—they're gonna need your help this morning."

Jug studied his players' faces, then continued, "Mike's daddy—Dr. Inouye—only wants him to throw sixty pitches today. Now, that ain't nothing new. But we don't have Smitty, and Ty can only pitch three innings in relief, if we need him. Big Phil is our DH and our closer, but Manny—or one of you other boys—may need to give us an inning or two somewhere along the way. In a championship game like this, you never can tell what's gonna happen, so be ready for anything."

In fact, Artie Bauer and Ty Green had already discussed this possibility at breakfast—that Manny Freeman, the team's utility player and pitcher of last resort, or some other position player might have to pitch, if the series went to a third game that afternoon. Now they faced the prospect of having to relieve Mike sooner than expected in Game Two—that is, if he couldn't keep his pitch count down. Artie and Ty knew that few high school pitchers could throw anything close to a complete game in under sixty pitches.

It was as if the Capital City batters knew about the parent-imposed limit. From the first hitter on, the Red Caps seemed determined to run Mike's pitch count up, taking more balls than usual and fouling more off than Artie had seen all season. Almost every batter took the count to full before swinging on a 3-2 pitch and either making contact or whiffing. To Mike and the Bruins' credit, only two batters reached base—on one walk and one single—in the two and two-thirds innings he threw before reaching his sixty-pitch maximum.

Counting pitches in the stands, Dr. Inouye had sent daughter Kimi to the dugout with a note for Coach Johnson as soon as Mike's pitch count reached fifty. "*Do not forget,*" read the index card, which Artie saw later on the mound, "*no more than 60 pitches — Kato Inouye.*"

After the sixtieth pitch, Jug Johnson called time and left the dugout, calling Artie Bauer to the mound with him. Showing his pitcher the index card and asking him for the ball, Jug said, "I'm sorry, son, but we're gonna have to do it your father's way. I know you don't want to come out, but this was part of the deal. Remember? We talked about this the very first day we met back at Easter. I'm proud of you, but we don't have no choice." Jug tossed the ball to Artie.

"Yes, I do," said Mike Inouye, shocking both the coach and his catcher. "I will finish this inning. It's too soon for Phil to come in, and we can't waste one of Ty's innings for just one batter—or two."

"Phil and Ty won't be relieving you," Jug Johnson explained, having discussed this strategy with Joe Carson in their motel room the night before. "It'll be Manny, and you'll be out in center for him. If Phil comes in, we'll lose our DH. Like you said, Ty can only pitch three innings—no matter how many pitches it takes. The way Mac's throwing, we need all your bats in the lineup."

That was definitely the case, because the Capital City ace, who had embarrassed the Arbor boys earlier in the season, was putting on a repeat performance that Sunday morning. To that point in the game, none of the Bruins batters had gotten the ball out of the infield, hitting pop-ups and groundouts if they made contact at all.

With the plate umpire headed toward the mound, Mike just shook his head and said nothing for a couple of seconds until the man in blue arrived. Then the boy surprised the others again by asking to borrow the ump's pencil. "What?" the confused umpire said. "You want my pencil?" But he handed it over when he saw the index card.

Mike's reply to his father—and to his coach—was a simple request: "*My teammates need me to finish this inning. Please. It is my duty. M.*" He returned the stub of a pencil to the ump, gave the card to Jug, and took back the ball from Artie. He finished the inning, and his father understood.

* * *

After a scoreless home half of the 3rd, Mike Inouye reported to center field for the top of the 4th, and Manny Freeman went to the hill to pitch. Jug Johnson had told the team's speedy jack of all trades that his prime objective was to get three outs—in other words, to last that one inning. What Artie knew that Jug had left unsaid was, *without letting them score too many runs.* As the Bruins could attest from their meeting a month earlier, the Capital City offense was potent against average pitching, especially their power hitters at the three, four and five positions in the batting order. But after contending with Mike's fiery pitches, the first two Red Caps sluggers—the three and four hitters—couldn't keep from getting out in front of Manny's weaker fastballs. They twisted themselves into human pretzels, flailing away at his inarguably off-speed pitches. Both struck out swinging. That was when Manny's luck ran out.

Cap City's number-five hitter—their stocky catcher with brawny arms and post-like legs—walked from the on-deck circle to the coaching box near third base. There he conferred with his coach for half a minute, the batter's red helmet nodding like a bobblehead toy as the man talked and pointed at Manny and at the boy's bat. After striding to the plate, the right-handed hitter stepped into the batter's box and dug his cleats into the red clay. With two outs and no one on base, Manny went into his full windup and threw the ball toward his target—Artie's mitt set low in the strike zone. The batter tapped his front foot once to hold himself back and then swung his arms and bat forward with all his might, connecting with the pitch and sending it rocketing toward the left-field corner. The ball rose toward the yellow foul pole, with left-fielder Brett Woods struggling to follow its flight high in the sun-drenched sky. Brett stopped at the base of the ivy-covered wall and turned to watch the ball sail just to the left of the pole. "Foul ball!" shouted the umpire. "Strike one!"

"Timeout!" Artie called, taking off his mask and jogging out to the mound. "You're doing great, Manny—really, you are. But I've got a question: can you throw any other pitches besides that fastball? Have you been working on anything else?"

Manny gave Artie an odd look. "Well," he said, holding his glove in front of his mouth, "me and some of the guys have been messing around with different stuff in warm-ups—you know, at the start of practice and before games. I'm getting pretty good throwing one thing, but it's kind of a junk-ball pitch."

"Junk ball?" asked Artie. "You mean, a spitball or something? That isn't legal."

"No," Manny replied, shaking his head, "a knuckleball—like in that baseball book."

"*Ball Four?*" Artie said, not knowing that his teammate was so widely read. "Well, okay," Artie said, with a shrug. "Let's give it a try. I think that boy has caught up with your fastball. We just need two more strikes—or an out any way we can get it." Artie managed to smile before turning to jog back to home.

The ump tossed Manny a new ball and shouted for play to continue. The batter took his practice swings. Manny looked down at the ball in his glove and arranged his grip, pursing his lips as if he wanted each fingernail in precisely the right spot. When he was satisfied, he reared back and stiff-armed the ball toward the plate, the sphere rotating in flight but landing in Artie's mitt more than just a bit outside. The count was now one ball and one strike. Three bad knuckleballs later, the Red Caps catcher walked, as did the next two batters on four pitches each. There were still two outs, but the bases were loaded.

This time, Jug Johnson stopped play and waved Ty Green in from right field. When they all stood together on the mound, Jug took the baseball from Manny. "You did fine, little man," Jug said. "Now, get out there in right field. We still need your glove, your bat and your speed." The old coach paused, then handed Ty the pill. "Now, I don't want to see no more knuckleballs or hanging curves," Jug said, "and if nothing else is working, just smoke 'em inside." He winked, turned and headed back to the dugout.

Capital City's number-eight hitter was up next, batting left. On the first pitch—a screwball—the boy took a cut and caught only part of the ball, popping it up into foul territory between third base and the Red Caps dugout. Third baseman Jimmy Gore scrambled laterally in hopes of catching the pop-foul and ending the inning. But the arc of the ball was higher and closer to the team's bench than Jimmy had thought, forcing him to lunge awkwardly toward the railing that kept players from falling into the dark dugout, its roof shading the cemented, rectangular interior from the sun. The former Solid Rock football star and State College recruit hit the railing just as he reached up and snagged the foul ball out of the air. His momentum flipped him over the top bar and into the dugout, halfway caught, halfway blocked by the boys closest to where he landed.

All three Red Caps baserunners took off—the one on third headed toward home—because they could advance and score if the impact of Jimmy's fall caused the ball to pop out of his glove. But as had happened the day before with Smitty's spectacular catch in right field, Jimmy quickly stood and lifted his clenched glove high in the air so that all could see; he opened it and showed that the ball was secure in the smooth pocket of his leather mitt. The half inning had ended, and Capital City's scoring threat was over. Arbor fans were overjoyed, while even Capital City's supporters were impressed with Jimmy's feat. However, seated in the stands, Coach Landis—livid at seeing one of his football recruits risk injury in any other sport—grumbled and swore, then threw up his hands and left the park, leaving the State College baseball coach sitting by himself. Artie looked back at Jimmy to see if he noticed, but the superhero of the moment was busy brushing himself off and laughing, as he climbed out of the other team's dugout.

* * *

Ty Green's 4th-inning relief appearance—though it had consisted of a single pitch—meant that he could throw only two more innings that day, even if the teams had to play another game to decide the state championship. Later in the dugout, Coach Jug Johnson had explained to his star pitcher and catcher—the team co-captains—that he felt it was better, in this pitchers' duel, to use Ty until his innings were spent. It would be different, Jug had said, if Arbor hadn't won Game One or if they weren't in contention right then in Game Two. Otherwise, Jug might have decided to pull Ty after the one pitch and save him to make an appearance—two innings early or late—in Game Three. "I'm glad Joe's here to help me with this," Jug had said. "All this thinking makes my head hurt."

Capital City's Big Mac McIntosh continued mowing Arbor batters down in the "home" halves of the 4th and 5th innings. Likewise, Ty Green picked up where he had left off on Saturday, and retired all three Red Caps in the 5th. Nothing changed on-field until the start of the 6th inning, when Jug Johnson switched Manny Freeman in right field with Ozzie Maye at shortstop. After two outs, Phil Waters subbed in for Ozzie Maye in right. That move meant, however, that the Bruins could no longer use a "designated hitter" for the rest of that particular game, but—since Phil had been the DH for weak-hitting Ozzie, anyway—it really didn't matter. Phil's bat was still in the lineup, and he now batted for himself.

At the start of the 7th inning with still no score, Phil Waters, as usual, took the mound, and Ty Green—whose day was done as a pitcher—took Phil's place in right field. Even though it wasn't a "save" situation, Arbor needed their best available pitcher on the hill in hopes of shutting down the Red Caps and then getting a run in the bottom of the final frame for a walk-off win. Phil, a lefty, was just the medicine for Arbor's ailing pitching staff that Jug and Joe—not to mention Dr. Inouye—had ordered. Mike Inouye, as much of a flamethrower as Mac McIntosh, might have matched the Cap City ace with a complete game that day. But Artie—and, likewise, Jug and Joe—knew that defying Mike's father would have had ramifications off the diamond, as well as on. It was good that Mike had found a way to be true to himself—in the spirit of *wa*—without pitting his father against the team's coach.

Big Phil Waters—a senior who had played alongside Artie Bauer on the Bruins offensive line the previous fall—possessed, like most football linemen, a good head for remembering the smallest details. And not having to play defense for six innings as the baseball team's designated hitter, Phil didn't just sit in the dugout and pick his nose; he always paid attention to the action on the field. That foresight came in handy on this day, because Phil Waters must have recalled how, early in the game, Capital City batters had run up Mike Inouye's pitch count—by taking pitches and fouling off more balls than usual. This bit of knowledge mattered, because Phil—after shutting down the Red Caps from the mound—would bat first for the Bruins in the bottom of the 7th. Sophomore Brett Woods, still wearing his Zorro mask, would be on deck. Freshman Tommy White would be in the hole, batting third. Brett and Tommy were rookies on the baseball team, and Artie worried when he saw that both boys looked nervous about facing the Red Caps fireballer at such a critical point in the game.

In the batter's box, Phil stood and watched Mac's first pitch zip past, low and away, for ball one. He then fouled off the next five pitches. With the count 1-and-2, Phil started to swing again but held up, and Mac just missed striking him out with a slider in the dirt. The 2-2 pitch was another ball, this one high and tight, so far inside that Phil had to jump back to keep from being hit. On the bench, Artie Bauer heard someone—maybe it was Ty Green—say something about "taking one for the team," but no one in the dugout, not even Mike Inouye, had enough *wa* in them to take one of Mac's fastballs in the helmet. But that fastball gave Artie an idea that he shared, first, with Tommy and then with Brett, calling him back from the on-deck circle. Joe Carson was coaching at first; Jug Johnson, at third, as usual.

"Brett, we've got to tire Mac out," said Artie, while the umpire called time to let Phil step out of the batter's box and gather himself after the close call. "Whether Phil gets on or not, take the first pitch and then protect the strike zone," Artie told Brett. "Foul off anything that's close. Run up his pitch count the best you can, unless he gives you something too good *not* to swing away at."

Behind the protective mask, Brett looked worried. "But what if Coach gives me a different sign?" he asked. "What if he says to swing at the first pitch?"

With a shrug, Artie replied, "Just tell him that facemask blocked your *perpendicular* vision."

"*Parenthetical*," Brett corrected.

"Whatever," said Artie. "Phil's too slow to steal second or to use the hit-and-run, so you need to get either a hit or a walk. And if we can tire Mac out for Tommy, that's even better." Brett nodded and returned to the circle.

At the plate, the count full, Mac McIntosh went into his windup and hurled a fastball that might have risen out of the strike zone if Phil Waters had been able to hold up his swing. But he could not, and he wheeled around, his bat nicking the ball as it flashed past and smacked securely in the catcher's mitt. "You're out!" cried the umpire. Phil shook his head, upset with himself and stomped back to the dugout.

Brett strode to the plate and took his time setting up in the batter's box. As

Artie, the team co-captain, had instructed, Brett took the first pitch for a strike, even though he might have been able to do something with it. Artie glanced over at Jug, who didn't appear upset but was busy clapping and tugging and brushing through his series of signs to tell Brett what to do next. Artie saw the masked batter nod at the coach, before stepping back in and fouling off the next pitch. The count was 0-2. Again, Jug was calm and did nothing now but clap twice, touch the bill of his cap, and clap once more. He had signaled Brett to swing away—which was basically what Artie had told his young teammate to do.

The next pitch was a fastball that Brett Woods swung on and drove straight back at the pitcher. The line drive left Brett's bat at an even higher velocity than Mac had thrown the ball from the mound, and it struck the gangly boy in the back as he completed his follow-through. But it was a glancing blow, and the ball caromed off Mac straight at the Red Caps third baseman, who snagged the rock in his bare hand and fired to first for the Bruins' second out of the final inning. The Capital City coach called timeout and rushed onto the field with his trainer to check on McIntosh. The boy looked okay, but he stretched and worked his left shoulder for a minute before nodding that he'd be fine. Satisfied, the trainer gave Mac's shoulder one last rub, and the coach waved to the umpire that his ace would stay in the game.

Tommy White walked to the plate. He stopped outside the batter's box and looked back at Artie standing on the top step of the dugout, the big catcher having not yet bothered to put back on any of his gear. Artie nodded to his young cousin and gave him a thumbs-up, hoping to calm the boy's nerves. Tommy nodded back, stepped into the box, tapped home plate with his bat and took his practice swings. Then he waited for the first pitch. "Strike one!" shouted the umpire.

Like Brett before him, Tommy followed Artie's instructions and tried to extend the at-bat for as long as he could. Mac's control wasn't what it had been, whether because of Brett's line drive off his shoulder or from having pitched almost a complete game. The count was 3-and-1 when Mac released an off-speed pitch whose initial path tempted Tommy to swing. He chased the slider, stepping into it and swinging from his toes. His front foot slid in the loose dirt of the batter's box, and he missed the ball completely, though it also sailed past the catcher untouched and hit the backstop. The umpire shouted, "Strike two!"

Instead of retrieving the ball, the Cap City catcher came out of his crouch and pointed first to his coach in the Red Caps dugout, and then at the ground before him. "It was a foul tip," yelled the catcher. "He stepped out of the box. His shoe touched the plate. He's out!" He made an *out* sign with his fist.

The ensuing discussion—between both coaches, the catcher and the ump— grew heated when first one side, then the other seemed to get the upper hand. Even though the game was being televised, there were no instant replays or official reviews allowed to ensure that the correct call was made. But this umpire was experienced—he was perhaps the best ump in the state—and he trusted his instincts and his initial call. Because Tommy had not made contact with the ball on his swing, the fact that he *had* stepped on home plate made no difference whatsoever. The count was now full at 3-and-2.

While the others argued, Tommy White drifted back toward the on-deck circle, where lead-off hitter Ricky Duran waited for his turn at bat. Of course, that depended on whether or not Tommy, the number-nine hitter in the lineup, got on base. Artie could see that Ricky was doing his best to encourage Tommy. Not only were they teammates, but they—and Artie as well—were friends at the Barf Table and neighbors on the Bauer farm.

Then Artie saw Ricky point toward the stands rising behind the Arbor dugout, directing Tommy's attention away from the argument at home. At the same time, Artie became aware of a sound—a kind of low hum—that was rising above the normal chatter and noise of the stadium crowd. Artie took a step in front of the dugout so that he could see over its roof, and there in the stands he saw the Solid Rock Church members standing up, all of them with both arms extended and both hands signing what Artie knew to be the letter *B*. Following the congregants' lead, the Arbor students lifted their own hands and also began to hum the same tone, increasing its intensity. Artie watched as a literal wave of support for his timid cousin spread from one section to the next around the ballpark. Even Grandpa Bauer and the Arbor parents stood and saluted Tommy "Buzz" White. He was *The Drone Ranger* no longer—or was he?

Ty Green stuck his head out of the dugout. "What's going on, Yogi?" he asked his friend.

"They're making *B*'s," Artie said, holding up his hand and tucking his thumb into his palm. "And they're buzzing like bees—like Tommy's bees. Come look guys." He waved his teammates up to the dugout railing so that they could see and hear for themselves this spontaneous display of spirit. In seconds, the whole team was signing and buzzing along with the Arbor faithful in the crowd.

And they didn't stop as the dispute at home plate was settled and Tommy stepped back into the batter's box once again. The sustained sound—like the drone of a bagpipe—seemed to unnerve Mac on the mound, but he shook off the distraction, nodded to his catcher, and went into his windup. Standing tall, then crouching a bit, Tommy kept his eyes on the pitcher, though he wanted to look down to make sure neither foot was close to stepping outside the box. The 3-2 pitch flew from Mac's hand and seemed to explode toward the strike zone as it approached the plate. Tommy saw the spinning ball's rotation. Its thick, crimson laces—sewn into the white, horsehide cover—gave the sphere a reddish glow, an aura of warmth and strength that Tommy said later he had never felt before, a thin atmosphere of pressure that stilled his nervousness in the moment and helped him breathe in and then out as he swung his bat.

The ball cleared the center-field wall and kept rising, rising until it disappeared into the glare of the midday sun. Tommy watched its flight for as long as he could before pitching his bat into the grass and starting his home-run trot. As he stepped on first base, he raised his arms—making the same sign that had given him strength—and turned toward second, then toward third, and then home, where he hopped with both feet on the plate, surrounded by a joyous, jumping throng of teammates, coaches, and students still streaming from the stands.

There was no denying now that the Arbor High Bruins were Solid Rock strong.

CHAPTER 26

BENNIE PRESSLER SUGGESTED 'MOZEL TOV MONDAY,' but he was voted down by Vicki Duke and the cheerleaders. Since *they* were making the banner, championship week at Arbor High School started with "Maniac Monday" in the cafeteria. Without telling the team in advance, everyone who had been at the game—including cashier Frankie Hughes—changed back into their green-and-gold *We Are Solid Rock Strong* T-shirts and celebrated Jug Johnson, Joe Carson and the baseball Bruins' big win. The cheerleaders' banner stated, "*GET CRAZY! WE ARE THE CHAMPIONS!,*" and Frankie Hughes hung it on the lunchroom wall above Jug and Joe's faculty recliners. Once everyone was through the lunch line, Vicki rousted the coaches from their easy chairs and called all the boys to the front, where they were saluted with a roomful of *B*'s and buzzing until Thelma Hopper quieted them and announced, "Honey buns for everybody!" The cheerleaders—with pipe-cleaner antennae attached to hair barrettes—handed out boxes of the treats to ensure that the student body spent the rest of the school day with a sugar buzz. But on this day the faculty understood why their students needed to get a bit crazy. Likewise, Principal Jerry Church was patient when several senior boys decided to fling their honey buns like flying discs across the cafeteria toward the Barf Table instead of eating them.

It was good that there was no sports practices that Monday—and for the rest of that week—because clouds rolled in shortly after noon and, according to the forecasts, looked like they would not clear until late in the workweek. A steady rain began to fall mid-afternoon, and when Artie, Tommy and Ricky ran from the school building to the old red pickup truck after the release bell, they splashed all the way across the parking lot. Artie wondered if sunny skies and dry conditions would return to Oleander County in time for that Saturday's benefit golf tournament at Sandpiper Shores. Working on the farm in downpours would be hard enough, but getting soaked to the skin on the golf course would be no fun at all. Artie made a mental note to ask Woody Woods about getting them all golf umbrellas, just in case.

In the pickup truck, all three boys laughed about the lunchroom scene that day. Artie and Ricky teased Tommy—in a good way—about being the "king bee," though he reminded them that females run the hive, as the queen bee and all the workers are girls. In a reflective mood, Ricky wondered out loud whether that made Vicki Duke or Miss Hopper their true queen—Vicki, he decided, since the students had voted her that honor at homecoming the previous fall. But Artie countered that Vicki's misbehavior with Josh Stark at the homecoming dance, and her embarrassment over the whole nasty affair had tarnished more than her queenly reputation; it had been a much-needed wakeup call for the girl, one that had forced her to work at being nicer to everyone in school, not just to those who might help her climb the school's social ladder. "Remember?" Artie said, as he stopped the truck at Ricky's house. "Her nickname used to be *Digger*. But you don't hear anybody call her that now. That's a good thing."

Almost home, Artie got out of the pickup and hurried across the highway to check the mailbox, in case his grandfather hadn't ventured out in the rain that afternoon for the mail. Inside were a couple of bills, an advertising circular, and the Mother's Day card that Tommy had mailed to Connie White the previous week. Back in the truck, Artie handed it to Tommy. "Sorry, buddy," Artie said, restarting the engine and pulling across the road to head down the farm lane.

Tommy looked at the yellow envelope bearing his loopy handwriting and the "Undeliverable as Addressed" sticker. "Gee," he said, shaking his head, "I hope she saw the game. I should've called. *After* the game yesterday, I asked Skip and Miss Hopper if they'd take me over to the prison—I figured Coach would let me go—but Skip said it was too late."

Artie nodded. "I thought you were kinda down yesterday at Sal's," he said, "but don't worry—if she didn't see the game on TV, she can read about it. It had to be in the Capital City paper this morning. I bet they even got your picture hitting that dinger."

To get Tommy back in a positive frame of mind, Artie continued, "Speaking of Sal's, did you see him and Woody hitting it off yesterday? I think Woody asked Sal for some of his recipes, and said he was going to add them to the grill's menu. When we were leaving, I *did* hear him invite Sal down here—to come talk about opening his own place at the beach."

"Is Woody getting tired of cooking for us?" asked Tommy, frowning a bit. "He wouldn't sell the surf shop and the grill, would he?"

"I don't think he would," Artie said, glancing toward the barn as they drove past it, "but he does own *three* surf shops. Maybe he wants to add a restaurant in either Mimosa Beach or Iron Harbor. They don't have grills like the one at the Sandpiper shop." Artie saw that despite the constant showers Minnie Marecek's pickup and *Moby* were both parked outside the doublewide trailer next to the corral, but that neither Minnie nor Wilma was outside.

"I wonder if Minnie has any therapy sessions scheduled this afternoon," Tommy said, turning to look back toward the trailer. "Maybe she'll need me to help them."

Artie, looking toward the farmhouse, said, "Nope, but Grandpa sure does have a bunch of company—looks like Abe Pressler's SUV and Skip Ross's rental car. I'm not sure about the other SUV. Gee, I wonder if Skip brought Miss Hopper, too. Then, with Minnie and Wilma, we'd have a real party."

Instead, as Artie and Tommy parked the pickup next to the other vehicles and got out, someone opened the porch door, and Brody the long-haired German Shepherd dashed down the ramp and up the sidewalk toward them. The dog met them halfway and started to jump to greet Tommy, but the screen door opened again and Marty Quinn stepped outside.

"Halt!" called Sgt. Quinn. "*Zitz!*" Brody stopped and sat. The officer looked up at the boys and smiled. "Looks like somebody's glad to see you two. Makes me glad I brought him back out here. Hey, Tommy, how about taking Brody for a walk—he needs a break—and then bring him back inside. We're in the kitchen."

The rain having stopped for the moment, Tommy agreed and led the big dog around the house, away from the yard. Artie followed Quinn onto the porch and into the kitchen, where he saw the other three men—Grandpa, Abe and Skip—all sitting around the table, as if a board meeting were underway. Artie realized then that they had wanted to talk to him alone for a minute and that what they had to say probably wasn't good.

Once Artie was seated, Harry Bauer did the talking. "Son, I just couldn't bring myself to tell you this yesterday," Grandpa began, "not with it being Mother's Day and all. And, the good Lord knows, I wasn't gonna tell you over the phone Saturday evening when you called. I'd just found this terrible thing out myself, and I had to deal with it all afternoon, making arrangements and such. Miss Minnie helped me with it—so, yes, she knows about this, and I apologize that she found out before you did."

Artie's spirits sank, but he said, "That's all right, Grandpa. What is it?" He could have guessed.

"There really *were* two graves out there in that clearing near Tommy's tree house," said Harry Bauer, "and they really did find the two pilots buried there. But . . ." The old man looked up toward the ceiling for an instant, then back at Artie. "But those two men—the two pilots—they were buried in the same grave." Again, he stopped, unable to find the right words.

"Was P.J. buried out there, too?" asked Artie. "In the other grave?" They were questions whose answers Artie hoped would be *yes*, but Grandpa still said nothing, his gray head unmoving, his blue eyes telling Artie that this was one of the worst things a grandfather would ever have to tell his grandson.

"No, son," said Harry Bauer. "They found your mother—my little Ingrid—in that second grave. She's been there for . . . eighteen years." Now Grandpa pursed his lips and looked away, trying to regain his composure. "She didn't leave you behind, Artie," he said at last, in a hoarse whisper, "and she didn't get upset with me and Mama, either, and run off like we always thought. She *couldn't* come home."

Artie had never really known his mother, or at least he remembered nothing from the months she had cared for him as a baby. He knew that it wasn't possible to truly miss something he'd never had, but he had always held deep within himself the hope that she was alive and well, and that she would someday return, maybe even that spring for his high school graduation. Even that year, he had dreamed that she might have read in the newspapers about his athletic successes— his football victories, and his wrestling and baseball championships—or that his mother might have watched him on TV, maybe even that very weekend, as Tommy's parents had had the opportunity.

"How did she die?" Artie asked. "Did he kill her?"

This time Harry Bauer shook his head, but motioned for Marty Quinn to answer. "We don't think so," Marty said. "I talked to the medical examiner this morning, and he told me that there were no signs of blunt-force trauma, or gunshot or knife wounds. I won't go into the details, but we're still waiting for toxicology results that *might* answer some questions. Skip? You want to tell him how she was found?"

"Sure," said Deputy Ross, turning to face both Artie and Grandpa. "Whoever buried Ingrid took care to *place* her in the grave—I'm not gonna say, with *love* or anything like that, but her little body was handled with respect. We could tell from the way her head and her hands were placed. The person had folded some clothes under her head—maybe extra clothes she'd kept at the Whites' house— and her arms were crossed, and her shoulder bag—you know, one of those big leather handbags with fringe—it looked like she was holding it. And, yes, it looked like all of her things were still in it."

Grandpa was shaking now, not bothering to hold back his tears. Artie spoke for him. "Was there anything else?" the boy asked. "Jewelry? Like a ring or a bracelet or a necklace?"

Skip hesitated and glanced over at Marty, then nodded for his colleague to take over again. "Not *her* jewelry," said Marty Quinn. "There was a ten-karat-gold class ring on her finger, an old one—and by *old* I mean not for what would have been Ingrid's graduating class if she had graduated. And it wasn't from the right school, either." He paused, but decided to tell Artie and Harry, anyway. "The ring was on her left hand, on her ring finger, placed there—we think—after she died. It was a man's ring in a large size—too big for a little girl like her to wear, not without wax or something like that to keep it from falling off. It was from E-ville High School, and the initials inside it were *PJW*. The year on the ring was the year P.J. White graduated. We found him in a school yearbook."

"Case closed," Artie said, hearing the screen door slam and then Tommy's footfalls and Brody's panting out on the porch as the boy and dog headed toward the kitchen door. "That explains why P.J. got so mad at Connie that morning after the robbery, right? You know, when she mentioned my mother to him. Didn't Connie say that—'No wonder Ingrid left you'—and slapped his face?"

"She did," said Grandpa, though the question hadn't been directed at him. He turned to greet Tommy and motioned for him to take a seat at the table. "Sit down here, Tommy boy. We need to have a little talk." Again, Harry Bauer looked to Skip Ross for help.

Not in uniform, the off-duty sheriff's deputy cleared his throat, as if what he had to say was again difficult and needed to be stated delicately. "Yesterday you asked if Thelma and I would take you to see your mother," Skip said, "and I told you *no*. Well, I need to explain. It was bec—"

"But it was Mother's Day," interrupted Tommy, "and everyone's been putting pressure on me to stay in touch with her—even though *I'm* the one in a foster home." He looked at Abe Pressler, his official foster father since the previous summer. "I'm sorry, Abe. You and Deborah and Bennie are family to me, but none of this would've happened if my real mom and dad weren't such . . . screw-ups."

Abe Pressler—in his shirtsleeves, his jacket on the back of his chair—shook his head. "No, no, Tommy," said Abe. "I know what you're saying, but none of us have control over what happened in the past—over the choices our parents made, good or bad. We just have to make the best of what we're left with. I'm trying to do that, myself."

"What'd'ya mean?" asked Tommy. "Are you talking about Bennie? He's doing good now."

Abe nodded. "And we have you to thank for that," he said, "for helping him after his surfing accident and the stroke. You helped him have more of a normal life—at school and at home. He calls you his brother from a different mother, whether you live here or at the beach with us." Abe glanced across the table at Harry and Artie, but said nothing more for the moment.

"Is that why you're here?" Tommy asked Abe. "To move me back home?"

Skip Ross spoke up again. "No, Tommy," said Skip. "I asked Abe to be here—because what we learned Saturday at the White farm and what I learned Sunday morning in Capital City affect Abe *and* you, as well as Artie and Harry."

The deputy took out a sheaf of photocopied pages on legal-sized paper. "This is Bob White's full confession," said Skip matter-of-factly. "He wrote this out after I told him who we'd found buried in that clearing near your tree house—two of the missing drug dealers . . . the two pilots. He said he wanted to make sure we know that he and his brother didn't kill *anyone*, not the two pilots and not, well, the *other* person whose remains we found buried out there."

"Another person?" asked Tommy White. "P.J.?"

"No," said Skip. "It was Artie's mother, from several years earlier. It was the smaller grave that was covered with those little flowers—what's it called, thrift?—off to one side." He cleared his throat and then continued, "The pilots were buried—in the same grave—under the cinderblocks where your beehives used to be."

Tommy looked confused. "But what does that have to do with Abe?" he said. "I mean, other than that he's my guardian, and he's managing the property out there?"

"That's enough reason," said Skip, "but we also found some of the stolen property from the Christmas Eve burglary at Pressler's Department Store. It was buried with the pilots."

"How did that happen?" pressed Tommy, looking from Skip Ross to Marty

Quinn to Abe Pressler.

Marty answered for the others. "That's all we can say right now," he offered, "because this new evidence is connected to two different on-going investigations. On the surface, they appear unrelated, but now we know they aren't. That yellow spiral notebook of yours—the one that Rocket Reep kept his diary in—contains the connection. He was harassing some of the people on that list you found in your notebook because of things that happened a long time ago—not naming any names right now."

"So, you found my notebook?" Tommy said. "Can I have it back?"

Marty shook his head. "No," he said, "we don't have the actual notebook— it's still missing, and we *are* going to get it back if we can. But, remember, I made copies, and I've given them to the state and federal investigators working these cases now. So, they know what Rocket Reep wrote in your notebook without actually having it."

The detective sergeant exchanged a look with the sheriff's deputy, then went on, "You two boys can do us a couple of favors. First of all, until we break these cases you must not talk to *anyone*, even in law enforcement, about what we've told you today, not unless one of us—either me or Skip—is present. If the wrong person hears the wrong information, you both could be in danger—like Bob White told you last winter, Tommy."

"I understand," the boy said. "What's the other favor?"

"You can tell us what all was in that storage container you boys found in your tree house," said Marty Quinn. "We know you kept the yellow notebook, but what else was in the container, and what else, if anything, did you boys keep? It's important that we know." He glanced over at Abe Pressler.

Artie Bauer noticed the look between the two men. "Bennie Pressler took pictures of everything in the storage tub that day," said Artie. "Bennie has the photos and negatives, and I have the duplicates. I'll go get them for you right now." He started to rise. "But we can do one better. We know where that storage tub is, and we know that some things were taken out of it, but Bennie's photos show everything that was in it to begin with. We can take you to the tub whenever you want to go get it."

Both Marty Quinn's and Abe Pressler's eyes lit up. The detective spoke for them both. "Yes, as soon as we're done here—definitely," Sgt. Quinn said, "but we have one last thing, one very important thing, to tell both of you. Skip?"

Though he was addressing both boys, the sheriff's deputy seemed to focus mainly on Tommy. Skip Ross said, "At the prison Sunday morning—at their requests—we administered polygraph tests to both Bob and Connie White as they were being questioned. As I said earlier, Bob was concerned about them being charged with murder in the disappearance of the three drug dealers— including his brother. Again, Tommy, I can't tell you everything, but I can say that the polygraphs—or lie-detector tests, if you prefer—supported their claims and Bob's confession."

Skip paused for a second. "There was only one, well, *glitch*, we'll call it, in the answers that your *mother* gave us," Skip said, "and when we called it to Connie's attention, she corrected the record, so to speak. The question had to do with her dealings with P.J. White—like, how close she was to P.J. and how well they got along, I guess you could say."

With mixed emotions, Artie Bauer had an odd feeling about where Skip Ross's story was headed. The deputy continued, "I asked her if she and P.J. had ever, well, *dated*. At first, her answer was *no*, but that was what registered as being less than truthful on the polygraph." He hesitated.

"So, Mom and P.J. dated?" asked Tommy. "Is that it?"

Skip raised his hand a bit. "Well, your mother told us it was more than dating, Tommy," he said. "You know, don't you, that Connie and Bob lived together before they were married. And you've known for a month now that you and Artie are cousins, right?" Tommy nodded, and Skip continued, "As it turns out, you and Artie aren't *cousins*. You're *brothers* . . . half-brothers. P.J. is your father, too, Tommy."

The boy said nothing for a few seconds. He just stared straight ahead. "Does Dad know?" asked Tommy. Still confused, he looked at Artie, then back at Skip.

Skip nodded his head. "Yes, he knows," the deputy replied. "Connie said he's known since their arrests last summer. But they thought you had enough to deal with. They gave me permission to tell you for them now. You can understand why, I'm sure. But that's another reason your mother didn't want to see you yesterday—because she wasn't sure how you'd react."

The deputy took out another paper, this one folded, a page from a yellow legal pad. "Bob did write you this letter yesterday," Skip said, handing it to Tommy. "You don't need to look at it now. But I can tell you that both of them *did* watch your games on TV this past weekend. I made sure they knew to watch. Yesterday morning before your game started, they both were excited about seeing you play in the state championship. I'm sure they were so proud when you hit that walk-off home run."

Tommy had opened the letter while Skip spoke and had begun scanning the scribbled lines on the yellow paper. "Yeah," Tommy said, "that's what Dad says here, that he's proud of me and can't wait to watch the game—and that I'm still his boy, no matter what."

Marty Quinn had the last word right then about the investigations. "Before you boys ask us any more questions about P.J. White," said Sgt. Quinn, "let me just say that our central focus right now is not on finding *him*. Our investigation is looking elsewhere. If what Bob White told us is true—and we think it is— then P.J. White is *not* the main person of interest in these murders. The Pressler's robbery, however, was a different matter. That was all P.J. White and Rocket Reep."

Still silent, his lip trembling, Tommy White looked first at Abe Pressler, then at Grandpa Bauer, the two father figures who had welcomed him into their homes. Abe spoke first, saying, "You shouldn't feel embarrassed about this, Tommy. You know what Bennie would say, right? Last summer you started out as an only child. And, now, *The Drone Ranger* has *two* brothers from other mothers." Abe smiled.

Harry Bauer added, "And Abe, I know baseball season's over, but, if you don't mind, I'd like to keep Tommy here on the farm with me and Artie for just a few more days. We'll be having a funeral for Ingrid later in the week—if this rain ever lets up—and, at a time like this, the three of us boys need to be together to help support each other."

"That's a good idea, Harry," said Abe, with a nod, "and don't you hesitate to ask if I can do anything to help out. Anything at all."

Grandpa thanked him, adding, "Yes, sir, this is gonna be some kind of week—for everybody."

Artie was afraid that his grandfather didn't know the half of it.

Right then, the telephone rang in the farmhouse kitchen. Artie hopped up and answered it. "Oh, hi, Coach," said Artie. "Thanks for calling. . . . Yes, that's right. Thank you for saying that. . . . Excuse me?" He looked around the room and held up his finger for the two lawmen to wait for him to finish the call. "Sure," Artie said on the phone. "I'll be glad to come see you tomorrow, Coach. I'll tell Grandpa, too."

Artie Bauer wondered how Jug Johnson had already heard the news about his mother, but then he realized that Jug hadn't mentioned her specifically— he'd referred to "what *they* found Saturday over on the White farm," and Artie had assumed he knew the whole story.

As it turned out, the big farm boy was the one who didn't know the half of what was going on in Oleander County.

CHAPTER 27

INGRID BAUER'S GRAVESIDE RITES WERE HELD that Friday afternoon under clearing skies in the Shin's Grove Church cemetery. She was laid to rest next to her mother, Pearl Bauer. Their graves were surrounded by floral arrangements sent to the private service by family friends, including a vase of homegrown flowers picked by Tommy White himself.

Other people present were Artie Bauer's Barf Table friends, many of their parents, and his closest teammates, as well as Harry Bauer's new best friend, Minnie Marecek. From Arbor High, Jerry Church, Thelma Hopper, Joe Carson, Frankie Hughes and, of course, Jug Johnson were there. Even that number of people would have filled the little white church to overflowing, so it was just as well that the funeral was held outside.

Artie's senior teammates—on the football, wrestling and baseball teams— had acted as pallbearers and had carried the small wooden coffin, topped with a handpicked spray of Ingrid's favorite red roses, from the white hearse to the gravesite. A half hour later, after the last expressions of sympathy had been spoken and everyone had driven away, Grandpa, Artie and Tommy returned to the graveside and stayed until the funeral director lowered the casket into the ground. It was then that they said their last goodbye.

* * *

Bright and early Saturday morning, the gang was together again, this time at Woody's Surf Shop & Grill on the beach, to discuss their plans for the day ahead. Still determined to stop the wastewater dumping that she had witnessed near the river, Leah Russo distributed an armful of disposable cameras to the others and instructed them to take pictures of every suspicious—or stinky—thing they might see while they were circulating around the golf course. She warned them, though, not to attract attention when using the cameras—to make sure at least one of them was in the shot, in order to give the impression that they were just being silly teenagers. Jamie Foxx took a camera and said she would use her unrestricted access as the course manager's daughter to prowl around inside the different buildings—the clubhouse, the pro shop, the locker rooms, the cart barn, even the country club's dining room and ballroom, where the next weekend's junior-senior banquet and prom would be held. "If they catch me," Jamie said, "I'll say I'm taking pictures for the prom committee."

Leah Russo informed the others that Vicki Duke's father—Vicki, not being there right then—had not come up with any leads on who was doing the actual waste dumping. "Her dad couldn't tell her who owns the septic trucks I saw—Tri-W Services," said Leah. "I don't know if it was *couldn't* or *wouldn't*, but we still need to find that out—who Tri-W Services is."

Bennie Pressler spoke up. "I'll get my dad to check that out," Bennie said. "He has to deal with all kinds of contractors and agencies as we rebuild the E-ville store—from architects to zoning boards. I wonder, though, what *Tri-W* stands for—*Waisin Wednesday Wentals*? Or, *We Wike Waste*?"

"Don't be silly, Bennie," said Leah, turning as the door to the kitchen swung open. Brett and Woody Woods walked in carrying boxes of sandwiches and canned drinks. "I know Vicki needs to get her cheerleaders in line this morning," Leah continued, "but I wish she was here right now. I'm worried that Josh Stark may show up today and cause trouble. He might have called and told her he was coming."

Hearing Leah's unease, Woody Woods set down the double-stacked boxes in his arms. "You kids don't have to worry about Josh Stark," said Woody, with a chuckle, "not today and not next Saturday at the junior-senior—matter of fact, not until he's eighteen years old in a couple years. Haven't you heard what he did—I mean, other than cause that wreck the other week and put Officer Ross in the hospital?"

When no one—not even his son—seemed to know, Woody explained, "Ol' Josh went to court on Tuesday over that wreck. I thought I'd have to be there, too—to testify that he was already drunk when he got here that night. For the first time in that boy's life, Joel Stark couldn't buy his son's way out of trouble. Josh was convicted of running the stop sign and DWI. But that's not all the news about him."

Woody smiled again. "His father *had* fixed it so that Josh could serve his jail time on weekends," said Woody. "They only gave him ten days in jail, and the rest of his sentence was probation. But ol' Josh went back to Hawthorn on Tuesday night, got stinking drunk again, and shot out every streetlamp in the administration building parking lot. He even shot out the academy commandant's office window—with the man still sitting at his desk working."

Woody laughed, but no one else did. "Wow!" said Artie Bauer. "Did he hit the commandant? I didn't hear anything about a shooting there. That would be big news."

"It would be if he'd used a gun," said Woody, "but he used a slingshot, and the only thing that hit the commandant was a little glass. Turns out, Josh learned how to use one from that guy who was always hanging around here out in the alley, that bum you kids called *The Pizza Guy*—Rocket Reep. In addition to dumpster diving, he 'worked' for Sandpiper Realty, from what Officer Ross told me."

"So, where's Josh now?" asked Artie, remembering all of Josh Stark's crimes of the past school year whose punishment the elder Stark had prevented—the homecoming dance fiasco, the Halloween festival assaults and arson, the incident at the season-ending Arbor/Solid Rock football game, his verbal and physical abuse of Vicki Duke at Woody's Grill, followed by the mainland car crash involving Thelma Hopper and Skip Ross.

"He's where he should have gone to begin with," Woody said. "He's at the School for Troubled Youth in Capital City. The judge from Tuesday revoked his probation on Wednesday morning, and by that night he was wearing a new uniform—cheap dungarees and a yellow work shirt. That's the only uniform he'll be wearing at *that* school, for the next two years."

* * *

That day's benefit golf tournament—the Sandpiper Shores Scramble for Solid Rock—teed off at nine o'clock. It was a shotgun start, with the maximum number of four-person teams on the eighteen-hole course. At $1,000 per team, the Solid Rock Foundation for Restoration and Recovery stood to make at least $18,000, not counting profits from the sale of merchandise and concessions. Vicki Duke and the cheerleaders sold almost a hundred *We Are Solid Rock Strong* T-shirts for a return of $1,000. Woody's helpers—the Barf Table gang—sold about a hundred BBQ sandwiches and more than two hundred soft drinks out on the course, making another $600 windfall. The players' awards luncheon at one o'clock—also catered by Woody's Grill—earned another $1,000 in profit for the Solid Rock foundation.

At the end of the lunch, course manager Jimmy Foxx presented age-group prizes—all of them donated—to the top teams, which included the winning 55-and-over foursome of Iron Harbor A&M's longtime president and its brand spanking new athletic director, as well as Jug Johnson and Joe Carson. The college had paid the old coaches' $250 entry fees.

Finally, Sandpiper Shores owner and tournament sponsor Joel Stark matched the amount raised. He put on a magnanimous if not entirely happy face for the moment, looked down one last time at the $20,000 matching check that Jimmy Foxx had just handed him, and presented it to foundation president Deborah Pressler.

While the golf awards and check presentations were underway, Jamie Foxx, Leah Russo, Bennie Pressler and Artie Bauer slipped into the office area of the country-club building. The foursome split into pairs—Leah and Bennie, Jamie and Artie—and searched Joel Stark's and Jimmy Foxx's separate offices, as well as their secretary's desk, for evidence that might connect them either with Tri-W Services or with Rocket Reep, based on what Woody Woods had told them that morning. As it turned out, the four teens found both—in one document.

"Hey, guys," hissed Bennie, who was looking through Joel Stark's closet while Leah searched the drawers of his polished walnut desk. "Get in here. I found it."

Artie and Jamie exited her father's adjoining office and hurried past the secretary's work station toward the owner's section of the suite, when a familiar voice boomed in the hallway outside. *"You need to cool your jets, Dedmon—you'll get paid,"* said Joel Stark. *"Do you think I carry the company checkbook in my golf bag? Idiot."* He muttered the last word instead of yelling it.

By the time the developer rounded the corner seconds later, Jamie had pushed Artie inside the man's office and closed the door behind him. Even from Artie, Leah and Bennie's hiding place in Stark's office closet, Artie could make out Jamie's loud, nervous chatter.

"Oh, hi, Mr. Stark," said Jamie, almost shouting. *"Boy, am I glad you're here. Dad told me I could use your fax machine—you know, to send tournament results to the TV stations and the newspaper—but I can't find it in either of your offices. Can you help me with that? "*

"It's right there, on Dorothy's desk," Stark said. *"Look, I'm in a hurry. Would you mind stepping out for a minute?"* Artie wondered if Red Dedmon had come into the office yet, or if the crooked deputy were still standing out in the hall. But Joel Stark must have been on the same wavelength, and said, *"No. Stay here. I'll grab what I need and go."*

"Your checkbook?" asked Jamie, still thinking fast. *"I saw it just now on Dad's desk. I didn't look at it—honest, I didn't—but didn't he just get done writing out some checks for prizes a few minutes ago? He probably forgot to put it back in your office. I hope I'm not getting him in any trouble."* Artie Bauer would have laughed to himself at Jamie's last line, if he hadn't been so scared of getting caught.

Joel Stark was silent for a few seconds—apparently as he retrieved the checkbook from Jimmy Foxx's office—and then he said, *"Well . . . thanks, I guess. Do you want me to send your father back in here to help you with the faxes?"*

"No, thanks, anyway," said Jamie. *"I'm sure Dad's busy giving out the*

awards. I've been meaning to tell you, Mr. Stark, what fun all us kids had today helping with your tournament. This golf course is so beautiful, even being a little bit wet from all the rain this week. But thank you for asking—and for giving Dad a job. He just loves working here! Mr. Stark? Hello? . . . Mr. Star-rk?"

Seconds later she opened the office door and told her three friends in the closet that the coast was clear for them to emerge. The door popped open, and all three took deep breaths as they came out.

"Jeez," said Bennie Pressler, "now I know what clowns at the circus feel like, when they hop out of the little car." The dark-haired boy grinned. "And I know how a magician feels when he pulls a rabbit out of his hat."

"You aren't wearing a hat," Leah Russo said, "or holding one. What are you talking about?"

Bennie lifted the bottom of his *Solid Rock Strong* tee just enough to take hold of an object tucked under his shirt. "Abracadabra, palsy-walsy, paraphernalia," he said, pulling the thin, flat object out and holding it up for the others to see.

It was Tommy White's yellow spiral notebook. Inside the front cover were the same two loose sheets of paper that they'd seen in it before—the old newspaper clipping about the White farm's public auction, and the curious list of names and addresses on Sandpiper Realty stationery—as well as another, newer piece of paper, the yellow carbon copy of a bill from Tri-W Services, dated that Friday and signed by Joel Stark himself, for "the pumping, hauling and disposal of storm-water runoff and assorted other waste removal services." The amount of the bill—marked *PAID IN FULL*—was $100,000.

After reading the bill aloud, Bennie looked up with a sly smile and said, "It's those *assorted other services* that get you every time."

CHAPTER 28

THANKS TO PRESSLER'S DEPARTMENT STORES, INC., the students who had received invitations to the original Arbor High School Junior-Senior Prom had no trouble postponing their tuxedo rentals and gown layaways for a month. This third week in May was now Arbor High's rescheduled junior-senior banquet and prom week. The event was still set for a Saturday night in the Sandpiper Shores Golf & Country Club's banquet hall and ballroom. The prom committee and other juniors spent Friday after school and most of Saturday decorating and setting up for the formal affair. The work crew included certain underclassmen like Bennie Pressler, who needed to set up his sound system in both rooms—to act as announcer for the banquet and disc jockey for the dance. The other Barf Table 9th and 10th graders, all of whom would be involved in the entertainment—mainly a skit and some song-and-dance numbers—were there to set up and practice, too. No seniors—not even members of the Barf Table gang—were allowed to see the skit being rehearsed. Prom committee members Jamie Foxx and Mike Inouye saw to that, even though Artie Bauer tried his best to sneak into the main country-club building Saturday morning when he dropped off Tommy White and Ricky Duran.

Back at the Barf Table clubhouse on the Bauer farm, Vicki Duke and Nicie Evans had set up two chairs late Saturday morning. For much of the afternoon, they had run an impromptu beauty salon for senior and junior girls wanting their hair and makeup done. After helping her aunt with three horse-therapy sessions, Wilma Marecek sat for a full makeover, getting attention from both of her senior friends. Kimi Inouye, a junior, talked her twin brother into driving her from skit practice to the farm so that Vicki and Nicie could braid her long, dark hair into two pigtails and then twist them into a fancier hairstyle atop her head. She refused to tell them why she needed pigtails when they suggested that a different hairdo might be more attractive, as Dr. and Mrs. Inouye had decided to let Kimi and Mike stay for the entire evening after all. "No," Kimi had said, "I need pigtails, not a ponytail and not a French braid—*pigtails*." Artie Bauer had walked into the clubhouse just in time to hear the end of the pigtail discussion, and he had suggested that Vicki and Nicie make Kimi's pigtails curly like Frick's and Frack's in the hog pen outside. That was when Artie Bauer was banned, at least temporarily, from his own clubhouse, by order of associate hairstylist Nicie Evans.

Just before the Barf Table gang's long, white limousine arrived at the farm, Jamie Foxx showed up for a quick makeover. Nicie Evans fixed her friend and former rival's short brown hair, while Vicki Duke applied makeup to the tomboyish girl's face. It was the first time since she had transferred to Arbor High that Jamie Foxx had made much of a fuss over her appearance. Jamie's lack of effort to look appealing might have been because her exchange sister, Julia Safin, possessed such natural beauty and was such a head-turner in whatever she wore. But Julia would be gone to another tennis tournament, and Jamie Foxx was Barf Table buddy Mike Inouye's prom date, at least until they walked into the country club together. She told Nicie and Vicki that she wanted to look good for Mike, even if it wasn't a real date.

When Jamie Foxx stepped outside the clubhouse trailer onto the front deck, Ty "*The Luuuvvv Machine*" Green and Jimmy Gore both wolf-whistled and started teasing Mike Inouye, until Artie Bauer told them to act like they had some manners, not like they were a couple of silly freshmen. Right then, Bennie Pressler ambled up after checking out the stretch limo's surround-sound stereo system, and he immediately noticed Jamie's striking new look. "Whoa, lookin' foxy, Ms. Foxx," complimented Benny, "or as my old grandfather would have said, 'What a *shayne maidel*.' What a lovely girl." Nicie and Vicki agreed, making Jamie blush. But she also smiled. Ty and Jimmy were red-faced, too, though from having been put in their places by Artie and Bennie. Mike just looked pleased at his hot date's appearance.

* * *

When the pearly white limousine pulled around the country club's circular drive and stopped under the main building's *porte cochere* to let out its passengers, every member of the Barf Table gang was ready for an unforgettable evening. The seniors were all dressed to the nines—in sharp, black tuxes and elegantly flirty dresses, some long, some short. Since they would be entertaining during the banquet, the juniors, sophomores and freshmen in the limo wore regular clothes and carried their costumes, as well as their prom attire, in garment bags that Bennie Pressler had gotten for them from his family's store. As for Bennie himself, he stepped out of the limo in his puffy, white shirt with its ruffled front, threw on his electric-blue, crushed-velvet tuxedo jacket with its flared, black-satin lapels, and reached back into the car for a garment bag of his own. He strutted straight over to Thelma Hopper and Hiroka Inouye, the two faculty members who had volunteered to work the check-in table in the lobby. "Looking good, Miss Hopper," complimented Bennie. "Looking good, Mrs. Inouye. Or as my old grandfather would have said, '*Ha cha-chaaaa!*'" Everyone laughed, especially when Miss Hopper said she wouldn't have guessed that Bennie was related to such a famous comedian.

The banquet dinner was catered by Woody's Grill, with indispensible help from Sal's Italian. As promised, Jug Johnson's old friend, favorite cook and former teammate, Salvatore Maggio, had driven down from Capital City early that morning to assist Woody Woods with entrees and desserts that Arbor girls wouldn't be afraid to eat in fancy dresses, and that Arbor boys wouldn't be tempted to pick up and eat with their fingers—or to throw. The answer was Fettuccine Alfredo topped with either chicken or fish, each plate with a single spear of broccoli added simply for color. The dessert was a square of tiramisu—large enough to satisfy any sweet tooth, but small enough to leave big farm boys like Artie Bauer and Tommy White wanting more. Having grown to like Sal's pasta dishes, Artie hoped the man would take Woody up on opening a Sal's

Italian at the beach, even if it were connected with Woody's store in Iron Harbor. Eating out at Sal's on a regular basis would be a streak that Artie would enjoy respecting and never breaking.

* * *

When the meal was over and all the plates were cleared, Bennie Pressler—in his electric-blue tuxedo—mounted the steps to the stage and stopped at a microphone set up to one side, at stage left.

"Welcome, everyone, to the First Annual Arbor Charter High School Junior-Senior Banquet and Prom," announced Bennie. "Wasn't that a great meal! Let's put our hands together for our fine chefs—Woody Woods and Sal Maggio." As the applause began to fade, he continued, "I want to ask the other members of the B.T. Experience—that's Brett, Nicie, Jimmy and Jamie—to hop on up here and grab their instruments so we can start tonight's entertainment. We'll be right back in two shakes of a bunny's tail."

The other members of the Barf Table combo hurried up the stage steps—even Nicie and Jamie, in their prom dresses and heels—and followed Bennie behind the drawn curtain. Seconds later, sounds of a drum set, bass guitar and keyboard filtered through the curtain's velvety, sand-colored fabric. When the curtain finally opened to reveal the stage, there stood the five friends, with the school's new ukulele choir in a semi-circle behind them.

Cradling his wooden ukulele, Brett Woods—now unmasked—stepped up to a microphone at center stage, leaned in and began to sing *a cappella*, "*A-ma-zing grace . . . how sweet . . . the sound . . . that saved . . . a guy . . . like me. . . .*" Muffling the tambourine she held to her chest, Nicie joined in to harmonize the next line, "*I once . . . was lost . . . but now . . . I'm found . . . was blind . . . but now . . . I see.*" The pair's voices, still entwined in harmony, faded as the first strums of Brett's uke changed the medley's rhythm from three beats to four, and led the combo into the song, "Some Days Are Diamonds (Some Days Are Stone)." On the second verse, the ukulele choir joined in. By the time the band and ukes repeated the last chorus, everyone in the banquet hall was singing along.

But Brett Woods wasn't finished. Nicie Evans stepped aside and gave her young friend the mic once again. Brett held his ukulele up and plucked the single strings of the last complete chord over and over, slowing the tempo with each repetition until he was joined by the soft strumming of the choir, to segue into the final song of the medley. "*Some-where . . . o-ver the rain-bow . . . way up high,*" crooned Brett softly, in an amplified near-whisper. The band took up the accompaniment, and, as with the other number, audience members sang along, almost from start to finish, as a wide, colorful banner that read, "*SEARCHING FOR RAINBOWS,*" was lowered from the flies.

Before singing the last lines of the song, Brett took hold of the mic stand and slid it forward. The curtain closed behind him, as he delivered the closing strains by himself. Then he bowed to Bennie, the master of ceremonies, who had returned to the microphone at stage left, and Brett exited stage right.

"That was Brett Woods and the B.T. Experience," said Bennie, clapping to prime the crowd, "and the Arbor High Ukulele Choir." As he waited through the applause, the lights dimmed, and he continued in his most somber voice, "Let's all step into the time machine—or, who knows, maybe it was a dream—and travel back to that fateful Good Friday evening in Oleander County, that we remember so well."

Behind the curtain, the sounds of props being moved into place could be heard. Bennie nodded to his assistant, Leah Russo, at the mixing board offstage, where she cued a low, engine-like roar of tornadic winds spinning and spinning. The curtain opened on a dark and stormy set, with brilliant flashes of stage lightning and ear-splitting crashes of metallic thunder. A spotlight fell upon a slight girl wearing a camouflage T-shirt and a pair of denim, bib-overall shorts—her long, dark hair pulled back into pigtails. She wore bright red, high-top sneakers. It was Kimi Inouye, as Solid Rock Christian Academy's answer to Dorothy Gale. Crouching at her feet was her twin brother Mike Inouye, wearing the Bruno mascot suit without its cartoon-bear head. Instead, he wore a white vest and Brett Woods's discarded facemask, fixed to look like the eyes, nose and jowls of a large dog. A sign that hung on a choke-chain around Mike's neck identified him as Bobo the Saint Bernard. Behind them, stage hands in all black shook and spun cardboard cutouts of shadowy agents in black tuxes, silhouettes of women in evening attire, fast cars, gun-barrel spirals and four madly swaying palm trees—all of these decorations held over from the prom committee's original, pre-banquet plan.

As the cyclone grew louder, Dorothy and Bobo pretended to be buffeted by its high winds, with the *License to Thrill* props blown here and there and off the stage one by one, until what was left were the two characters in each other's arms and the four cardboard palms surrounding the pair and bending down to shelter them from the passing remnants of the storm. Over the sound system came the din of sirens, chainsaws, emergency radio traffic and random shouts for help. Dorothy and Bobo now lay down under the trees and appeared to fall into a restless sleep. The spotlight grew smaller and smaller until its pinpoint of illumination disappeared into darkness. For long seconds—the time it took for Leah Russo to cue a different tape—there was deathly quiet.

"It was a long and scary night in Oleander County," said Bennie Pressler. "The terrible storm was over, and the long recovery was just beginning." The stage lights slowly started to rise. "And when the sun came up that Easter Saturday morning—on Ebenezerville and on all of Oleander County—we knew that our lives as friends and neighbors would never be the same again."

Filtered floodlights filled the banquet hall with the rainbow's four main colors—red, yellow, blue and green. Up on stage, Dorothy and Bobo stood, linked arms and skipped on a long, yellow, carpet runner into another circle of light, this one more brilliant than the first. "Oh, Bobo," said Dorothy to her best friend, "I think we're lost. Where are we?"

After a couple of tongue-wagging pants, Mike turned and looked at the audience. "I don't know, Dorothy," he said, in a doggy voice, "but we sure aren't in Ebenezerville anymore. *Woof!*" Girls in the audience giggled and whispered to each other.

Jenny Gore jumped into the spotlight. Her outfit was similar to Dorothy's—a camouflage T-shirt and bib-overall shorts—except that her camo was pink, her overalls bore a floral print, and straw poked out of her neckline, sleeves and shorts. Also, instead of dark pigtails, she sported a backward-facing ball cap. It was a burgundy-and-gold Solid Rock hat with an interlinked S and R on the front panel. That cap was the very one her brother Jimmy Gore had worn earlier in the season when the Harvesters still had their own team. Jenny did a slow spin in place to show everyone her outfit, but, more than anything, she wanted them to see the Solid Rock emblem of which she, her brother and all their fellow transfers were still so proud. Everyone in the crowd cheered.

"I've been out standing in my field," said Jenny, as the Scarecrow, "but everything is different now, and I have no idea what to do. Why? Because I have no *brain*—just straw—and there are so many forms to fill out, so much paperwork to do." She lifted her cap, and a handful of straw fell out.

As the two girls continued to talk, they turned around and—with Bobo at their heels—skipped back along the yellow carpet runner to where the first spotlight had illumined the stage. There they met Tommy White in character, wearing forest-camo pants and the blaze-orange gear of a tree cutter, and carrying an orange chainsaw. On his head was a yellow hard hat emblazoned with an Oleander Power & Light crest. Saying nothing at first, Tommy slowly pulled the chainsaw's starter rope, then again, and for a third time, but wasn't pulling hard enough to start the saw.

"Do you need some help?" asked Dorothy. "Are you out of gas?"

"Well, no, not exactly," the Camo Tree Cutter said sadly. "It's just that so many trees were blown down in the storm and need to be cut and cleared away now, that I just don't have the *heart* to keep on going—not by myself, anyway."

The three new friends—and their big dog, too—turned back around and crossed the stage again on the yellow carpet runner. Back in the other spotlight, they met little Ricky Duran, dressed as a singing cowboy in an all-white outfit, complete with tan chaps and a white, ten-gallon hat. Instead of a gun belt and six-shooter, he carried a white, plastic ukulele slung over his back on a black cord.

"What's the matter?" Dorothy asked the diminutive cowpoke. "Are you afraid to play your little guitar? Is that why you carry it on your back? Or are you afraid to sing?"

"No, ma'am," said Ricky "The Shooter" Duran, in cowboy talk. "I ain't afraid to play and sing, and I ain't afraid to dance, either." He flipped his ukulele around and began to strum the opening chords of an old western tune. "No," he said, "I'm afraid that the people here need more cheerin' up than a song-and-dance man like me can give 'em. But I'm gonna keep on searchin' for that rainbow, anyway."

Tapping his tan, pointy-toed boot in exaggerated fashion as he played and sang, the courageous little cowboy finished the first verse and the chorus of his song, before announcing to his new friends: "I hear there's a great magician, a mountain of a man who monitors the skies for us and chases the storms of life away. He and a friend live beneath a rainbow and drink from a big golden cup that this wonderful wizard, this magical monitor, searched for his whole life and finally found. Hey, you know what? Maybe he can help us, if we can find him. What do you say, guys?"

They all nodded—even Bobo—and after locking arms, the five friends skipped back across the yellow carpet runner and into the wings, at stage right. The curtain closed, the audience applauded, and Bennie Pressler stepped back up to his mic stand on the left.

"Our fearless friends searched high and low for the great magician's lair," said MC Bennie, "for the magical monitor's den, for the place beneath the rainbow where he and his friend, well, where they *reclined*, as it were, all the day long."

Bennie Pressler nodded to Leah Russo, who started a tape of sounds from the beach—children laughing, seagulls calling and gentle waves breaking on the strand. From behind the curtain, the ukulele choir began another tune. Brett Woods's mellow voice sang, *"I can see clearly now, the rain is gone. . . ."* He and Nicie Evans alternated verses, harmonizing on the last, optimistic line of each stanza. This time, the audience didn't sing along, except for that last line. Instead, they clapped on the second and fourth beats, as soon as they recognized the familiar song.

From stage right, the five friends skipped back into view, in front of the drawn curtain. "Oh, my," said Dorothy to her fellow travelers. "It really is a bright, bright sun-shiny day! But we're searching for a rainbow. How can we possibly find one on such a warm, sunny afternoon?"

Behind the drawn curtain, someone moved from stage right to its part at center stage, ruffling the sand-colored fabric the whole way. Two white-gloved hands pushed through the curtain, each grasping a side and opening a hole just large enough for a dark-haired boy to stick his head through. It was the Bruins baseball team's best middle infielder. Wearing khaki-colored cargo shorts and a yellow Hawaiian shirt of green palm trees, the great Ozzie Maye parted the curtains and stepped forward.

Dorothy repeated, "Does anyone know where we can find a rainbow?"

"Ozzie Maye!" shouted the other four friends in unison, as they recognized their classmate.

"Or he may not!" the pint-sized shortstop replied. "I may be a defensive wizard on the diamond, but I'm not the *magical monitor* you seek. He and all his friends are here, though—in the Land of Ozzie. Come on back, and I'll introduce you!" He waved for his five classmates to follow him.

As the curtains slowly opened, a titter began to run through the audience, starting down front and spreading to the back and sides of the banquet room, like the Wave in a stadium. Its intensity grew into laughs and cheers when everyone saw who the *magical monitor* and his friend were. Seated in their twin recliners—direct from the Arbor High cafeteria—beneath the "*SEARCHING FOR RAINBOWS*" banner were coaches Jug Johnson and Joe Carson. Like Ozzie, they, too, wore colorful, floral-print shirts. On the floor between the two recliners sat the large, gold trophy—a gigantic loving cup—symbol of the Bruins' freshly minted state championship. Around them were Arbor underclassmen wearing shorts and tie-dyed tees or Hawaiian shirts of all colors. With the exception of Jug and Joe, they all danced and sang along as Brett, Nicie and the ukulele choir reprised their last song. Despite the late hour, the feeling really was one of sunshine and rainbows. The curtains closed again to thundering applause.

* * *

Bennie Pressler stepped aside for Principal Jerry Church. "Thank you, Bennie," said the principal. "And thank you, everyone, for coming out tonight to our first-annual banquet and prom. Bennie will be back out in just a minute to lead you over to the ballroom—only our seniors and their dates, and our juniors are allowed—but first we have several very important announcements to pass along while everyone is still here together. Miss Thelma Hopper? If you will please come on up."

Bennie Pressler disappeared behind the curtain, and Mr. Church took a step back to make room on-stage for the perky guidance counselor. "Thank you so very much, everyone," Miss Hopper said. "On behalf of the Arbor High guidance office, I'm honored to announce the graduating class's two highest-achieving scholars—first our salutatorian and then our valedictorian. Oh, my, those words almost made me tongue-tied." She giggled and, a bit self-consciously, put on a pair of reading glasses.

"With a perfect 4.0 grade-point average," said Miss Hopper, "this year's salutatorian—tied for number one in the senior class—is Mr. Harold Arthur Bauer the Second. Congratulations, Artie Bauer!" The guidance counselor held up her hands and led the students in clapping for Artie. He half-stood and gave them a little wave and sat back down quickly.

"And now," continued Miss Hopper, "Arbor High's top scholar—also with a perfect 4.0 grade-point average and tied with Artie for number one in the graduating class—this year's valedictorian is Miss Wilhelmina Magdalena Marecek. Way to go, Wilma Marecek!" Miss Hopper took off her glasses and tucked them away in one fist, clapping with only two fingers on that hand. At her seat with Artie and the other Barf Table seniors, Wilma smiled and stood, nodding to others around the room.

Relieved that he would *not* be giving the big speech at the upcoming graduation ceremony, Artie shouted his congratulations and whistled a couple of times to show his support for Wilma's selection. He figured that her thoughtful Ebenezer Endowment essay surely was better than his hastily written one, based on what Miss Hopper had told them about a potential tie-breaker. He remembered Wilma telling him that in her essay she had compared her life to that of Henry David Thoreau and that she intended to live deliberately from then on, not by accident—to take her time and make the best choices about how to help her family, her friends, her neighbors, and herself. Artie, on the other hand, had written about sitting at the Barf Table for four years and trying to be everyone's solid rock—an idea that the scholarship committee must have judged as less impressive, he guessed. So, Wilma would also get the Ebenezer, Artie assumed. *That's good*, he thought. *She deserves it.*

Principal Church held Miss Hopper's hand as she took her first step down the stairs. He turned back to the microphone. "Our next announcement tonight," the principal went on, "involves a related matter—this year's recipients of the prestigious Ebenezer Endowment, a four-year, full scholarship to Iron Harbor Agricultural & Mechanical University, given to the top student-athletes in Oleander County's Suncoast Conference, one recipient for each of the five member schools." He paused to catch his breath.

"Tonight, we are again honored to recognize two Arbor High students—one, a student-athlete who transferred to us from Solid Rock Christian Academy after the recent storm; the other honoree, a distinguished scholar and athlete here at Arbor High for four years. The Solid Rock recipient—who, by the way, has also signed a letter of intent to play football at State College—is Jameson 'Jimmy' Gore, an all-state linebacker in football and a member of our Arbor High state championship baseball team."

As the crowd roared, Mr. Church found the Barf Table gang in the dim light offstage, and he added, "So, Jimmy, if things don't work out with Coach Landis at three-a-days this summer, A&M has a spot waiting for you. But I'm sure you'll do fine."

The principal looked up again. "Did I mention that A&M is one of my alma maters?" he said with a smile. "Without further ado, the Arbor High recipient was an important member of the Fighting Bruins wrestling team for four years and, this year, played significant roles in the success of Coach Joe Carson's

Bruinettes basketball and softball teams. Our scholarship winner is Miss Wilma Marecek—this year's valedictorian. Again, congratulations, Wilma. We're proud of you and Jimmy both."

Even though it was what Artie Bauer had expected, his spirits sank, as he now feared he would not be able to afford the college education he wanted and needed. It was the same feeling as when his grandfather had confirmed his lifelong fears about his missing mother, that she wasn't just hiding away somewhere and secretly applauding his scholastic, athletic and personal triumphs. But Artie still wasn't ready to give up, and he knew that his best friend, Ty Green, who hadn't received a scholarship offer yet either, also wouldn't throw in the towel. There was some time left on the clock for them both.

"Now," Principal Church said, "I'd like to call Mrs. Deborah Pressler to the microphone for our last announcements this evening. Mrs. Pressler, as we all know, is one of our parents. I'm proud to say that she, too, is a graduate of Iron Harbor A&M, and she is the executive vice-president of community outreach and public relations for Pressler's Department Stores, Incorporated." By then, Bennie's mom had mounted the steps and reached the microphone.

"Thank you, Mr. Church," said Deborah Pressler. "First, I'd like to go on record stating that I had absolutely no input into my son's choice of attire tonight. If you didn't notice that electric-blue, crushed-velvet tux, well, just hang around until he gets back up here. As they say, you ain't seen nothin' yet." The crowd laughed.

Smiling, she went on, "No, tonight I'm here to tell you a little story—a quick one, because I know that you can't wait for your prom to begin. This sounds like a sad story, but it has a happy ending. It's partly about my husband's grandfather—his name was Noah Pressler—who came to Ebenezerville from Germany years ago to make a new life for himself and for his family. He and his wife left Bavaria with a single suitcase between them, but also with a secret that Noah, a jeweler, kept hidden away for many years. That secret was stolen almost sixteen years ago, but thanks, in part, to the Good Friday Storm, which, as you know, destroyed our original store in Ebenezerville, his secret has come to light.

And now it will help make new lives for others through what we're calling the Stepping Stones Scholarships, two-year grants covering tuition and all expenses at Suncoast Community College in Port Oleander."

Mrs. Pressler paused for a moment, then continued, "Our first two recipients of the Stepping Stones Scholarships are . . . Miss Victoria Duke, who plans to study cosmetology . . . and Miss Donicia Evans, who will begin her nursing studies at SCC. Let's give Vicki and Nicie a big hand! And, finally, I'd like to ask my husband, Abe, to come up here and close this out—that is, before we turn things over to our son again, to Bennie . . . the comedian in our family. Again, I apologize for what you're about to see."

Abe Pressler was laughing as he took the stage. "Now I know where Bennie gets his sense of humor," he said, with a smile. "Deborah, my wife, told you just *part* of my grandfather's story. Well, here's an even more exciting part. That big secret of his? Actually, there were *four* secrets that Noah Pressler had hidden away in his suitcase . . . and then in the false bottom of an old safe in that old store building in Ebenezerville—four uncut diamonds from the Old Country, from Bavaria. They were stolen sixteen years ago—on Christmas Eve, actually. And this week . . . we found them."

The businessman explained that the four uncut diamonds—which in this form looked nothing like what one might see in an engagement ring, more like quartz crystals stuck in river rock—would be cut and sold, he said, with the proceeds going toward yet another annual endowment for a deserving Oleander County student. Abe announced that the Noah A. Pressler Uncut Diamond Award—for four years of expense-paid study at any publicly funded college or university in the state—was based on the winning student's "potential for serving the people of this state, not just this community, in the future."

Abe Pressler peered into the audience to find the scholarship winner. He looked past the Barf Table gang to where another group of seniors sat, and he asked Mel Grayson to stand. "Miss Grayson will be a pre-med student next fall at State College," said Abe, "whose business college, by the way, is where I received my MBA, Mr. Church—that's one of *my* alma maters. But that's not why we've selected Melanie for this award. It's because she—like so many of our fine graduates—needs our encouragement on this road to the future that she has chosen. Congratulations, Mel."

As the applause rose and fell, Abe Pressler stepped down the short set of stairs and headed back to his table with the other adults. His son, the master of ceremonies—now wearing a pink, full-length bunny suit, complete with hood and long ears—parted the curtains at center stage and hopped down onto the floor. "Let's do the bunny hop!" Bennie Pressler shouted. "Get out your invitations, and follow me to the ballroom!" He pointed across the room to Leah Russo, who punched a button and started the next song.

With "The Bunny Hop" blasting from the big speakers next door, Bennie Pressler led the growing line of dancers—first Vicki Duke and her senior cheerleaders, then the Barf Table friends—around the perimeter of the banquet hall, through the opening in the floor-to-ceiling partition, and into the ballroom. Artie Bauer felt the weight of Wilma Marecek's hands on his hips as his tall friend danced and hopped behind him. Once when the line slowed, he felt her lips touch his ear, and she whispered, "This doesn't count as our dance, big guy. You still owe me one from Valentine's Day."

Artie smiled as he turned to glance back at her. "You bet I do," he said, but then he laughed and hopped three times to the music.

CHAPTER 29

SUPERVISED BY CASHIER FRANKIE HUGHES—whose black, death-metal T-shirt was almost appropriate for a change—juniors from the banquet/prom committee and underclassmen moved tables and chairs around the dining room, as the conga line of bunny hoppers danced into the ballroom. At the same time, a handful of Solid Rock transfers whose parents didn't approve of dancing chatted and laughed together as they left the country-club building. Tables were pushed to the margins of the dining area, and the big partition separating the two sides of the event space was moved panel by panel to enlarge the ballroom.

Bennie Pressler's disc-jockey booth, with his sound system and speakers, sat on a low platform on the far side. Still in his bunny suit, Bennie grabbed a mic and called out to the prom goers, "Wasn't that fun? While the ukulele choir and our dance leaders take their places, let's put your hands together one more time for my buddy, Brett Woods, the *Pele of the Ukulele*!" Everyone clapped and whistled, as Brett, uke in hand, stepped up onto the platform and plugged his instrument into a small amplifier.

"Lovers and dreamers," announced Bennie, "it's time to crown the queen and king of the prom, and to give them this first dance together. Miss Thelma Hopper—or soon to be Mrs. Skip Ross—will you please come help Brett and me do the honors?" Standing next to her fiancé across the ballroom, Thelma smiled and nodded, a crown in each hand. She hurried across the floor to stand just below the two boys.

Bennie went on, "First, our prom king—what can I say about him . . . that he hasn't already said about himself? He's a great athlete, a great baseball player.

He's a great dreamer, with a great future ahead of him. He's a great lover (he says) of great books like *Moby-Dick*—now, don't laugh, folks, don't laugh—and two other great fish tales called *Jaws* and *The Old Man and the Sea*, which is also about baseball, by the way. . . . The only thing our king isn't great at, is knowing when he's got enough gas to get home on a date. Say it ain't so, Tyrone Green. Say it ain't so, *Luv Machine*. Come on over here, Ty."

Ty Green was laughing too hard to act mad at his young friend. He crouched slightly to let Miss Hopper put the larger of the two crowns on his head, and then he stood to face the smiling crowd and to await the coronation of his queen.

"And, now, I *really* don't know what to say about our queen," said Bennie. "She's a dear friend of mine, but if I say the wrong thing, I'm afraid she'll beat me up. And so will Ty Green. Why? Because the queen of this year's prom—a young lady you've already heard about tonight—is one of the toughest competitors I've ever seen on the basketball and beach volleyball courts, and on the softball field. She's a real fighter, especially for friends like me who owe her so much. She and Ty belong together. The star and queen of Prom Night . . . is Nicie Evans. We love you, Nicie. Come on over here . . . please?"

Tears streamed down Nicie's face as she was crowned. She turned to let Miss Hopper give her a peck on the cheek. Then Ty Green took his queen's hand and led her onto the dance floor, where they were encircled by a throng of students from the school's dance group. Brett Woods stepped up to the microphone and began to pick out the first notes of the waltz to which the queen and king would dance. The ukulele choir joined in as Brett sang the opening lines of "The Rainbow Connection," and as Ty and Nicie and the other waltzing couples twirled dreamily around the dance floor.

When other couples took their cue to dance, Artie Bauer approached Wilma Marecek, his rival and friend, and held out his hand to her. "Will this song do?" he asked. Her smile was her answer, and she put her hand in his and let him take her into his arms. They danced to the wistful tune that others, whether they were lovers and dreamers or not, sang along with Brett, all of them under the melancholy song's magic spell.

"I need to ask a favor, Wilma," said Artie, as the song ended and the pair left the dance floor. "Thank you for the dance, by the way. I'm sorry it was so long in coming. But . . . ."

"You're welcome, Artie," replied Wilma, "and thank you, too. That was fun. What's the favor? Why do I get the feeling it isn't for you?"

Artie's eyebrows rose a bit. "Well, you're right," he said. "The favor isn't for me. It's for Tommy." He paused. "You know we're brothers, right? Well, I was wondering if you would ask *him* to dance. You know how shy he is. And I can tell that he likes you a lot. Will you do that for me?"

"Sure," she said softly, leaning up just a bit to give him a friendly kiss. "Wow, Artie, in these high heels you and I are about the same height." They laughed, and she added, "I do wish Julia was here, not at that tournament. You know, Artie, she really does love you."

"I know," he said, "but she has to follow her dream—like in the song, right?"

"We all do," said Wilma, releasing his hand and letting him drift away. "Don't worry, buddy. I know how to get Tommy boy out there on the dance floor. We've been working together on the farm for the past year, and—if you remember—I helped teach him to wrestle last winter. I have his number."

Wilma winked and waved, as Artie turned to leave. For whatever reason, he had to get out of the ballroom and out the building right then. He needed some fresh air, because after everything that had happened to him so far that evening—both the surprises and the disappointments—he wasn't too sure about his own dreams and his own future.

* * *

Artie Bauer wandered outside to a covered porch area on the side that faced the clubhouse and offices. The porch's only illumination came from lantern-style sconces at regular intervals, casting a minimum of light on the walkway. When he turned the corner, the big farm boy was somewhat surprised to spy Jug Johnson and Joe Carson standing there at the porch railing—Jug, a red plastic cup in one hand; Joe, a lit cigarette in his fingers, holding it up to his mouth. Jug spat into the cup. Joe exhaled a stream of smoke into the night air. Jug turned as

Artie approached.

"Yogi," said Jug, "what're you doing out here, sneaking up on us like Pearl Harbor? I almost jumped off this porch when you came around that corner."

Artie chuckled. "Lucky thing you have such good parenthetical vision, huh," said the boy.

"*Peripheral* vision, kid," said Jug. "I thought you were smart—*Mr. Number One In Your Class.*"

"Whatever," Artie said, with a laugh, "and that's *tied* for number one, Coach, just like the state wrestling title. That's the story of my life—except for the baseball team."

Joe Carson dropped his cigarette butt on the cement floor of the porch and ground it out under his shoe. "Funny you should mention that, Artie—not baseball, but wrestling," said Carson. "I gave your co-champion, Mr. Hines, a call the other day, and he said to tell you hello."

"Why did you call Louis?" asked Artie, confused.

Jug Johnson interrupted. "Hold on a second, Joe," said Jug. "We're getting the cart in front of the horse right now. I'll take it from here." Jug spat out his dip and set the red cup on the floor. "So, why didn't you come see me last week, Yogi?" asked Jug. "You told me on the phone you'd stop by."

"I don't know, Coach," said Artie. "By the way, thanks for coming to my mother's funeral. I guess I'm just feeling kinda weird these days, what with that and everything else going on right now. I'm sorry I didn't stop by your office."

"Well, you should be," Jug said with a straight face, "because I had something important to tell you. Actually, you wouldn't be feeling so *weird* right now if we'd talked. But I gotta ask—are you feeling weird because you didn't get any of those big scholarships, and because no coaches in this blessed state seem to give two hoots about you?"

Artie shrugged, then nodded. "Well," continued Jug, "you ain't no Lone Ranger that way. I know he hasn't told you yet—because I made him promise not to—but your best buddy, Ty Green, is the best friend you could ever have. He went to bat for you with the State College coach—the *baseball* coach—

because when they refused to get you up there with Ty, he told that coach what he could do with their scholarship offer. Ty told them he could always sign a minor-league contract and play pro ball."

"So, they *were* going to offer him a scholarship?" said Artie.

"They sure were," Jug replied. "And then there's your other buddy—Jimmy Gore. Remember how Jimmy was the one who called and warned you about what Josh Stark and those other Solid Rock boys were planning to do at Halloween? Well, Jimmy stood up for you again, this time with that high and mighty football coach they got up there at State."

"With Landis?" asked Artie.

"None other than," Jug said. "Jimbo told Landis that he had put him and you and Ty in a bad spot—not just that once, you know, that first time we played Cap City last month, but last weekend at the state championship, trying to talk to you boys before the game. Now, this isn't common knowledge yet, but Jimmy told Landis he's withdrawing his letter of intent to play football at State, and—between me, you and porch rail—he's going to A&M, for football *and* baseball. Wha'd'ya think of that?"

Artie didn't know *what* to say, because it has all news to him. Jug said, "Okay, Joe, *now* you can tell him why you called Louis Hines this week."

Carson nodded and said, "Well, Artie, as I was telling you, I called Louis to talk to the young man about playing football and baseball for *us*." Joe let that sink in for a second. "Now, by *us*," he said, "I'm not talking about Arbor High. No, I'm referring to Iron Harbor Agricultural & Mechanical University—the A&M Monitors. That's our school now, and it could be yours and Ty's, too."

Now Artie *was* confused. "What?" he said, looking from Joe Carson to Jug Johnson.

The smile on Jug's face was broader and prouder than Artie had ever seen on him. "That's right, son," said Jug Johnson. "You're looking at A&M's new head baseball coach, and Joe, here, is my assistant coach and A&M's new recruiting coordinator. We don't have a new football coach yet, but he'll be a good one—I promise. Our first four prospects—for both football and baseball—

are Jimmy Gore, Louis Hines, Ty Green and you. When Jimbo called Louis and told him he had changed his mind about State, Louis said he was leaving, too. He never liked Landis, either, not after the mess last winter at the state wrestling championships."

Artie's heart leapt. "So, all four of us can play both sports?" he asked. When Jug nodded, Artie followed up with, "So, how many scholarships does each of us get? One? Or two?"

Jug laughed. "You only get one scholarship, Yogi," he said, "and just so you know, Joe even gave that pretty girl you dated a call, just to see if she'd be interested in playing tennis for A&M. She said, no, not just yet, but for Joe could keep her in mind for a spot on the ladies' basketball team—or even for the mascot job. That'd be in about a year after she gives the tennis tour a try. *She's* leaving State, too."

Joe picked up the story there. "Yeah, Artie," he said, "I wished Julia luck, and then I laughed and told her that if anybody could look good in a lizard costume—as Lizzy the Monitor Lizard—it would be her, and she laughed about that. I like that girl, even if she *is* Russian. You do, too—don't you, Jug?"

"I do indeed," said Jug. "Now, Yogi, everybody here's telling stories tonight about little secrets, so let me tell you another one right now about the very thing you just mentioned—double scholarships. The reason we're in this position right now is because one man couldn't keep his mouth shut, and one other man decided to do what was right." He looked down at his spit cup, but decided to leave it sitting there.

"The first man was Jimmy Foxx," explained Jug Johnson. "He was so busy running his mouth and running down some of our best athletes—I won't say who, but you know who they are—that word got out about the *former* A&M athletic director handing out two scholarships at a time to recruits who were willing to play two sports. Well, when that word got to Mr. Abe Pressler—who, by the by, is on the A&M Board of Trustees—well, that little bit of information didn't go over too well. That sorry athletic director got fired; the even sorrier football and baseball coaches got fired; and here we all are. It's Joe's job now to make sure nobody plays fast and loose with the scholarships again."

Jug looked at Artie, his protégé, and smiled. "When I was hired the other day," Jug said, "Abe Pressler told me that I should have a talk with you. He said when your granddaddy had that terrible accident last fall, he told you not to worry about nothing, that he owed you big-time for looking after Bennie and for being his friend from the very first day of school, even when you didn't know who that mouthy little boy in the wheelchair was. I was gonna talk to you, anyway, but this is Mr. Abe Pressler's way of thanking you for being a good person, Yogi. Yessir, he's a rich and powerful man, but he's the finest kind of rich. And he and his wife are the finest kind of people."

"I wish more people were like them," said Artie.

Jug nodded. "From your lips to God's ears, Yogi," the coach said. "This world would be a better place if everybody tried to help other folks instead of just helping themselves."

Now Artie didn't know if he should laugh or cry. He wasn't sure if he could succeed as a two-sport athlete at the college level, but he was willing to try, especially if it helped this old coach and mentor to whom he owed so much himself. As with his friends—with both Ty Green's and Julia Safin's dreams of becoming professional athletes, and as it had been with Brett Woods's resolve to surf the big waves in Hawaii the previous winter—Artie knew that he had to try his best to reach his goals, and that winning and losing were defined in different ways. Also, remembering what Ricky Duran—a state wrestling champion in his own right—had said about facing the best competition, Artie Bauer reminded himself, *I know I can win, if I'm given a fair shot.*

* * *

After Jug Johnson and Joe Carson had gone back into the building to act as chaperones—and after Artie Bauer had reminded his coach to be careful where he set his spit cup down, especially around twice-shy Vicki Duke—Artie went hunting for a public telephone he could use to call his grandfather and give him the good news that Jug had shared. Back in the main building's lobby, he couldn't find a pay phone, but he did run into Ty Green.

"Hey, man," said Ty. "I just saw Coach Johnson, and he said I can talk to you now—you know, about playing ball next year at A&M."

Artie beamed. "Yeah," he said, "that's a load off my mind. I was starting to panic." Then he realized the assumption he was making about his friend. "You *are* gonna go there, right?" asked Artie. You can study kinesiology there, too, can't you? And, hey, I'm sorry I messed up your offer from State."

Ty waved it off. "Don't worry about that, Artie," said Ty. "You didn't mess anything up. But right now, I need you to help me make a decision. Will I have my catcher—and my center—at A&M? Or will I have to get used to someone new on *both* teams? If that's what I'm looking at, then I may as well go pro now and see if I can make it to the show that way, just like Julia's doing in tennis."

Artie assured his best friend that attending A&M had always been his own dream—to study agriculture any way he could and to play sports, if that was the best way he could pay for his college education. Unlike Ty and Julia, Artie didn't want to be a professional athlete. He enjoyed the thrill of competition and the challenge of knowing when to lead the team and when to follow—to understand the *wa* of being a team player. It had been that way in every sport that Artie had played at Arbor High, and it was that way on the Bauer farm as well, with Artie always having to decide whether to be a leader or a follower—or as Harry Bauer would say, whether to be the big chief or one of the braves, the general or one of the grunts, the lead dog or one of the younger pups pulling the sled. Artie preferred his half-brother Tommy's metaphor on that topic—whether it's better to be the queen bee in the hive or just one of the workers. Artie knew that everyone on a winning team was important and had a job to do.

Just then, Officer Skip Ross—looking like a secret agent in his black tux—left the ballroom in a hurry, with Tommy White in tow. They were headed straight for the door out of the building. As they drew closer to the two friends, Skip pointed at Artie and ordered, "You need to come with us. Just you, Artie. This may take a while. Sorry, Ty." With a worried look, Ty nodded and returned to the ballroom.

Officer Ross led Artie and Tommy down the main building's front steps and across the courtyard to the clubhouse and offices, where yellow crime-scene tape had been strung across the front entrance. Skip moved the tape. He opened the door for Artie and Tommy to enter. "You're not in any trouble, guys—not now," the deputy said. "As a matter of fact, I think you both need to know what's been going on here. Just head on down the hall to Mr. Joel Stark's office, Artie. You do remember where that is from the other day, right?"

In the lead, Artie stopped in his tracks, too quickly for Tommy to keep from bumping into him. "Are you talking about last Saturday when we found Tommy's notebook in there?" asked Artie. "Yeah, we should have told you how we got it—that we snuck in while the golf tournament was going on. Is Mr. Stark charging us with breaking into his office?"

"He tried to," Skip said, "but . . . just hang on a second, and you'll understand everything. We've been working on this ever since you brought us that notebook last weekend and the other stuff from Rocket Reep's storage container before that. And all those photos you kids took of the waste dumping were a big help, too." He nodded toward Joel Stark's closed office door. "Just go on in. It's unlocked, and you don't have to knock. They know we're coming."

This is just great, Artie thought, not ready to open the door yet. *Stark's gonna get us in trouble for stealing back our own property, and he's gonna get off scot-free again. This will never end.*

"Go ahead and open the door, Artie," said Skip. "We need to get this thing over with. My date's waiting for me back there. She thinks the only reason I came tonight was to be with her. Thelma doesn't know I'm working. But go on in. Don't worry."

Artie Bauer turned the knob and slowly pushed open the door to Joel Stark's office. In much the same way that little Ozzie Maye had introduced himself during that evening's skit, big Artie Bauer stuck his head through the door opening just enough to see who was inside. He was relieved to see Sgt. Marty Quinn sitting in a chair off to one side, with Brody the German Shepherd at his feet; Abe Pressler, seated next to Marty; and Harry Bauer sitting on Marty's other side. Grandpa was bent down, running his hand over Brody's neck and back. He didn't stop but looked up to acknowledge Artie's entrance. The leather executive's chair behind the large, polished desk was empty. The executive himself, Joel Stark, was not in the room.

"Well, it's about time," said Harry Bauer to his grandson. "Brody and I have been in protective custody all evening, it seems like. Haven't you kids danced enough tonight?"

Skip smiled at the old man. "It was for your own good, Harry," the deputy said. "I'm sure Marty explained part of why we needed to keep an eye on you and Abe and the boys. But he can tell you the whole story now. Right, Marty?"

The detective nodded and rose to his feet, moving toward the desk. "That's right," Quinn said, motioning for either Skip or one of the boys to take his chair. Quinn leaned against the front of the desk. "A few hours ago, we weren't sure how everything was gonna shake out, and we would have picked any other time if we could have. But it is what it is."

Sgt. Quinn raised up enough to sit on the desktop. "Skip got a call late last night that he referred to me," said Quinn. "It was Jimmy Foxx, and he was mad as a hornet about something he finally figured out. You see, when Joel Stark realized that Tommy's notebook was gone, that *somebody*—probably you kids—had snuck into his office last Saturday, he chewed Jimmy out for letting his daughter have the run of the building. He remembered talking to her in the outer office when he came inside late in the day."

"That's right," said Skip Ross, "and I've been keeping an eye on Jamie Foxx tonight, too. What made her father so angry was when Stark showed him another copy of that list you guys found in the notebook—you know, all those names and addresses."

"Yeah, it included us and the Greens," said Artie, "and the Russos, too."

Marty Quinn picked up the story again. "And there were a bunch of other houses on the list that had something in common with the Russo house," he said. "All of them had been built on lots that didn't perc—that never should have been built on. That's where Rocket Reep came in. Joel Stark had hired him to harass all those property owners into selling their houses back to Sandpiper Realty—

what used to be called *Stark* Realty before this year." He looked at Grandpa.

"As far as your farm and the Greens' farm went," Quinn added, "Stark wanted your properties for more development—golf courses and housing subdivisions. He wanted the old White place for that, too, and he figured Rocket Reep could convince all you folks to sell, by giving everyone a hard time with that stupid slingshot of his."

Oddly, at that point in the story, a smile crept across Quinn's face. "That's where Stark messed up," he said. "Remember how Rocket Reep was killing people's dogs?"

"I sure do," said Grandpa, jumping in. "That rascal killed *my* dog with his slingshot—but that was years ago, back when Artie, here, was just a baby."

Quinn nodded and continued, "Well, it turns out that one of the houses on the list was the Foxx family's neighbor, and one of the dogs that Rocket Reep killed was the Foxxes' little dachshund, to keep the dog quiet while he broke into the neighbor's backyard."

"I remember that," said Artie. "His name was Nathan—like the hot dogs."

"You have a good memory," Quinn said, "but Joel Stark apparently doesn't, because he started laughing to Jimmy Foxx about Rocket's little crime spree, and Stark didn't remember how much Foxx's family had been affected. Stark said his only regret was that he had let Reep teach his boy Josh how to use a slingshot, which was what got the Stark kid kicked out of military school. That's when Jimmy Foxx decided to talk to us. He also put us in touch with the county health inspector who let Stark build on lots that couldn't handle a regular septic tank. We had no trouble getting Victor Duke to flip on Joel Stark, especially after Skip, here, reminded him about all the bad things Josh Stark had done to Vic's daughter."

"Yes, sir," Skip Ross said, "Victor was champing at the bit to tell us about all the bogus permits that Stark had pushed him to issue. That includes for this whole place here—all of Sandpiper Shores—which is why we're shutting it down tonight . . . well, as soon as the prom's over. Thelma would kill me if we stopped the prom after what happened at homecoming." Now he smiled a bit, looked back at Marty Quinn, and nodded for him to tell the rest of the story.

The detective's face grew somber. "This is the part I don't enjoy telling you about," Quinn said, preparing them for bad news. "This wasn't just a land development scheme that Joel Stark was running. It goes way back—at least twenty years—when Stark was just getting started in the real estate business here in Oleander County, down toward Mimosa Beach, actually. He needed financing to get his business up and running, and he got it by laundering drug money through a company he started. It was called Tri-W Services, for *water*, *waste* and *weed*. That didn't last long—the *weed* part, once they got into cocaine and crack. They're legitimate now—you've seen their trucks, I'm sure—but back then it was basically a shell company that handled all the dirty money—and the dirty water—flowing into Oleander County. One of Stark's other properties then was a flophouse and dive bar off the beach called the Four Palms Motel & Lounge. For years, it was the unofficial headquarters for the local drug trade—until it burned down. That is, everything but two little tourist cabins out back."

"What is it now?" asked Abe Pressler, speaking up for the first time. "I think I know the answer, Marty, but I want to hear it from you."

Quinn looked Abe straight in the eye. "Stark Stables," he replied. "And the two cabins are still there. That's where Brody and I found another old grave this afternoon—at the back of the property behind the cabins." Quinn turned to Artie and Tommy. "And while we were there, we got a little visit from someone you boys know well enough—from Deputy Red Dedmon. One of the stable hands called the sheriff to say someone was snooping around, and he tipped Dedmon off that we were there."

"What happened?" asked Abe Pressler.

"Well, let's put it this way," said Quinn, not smiling at all. "Nobody was using slingshots when the shooting started. Luckily, Brody and I weren't there alone. The state police had sent a car, and the FBI office out of Capital City sent two agents. So when Dedmon tried to sneak up on us, we were ready for him. We had more firepower than he could handle. He holed up in one of the cabins. We tried to talk him out, but he wasn't having it. He kept trying to hold us off until he was all but out of ammo."

"Did you kill him?" Harry Bauer asked. "Or is he locked up now?"

"The answer is *no*, to both questions," said Quinn. "I said he was *all but* out of ammo. He saved one bullet for himself—and he used it—because he knew we had the goods on him. Bob White told us in his confession to Skip what happened sixteen years ago to the two drug-running pilots and to P.J. White after the Christmas Eve robbery at Pressler's Department Store. Dedmon had tried to frame P.J. for the pilots' murders, but Bob came home and found P.J. out in the barn—with Dedmon's gun lying there next to him—revived him, and then got Rocket Reep to take P.J. to the Four Palms after they buried the two pilots. They also buried with them what was left of the evidence from the robbery—credit-card slips and personal checks—as well as that ridiculous forty-four magnum that Dedmon used as his service revolver, the gun he reported stolen. Dedmon had taken the engagement rings, wedding bands, and all the hard currency. He used some of that money to pay off the drug runners."

"And that was thousands of dollars in cash alone that the store lost," said Abe Pressler, "but I still don't understand how Rocket Reep ended up with the uncut diamonds and why he kept them in a pickle jar full of rocks. He could have accidentally used one as slingshot ammo." The businessman shook his head in amazement at the odds of getting all four stones back.

"That little man wasn't the sharpest pencil in the box," said Sgt. Quinn, "but he did know how to write—he even saw himself as a poet—and, in the end, that's how we figured all this out, in the journal entries he recorded in Tommy's notebook."

Quinn took out the photocopies that he'd made of those notebook pages, and studied them for a second. "After Rocket Reep drove P.J. White down to the Four Palms, to one of those tourist cabins, P.J. either gave Rocket the four uncut diamonds or Rocket found them on him—we're not sure which. That's where we found P.J. buried, and we think that's where he was shot and killed by Red Dedmon. The M.E.'s preliminary report found gunshot wounds to P.J.'s head and chest, and we also found one bullet with his remains. It appears to be from a gun like Dedmon's forty-caliber semi-automatic, which was the only pistol Red carried in all his years other than that cannon we found in the pilots' grave."

Tommy White—who had read all of Rocket Reep's scribblings the night before they turned the notebook over to Marty Quinn—waved for the detective to hold up. "How did you get *that* from what he wrote in my notebook?" asked Tommy. "I couldn't make heads or tails out of some pages—like he was writing in code or something."

Quinn chuckled. "Yeah, well, back in senior English," he said, "I thought a lot of the poems in our lit book had been written in code. But, fortunately, the state crime lab up in Cap City has smart people who can decipher this kind of stuff. Here's what Rocket wrote: '*Rocks in his socks / One for each palm / When in a pickle / That keeps them calm.*' So, P.J. White must have hidden the uncut diamonds in his socks—which was how Dedmon missed them back in the barn—and the poem's other lines deal with something Bob White told us in his confession. Skip? You want to elaborate?"

"Sure," said Officer Ross, turning toward the two boys. "Bob told me that the Four Palms got its name, not from actual palm trees but from 'the four palms that had to be greased' if somebody wanted a piece of the drug action in Oleander County. Those *four palms* were P.J. White, the local drug connection, the link between the locals and the drug cartels; the county sheriff, the one back then who has since died, and the one now, who wishes he was dead, because he just got arrested; the enforcer, who was *always* Red Dedmon, to his dying day; and the money man, who put together all the deals and laundered all the money. That man was Mr. Joel Stark—who the FBI arrested less than an hour ago at his nice, new, country-club mansion—which, according to Marty, also has septic-system problems." He made a face and waved a hand in front of his own nose.

"So then, did Dad—I mean, Bob—did he take over for P.J.?" asked Tommy. "I don't remember him doing *that* much—honest—at least not after I was old enough to know what was going on. I mean, people came around sometimes, but I didn't think Bob was one of the bosses. And he and Red Dedmon *never* got along. Dad hated him." Tommy knew what he'd just said, but didn't correct himself again.

Skip Ross studied Tommy White's worried expression for a moment. "The whole setup changed after all that happened at your family's farm, Tommy," said Skip. "Stark *did* want Bob to take over, but—you're right—there was a lot of friction between Bob and Red Dedmon and the old sheriff. Bob had even burned down his own barn, hoping that Dedmon would think the pilots' and P.J.'s bodies burned up with it. You see, after killing the two pilots, Red beat P.J. to a pulp, took what he could of the robbery loot, and then left P.J. for dead there in the barn, with the murder weapon—that forty-four magnum—on the ground near him. Then P.J. was taken to the Four Palms. Why Bob White told Rocket to take him there isn't clear, unless they thought Joel Stark could protect him. Obviously, he couldn't—or wouldn't. In fact, there's some evidence—phone records and call logs—indicating that Stark called the sheriff around the same time the fire was reported at your folks' barn. As far as Bob has ever known, P.J. just disappeared from the Four Palms and never came back. And your mom Connie didn't even know *that* much, Tommy."

"That's right," said Sgt. Quinn. "The drug activity—or most of it, anyway—shifted from the farm to the Four Palms. Bob White was more or less pushed out, and Joel Stark took over that end of the local drug trade, too, along with handling the money. I guess that was more efficient."

Quinn continued, "Anyway, as far as Rocket Reep was concerned, he knew enough to keep his mouth shut and to do whatever Stark told him to do. He was in and out of jail, and he even did some hard time. But last year when he started getting too much attention—from all the break-ins and the dead pets—Red Dedmon decided to put a stop to it. Rocket knew he was in danger, but he didn't stop, because Stark wouldn't let him. Rocket wrote this cryptic poem in the notebook: '*I'll turn on the dead man / Whose bite is like his bark / And take the White rock show / To grease the palm of old Stark.*' Turned out, Rocket was the one who got greased before he could take the uncut diamonds to Joel Stark and buy his way out of the mess."

"I don't wish that fate on anyone," said Abe Pressler, "but it's just as well, considering everyone that little man hurt. And the stones would have been cut and sold by now and used to build another stinking golf resort—literally."

Artie Bauer had one last question about the diamonds. He remembered his earlier talk with Bennie Pressler about the mysterious treasure in the safe's false bottom—the family secret that had died with Bennie's grandfather before it could be passed down. "So, Mr. Pressler," Artie asked Abe, "how did you figure out that those four rocks in Rocket's pickle jar were uncut diamonds, and that they had come from the safe at the E-ville store—I mean, if you didn't already know what the treasure was?"

"Simple," said Abe Pressler. "A letter in my grandfather Noah's handwriting that identified the stones was found with the checks and credit-card receipts that were buried with the two pilots. It had to have been in the safe with the diamonds, and P.J. White had to have read it. Bob White didn't, though. He doesn't even remember seeing the letter—just that he and Rocket were in a hurry to bury the bodies and get P.J. on down to the Four Palms. The letter even refers to an article in that old German newspaper we found in the safe. The article—in German, of course—describes the diamonds and includes an illustration of them, and lists my grandfather as the owner. We figure P.J. had to have told Rocket something about the stones, but we don't know what—enough that Rocket hid them away all these years and never told anyone else about them."

Artie nodded, then turned to Marty Quinn and asked, "Is this over now?"

"Yeah, it is," the detective said. "All the bad guys are either dead or in jail, where they're gonna be for a long time—and, I'm sorry to say, Tommy, that includes Bob and Connie White. They'll probably get a few more years apiece. More than likely, Jimmy Foxx and Victor Duke will get off with probation for helping us out, but they'll both be looking for new jobs. And the good guys? Well, one good guy got his family's diamonds back, and, from what I heard, he's using them to help people, not to hurt them. Two good guys I know won a big championship two weeks ago, and I'll bet my bottom dollar we hear more good things about those two in the years to come. Don't you think so, Mr. Bauer?" He looked first at Grandpa, then down at Brody on the floor between them, then back up at the old man.

"Well, I certainly hope so," said Grandpa, "but it's gonna be awful lonely out there on that farm if Artie goes off to college. As of right now, though, that's still up in the air—ain't it, son?"

Abe Pressler held up his hand for the honor of telling Grandpa Bauer about the changes at Iron Harbor A&M. "As you know, Harry," said Abe, "I'm a trustee up the road at A&M, and I happen to know that Artie has been offered a full ride to play ball there—for his old coach, Jug Johnson. That hasn't been in the news yet, but it *will* happen—if Artie wants it to."

"Yeah, buddy," said Grandpa. Then he got quiet for a second. "So, I guess I'd better get all the work out of Artie I can this summer, if I'm gonna be running that whole farm by myself come fall—well, me and Ricardo . . . and Miss Gabby . . . and Miss Minnie." He smiled sheepishly.

Tommy White reached over and playfully popped Harry Bauer on the knee. "You won't be alone, Grandpa," said Tommy, "and I can be there, too—if you want me. Right, Abe?" The businessman nodded and smiled. Tommy went on, "Besides, Bessie and Bossie are used to having me milk them now. And you still need help with Frick and Frack, not to mention with Tom and Dick, and all those chickens. And, hey, I can keep working for Minnie. She'll need help with Wilma off at college."

The penultimate word was Marty Quinn's. "And you won't be lonely in that big old farmhouse, Mr. Bauer, not even when Tommy, here, goes off to college himself in a few years. I hear that a certain long-haired German Shepherd named Brody wants to come live out there on that beautiful farm with you—for keeps. I'm starting a new job soon—it's with the regional FBI office in Capital City— and I can't bear the thought of Brody being cooped up in an apartment all day. So, you'd be doing both of us a big favor if you'll take him in, and then you—or Tommy—can be Brody's new handler. What do you say?"

Now it was old Harry Bauer who didn't know whether to laugh or cry with joy. All he could say was, "Hallelujah."

CHAPTER 30

FINAL-EXAM WEEK BEGAN THAT MONDAY at Arbor High, with graduation exercises scheduled for Friday night under the lights in Reuben Russo Memorial Stadium. The exam schedule was such that lunch period each day was shorter than usual—only twenty minutes in three shifts—and the Barf Table gang didn't get as much sit-down time together as they had gotten during the year. They also didn't meet at the Bauer farm that week, because they all were busy finishing final projects, writing papers and studying for final exams.

That word—*final*—hovered over Artie Bauer's head like a gray cloud all week, keeping him from being too excited about his future at A&M. He didn't have to say goodbye to Ty Green and Jimmy Gore, who would still be his teammates in the years to come, and he would see Wilma Marecek either at A&M or on weekends when she might help her aunt with horse-therapy sessions on the farm. And, of course, he would spend time whenever he could get back home with Tommy White and Ricky Duran. With a couple of exceptions, Artie Bauer managed to find and say personal goodbyes to the remaining tablemates—to the Inouye twins, Jamie Foxx and Vicki Duke; to Jenny Gore and Nicie Evans, both of whom would surely attend A&M Monitors games in the fall and spring to see Jimmy and Ty play; and, finally, to Bennie Pressler and Brett Woods.

Russian exchange student Julia Safin, also a senior, had made arrangements to take her exams early and wouldn't even be attending Friday's graduation. Artie learned early in the week that Julia had been runner-up in her tennis tournament over prom weekend, and that she had already flown to Florida to continue training for two more qualifying tournaments that summer. According to the letter that she left Artie, her goal was to test herself in the national championships—first, to qualify for the tournament and, finally, to win at least her first-round match against an actual pro. Her handwritten letter was short, but it was signed, "Love, Julia," and she included a postscript asking him to extend her best wishes to his grandfather. In his mind, Artie could hear Julia saying, *"Please give Meester Bauer my best."*

The commencement exercises on Friday night came off without a hitch. Salutatorian Artie Bauer kept his speech short and sweet, reminding his fellow graduates to be kind to everyone they passed on the road of life or on their climb up the ladder of success. Artie knew that traveling roads and climbing ladders were both commencement clichés, but he changed the punchline by finishing with, *"because you never know when you might run out of gas or fall off that ladder, and need someone, anyone, to pick you up—something I know from experience."*

Wilma's valedictory speech was almost a reprise of her winning Ebenezer Endowment essay, in which she encouraged the seniors to *"live deliberately and not stumble through their lives."* Like Artie before her, Wilma turned the graduation evergreen on its head with, *"For practice, I gave this speech to my aunt all week, but with a different ending. Then, just this morning, Aunt Minnie reminded me not to be so headstrong or so driven to succeed that I don't leave room for serendipity in my life—for those happy little accidents that make life worth living. I've learned a lot about serendipity this year at Arbor High— playing two new sports that I had never thought to try before, leading a creative- therapy group to help the many of us who were impacted by the Good Friday Storm, but, first and foremost, deciding to pick up my lunch tray and to carry it to another seat in the school cafeteria, a seat where almost no one else wanted to sit. There—sitting with Artie Bauer and others—I grew close to a whole new group of friends whom I never would have come to care so deeply about if Aunt Minnie hadn't dared me to sit at a place called the Barf Table. I will always be glad she did."*

Guidance counselor Thelma Hopper—not so perky by the time she got to

"*Phillip Roy Waters*"—read, in alphabetical order, each grad's name as they walked across the portable stage, and as Principal Jerry Church shook their hands and gave them their diplomas. In their forest green gowns, the seniors stood together one final time, turned the golden tassels on their flat hats from the right side to the left, and then flung the heavy mortarboards into the night air when Principal Church proclaimed them official graduates of Arbor Charter High School. Near the front of the line as they processed out of the stadium to "Pomp and Circumstance," Artie Bauer didn't look back. He knew that Grandpa Bauer was sitting with Minnie and Lena Marecek, Wilma's mother, and that they would help him out of the stands and back to the parking lot so that Grandpa and Tommy White could ride home with the Durans.

When Harry Bauer had asked his grandson what he wanted as a graduation present—besides the old, red pickup truck—the big farm boy had said, "Not a thing, Grandpa. I have you. You've always been like a father to me. And I have a real brother now. And Brody—the best dog in the world. I live on the best farm in the best state in the best country on Earth, and I have a plan for the future." But Artie decided that he did want one other thing that Friday night before Memorial Day. After hearing Wilma's valediction, he wanted to go to the one place where he could travel back in time and revisit the scene of his greatest triumph at Arbor High School.

* * *

The cafeteria was dark when Artie Bauer pushed through the heavy double doors from the hallway and eased himself inside, as if he feared he might set off a nonexistent alarm. But no one in the brightly lit hallway cared about his detour, as they were busy celebrating their long-awaited rite of passage. The somber young man stood for a moment and peered past the long tables that for months had held rows of noisy underclassmen. He squinted in the dim light toward the area down front where the serving line, the cashier's stand, the tray-return window and the now-empty trash bins were. Everything was clean and back in its old place, ready for the next school year. The two coaches' recliners were gone, having been trucked up the road to Iron Harbor A&M. The two round tables—one that had originally been for the faculty, the other for misfit students like Artie Bauer himself had once been—stood apart again, as had been the case on the very first day of classes, that year and every other year of Artie's high school career.

Then he saw her—the girl he would miss the most.

Leah Russo's head was in her hands. She was sitting alone at the old Barf Table, in the very same seat she had picked for herself on the first day of school. Leah looked up when she heard Artie's footfalls on the tile floor. "Hi, Artie," she said. "Imagine meeting you here."

"I missed you this week," he said, trying to sound cheerful. "I even drove over to Woody's one afternoon looking for you."

"Honest?" she asked.

Grinning, he replied, *"As honest as you can expect a man to be . . ."*

". . . *in a world where it's going out of style*," she said, completing the quotation with a laugh. "I'm surprised you remember that."

"Really?" he said. "I'll never forget that day. You were sitting there reading that paperback, and you couldn't wait for the bell to ring. It was *The Big Sleep*, and I thought that was funny because you looked bored to death with every-*thing* and every-*body*, like you were already asleep."

"So, when did you read it?" she asked. "You must have liked it, to remember the best line."

Artie nodded and said, "Yeah, I checked it out after I saw you with it . . . but I like *The Long Goodbye* better. Ty even made Grandpa, Tommy and me watch that movie on TV one night—because it had that ballplayer, the writer, acting in it. Yeah, I understand *The Long Goodbye*—especially now. Know what I mean?"

"Yes," she said, "and it *does* hurt. '*To say goodbye is to die a little.*' You *do* understand. But you and I are survivors, and I finally figured that out, us losing Reuben, and then me and Dad watching Mom give up. You know, Artie, I'm sorry about what you had to go through this year—I mean, you almost lost your grandpa, you did lose your grandmother, and then things didn't work out with

Julia."

"I don't guess Julia and I were meant to be," he said, "not right now, anyway. She needs to find out if she has what it takes to compete with the best—like Brett did last winter surfing in Hawaii. Maybe she'll come back sooner or later, and we can pick up where we left off, like you guys did."

"I hope so," she said, "because you two were good together. I have to admit, though, I did get kind of jealous. You more or less took Reuben's place—worrying about me and giving me advice and all—and it was awfully hard to give up another big brother, even though all I had to do was ask for your help. You were always there for me. I just didn't see it sometimes."

Artie didn't know what to say, except that he felt the same way about Leah.

"I appreciate you mentioning me in the Class Will," she said, "but I can't accept—I mean, I can't take your place here at the table."

"Why not?" he asked. "You'd be great with next year's 9th graders. Maybe if you get some help from Bennie? Your tough love and his wisecracks? That's a winning combination." They both laughed.

"No," she said, "because I won't be here. Dad and I are gonna travel this summer—out to see Mom near St. Louis—and then we're gonna go all over the country. She can come, too, if she wants, but Dad says if I want to be a writer, I should see a lot of different places and do a lot of different things."

"But that's this summer," Artie said. "You'll be back here in the fall."

"No, I won't," said Leah. "I learned three things from Julia Safin. One was, not to be afraid to love somebody if they're the right person. The second thing was, to be willing to go halfway around the world, if necessary, to chase down your dream—even if it is over the rainbow. That's why I applied to be an exchange student next year, and I found out last week I've been accepted. Pretty neat, huh?"

Artie was taken aback for a second. "Yes," he finally replied, "but I'm sure everyone—especially Bennie and Brett—will miss you. I *already* miss you." Then he raised an eyebrow and said, "I'm almost afraid to ask what the third thing you learned from Julia was. Does it have anything to do with where you're going in the fall?"

She nodded. "It sure does," she said. "They asked me where I want to live next year. I told them anywhere but Paris, so people won't think I'm trying to be like Ernest Hemingway or Gertrude Stein. I told them anywhere else would be fine. They suggested Russia, and I said that would be okay, as long as they didn't send me to Siberia—you know, where Julia used to live. Did she ever tell you about that?"

"Well, we didn't really talk about Siberia—or even Russia—on our dates," said Artie, blushing. "Didn't she like living there? In Siberia?"

Even in the dark, the girl's sultry look made the young man's face turn a deeper shade of red. *"Meester Bauer,"* said Leah Russo, in her best impression of Artie's old girlfriend, *"no one* likes *living in Siberia.* That was the third thing I learned from Julia—you need to like where you live. But don't worry, Artie. She told Wilma and me how much she likes Oleander County, because all of her friends are here. She'll be back someday. And so will I."

The pair sat quietly for a few seconds, both of them looking around the dark lunchroom and all but hearing the old chatter; breathing in—almost tasting— their memories of lunchtime smells; recalling the faces of three, then six, then nine, then fourteen other scared teenagers besides themselves, first around that one table, then around the two tables that when pushed together looked like infinity. As their camaraderie had grown, the anxious outsiders' fears and doubts had faded into a confidence and pride that would continue to grow within them all. Despite their differences—or perhaps because of their diversity—Artie and Leah and the others had forged bonds that mere separation could not break.

"By the way," Artie said, breaking the silence, "have you seen the drawing that Kimi did of us? I wondered why she put you in with all of us seniors. They brought the picture over to the farm the other day. They had it framed—well, their folks did—and so we hung it in the clubhouse. You'll have to come see it before you and your dad take off for the summer."

"I will," Leah said. "I promise."

"Yeah, you'll get a kick out of it," said Artie. "She drew us all as manga characters—you know, like that picture she did of Mike on the mound? What did she call him—Zircon or something?"

"What?" Leah said with a snort. "As manga superheroes? I'm not sure I want to see what my superpower is." Then she smiled. "But you're like Mike was in our skit—you know, Bobo the Saint Bernard? Whenever someone needs help, you always come to the rescue."

"No, not superheroes," said Artie. "Just regular characters. I mean, she drew me like a big bear, but I look like a wide-eyed farmer with a milk pail in one hand and a pitchfork in the other." He grinned. "I won't say how she drew you, Leah. But you're standing beside me in the picture."

"As it should be," she said, with a nod. "As it'll *always* be—wherever I am. Honest."

The two friends laughed. The two friends cried. Their love and respect—for each other and for the whole Barf Table gang—had become more than just a part of them. It was everything.

THE END

Barf Table seniors and Leah Russo (manga illustration by Amelia Dowdle)

Tommy White's notebook, ABC's in sign language, and
Bennie Pressler in his bunny suit

Mike Inouye dressed as Bobo the Saint Bernard.

Acknowledgements

*Special thanks to friends and former teaching colleagues **Carolina Elliott** and **Sandy Deal** for reading and commenting on all or part of the books in this series; to best friend and baseball coach **Roger Knight** for his advice about high school baseball and game situations; to artist **Amelia Dowdle** for her manga sketch of the Barf Table seniors that appears at the end of the text; and to Sandy's long-haired German Shepherd, **Levon**, for inspiring our canine character, Brody, the police dog.*

Also by Rahn & Timberley Adams

Tales of the Barf Table, Book Two: Trouble Shooters

Tales of the Barf Table, Book One: From the Gridiron to the Fire

Night Lights; or, Golf, the Blues, and the Brown Mountain Light

Also by Timberley Gilliam Adams

Henry Heron Finds His Home and *Turtle Beach*